CHEKHOV'S SISTER

CHEKHOV'S SISTER

A Novel by
W. D. WETHERELL

LITTLE, BROWN AND COMPANY

BOSTON   TORONTO   LONDON

The author would like to thank the National Endowment for the Arts for their support during the completion of this work.

First edition

Chekhov's Sister is a work of fiction. Names, characters, places, and incidents are either the product of the author's imagination or, if real, are used fictitiously.

The excerpt from *Anton Chekhov's Life and Thought: Selected Letters and Commentary* by Simon Karlinsky and Michael Heim, Copyright © 1976 by the Regents of the University of California, is reprinted by permission.

Library of Congress Cataloging-in-Publication Data
Wetherell, W. D.
Chekhov's sister: a novel/by W. D. Wetherell. — 1st ed.
p.   cm.
ISBN 0-316-93162-4
1. Chekhova, M. P. (Maria Pavlovna), 1863-1957 — Fiction.
2. World War, 1939-1945 — Fiction. I. Title.
PS3573.E9248C47   1990
813'.54 — dc20   89-37990
                                                          CIP

10   9   8   7   6   5   4   3   2

Design by Joyce C. Weston

FG

Published simultaneously in Canada by Little, Brown & Company (Canada) Limited

Printed in the United States of America

For Erin

Dear Maria,

I bequeath to you my house in Yalta for as long as
you live, my money and the income from my dramatic
works. You may sell the house if you so desire. After
you and Mother die, all that remains is to be put at the
disposal of the Taganrog municipal administration for
the purpose of aiding public education. I have promised
one hundred rubles to the peasants of Melikhovo to help
pay for the highway.

Help the poor. Take care of Mother. Live in peace
among yourselves.

Anton Chekhov
Yalta August 3, 1901

CHEKHOV'S SISTER

KUNIN

YALTA, IN TROUBLED TIMES.
Curtain of rising mist colored by what backs it. By the sea, a heaving gray turbulence thick as fabric. Incoming tide surges inland, staining it white. Grainy effects. By the promenade, soft flesh tones, paleness, the first teasing transparencies. Rising higher. From the palms, touches of lushness, pliancy, tropic crimsons. From the hotels and sanatoria, a stuccoed warmth, creamy flashes, the motion of smoke. From the casinos-turned-collectives, various humpings juttings archings, a canopy of veil-like

clingings. Higher and higher. From the cliff backing the Old Town, vertical seams, mica sparklings, rocky streamers. From the cypress lining the top, a tossing of daylight, scrimlike dispellings — the mist shot through with blueness, a breeze away now from sky.

Curtain of fragrance. A smothering iodine at the base matches the gray. Inland the wetter smell of seaweed against sand. Lighter resin of weathered boards. From the left, coal fires, frying sunflower oil. From the right, wood smoke, acrid and sharper. Oleander. Soft cinnamons. Damp earth, cold rock. A ceiling of sweetness vaguely citrus.

Curtain of sound. The call of a bird. A lonely bell from an anchored ship or distant lighthouse. The cry of a *muezzin* off toward Massandra. They blend into a rolling sound as liquid and soft as the tide — a tide that is louder and drier with each incoming beat, until the friction becomes a clanking, a harsh metallic superimposition as asperate as steel against flesh. When the clanking becomes unbearable it stops — suddenly, with no echo.

Curtain of sunlight.

The scene is of a steep hillside overlooking the Black Sea. At center, framed by a crescent of acacia, a large white villa two stories high. Numerous gables and wings give an eccentric but pleasing effect; miniature balconies are tucked away beneath arches and there are large sunlit terraces of pinkish rock. Most noticeable are the windows — windows of every size, shape, and pattern, as if inserted by someone who craved light and shifting perspectives. The larger ones are shaded by awnings striped a delicate manila; the smaller, by shutters of tin. Gables and windows reach their peak in a three-story tower facing south. In the simplicity of the wisteria-covered base, the ornamental fluting of the top, it suggests the influence of both the Genoese who first colonized the Yalta seacoast and the Turks who came after.

The villa is the home of the late Anton Pavlovich Chekhov, now run as a museum dedicated to his memory by his sister, Maria Pavlovna.

At right is a grove of various fruit trees: orange, lemon, quince. The branches toward the bottom are for the most part neatly trimmed, but higher up they become tangled and the branches intertwine. Attached to the trunks are conspicuous labels. *This peach tree planted in March 1899 by the hand of the dramatist Anton P. Chekhov. This apricot planted in April 1900 by the hand of the storyteller A. P. Chekhov and transplanted to the present location in the autumn of the same year.*

Beneath the lush foliage an assemblage of lawn chairs lie tilted on their sides, suggesting a party that has hurriedly broken up — not recently, but in the past. The grass is uncut and high. Rusty stanchions with sagging velvet ropes lead toward the villa's entrance and a small ticket kiosk shuttered close.

The sun, rising fully, provides enough light to see clearly the left. It is apparent now that not only does the villa sit on a cliff, but the drop is an enormous one over which nothing can be seen. Dawn brings warmth to the center and right, sharpening the detail of orchard, house, and garden, but over the rocks the mist remains, impenetrable and chilling. On the edge of the cliff a brass telescope is mounted on a wooden tripod — the ancient kind of spyglass that might have come off a derelict man-of-war.

A door tentatively opens. In quick succession, three shapes, seen only in silhouette, move from the house through the garden to the cliff. They seem torn between tiptoeing and marching — there is a jerky, hesitant quality to their progress as a result. Each peers through the telescope toward the void; each shows evidence of great anxiety and distress. In the dawn's fragmented light, none becomes recognizable before disappearing again into the villa.

There is an interval of five full minutes before another figure emerges from the door. During this time, the clanking sound returns, this time localized on the left from the void. Less harsh than before, the sound is heavier, with an engine's unmistakable throb. The figure emerging from the door is aware of it instantly, and — stooping under an unpruned tree limb — walks across to the telescope with the obvious intention of finding out what it is.

This is Peter Sergeich Kunin, a medical student aged twenty-one. His features, while handsome enough in the Slavic way, are soft and undefined, showing evidence of his unfinished personality; for him, all is potential and turning into and becoming. At least his face. His body suggests something older and more complete — strong torso, tight chest, broad shoulders. The workman's blouse he wears emphasizes this thick, manly quality, as does his broad leather belt. Further down, the effect is contradicted again, this time by a limp that becomes apparent as he crosses to the telescope. He is clubfooted, and rather than drag the crippled leg behind him like an anchor, he leads off with it like a ram. He stops, rests, then starts off again, the effort obvious in his strained expression.

Reaches the telescope. Rather than use it, he peers down over the precipice with his hand shading his eyes.

A play, or perhaps a story instead.

In the late autumn of 1941, at the Black Sea resort of Y____, a young clubfooted student named Kunin stood peering down over a cliff toward the streets leading into town. On his pale, average-looking face his eyes were by far the most active part, alternately darting out looks of defiance, bashfulness, and hurt. For the most part, however, they were set with a peculiar blue thinness that gave him an expression of curiosity and interest, as if nothing should be missed. At the present moment, these eyes were shaded by his hand as he sought movement in the deserted streets below. The morning sun sent the sea aglitter so that much was lost in the sparkle that would otherwise have been revealed. Along the famous promenade seabirds pecked at hard stale bits of leftover buns. A shutter flapped at Shavrov's, the confectioner's, as if the shop were lonely and in need of comfort. By the Oreanda Hotel, a cat of ugly complexion rooted for garbage along the curb. On Pushkin Street, a trolley stood stalled and empty, its cables slack. Along the bright curve of the seafront, not a human stirred.

Or perhaps this.

Peter Sergeich Kunin well remembers the day forty years ago when the German infantry came to town. It was one of those soft Crimean days when the sun seems endless, Moscow with its frosts as distant and uninhabitable as Mars. He was a boy then, with a boy's foolish pride that was intensified both by the clubfoot he was born with and the literary ambitions that had become all-consuming since he had left the university at the precocious age of nineteen. Now, on this fine and typical Yalta morning, he had been sent by his patroness and protector, Maria Pavlovna Chekhov, to keep watch for the advance armored units that — the war being what it was — were momentarily expected.

Or this.

As a young man, Peter Sergeich Kunin was in the habit of playing a game with himself. This game consisted of imagining everything not as it came to him, mundane, colorless, and tame, but as it might have appeared in the plays and short stories of his hero, the writer Anton Chekhov. A cake would be served him at dinner. *A cake greedy with raisins,* he thought, smiling to himself in satisfaction. Moonlight would come through his window as he tossed restlessly before sleep. *The moon,* he decided, *laid its rays on the windowsill in the jagged pattern of new-cut cloth.* A peasant would stop him in one of the Tartar villages, selling icons. "Only suffering can redeem us, grandfather," he said, or some such nonsense, puffing up his chest like a pompous character in one of the plays.

It was an innocent game, and it helped him forget the twin obsessions that otherwise tortured him: his youth with its lack of accomplishment; his lame foot and the laughter it caused among the girls.

But at one particular moment in history, the November morning forty years before when he had stood looking down toward Yalta's harbor for the first signs of German troops, the game was something more than that, something very important indeed. Yalta was undefended, the Red Army in retreat all across Russia, the entire Crimea open to the Wehrmacht's advance, and yet it was just this very hopelessness that made his heart beat wildly, his head so joyously throb. For here he was in the melodrama he had always longed for — in a drama, and not as a bit player but in a prominent role. There was Mother Russia trampled by a million fascist boots, and here was one small corner left undefiled, and between the two stood a crippled boy armed with daydreams of a dead master's art.

So he played the game right up to the moment of the Germans' arrival and all that happened then. He stared over the cliff and saw the Yalta seafront with the abandoned, slightly down-in-the-mouth look a resort wears a month out of season. He stared through the telescope and saw cypress trembling in the wind like beauties waiting to dance. He saw a street clean and bright as a woodsaw — saw the paving stones tremble as if from the approach of an unseen elephant. He saw these things and transformed them into phrases, and so foolish was he at twenty-one that his shoulders spasmed as if it were bullets he were firing and not words.

And what was odd, this habit survived long after everything else about his youth had been torn away — his idealism, his romantic posturing, the feeling deep inside himself that despite a crippled foot and a world in flames, everything would come right in the end. Years later, when he had given up directorship of the Chekhov Museum and retired to Moscow, he would stroll down the Petrovka on winter afternoons, his overcoat gathered around him to muffle the cold, exchanging with fellow pensioners those proud, slightly amazed nods of recognition men his age always exchanged, as if each were surprised to find any of his generation still alive. He would find a bench halfway along, bend over to clear the snow off, sit down to stare toward the steamy shop windows and the people hurrying past: the harried officials late from their lunch breaks, the bashful couples hand in hand, the children swaddled too tightly in cheap nylon suits. He would watch them and try to picture them in stories, not just as Anton Pavlovich would have described them, but as Gogol would have or Pasternak or Tolstoy.

His passion for literature had survived, a private personal thing that formed his chief defense against the loneliness and cold. Later, when he returned to the simple, book-crammed flat he shared with his sister, a widowed schoolteacher, he gave himself over to other moods, not cynical so much as cold-blooded, when he would try quite deliberately to total up what had survived besides that. The men his age on the street seemed satisfied merely to have survived at all; they inhaled each new lungful of air with such relish it was clear that for them physical existence was reward enough. But Kunin had a cripple's contempt for his body, and the physical fact of his continuation interested him not the slightest. Their tough hides had survived the war, but what of it? What had they brought into this new world with them? What prompted those proud erect postures, those chests swollen with ribbons, that right precious beyond all rights to move to the head of the queue?

What, if anything, had survived the Great Patriotic War?

He took out pencil and pad, started his list at the very beginning. The earth itself, with roughly the same diameter and circumference, density and mass in the year 1945 as it had displayed in the year 1939. The earth, though not as smooth as it was priorly, with numerous chips and indentations caused by the erosion of shells, and the various scoops and tunnels attendant upon mass graves. The earth, though not the same unpolluted color as before. The earth — checking it off — indisputably.

Certain arbitrary entities on that same earth, i.e., countries such as Poland and Czechoslovakia and the Union of Soviet Socialist Republics. These survived, albeit with their arbitrary lines somewhat altered in respect to where they were antecedently, particularly in regard to certain countries lying east of the arbitrary entity called Germany, i.e., Poland, Czechoslovakia, and the Union of Soviet Socialist Republics.

Certain people in these countries, probably the majority minus thirty million.

Certain moods of these same people, certain habits and states of being. Happiness, rather less than before. Decency, less. Sorrow, rather more. Anger, more. Hopelessness, more. Violence, more. Rather more of everything bad, as if the war hadn't cleansed out the old infections but injected fresh ones instead.

Certain buildings, though from a line drawn from the western border of Germany to the city of Volgograd, née Stalingrad, two thousand miles to the east, very few indeed, chiefly those made of stone. Villas, brothels, dachas, farms, hospitals, libraries, homes of famous authors. These by and large had not survived.

The Anton P. Chekhov Museum of Yalta, open 0830

to 1630, Sunday through Thursday and on special patriotic occasions. This, by a miracle, had survived.

Miscellaneous things. Printing presses. Theatres. Orchestras. Ballet in the major cities. Books, minus the banned ones. Paintings, those that were hidden. Philistines, charlatans, literary bureaucrats. The shell of culture.

The life within the shell?

Art?

This was the question that concerned him most, stripping away all his cynicism so that he had to face the question square, without verbal games. Had art survived the war? Art, namely the grace that gave a few scattered men and women the ability to wrench from the horror something immaculate and lasting and true? Had it survived or was it buried away beneath the decomposed bodies and vanished buildings of this abomination of a century, the 20th, these fat gloating numerals over a tragic mass grave?

The questions absorbed all his imagining, so there were few moments during the day when he wasn't reconstructing in his mind what had happened. As a young man he had witnessed a battle for art, a battle that was to him every bit as desperate and vital as any fought during the war — one so fierce that even now, forty years later, the opposing forces still struggled for domination in his memory. It was a battle with its own heroes and villains, though the older he got the hazier these distinctions became. It was a battle in which only one man had died, though the stakes had been enormous. It was a battle so unlikely as to be glorious — a battle worthy of its own epic, though whether or not epics had survived was exactly the point.

It was a battle that in many respects was lost before it began. For on that November morning when Maria Pavlovna sent him out to keep watch for the German troops, his literary game had not been weapon enough. It was as if the tower of art his favorite writers had constructed so beautifully in his heart had crumbled at the very whisper of their approach, so that he was left alone and unsupported before the enemy's advance. After Chekhov, he could describe the Yalta seafront lying there below the villa with the lonely, down-in-the-mouth look a resort wears a month out of season. He could see the avenues lined with cypress swaying in the wind like beauties waiting to dance. He could focus the telescope toward a side street clean and bright as a woodsaw — see the paving stones tremble as if from the approach of an unseen elephant.

But what happened next was much harder. For a while he was able to construct images fast enough to act as a barrier, so there were still a few seconds left in which things made sense. The clanking sound increased and diminished like the buzz of a monstrous fly. The paving stones trembled, then went flat and still, as if prostrating themselves in worship. There was the slap of a metallic something being slammed shut, then from around the corner — swiveling from side to side like a challenged bull — appeared the most un-Chekhovian thing it was possible to imagine, something there were no bright similes to fire at, no metaphors to entrap — something that in its squat simplicity might have stood for the very epitome of naked, nonliterary fact.

Tank. German. Machine gun. Death's-head insignia. Gun.

ACT ONE

THE DRAWING ROOM of the Chekhov Museum in
Yalta, November 1941. Couch, armchairs, and tables are
the brown, leathery kind to be found in a private men's
club. Vases of yellow flowers and extravagant wallpaper
add a lighter, more feminine effect. At left, floor-to-
ceiling bookcase crammed full. At right, stairway with
Persian red carpeting. Massive oak door beyond is closed,
leading to what a large, neatly printed sign announces as
Study and Writing Room of Anton P. Chekhov. Sign and

arrow opposite point toward *Kitchen and Pantry of Anton P. Chekhov*. There's an enamel stove in one corner, the grate open to reveal the glowing embers. A crescent-shaped window overlooks the back garden and the drooping foliage of the fruit trees.

Scattered about in a deliberately haphazard way, souvenirs from Chekhov's career and travels. An ivory walking stick. A stuffed fox. Moscow playbills, mounted and framed. A miniature samovar crafted of silver. Various icons. Gardening catalogs and stakes. A fishing pole.

Photographs on the walls. To the left and very prominent, Maxim Gorky. To the right and equally prominent, Maxim Gorky. Smaller Gorky pictures on the doors. By the bookcase, oil portrait of Count Leo Tolstoy. On the bookcase in matching round frames, Vladimir Ilyich Lenin and Karl Marx.

At center, a table piled with printer's proofs weighed down by a golden pince-nez.

While the effect is at first static, as that of a museum room undisturbed by dust, a sense of agitation is soon apparent. This is created by loud, hurried footsteps in the wings and above the stairway; inarticulate, repeated cries; doors being slammed; the crunch of breaking wood; a fire, which grows visible out in the garden, dwarfing the punier flames in the smoldering stove.

Enter Alexander Potapov, a retired actor. He is a man of about sixty, with finely chiseled features that he displays by walking with his head held unnaturally straight, as if it is being served on a tray. His silver hair is almost shoulder length, giving him a flamboyant, artistic air that is softened by his plain, rather threadbare linen suit. As handsome as he is, his girth is enormous. When he walks, he slaps his sides with his hands, as if trying to regain control over something he has long since let slip away.

Goes right to the window overlooking the garden, presses his face against the glass, taps plaintively, then goes over to peer up the stairway in obvious confusion.

POTAPOV: *softly.* Maria Pavlovna?

Pause.

POTAPOV: *a bit louder, with a trace of condescension.* Peter Sergeich, old man?

Pause.

POTAPOV: *with irritation and pompous command.* Gerassim! Downstairs at once!

Shrugs in resignation and wanders over to the stove. Stands there warming his hands, then suddenly remembers something and hurries over to the bookcase. Squats with difficulty to examine the lowest shelf, then boosts himself up each succeeding shelf in turn. When he gets to the top, yells in triumph and plucks out a book bound in red. Opens and begins to read at random.

POTAPOV: When the dialectic of the capitalist inverts to form a continuum. *Hesitates, in obvious bewilderment.* When the dialectic of the capitalist inverts to form a continuum . . .

For the next few minutes he repeats the phrase, each time emphasizing a different word like an actor trying to make sense of his lines. As he does so, he is taking books over to the stove and burning them. When the last is gone, reaches into his pocket, takes out a list and a pen. Checks something off with flourish of satisfaction.

POTAPOV: So much for the collected works of you, Comrade Lenin! *Consults list.* Lenin burned, Marx burned,

Red flag burned . . . That leaves only . . . Ah! *Crosses to the largest of the Gorky photographs. Stops, makes a low, mocking bow.* I am here on an important mission, Comrade Gorky. I am sent as a representative of the people you were so kind as to portray yourself the savior of which . . . I am sent to give you your rightful place in Russian literary history . . . I bow to you, Comrade Gorky, prior to . . .

Reaches up and pulls down picture with a vicious tug, then rips it into shreds. Finishing, he goes and rips apart all the other Gorky pictures in turn. By the time they're destroyed, he's exhausted. Even when his breath returns, his stomach keeps spasming with a life and will all its own.

POTAPOV: *consulting list.* Destroy Gorky pictures. Destroy . . . *He does a double take and holds the list closer to his eyes.* But why? Why, Maria Pavlovna?

Shrugs. Walks diffidently to the bookcase and the handsome oil portrait of Tolstoy.

POTAPOV: *sadly.* I'm sorry, Lev Nikolayevich.

Reaches up to remove picture, but at the last moment can't, and brings his arms back down to his sides. Takes a deep breath and tries again, with the same result. Walks a few steps to the side, approaches from different angle, spits on his hands, averts head to avoid Tolstoy's eyes, but none of this is of any help. He can't bring himself to take the picture down.

While all this is going on, Varka, maid to Maria Pavlovna, enters left. She looks about with a stern expression, pulls a cloth from her apron, advances across the room, her hand shooting out toward the furniture to swab away stray bits of dust. Checks to see the Lenin is gone from the bookcase; checks to see Gorky's photographs have all been destroyed. Comes to a stop behind Potapov, who is still not aware of her presence.

POTAPOV: If only your eyes didn't shine so, Lev Nikolayevich. It's like God, like staring at God. That patriarchal beard. And why does Maria Pavlovna want you taken down in the first place? Have they never heard of Tolstoy in Germany? *Reaches up.* Here you go, my good count. We'll just take you down for a quiet nap and . . . *Again, his arms collapse to his side.*

VARKA: Burn him.

POTAPOV: Eh, what's that? *Jumps back as if the picture has spoken.*

VARKA: *with intense passion.* The Germans will be here at any moment. Burn him!

When Potapov still hesitates, she pulls over a heavily varnished stepladder and climbs up to remove the painting herself. She has it unhinged — is about to lift it free — when her face brushes against the painting's surface. Her head jerks back as if she has just been improperly kissed. Stands there looking at the portrait in awe, only now seeing it. Crosses herself secretly.

POTAPOV: *triumphantly.* See! It's not so easy is it? Like looking at the face of God, as I said. *Extends hand to help her down.* And what's more, the man was a writer. Do you know that chapter in *Anna Karenina* where Levin's brother wants to propose to that nice young woman whose name escapes me? He wants to propose and she longs for it herself, but they are busy picking mushrooms and the moment passes and we understand that both are irremediably alone. Masterful! Even Anton Pavlovich himself couldn't bring off such an effect.

Away from the picture, Varka once more assumes her busy, no-nonsense air. She is a plump woman in her early fifties, of Polish extraction, with sunburned arms and a shoulder that droops to the side as if she is perpetually carrying a basket. Though her hair is long and beautifully silky, her face is pockmarked with an intense ugliness that makes people upon first seeing her want to turn away. She is used to pity; her severity is her defense. She carries herself with the pride and gravity of the saintly or single-minded.

VARKA: The mistress will not be pleased.

POTAPOV: *moving toward stove.* I was in a play once in Odessa. Molière. This was before the Revolution, of course. But why I mention it at such a perilous time . . . *Stops, rubs his head, then turns toward Varka with an expression that is heartbreakingly open.* Why isn't Maria Pavlovna here? We need her, Varka. I feel very afraid without her.

VARKA: In his study. There are letters with favorable references to some Germans and unfavorable references to others. She is rearranging them accordingly.

POTAPOV: And Kunin?

VARKA: Keeping watch.

Reassured, Potapov resumes his lighthearted air. When he lights a cigar, Varka looks at him in disapproval, but he puffs away in boyish defiance.

POTAPOV: One thing puzzles me. The Germans. Now tell me something, Varka my dear. The Germans may be the invaders, this Hitler man the reincarnation of Genghis Khan, but they aren't Reds, correct? What isn't Red is White. Hence the Germans are Whites. So rather than cower here in mortal terror we should be rushing out to greet them with bread and salt.

Varka mumbles something under her breath, but Potapov rushes on, getting carried away with the beauty of his own voice.

POTAPOV: And even should these Nazis be as bad as some claim, Yalta . . . Well, we know what Yalta does, eh? Not for nothing is it the resort of emperors. The barbarian comes hirsute and savage, he glowers in fierce wildness, then the balmy sea breeze, the swaying palms, the fragrant magnolia . . . these things work their magic and a minute goes by and our hairy barbarian is strolling down the promenade with a yellow parasol like a fat merchant prince. The Bolsheviks came, and did they tear the casinos down, close the hotels? They splashed their filthy banners all across Pushkin Street, but in every other respect they aped the Tsars. No, my dear Varka. We have nothing to fear from mere Nazis.

During this monologue, Varka becomes increasingly agitated, and now her excitement can no longer be contained.

VARKA: The Bolsheviks? They were so tame then? They were only here to soak up the sun? This villa that shelters you, Alexander Ivanovich. Did they not send their looters to sack it after the Revolution? Did they not try to make it into a dacha where party bosses could entertain their whores? Did they not try to cut down Anton Pavlovich's beautiful trees? You forget too easily. You forget that it was Maria Pavlovna alone who held them off.

POTAPOV: *flustered.* Of course. Of course, there's no . . . Maria Pavlovna is a remarkable woman. Remarkable.

VARKA: Rush to meet your Germans then, Alexander Ivanovich. You will see. There are stories.

POTAPOV: Propaganda.

VARKA: Stories the old people would tell about Prussians who rode into the villages and what happened then. They would talk late at night when they thought we children were asleep. They would curse and weep at the memory. *Impatiently shakes head.* I know about Germans. I know here. *Thumps her heart.*

A door slams open behind the staircase. Enter Kunin at a clumsy trot, his face screwed up in effort. He looks wildly about the room.

KUNIN: Maria Pavlovna?

Varka tilts her head toward the study. Kunin starts in that direction, then comes back.

KUNIN: They're in town now. I watched them for ten minutes. One of the soldiers crossed the sand to wade in the water and throw apart his arms in victory. Like this. *Gestures.*

POTAPOV: *to Varka.* You see! Seabathing already!

KUNIN: We must get ready for their arrival.

His tone and manner indicate he would like to take charge; he nervously closes and opens his fists; he clears his throat trying to find the proper register of command. During all that follows he keeps glancing toward the closed door of the study for reassurance.

KUNIN: Is the Lenin destroyed? The Gorky? Maria Pavlovna gave strict orders. There must be no traces of anything that would offend the Germans.

VARKA: *mumbling.* Cut down the trees.

KUNIN: What's that?

VARKA: Tear up the gardens, burn down the house. It is beauty that offends them. I have seen it all before.

KUNIN: *to Potapov.* It was my understanding that the Tolstoy was to come down as well.

POTAPOV: We were just getting to it, Peter. Perhaps you could assist. *Cynically.* We know you are master here.

Makes a great show of steadying the stepladder. Kunin ignores it and reaches up to take the picture down by himself.

POTAPOV: *softly and ironically.* He has the hook loose. He is beginning to lift the frame off. He sees the face. He hesitates . . . *Loudly now.* What's that, Peter? Is it too heavy then?

Kunin looks at him with the fury of a boy faced with the knowing smugness of a man. He grabs the stepladder and is about to climb up when there's a loud crashing sound from the pantry. All three of them start. Enter Gerassim, a servant.

He's in his early twenties, but looks a decade older, with a Tartar's dark complexion and the matted beginnings of a beard. He wears a shabby gray suit that is too small for him; his sharp bony shoulders and barrel-like chest combine to give the effect of a wedge. Despite this, he moves lightly, with a feline grace.

In his right hand is a double-bladed axe. He stops in the middle of the drawing room showing neither fear, anxiety, nor any human emotion at all.

VARKA: Have you destroyed the china then? *Turning to Kunin.* Made in England. The mistress's command.

POTAPOV: *to Gerassim, with the tone someone would use in teasing a chained lion.* What's that, boy? Your mumble is exceedingly indistinct today.

Gerassim sees now that the portrait of Tolstoy still hangs. Crosses to it, pulls it down, then immediately begins hacking it apart with his axe. There is no passion in the way he does this; rather, it is the very absence of passion that makes his action so brutal. His arm rises and falls like a piston.

Gerassim is kicking the fragments into a pile when Maria Pavlovna enters from the right, carrying beneath her arm two pictures in ornate gold frames. She is a youthful woman in her seventies, taller than average, with traces of auburn in her otherwise gray hair. Her forehead is wrinkled, but tightly; her cheeks are as smooth as a young girl's. Childless, a spinster, there is about her a strength and directness that suggest great fecundity; her hips and breasts are full, for instance, and the only sign of her solitude is the yearning, absentminded way she strokes herself, even in company. Her eyes are brown flecked with blue and remarkably coquettish; her smile ironic, as if she knows full well how ludicrous the effect is. In this irony, in the curious tilt of her head and her dark eyebrows (thick and brooding by the bridge of the nose; thin and merry by the edges), she resembles her brother, Anton Pavlovich Chekhov.

She is dressed in the graceful style of the 1890s: striped cotton blouse over long black skirt, a simple belt at the narrow waist where they join. Of the five people on stage, she is the only one who blends into the villa's decor and seems part of it; it is precisely this quality that gives her physical dominance of any scene in which she appears.

Approaching the others, she takes in the situation in a glance.

MARIA: *to Kunin.* How much longer before they come?

KUNIN: They're in the lower town. If they come directly? *Shrugs.* Even without resistance they're cautious. They check each street for partisans.

MARIA: *to Gerassim, indicating debris on the floor.* Take everything out to the garden and add it to the fire. Go and add some dead limbs, too. If the Germans question you, say that you are burning brush in the autumn pruning.

Gerassim cradles the broken frames in his arms, then exits behind the stairway.

MARIA: *to Potapov.* Here, put these up. The small one first in the empty spot by the sofa.

Hands him a picture. Potapov examines it at arm's length.

POTAPOV: Gerhart Hauptmann! I was in his *Lonely Lives,* did you know that, Maria Pavlovna? Stanislavsky directed it himself with his usual acumen. Ah, and I see that it is inscribed! *Translates awkwardly from German.* To my friend, Anton Pavlovich Chekhov . . . with . . . whose plays shine . . . with a brightness . . . that endures. Whose plays shine with a brightness that endures.

MARIA: *with obvious satisfaction.* They will see this first upon entering. I will receive them here, they will see the German, then they will follow me over to the bookcase, where they will see this.

Hands Potapov the second, smaller picture. It's of Chekhov at the family home in Melikhovo — the famous photograph, taken before illness marked his face, that shows him lounging on the steps in a double-breasted overcoat, one hand holding a thin and elegant walking stick, the other affectionately cradling a squirming dachshund.

POTAPOV: What a charming likeness! Those sad and

sensitive eyes! I well remember the time he gave the Art Theatre the honor of his attendance. We were doing *Three Sisters* in Petersburg and your brother's wife, Olga Knipper . . .

MARIA: Your opinion, Peter?

KUNIN: *with an appraising glance around.* The Hauptmann first, then the portrait with the dachshund. The German dramatist, then the German dog.

MARIA: You say that with irony, but for Germans irony does not exist. They look in a mirror and see nothing but themselves. *Smiles.* We shall give them that mirror.

Moves toward photograph and looks at it for a long time. No one disturbs her silence. Potapov and Kunin watch with the vaguely uncomfortable look men wear when a woman prays.

MARIA: Varka?

VARKA: *looking at her the same intense way Maria Pavlovna looks at the picture.* I am here, mistress.

MARIA: See that tea is served the officers when they arrive.

VARKA: *indistinctly.* It is not tea they will want. *Louder.* I will serve them tea.

MARIA: *spinning around with a quickness surprising in someone her age.* And do not leave me alone, Varka. Stand with me. I need you here. I can be strong to face them, but only with your help.

Varka nods and exits toward pantry. Maria Pavlovna turns back toward the picture, and instantly her mood is transformed into something lighthearted. These swings in tone — from irony to sentimentality, command to supplication — are characteristic of her and perfectly sincere, though the effect is exactly the opposite: to make her seem insincere and manipulative.

MARIA: *touching the picture lightly with her hand.* The dog's name was Bromide. Antosha liked dachshunds and so we ordered it especially for his birthday. They have such busybody airs, and yet they're fearless, do you know that, Peter? It came all the way from Berlin on the train. When it arrived, Michael put it in a little sausage box and served it for breakfast! When he wiggled out, I thought Antosha would die from laughter. *Shakes head in memory.* He was still alive when Antosha died. We gave him to Gorky, but Gorky forgot to feed him and he starved.

Steps back to study the effect. Nods her head in satisfaction, but then her glance falls upon the bare spot above the bookcase where Tolstoy's picture has been removed. It's obvious from the lighter patch of wallpaper that something is missing.

MARIA: *softly to herself, rehearsing the phrase.* We at the Chekhov Museum in Yalta . . . I, the sister of Anton Pavlovich Chekhov . . . *Turning to Kunin.* They will hear from my own lips the respect all Germany has for him. In his study I have displayed the German editions of his work. I have made prominent the programs from his plays as performed in Berlin. I have left open on his desk the notebooks from his trips to Germany in 1897 and 1901. They will learn of his affection for Hauptmann and for Schiller and for the great genius Goethe himself. They will come expecting our hostility and they will see this and we shall greet them as saviors.

POTAPOV: *puzzled.* Goethe? *Brightening.* Ah, Werther! *Turns to Kunin.* Werther, my lad! Werther and Faust!

KUNIN: I didn't realize there were any traces of Goethe in your brother's work.

Maria Pavlovna closes her eyes and presses her lips together with the look of someone who is enduring unendurable pain. In a moment she opens them again and is quite calm.

MARIA: *very slowly, as if to burn the words' impression on Kunin's memory.* My brother owed a great debt to the German master. Understand that, Peter? We in the museum cannot speak of my brother's work without frequently alluding to this debt.

KUNIN: *finally nodding.* Yes, Maria Pavlovna. I understand.

MARIA: And so the Germans can see this debt for themselves, it is necessary to hang a portrait of Goethe in Tolstoy's place. I see you smile. But there is such a portrait in Yalta. It was painted by that Krizlovnov, do you remember him, Alexander? A little man whose mustache reeked of sardines, but he could be charming. Was it before your time? My brother had no use for the man. But it was commissioned for the theatre and before the Revolution hung over the proscenium with Shakespeare and Pushkin.

KUNIN: The Gorky Theatre?

MARIA: So-called. The Imperial Theatre in our more innocent day. But it seems to me that this portrait may still be there. If we could obtain it while there is still time, our preparations would be complete.

KUNIN: *with boyish bravado, very conscious of the effect he is making.* I will go for the picture.

MARIA: Not above the proscenium now. There will be Marx and Lenin and Gorky above the proscenium. But backstage somewhere. In the storeroom, perhaps? Mur-kina, the last director, was a party hack but a miser as well — he would never throw anything away. *Finally noticing Kunin.* Bravo, Peter! You are my savior once again.

POTAPOV: Yes, very brave of you, Peter Sergeich. I'd go myself except for this cursed gout. *Looks at Maria Pavlovna.* Uh, bravo! Bravo!

MARIA: You'll be careful?

KUNIN: I know the way. The back streets. No one will see me.

MARIA: You see, Alexander? He is young, but I lean on him. He is indispensable to the museum and I lean on him. And just fancy how he came here! On a pilgrimage all the way from Leningrad. A young medical student, a writer of humorous sketches like Anton Pavlovich himself, his hero. And that was two years ago and he has been here ever since and I look upon him now as my brother's successor.

Kunin acts embarrassed, but there is no mistaking his pleasure at the last words. As he leaves, Maria Pavlovna raises her hand as if in benediction. In reflex, Kunin bows his head. Exits limping past the stairs.

POTAPOV: A glorious gesture! But he is rather a young man, Maria Pavlovna. To speak of him as your brother's successor? The boy may have talent, but surely it's premature to . . . *Sees Maria Pavlovna isn't paying attention.* He's a pompous young ass.

Maria Pavlovna walks hurriedly to the window overlooking the garden.

MARIA: Peter! *There is no answer. She waves her hand at the smoke blowing in from the fire.* Gerassim! Keep watch. At the first sign of their approach, let us know.

She walks back toward the bookcase, not in a straight line but in a loop that takes in the entire room. She straightens the fishing pole in the corner, turns the fox to a different angle.

MARIA: *to herself.* Everything must be ready for them. They must be made to understand how important the museum is. *Absentmindedly strokes her hair.* Alexander? I had that dream last night.

POTAPOV: Ah, the dream.

MARIA: Of our father, but that is usual. He wasn't a bad man, Alexander. Life moved too fast for him and so he was harsh. But do you know what he said when my brother published his first story? A scribbler and a lazy dog! He screwed his eyes up when he said it, so that none of us could tell whether he was joking. But I remember when the Art Theatre surprised Antosha between acts at *The Cherry Orchard*'s premiere with a jubilee celebration honoring his work. His admirers were there, there were countless ovations, and during the midst of it all Antosha winked at me and mouthed the words with his lips. A scribbler and a lazy dog!

Again, she starts on that same fussy circuit about the room, but this time there is something mannered and more graceful about her movement, making it seem she is dancing a quadrille with a partner who isn't there. Halfway across the room, she recollects herself and stops.

MARIA: I dreamed that my brother's books were all piled there on the seaside off Gurzuf and a wave came in and washed them all away. Not intact, but dissolved. The sea dissolved them, all the words, so that I cried to see them float apart. And what was so odd was that people were swimming in them, all kinds of people — old boyars, peasant soldiers, little girls in lacy frocks. They were splashing about in thick black ink and laughing and yet I was helpless and my heart wanted to break.

POTAPOV: *approaching her timidly.* Maria Pavlovna? Peter says the Germans will be here soon. I know there is nothing . . . Well, I'm quite old, hardly a soldier. But do you think . . . That is . . . Will they hurt me? I shouldn't like that if they hurt me. You see, I'm a great old trouper, but I'm not . . . What's the expression the posters use? A stern patriotic fighter for the Motherland. I'm an actor of no particular consequence and . . . You know me, Maria Pavlovna. You're the only one here who does.

Maria Pavlovna makes a little dismissing motion with her hand, but it isn't clear whether she's heard him or not. Again, she makes a circuit about the room, stopping at each labeled memento and furnishing, more slowly this time, so that she now resembles a woman making the stations of the cross. The light in the drawing room fades into the soft dusk visible out the window, until Alexander Potapov and the rest of the room are gone, and Maria Pavlovna is alone by the window, trembling, her hand resting on a high-backed leather chair for support.

MARIA: *softly, to no one in particular.* Last night I saw lanterns out on the ocean. Do the fishing boats go out even in war? *Hugs herself in the chill.* Peter? Have you brought the painting?

Stands there in silence, then makes an impatient gesture toward the window like someone yanking something in. She stands straighter. Smooths her dress down and throws her head back as if casting something off. By sheer force of will she makes herself seem younger and more resolute, so that the impression of a solitary old woman is only a glimpse, and she is quickly back to her proud, defiant self.

MARIA: He died in Germany, did you know that? He couldn't sleep at night, his chest was much worse, and the doctor began giving him arsenic injections so he could walk. He wrote me he was getting better — that his tuberculosis had miraculously vanished . . . There's a park called the Tiergarten. He took Olga there and wrote me describing how pleasant it was. I have the letter just as it came. You can see how labored his handwriting had become. But that was so odd. He thought he was getting better right until the end. He planned a new play about an exploring expedition to Spitsbergen and his fever was soothed by images of snow.

Again, she walks around the room, but this time she pays no attention to the furnishings and it is clear she is lost in her own thoughts.

MARIA: I remember the doctor's name was Professor Ewald, an internal specialist. Antosha wrote that he liked Berlin very much, though it was insufferably hot. They went to Badenweiler to escape it. There were Russian students in the next room and they sang for him when he couldn't sleep. He needed a summer suit so Olga was sent to Freiburg to fetch one. The food was very tasty, he wrote me. German food is very tasty. *Pauses.* They were the last words he ever wrote.

Her circuit has carried her to the bookcase and the picture propped there on the shelf. Slowly reaches out her hand to it, then taps its surface very lightly — not her brother, but the head of the dachshund.

MARIA: German food is very tasty. Very . . .

She touches the dog again.
The light fades.
The clanking sound.
Curtain.

KUNIN

AT NIGHT when his widowed sister was asleep behind the bookcase that partitioned their room, when the
sibilance of her breathing joined the quieter puffing of
the heat, when the soccer games he listened to on the
shortwave had ended and his music come on (Bartók if
he was lucky, Tchaikovsky if he was not); when, in short,
the present had faded away into a blank white nothing
that made no claim, he remembered like this, in acts,
scenes, and monologues, all of which were directed by
himself. People entered at his prompting, exited at his

cue. A wave of the hand and light appeared; a nod and the curtain came solemnly down. Casting, costumes, sets — these were all in his hands. Peter Sergeich Kunin, playwright of memory, sometime insomniac, writer in dreams.

On good nights. For there were nights when the voices of arguing families rose through the flat with the blare of pop music, his sister called restlessly in her sleep for her missing husband (killed in the Kursk tank battle — not when it happened but thirty years later when, weary of his blindness, he let himself down into the Moscow River ice), the shortwave brought in nothing but static. The memories he staged with such perfection scattered apart like snowflakes dispersing themselves into the dreary yellow of everyday. It was a tragedy he wanted, with all a tragedy's glory and pomp, and instead the memories came to him like lumps of potato in a cold cabbage soup.

At these times there was nothing for it but to wait. If he fought the noise too furiously, his angina would start up, the pain spreading in a warm flush right to left across his chest. At first, it was soft enough that he could dismiss it as indigestion, but after that the real pain began, and he doubled over in the chair with his arms clutched to his middle like a woman in a difficult birth. "Peter?" his sister called, but only in her dream, and he had to stumble across the room for his glycerine tablets by himself.

Of all the discoveries of his old age, this was by far the worst: that he couldn't remember during pain. In those vague prescient clutchings that told him an attack was on its way, he attempted to focus on a soothing detail from the past — the copper tint of the Yaila Mountains behind the villa, the picnics Maria Pavlovna hosted on the rolling lawns of the old Imperial Palace at Livadia, the exhilarating cold of the ocean when they plunged in off the rocks. He would find these, but only for a second, and then the pain would take them away with an obscuring rush of blackness he was powerless to stop.

At these times he tried to draw courage from the example of Anton Pavlovich himself. For if his own task was merely to shape the past in his heart so that its meaning became clear to him alone, how much harder to take what was there and give it a form the entire world could share. And yet this was exactly what Anton Pavlovich was faced with every morning. To write while his hemorrhoids tormented him, his headaches were increasing, his lungs — at forty-two — rapidly giving out. There must have been moments when his inspiration came so furiously it outraced his nerves, attenuating the pain. But more frequent would have been those other mornings, mornings when his words must have come in rhythm to whatever attack he was suffering, so that it took courage and sheer force of will to detach them from the throb. His ass burned and he wrote about flowers; his chest hemorrhaged and it came out art.

This was where the lesson was, at least so far as it applied to Kunin's old age. For forty years he had been trying to find a common ground with the writer whose memory he had devoted his life to serving, and it was only now that he had left Yalta — left the possessions of the man, left the very air he had breathed — that he had found it at last. His chest hurt, but he could still remember, fight through the spasming to seize the memories and give them life — not all of them, but the essential few.

Be their witness, that is. Be Peter Sergeich Kunin, aged sixty-five, retired Director of the Chekhov Museum of Yalta, overseer of Chekhov's estate, custodian of his papers, secretary and confidant to his sister, Maria Pavlovna, her successor upon her death in 1957 at the age of ninety-four. Be a man who kept up a busy correspondence with Chekhov scholars all over the world, attended frequent conferences on his life and work, published memoirs by lesser members of the Chekhov group, supervised in 1971 the first complete edition of his letters in this century, had the villa's tower repaired in 1962 with money all but extorted from the Lenin Library in Moscow, saw to it that Komsomol youth groups were ushered safely about the grounds without littering, welcomed the writer Alexander Solzhenitsyn to the museum a month before his exile and gave the identical tour to Leonid Brezhnev in August of the following year. Be, that is, a man who often repaired the window sashes by himself, cleaned the leaves out from the villa's cistern, pruned the orchard when it became overgrown. Be a survivor of the Great Patriotic War with a story to tell that came to him in so many ways he was never satisfied with telling it to himself, but would double back to tell it again, now as a play, now as a short story, then neither but a selective crazy-quilt blending that was his own private form.

Be, that is, not an artist but a servant to art. And it had all started on the September morning in 1941 when Maria Pavlovna, to appease the invading Germans, had sent a crippled boy to fetch a portrait of Goethe.

KUNIN FOLLOWED the cliff trail to town. The road past the old Tartar cemetery was easier, winding lazily across the plateau through young orange trees, but it was open and exposed to German patrols. Though steep, the cliff was covered in vines that would hide him until he reached the first streets. Then, too, there was something dramatic about descending this way that suited his mood. The brutal mysterious thing called war; his egocentricity, which pictured every involvement as titanic; the tension in the villa as the Germans approached. They swelled up in him until the excitement became unbearable, and he felt that indescribable emotion a boy knows when he is embarked on the first great adventure of his life. Though not a believer, he crossed himself for luck in the old way, moved toward the edge of the cliff, brought his arms together like a diver about to plunge into the abyss, then started down.

At first, the going was easy. The vines were coiled into hoops, so that moving through them was like being in a tunnel. There were thorns, but by pressing himself close to the rock he was able to keep free of them and make good time.

The heat was the difficult part. Past the lip of the cliff the breeze vanished, and the rocks held the sun like an oven. There was a shady pocket beneath a cypress halfway down, and it was here he stopped to rest — eyes closed, hands behind head, his breaths gradually slowing.

When he did open his eyes it was to look out toward sea. The famous harbor was as neat and round as ever, something from a painting, but farther out the ocean looked peculiarly blue and cold, as if it wasn't the Black Sea at all but one transported from the Arctic. He saw what he thought were whitecaps, but then they lifted themselves from the blue and slanted past the softer light of the horizon. Pelicans and gulls, he decided. He was watching them, trying to spot the lacy shape of ibis, when something stubbier penetrated the birds' plane — something stubby and yellow flying an unswerving horizontal line.

A biplane. A yellow biplane, the kind you might see at a fair. It circled the harbor, then floated back out again toward sea, with no menace in it but a stately, old-fashioned grace. With the sea and the seabirds and the red tile roofs of town, it formed a picture that was soothing and somehow literary, one that fitted in neatly with his childish sense of things.

And then something happened that was very odd.

Out to sea was a flash. A bright amber flash as if the friction of waves had created a spark. A few seconds later there was a thump around to the east of town where the vineyards began. A column of dirt shot into the air like a geyser, froze at its apogee, then wistfully collapsed. So sudden was it, so harmless the effect, that it was a few minutes before he realized what he had just seen was a shell coming ashore from a distant warship.

It was impossible to say how much this affected him. Not so much the explosion, which after all was quite minor, but what happened next. Or rather what didn't happen next. For there was no follow-up shell, no reply from shore, no furious exchange of cannonading. The gulls, momentarily ruffled, resumed their gliding. The seamless ether, bumped, returned flatter than ever. For all the difference it made, the explosion could have been that of a baker's oven, purely local in effect.

This was the odd part. All along he had thought of war as something vast and cataclysmic, a barrage of indescribable chaos, and now his first glimpse showed him war could be soft, even secret, the explosive equivalent of a shrug. But it was just this unlooked-for quality — this absentminded shell fired by a retreating Black Sea fleet — that convinced him the war really existed and wasn't just something from newspapers and radio broadcasts and posters. To see Yalta dive-bombed and strafed would have confirmed his previous conception of war and crystallized it so he wouldn't have been forced to reconsider it as a new, potentially dangerous fact. But to see war presented so offhandedly confused him and made him uncertain how to proceed.

The trail had become a goat path now, so at least the footing was better. After a short distance he reached the first street. It was little more than a dirty lane choked with refuse even the Tartars had no use for, but he was quickly past it to the New Town and the wide macadam avenues that led to the harbor.

As yet the only signs of the German presence were negative ones. That is to say, it was apparent from the complete lack of any activity that a new and hostile force had been superimposed over the normal course of things. Even the Yalta dogs, famous for their bad temper, were mute and invisible. No longer quite this, the atmosphere seemed to say, but not quite this either.

Kunin, for his part, stayed in close to the buildings, fighting down the urge to hurry. Half of him felt that way — felt impelled to complete Maria Pavlovna's commission as quickly as possible — but the other half, the prudent medical-student half, knew his safety depended on caution, on choking back the very adrenaline that had started him off in the first place. Slowly, in gradual increments, he was approaching the war. There was a handful of bullet casings strewn across the pavement like seeds the birds couldn't eat; smoke again, vague acrid wisps of it; the distant, angry sound of a mother scolding her child. His imagining seized these things and raced with them, but reality — having captured the city, having toyed with it — was in no hurry at all.

After ten minutes — ten minutes that seemed like hours — he came to the little bridge across the Bystraya, then Primorsky Park with the concealment of its coarse, steppe-like grass. Past it was the fashionable quarter of town, the Zarechye, with its aristocratic white villas and immaculately scrubbed streets. The larger houses had been collectivized into sanatoria for consumptives fleeing the north, but most were merely boarded up with shutters, as if the Revolution were as temporary as winter and their rightful owners would soon be back. It was easy to imagine snipers hiding behind the shutters; Kunin, walking even slower now, crossed in front of them ready to flatten himself on the ground at the slightest sound.

The Imperial Theatre was in a square of its own off Litkens Street, opposite the promenade. It had opened in 1898, just in time for the Moscow Art Theatre to perform *Uncle Vanya* there on its Crimean tour of that summer. Like most examples of Tsarist art, it was at its most ostentatious and massive at the very moment the monarchy was weakest. So beside the heavy pillars supporting the portico (the effect, Anton Pavlovich claimed in a letter to Suvorin, his publisher, was that of Atlantis awaiting the waves), there were overhanging cornices and elaborate balustrades, marble griffins and prancing copper stags.

To get there, Kunin had to cross the street — a full ten meters without cover. A German patrol, rounding the casino, would have found him a perfect target against the promenade. But there was nothing for it. Taking a deep breath, he crossed the street quite openly, twirling his hand about as though it held a cane. When he reached the theatre, he pressed himself against the wall and began inching his way toward the entrance, his heart beating wildly, the cold chill of the limestone matching the cold panic down his back.

The entrance was a revolving glass door barricaded with beams. He tried pulling the thinnest of these away, but it refused to budge. Off to the side was a smaller door used as an exit. It was barricaded, too, but with flimsier boards. He pulled them furiously apart, not stopping until his hands bled and there was an opening big enough for him to wedge his way through.

It was dark after the street, and it took a few seconds for his eyes to adjust to the gloom. As curious as he was about the theatre, as often as he had walked past it on the promenade, this was the first time he had actually been inside. It had been closed around the time of the show trials in 1936 — the shutters had nothing to do with the Germans. Maria Pavlovna, feeling the shame of its neglect, had been worrying the authorities to have it reopened, but the outbreak of war had put an end to that. Now it was musty and cold, stale with green air like a dirty bottle.

Kunin wandered around the lobby trying to get his bearings. The only light was a pale yellowing that fell from windows in the domed ceiling high above. In it, everything was shambles. The silver grillwork on the walls had been pried back and broken. The elegant mahogany bar was splintered and holed, as if by cannonballs, and the top was covered with broken glass. By the ticket window was a huge pyramid of blackened kindling; past it, the carpet was in shreds. Over everything, vile and bitter, lay the acid smell of cat.

It was the kind of atmosphere that made you tiptoe, not out of reverence but disgust. To the lobby's side were the doors to the orchestra seats; they were padded in thick maroon leather and so heavy it took a determined shove to force them open. Kunin hesitated on the opposite side like a timid gate-crasher — surely an usher would materialize out of the gloom to demand his ticket! — then with a little smile at his foolishness, walked boldly down the center aisle toward the stage.

It was even darker here than in the lobby. What light managed to filter its way inside came in the long slanting shafts of November, so that the vandalism had a surreal, exaggerated effect. And since the aisle was littered with the flat brown tobacco tins favored by the Red Cavalry, it wasn't hard to assign responsibility. They had bivouacked here obviously, probably during their retreat. They had managed to rip the gold edging from the seats, slash the cushions into ribbons. Higher up the gilt had been scraped from the parterre boxes, the chandeliers torn from their fixtures. On the ceiling, the twin frescoes of Tragedy and Comedy were pockmarked with bullet holes; Comedy, the fatter and sadder-looking mask, bled plaster in a dusty white drip.

Only the stage was unharmed. It was hung with a velvet curtain almost vulgar in its redness, the folds so heavy-looking and rigid it seemed spun of steel. Above it, set in mammoth gold frames, were the three portraits Maria Pavlovna had predicted would be there: Lenin, Gorky, and Marx, their faces staring down from the proscenium like disapproving gods.

Kunin edged past the first row of seats, his shoes scuffing up sparks of electricity from the carpet's thick damask. Even with all the destruction, the broken glass, the smothering smell, there was a plush romantic something about the place that made him think of Tolstoy and bare-shouldered women and uniformed hussars. The dusky, anticipatory light; the horseshoe curve of the mezzanine boxes; the way the slightest sound reverberated through the hall, evidence of a great acoustic power waiting to be tapped. All this seemed the prelude to excited stirrings and great applause.

And there was something else there, too, something so new and unexpected it made him find a seat in order to slow its progress down. A sensation that had been building ever since he had first tiptoed his way in, something to do with the plushness and the quiet but went beyond both of these, so that what he felt was a delicious, all-enveloping sense of safety. Safety, the kind a refugee feels crossing the border, but deeper and more essential than this, too — the safety a shivering child knows when it's placed by strong arms into a warm, clean-sheeted bed. The war, the urgency of his mission — it was as if neither existed. Only here, the feeling seemed to say. Here and nowhere else.

He was afraid to analyze its cause too closely, but it had something to do with what little effect the vandalism had on the overall grace of the theatre itself. Eternal art, the undying muse — all the phrases that came to him were stilted. And yet something of this is exactly what he felt. Regimes rose and fell, armies came and went, and yet this inarticulate thing latent in the theatre's amber light went on forever, and in its midst he could not be harmed.

The Imperial Theatre of Yalta! Scene of *The Cherry Orchard* and *Uncle Vanya* and *The Three Sisters*. The Imperial Theatre, where in 1898, after *The Seagull* had been laughed off the stage at the Petersburg premiere, the Art Theatre had given the triumphant revival that had stamped it as a masterpiece; the theatre where in 1901, an invalid now, Chekhov had been tricked into attending a literary testimonial in honor of his career. The Imperial Theatre, where the great Vasily Kachalov had performed, Vsevolod Meyerhold and Catherine Samarov, Constantine Stanislavsky and Olga Knipper, earning ovations in her husband's work long after Anton Pavlovich had died.

No wonder then that the atmosphere was electric — that the air finding its way through the ventilating shafts should rustle like programs being expectantly fanned. Something had happened here so beautiful that it would happen again — Kunin was certain of this — and the longer he searched, the more certain he became. The pulleys and levers that crowded the wings; the open dressing rooms with their trays of greasepaint; the prompter's box with its overturned stool. Everything stood waiting for the vital spark.

He prowled the back corridors like a stagestruck boy in search of autographs — it was all he could do not to respectfully knock before prying open the various doors. He had to force himself to remember what he was there for; each time he entered a new room he searched it diligently for the missing portraits. He found ancient flats from long-forgotten productions, costumes that must have been new in the time of Catherine the Great, photographs of party hacks, but of Shakespeare, Goethe, and Pushkin there was no sign.

The last room he checked wasn't a room at all but a glorified closet, filled with buckets and brooms and the smell of camphor. He was backing out again when a glint of something gold made him press on toward the back. In the corner, draped beneath the kind of gauzy silk gown a ballerina might have worn, were the missing portraits, their frames padded in cotton to protect them from scratches. He slid them out to the corridor to examine them more closely. Thanks to the care of some unknown someone they were intact and unharmed.

It was only now that he had them out in the light that he realized he didn't know what Goethe looked like. Shakespeare, though, was easy, as was Pushkin, so the third — the somber personage in the curly white wig — must surely be the German master himself. Returning the other two to the closet, he cradled Goethe beneath his arm, retraced his steps through the vandalized theatre, then by the dint of much pushing and shoving managed to wedge both the picture and his body back through the barricaded door outside.

Outside into what he realized with amazement was dusk. The light on the street wasn't much brighter than it was in the theatre, and it was colored by that same amber in-betweenness — the sense that any second it might flare up into light.

Maria Pavlovna will be worried, he thought. Between this and the protective twilight, the lingering sensation of safety instilled by the theatre, he was much less cautious than before and hurried through the arcades counting on their shadows for cover. There was a short-cut he knew that involved crossing the Vodopadnaya on a footbridge, then zigzagging past the docks to the promenade. He was to the end of Litkens Street — he was waiting for the fog to thicken before crossing the dozen meters to the river — when a flash of something yellow made him glance around to his right.

On a corner building, halfway up the stuccoed wall, was a sign printed neatly in German — a road sign with an arrow pointing toward the harbor. As harmless looking as it was, its effect was exactly that of the exploding shell, an unlikely detail that convinced him as no battle scene could of the war's reality.

Carefully now, he told himself, but just as the thought formed, he heard girlish laughter down the street to his left. He spun around in embarrassment, and was just in time to see who was standing there a moment before they saw him. Three local girls in high heels and stockings, their shiny red dresses wrapped tight around their legs to emphasize their figures. Tarts, the cheaper kind you never saw in the elegant part of town. Beside them were two German soldiers in gray combat dress, rifles held loosely at their sides. They were joking with the girls, bringing up matches to their cigarettes, then jerking them teasingly back.

One of the tarts looked up and saw Kunin standing there watching. There was a moment when their eyes met that Kunin was sure she wouldn't give him away, but that moment passed in an instant; the girl said something to the soldiers and they both spun around, bringing their rifles to their shoulders with a motion that was oddly graceful, like musicians taking up their violins. The taller

of the two put his immediately back down, but the shorter
one kept his aimed at Kunin's chest.

"*Schnell! Schnell!*" he yelled, cocking his head to one
side.

Kunin felt the cords of his arms tighten as if they
were reaching for something, and at the same time the
kind of damp, chilling sensation down the ribs as is only
experienced in nightmares. I must meet his eyes, he remembered thinking, but the soldier's face was pressed now
to the sights, and there was nothing to meet but a de-
formed brown cheek of flesh, wood, and steel.

It wasn't so much fear Kunin felt as a helpless sense
of failure. So this is how it ends, he thought. He brought
the picture around to his other arm to shift the weight,
and in doing so the frame slipped from his sweaty grip,
catapulting down onto the pavement with a noise that
reverberated through the alley. Startled, the other soldier
brought his rifle back up and aimed it in Kunin's direction, the bolt sliding back with a click that was like fingers snapping against his heart.

For a full thirty seconds they faced each other —
and then Kunin made the motion that saved his life. Not
understanding their shouts, feeling shy at the girls' giggles, he crossed to the fallen portrait, reached down and
grabbed its corner, straightened, tucked it carefully beneath his arm, then began walking backward the way he
had come, keeping his face toward them like a wary pic-
nicker retreating from a bear. Not in the back, he remembered thinking. In the chest and quick.

But the soldiers didn't fire. They lowered their rifles
and began laughing. The shorter one pointed and said
something — the tarts started laughing, too. A moment

more and the taller one was hobbling around in an exaggerated imitation of Kunin's limp, holding his leg with both hands, swinging it stiffly out in front of him, screwing up his face in mock-terror and alarm.

There was a moment of instinctive relief when Kunin saw the guns lowered, but it was immediately replaced by a sense of humiliation so intense it made him literally double over, as if he had been shot in the stomach after all. The soldiers limped back and forth along the curb, laughing and pointing, and there was nothing he could do to stop them, no revenge he could administer, no way to wipe the laughter off the prettiest girl's face. He turned his back on them and walked slowly away, hating his leg as he had never hated it before, hating the Germans and Yalta and everything that crossed his path.

And later, as he walked the New Town streets quite openly, hoping with a fierce, suicidal defiance to be stopped again, he sensed a different feeling that wasn't as overpowering as the others, yet in its implications much more frightening. For at that moment when the German infantrymen had aimed their rifles at his heart, in the moment of shame when the muscles of his arm had involuntarily tightened, he had been reaching for something after all — something inside himself that should have been there but wasn't. The sense of safety he had felt in the theatre — the refuge of beauty created in him by poetry and books. It had protected him in his childhood when his parents were arrested, protected him again at the university when no one thought of anything but the need to toe the line. In loneliness and fear he had sought for its shelter and never been refused, but now he had been refused, refused for the second time that day, and the chill he had felt was the bewildered hollow of his faith's passing.

He was exhausted now — guilty at lingering so long in the theatre, certain he would find the villa surrounded by machine guns or set ablaze. He tried running in his ludicrous, stumbly way, but the streets were crowded with peddlers and whores, and he kept having to swerve to avoid knocking into them. They were everywhere now, selling what they could to bored German soldiers who paid them scant attention. In the dark of the blackout, only the lapping waves created any light, so most of these first encounters were on the beach; there were little knots of soldiers and civilians every few meters, their heads huddled together like fishermen discussing their catch. A short distance inland all was blackness and shadow and damp. Kunin swerved into it so there was no separation between the emptiness he felt and the emptiness of the night, and he was able to take a perverse satisfaction in their matching. Occupied city, he remembered thinking. Occupied hearts.

And then without realizing it he had come to the end of the promenade. Directly above him towered the darker richness of the cliff. But it wasn't this he thought of forty years later when he fiddled impatiently with the shortwave, trying to fit his memories into the proper form and so understand. It wasn't the convoluted pattern of the vines that salved his pain, not the silver iridescence of the mica halfway up.

It was the villa that topped the cliff, the Chekhov

villa, with a light blazing in every window, the whiteness streaming through the wind-tossed cypress to give it motion, so that it sailed above the blacked-out town like a solitary liner embarked on a still and mysterious sea.

VARKA'S STORY

VARKA'S LIFE came in two parts, the first sad and easily told; the second happier, but told with more difficulty.

Of her early childhood she remembered little. She was born in Cracow in 1891. Her father was a violinist who played at weddings and bar mitzvahs — a happy, feckless man who would sit her on his knee and make his violin talk to her in funny voices. Other than that, all she remembered about him was the cologne he wore, the amazement she felt when she nuzzled him to find the smell there in the small floppy hollows of his ears.

Her mother played the ant to his cricket. She was always bent over something — the wash, the coal for the fireplace, another baby. By the time Varka was ten, there were six other children to care for, and, like most girls on that street, she was sent out to service in a wealthy family.

This would have been bearable had it been in Cracow, where she could come home occasionally to hear her father make squeaky voices for the little ones. Unfortunately for Varka, it was the fashion among wealthy Russians of those days to send to Poland for their domestic help, prizing as they did the intelligence and pious Catholicism of the servants thus obtained. There was a regular trade in it, with agents in the poor quarter of every Polish city. It was one of these agents, a catlike man named Pomerwitz, who arranged for Varka's employment and came with a cart to take her to the train.

That train ride across Russia was the first fully colored memory of her life. The straw seats that crackled in the heat. The peasant woman sitting opposite nursing twins at her pendulous red breasts. The tepid water a hunchback in uniform would bring around in a pewter bowl. The sunburned children that appeared when the train stopped for coal, pressing raspberries to the windows in exchange for pennies or bits of bread. In later years, she would go over these things again and again, feeling something important rested on her keeping their vividness alive.

After three days, the train stopped in Kiev. Long after all the other passengers had left, a cart appeared — a cart like the one that had delivered her to the train in Cracow. In it was a man who rubbed his hands together the same feline way Pomerwitz had, though he was less talkative and more abrupt.

"The Cracow girl?" he said, grabbing her satchel. "This way then and quick."

He drove her to a section of mansions that were larger than any she had seen in her native city, though she learned later they were far from being the largest in Kiev. The family she was to work for consisted of a doctor of internal medicine named Antip Polugradev, his wife, Olga, and their three adolescent daughters, ages seven, nine, and twelve. Because of confusion over her arrival date, there wasn't a place ready for her, so for the first five nights she was lodged with the children in the nursery. In a way, this was the cruelest of the many cruelties practiced on her there. For five nights, cuddling in bed with the two smallest girls, sharing their stories and toys, she was able to live under the illusion she was part of the family — that the miraculous, frightening journey across the vast Russian grassland had had as its purpose a coziness and sense of belonging that went beyond anything she had ever dreamed.

On the sixth day she was given a mat in the servants' hall beneath the bed of the cook, Marfa Tarayena. She was put to work scrubbing floors and washing dishes, and treated with icy superiority by the girls whose playthings she had recently shared. At dawn, she was shaken from her mat by the rough hand of Marfa Tarayena; at midnight, she was allowed to retreat there while the cook entertained her butcher friends on the bulging mattress six inches above her face.

In time, Varka became inured to this, as she did the

cracked hands from scalding water, the scabby hot patches on her knees, the bitter taunts of the Polugradev girls. What was harder was her own ugliness — an ugliness made apparent not so much by the mocking as by the kindness shown her by the manservants and maids. They pitied her for her crooked nose and square, ungainly jaw — they went out of their way not to stare — but later, when their pity made no difference and she was just as ugly and awkward as ever, their pity recoiled into harshness and she became the victim of everyone's bad moods.

These were frequent. Antip Polugradev had a face so round and open he could draw smiles from a stone, but he was a stern man, fussy over small things, and ridiculously vain in his appearance. Olga Nikolovna was if anything even vainer, but with less reason. She spent the daylight hours eating chocolates under the attention of her masseuse.

When Varka was fourteen, the entire household moved to the resort city of Yalta in the Crimea. It was a villa in the Zarechye district, and it was soon apparent that Antip Polugradev's practice was flourishing even more than it had in Kiev. Through certain stories told by the tradesmen — by the frequency with which carriages pulled up at the villa at night to discharge heavily veiled women — it was clear this practice consisted of giving abortions to the aristocratic women who made Yalta their winter home.

The money brought in by this acted like water on dusty, shriveled-up weeds. Antip Polugradev was less harsh to the servants, Olga Nikolovna stopped eating chocolates, and the three daughters made their debuts in expensive gowns. Even Varka reaped some benefit. Though it was small as a closet, she was given her own room, and on Wednesday afternoons was allowed to leave the house to do as she pleased.

Since she had no money, this consisted entirely of walking up and down the promenade along Yalta's famous harbor, staying in tight to the rail so as not to interfere with the grand couples strolling self-confidently down the center. She liked staring at the women, comparing their dresses. She liked the cidery smell of the ocean, the shade of the silk trees, the busy way the provision boats chugged out to the anchored white yachts with their slanting masts. Most of all she liked the openness of the horizon — how staring at it undid the hopelessness in her and gave her the feeling anything was possible.

Everything, in short, was fine, at least for a while. On her fifteenth birthday, meaning to give herself a treat, she woke up early and took a bath in the small pantry to the back of the kitchen. At the time she wasn't positive, but it seemed to her the pantry door had opened slightly while she was drying herself, then slowly closed. When she dressed and went back to the kitchen, she thought she caught the scent of Antip Polugradev's cigar.

That night after the last of his patients had left he came to her room and raped her, muttering all the while the filthiest obscenities, of which the gentlest was "You're repulsive. Repulsive, repulsive . . ." When he finished, he told her that if she went to Olga Nikolovna and complained, she would be immediately dismissed.

Two months later when it became obvious she was pregnant, she went to the mistress anyway, but only to timidly ask if the doctor might not remove her baby before it grew larger. She expected Olga Nikolovna to be angry, possibly yell, but instead she had listened to her story with her fleshy face puckered up in curiosity and excitement. She began asking detailed questions about what had happened, not letting off until Varka began crying in shame. When Varka asked again about having the baby removed, Olga Nikolovna swept her hand back through her hair in obvious impatience.

"Of course. Of course . . . The child? No, there's no question of that. It is God's will. Dr. Polugradev and I will raise it as our own."

The result was that she was treated much better than before, allowed two afternoons off a week, and stuffed with sweetmeats like a prize cow. She went into labor a month before she was due, but the boy survived and was immediately taken away from her, to be raised in the nursery by an English nurse. Once Varka was on her feet again, she was sent back to her duties in the kitchen. As before, her walks along the promenade were her only recreation.

All was exactly the same, but not quite. For she no longer looked upon the strolling couples with envy and admiration but with a cool, realistic disapproval, seeing them in all their selfishness, insignificance, and pride. Their kind had taken her childhood away but given her something priceless in return, something that only comes to those without hope: the ability to see beyond the husk of appearances to the essential kernel within.

And of these strollers along the promenade, only one met the test of her unsparing green eyes — a woman, nameless, she began thinking of simply as "her." It was a woman of about forty, with luxurious auburn hair, a smile of mild amusement, and a graceful, purposeful way of walking that managed to suggest both the prance of a

Petersburg princess and the headlong rush of a boisterous girl. In a world of couples, she always walked alone, following a habitual route along the promenade, then along the beach. Occasionally she might stop for an hour at one of the outdoor cafes; once she bought a paper and read it with a severe frown that darkened her face into something very formidable. The older and more dignified of the men bowed to her in recognition, but she had little time for chatting and always moved quickly on.

She was there every Wednesday at the same time, and Varka soon began counting on her arrival as the highlight of the afternoon. What attracted her to this woman was her nobility of bearing among so many fake nobles, her true beauty amid so much that was false, her perfect self-sufficiency and contentment, the thoughtful way she tilted her head as she stared out to sea. For the first time in her life, Varka had a person she could admire with her entire heart.

Like a schoolgirl with a crush, she would plan ways of positioning herself so as to come into the unknown woman's view. One Wednesday she actually got up the nerve to stop her and ask the way to the Oreanda Hotel, and was rewarded with two memories she cherished the rest of the week: the gentle, musical sound of the woman's voice; the understanding way she met her eyes, as if she knew everything there was to know without explanation.

This bright something that stood aside from the Polugradevs' helped sustain Varka through the difficult times of that spring. One by one the servants were being let go without explanation. The doctor's wife resumed her orgies of eating, and this time the doctor joined in, until they soon resembled the fat, wicked capitalists that were beginning to show up on posters splashed across the Old Town walls. At dinner, they talked of money to the exclusion of all else, exchanging lewd glances as they did so, dropping their voices to a whisper whenever one of the remaining servants entered with more food. There was a hurried, secret something in the air that boded no good for anyone connected with that house.

On the first day of June, Varka was summoned to the mistress's presence. The baby was playing by the sofa, sucking its mouth with a happy sound against the round bulge of Olga Nikolovna's ankle.

"Varka, my dear," she said cheerfully. "Do you know the Tartar village out beyond town, the one they call Kuchukoy? The elder has a rug made especially for me. As a relief from your usual chores, I am sending you there to pick it up."

To get to the village took her all morning and half the afternoon. At first, she enjoyed it — the air with its haze, the way the sea spread out the higher she climbed, the view of Ai-Petri and the distant Yailas. There was a ruined Genoese tower halfway up the path, and she spent a pleasant half hour resting in its shade. But by the time she reached the crest of the plateau, it was very hot and her legs throbbed in fatigue.

Kuchukoy turned out to be a collection of dirty hovels clouded with midges. No one knew anything about a rug, and the village children laughed at her and put their thumbs to their faces in imitation of her nose. By the time she trudged back to the Zarechye, it was well past dark. There were no lights on in the villa, but weary, thinking nothing of it, she walked around to the kitchen door.

Later, when the enormity of what had happened sunk in, it was this moment of opening the kitchen door that she thought of first. For in the strange way it creaked — in the hollow of quiet waiting for her on the other side, the blinding scent of disinfectant — everything was apparent.

It took a moment to grope for the light and switch it on. She saw first that the knives were not on the counter where she had left them. She noticed next that the sausage she had hung over the breadbox was gone — that there was no breadbox, only its square outline in the dust. No breadbox, no icebox, no plates. Nothing. The cupboards were open and empty; the pots and pans were gone from their rack by the stove. Someone had even taken down the fly tapes that hung over the table. The keeping room, the pantry. Empty.

Upstairs was the same. No furniture, no clothing, not the slightest trace of anyone's presence. She hurried from room to room, not believing the evidence of her eyes. The closets, the shelves. All were empty and swept clean. Between her departure that morning and her return, the house had been completely abandoned. She ran her hands over the wood, but still couldn't believe it, and it was only when she called the baby's name that she became convinced. Incredibly, the Polugradevs had fled. And even then she didn't think of why this was so or what would happen to her next, but of something totally different that came over her like a chill.

She thought of the time crossing Russia on the train

as a small girl, how the sun had poured down all day without anything to interrupt it, the sense the rolling grassland had given her of the utter emptiness of space, only she realized now it wasn't just space that was empty, but time and memory and being as well, so there was nothing in life but quicksand and beneath it a bottomless void. And knowing this — raising her arms in a vain clutching motion; listening to the echo of her baby's name diminish its way through the darkened halls — into this terrible emptiness she felt herself fall.

THAT WAS the first part of Varka's life. The second part started the afternoon of the following day. Like many people who experience great change, she would always look back on her early years with a mixture of wonder and disbelief, and something of this feeling was present right from the start. She spent the night in the deserted villa. She spent the next morning there as well, cleaning from habit, paying particular attention to the dust above the doorsills, and by the time she had finished dusting, she had finished with her youth.

It was a Tuesday, but she went to the promenade anyway, having nowhere else to go. For a long time she walked as she always did, staying well to the outside so as not to get in anyone's way. It wasn't fear she felt — fear attacks those who are fixed, and she floated unattached as a leaf — but the desperate exhilaration a gambler knows when he's staked everything on one card.

Precisely at three, the beautiful woman with the auburn hair appeared from behind the newspaper kiosk, walking rapidly toward the beach. Varka, her heart pounding, waited until she was almost up to her, then stepped out from the railing into her path.

The woman was startled, but only momentarily. "You're the girl who asked me about the Oreanda," she said, tilting her head to the side and smiling.

Varka stared at the ground.

"Yes?" the woman said pleasantly. "What is it?"

"Help me."

And what was odd, in later years Varka could never remember actually saying the words out loud — was sure in fact she hadn't — but so obvious was the desperation in her eyes, so skilled was Maria Pavlovna at reading them, that it was exactly as if she had.

Her look had instantly darkened. Not wasting any time, she took Varka firmly by the arm and led her over to the Artynov Cafe.

There were no empty tables on the terrace. Maria Pavlovna, who had introduced herself on their walk across the promenade, said something to the headwaiter and instantly a table was cleared.

"I think coffee for the young lady," she said. "That and some of your buns. I will have my usual two cups of tea, Henri. See that no one sits near us."

"There," she said, when he had gone. "They think me very odd here. The lady of two teas. But I am old enough now that I have the privilege of not caring what young waiters think. When the tea comes I will drink the first cup very slowly. I will drink the second cup even more slowly. While I am doing this, I want you to tell me everything."

This Varka did, though with the greatest difficulty.

Maria Pavlovna listened patiently, breaking in only when she came to the part about the Polugradevs abandoning the house.

"Rats from a sinking ship," she mumbled, her eyes flashing in anger. "To France probably. I'll wager they're halfway to Sevastopol already. They know what the future holds for rich abortionists." She waved her hand. "Go on, my dear."

But Varka had nothing more to say. Again, Maria Pavlovna stared at her as if she did — as if by the intensity of her gaze she could elicit everything. At last, with a little nod, she pushed back her chair.

"I have to be going," she said. "There's a performance of *Three Sisters* tonight and they tend to get sloppy if I don't attend. But thank you for your frankness."

She put a ruble note down on the table. Varka's heart sank as she saw her leave. She was all the way to the stairway leading down from the terrace, on the point of disappearing behind an ornamental palm, when she suddenly stopped and glanced back over her shoulder in Varka's direction.

"Well, are you coming or not?" she said impatiently. "The new maid of the Chekhov household does not waste her time in fashionable cafes."

Things happened very fast after that. A hansom driven by a walrus of a man drove them up the cliff behind town. There were views of the sea and mountains; a breeze that came in the window and teased loose Maria Pavlovna's hair. At the top of the cliff set alone in a little park was a white villa smaller than the Polugradevs', but happier looking, with curious wings jutting out at unexpected an-gles and a funny round tower of stucco-like brick. Maria Pavlovna paid the driver, then led Varka inside. The smell of oranges, so noticeable in the garden, carried in with them to the hall.

"This was my brother's library," Maria Pavlovna said, taking her into the first of the rooms. "He didn't like his books dusted, so you are not to dust them. The dust was the only way he could remember which ones he had read. Here, this was his reading glass. You're to leave it exactly like this on the table, do you understand? The girl you are replacing took it upon herself to rearrange his things and she was immediately dismissed."

Varka, bewildered by the severity in her tone, nodded dumbly.

"This way then."

They went from room to room, and in each one Maria Pavlovna's instructions were just as insistent and precise. Her brother liked to have his inkwells filled at night so as not to be disturbed in the morning. Her brother abhorred the scent of camphor, so all the cleaning was to be done by lemon oil and wax. Her brother hated to watch the wind blow and not feel it on his face, so the windows were to remain open. Her brother had always enjoyed flowers, and so Varka was to cut some fresh each morning and put them in the Oriental blue vase on his shelf.

"Do you understand?" Maria Pavlovna kept repeating. "Do I make myself plain?"

Varka nodded. As for understanding, she felt as though this brother, whoever he was, was about to jump out at her from the walls. After saying for the hundredth time "My brother wouldn't want this disturbed in any way," Maria Pavlovna caught herself and looked at Varka with the ironic little smile that was soon to become so familiar.

"This must be hard for you, but . . . ." She shook her head. "Not here. Out in the garden."

They sat on a bench beneath a lemon tree. It was quiet there, and the dappled shadows played like butterflies across Maria Pavlovna's throat. She took her time explaining, but still it was difficult for Varka to follow.

"My brother was a writer. He was also a doctor, and a good one, but he was a writer above all. He was a writer of stories and plays. He would see something, just a glimpse in passing, or hear something, just a phrase, and out of this he would make his tales. When he was alive I was able to help him in small things, and now that he is gone, I will help in big things. Do you see?"

Varka shook her head from side to side, then looked away in embarrassment.

But Maria Pavlovna wouldn't let her be ashamed. She reached over until she had both Varka's hands in her own, then turned her around so they were facing each other and there could be no mistake.

"Don't listen to my words," she said softly. "I will tell you about him, but you must listen here, through your heart."

And so she talked. And so she talked and so Varka listened, not with her ears but her heart, and through this she gradually began understanding that what Maria Pavlovna was asking wasn't complicated at all, but something very simple: she needed her help. She couldn't understand who this brother was and why it was so important to keep his things exactly the way they were when he was alive, but this direct, simple appeal touched her in the deepest part of her soul. She, Varka, for the first time in her life was being asked by another human being for help. It was a miracle, and this strong kindly woman was a miracle, and these two fixed beliefs came to her so instinctively that through all that happened afterward she never lost faith in their truth.

"I understand," she mumbled, her throat thick with tears.

Maria Pavlovna, too, seemed moved, and it was a long time before she let Varka's hand fall from hers.

"Then it's settled," she said, helping her up. "In the future you are to be my helper, but tonight you are to be my guest."

"I'm sorry, mistress?"

"We are going to the theatre. There's a dress you can borrow. You shall see for yourself what my brother was about."

From the time Maria Pavlovna helped pull the soft billowy dress over her shoulders to the time they came home after midnight, the taxi driver entertaining them with stories of his days as a thief, Varka never lost the sense that she was living a dream. It wasn't a fairy tale she felt herself in, but a stage before that: the delightful, awesome moment when a girl first becomes aware fairy tales even exist.

There had been the theatre crowded with people, and there had been Maria Pavlovna radiant in a simply cut gown of black satin, and there Varka had been beside her, her skin rising up in goose bumps of fear and pride. Everyone treated Maria Pavlovna with the greatest deference, and a special usher had been assigned to escort them to a private box to the left of the stage. "Bravo Chekhova!" someone in the audience yelled, and all the fashionably dressed ladies and gentlemen rose to their feet to applaud in their direction.

Of the performance itself, Varka understood little. The actors, whoever they were, talked very fast and moved about in unaccountable ways. One of the three sisters was quite attractive, but her hair was unkempt and she looked as though she needed a good meal. There were some soldiers, and a great deal of time was spent at lunch.

For her part, Maria Pavlovna kept up a steady stream of comments the entire time.

"That numbskull!" she said, not bothering to hide her voice. "My brother wanted a white dress. He specifically said white! . . . Weaker! Too strong, far too strong! Prosorov is meant to be spineless . . . A disaster, my dear. A complete and savage mockery of my brother's intentions."

And yet at the end she applauded as loudly as anyone, and nodded her head in satisfaction the way someone will at the completion of a familiar ritual. Beside her, Varka applauded, too, the sheer physical pleasure of it making her get quite carried away. As carefully as she listened, she had never made sense of what the actors were saying, but by remembering Maria Pavlovna's advice — by listening with her heart — she was able to understand something deeper than the words.

The three sisters. The army officer with his frowns. The way everyone seemed waiting, always waiting. She could sense all of them yearned for something, yearned with all their soul, and this yearning for an unknown, unreachable something matched what had been in her own soul and made it rise through her throat in a sob.

It wasn't important now to worry about this brother and who he had been. He had had some connection to this yearning — that was good enough for Varka — and the memory of that magic night when she rose with his sister to accept the audience's applause joined with the miracle of the day and the strength of Maria Pavlovna to become the third enduring pillar of her faith.

THOSE FIRST years at the villa were busy ones. Many of Anton Pavlovich's friends were still alive, there were relatives always visiting, complete strangers were apt to call, and at times there were upwards of thirty sitting down to dinner. Maria Pavlovna always worried about the arrangements, vowed there wasn't space to accommodate one more, but Varka soon learned to reassure her and before long was taking all the domestic details into her own hands.

Maria Pavlovna did a lot of traveling in those days, leaving Varka in charge for weeks at a time. An obscure poet would die of typhus in Central Asia and immediately her bags must be packed and off she would race to Bakchisarai to catch the train. The moment she got back, a minor playwright would die of consumption in Moscow and off she must go again, only stopping to pick up fresh clothes. Days later, she returned in a state bordering collapse, cursing Russian railroads and Russian hotels and everything that had happened.

"At least it was a well-represented affair," she said once she calmed down. "The critic Meyer and his circle?

Arkhipova, who wrote that lovely memoir of Antosha's youth? I fancy she was in love with him at one time — all on her side, of course. For him there was really no one until Knipper. But all of them were most careful to assure me how popular his work remains."

She saw it as her duty to represent her brother at these occasions — to provide with her presence the physical evidence of his immortality. What difference did it make if no one had ever heard of the poet, for didn't poets sometimes become famous after their deaths? It wouldn't be right that a soon-to-be-famous poet died and Anton Pavlovich was not represented at the funeral . . . or so Maria Pavlovna tried to explain. Each time, Varka smiled and nodded and went about her own duty: to knead her mistress's muscles with warm oil until they lost their bunched feeling and began to soften.

The constant concern about the house, the worry over finances, the vast correspondence that occupied her from dawn until noon, the journeys, not only to funerals but to performances of her brother's plays . . . these things were adding up. Maria Pavlovna's luxurious hair went to gray overnight, her eyesight worsened, and her temper, never her strong point, became at times unbearable. All this happened very fast, then was over with, as if she had no time for aging and must be finished with the process as quickly as possible. By the beginning of 1914, the girlish quality that had so attracted Varka was completely gone, but in its place was a beauty and grace that were ageless.

In a way, it was as though she had a premonition of what was coming and wanted to steel herself for the ordeal, cast aside anything that wasn't tempered and capable of hard abuse. For odd things were happening now.

Less and less did visitors come to the house. Invitations came back marked *Address unknown* and there was no longer any tracing many of Anton Pavlovich's friends. In Yalta itself, the tourists were as numerous and splendid as ever, but there was a frantic quality to the atmosphere that set everyone to longing for the old days when everything was calm.

"It's bewildering," Maria Pavlovna said as they walked past the shops on the Naberezhnaya. "Where is everyone I know? Why are things so expensive? Why do those women wear those unbecoming skirts?"

"It's the modern age, mistress. People's heads have been turned. Here, I know a cheaper place further along."

"The modern age?" Maria Pavlovna turned away. "Perhaps."

Mobilization came in August, then the Tsar declared war, then things started changing at a faster pace. Ever since Varka had gone into service at the villa, there had been one or more manservants — stupid, rough men who accepted their wages grudgingly and never stayed for long. Now, with the war, there was no obtaining any help, and Varka and Maria Pavlovna were forced to do all the heavy work themselves. For long hours they toiled in the orchard pruning all the trees, propping up the sagging branches, working until the skin on their palms split and became crusted over with blood. After this might come repairs to the walkways or the cisterns or any of the thousand jobs necessary to keep the house functioning. By nightfall, neither had the strength to prepare dinner, and they slept exhausted until dawn.

In January, Maria Pavlovna bought a map of Eastern Europe and hung it in the library over a portrait of Grigorovich, her brother's early patron and friend. On it, she traced the lines of the respective armies and each day would study the paper in order to update the positions.

This was a source of great amusement to those of her friends who still called. One of these, Pavel Rashevitch, was a minor official in town who over the years had been helpful in various small ways. He was a widower, still handsome, fond of flirting with Maria Pavlovna though she paid him little attention.

"Ah, I see your lines are inching eastward," he said, pulling his whiskers in mock-alarm. "Now tell me this, Maria, my adored. You have no interest in world events. Why then this sudden fascination?"

He paused, then went on to answer the question himself.

"Because you want to know where the armies are in relation to the Chekhov villa. Because at the center of the universe stands not the sun, not the earth, but this glorious white villa here above the bay. The world may crumble, kingdoms fall, but the Kaiser — God blast him! — will never capture the house of Anton Chekhov!"

The lines became choppier as the spring came. It was harder to obtain definite information from the newspapers, and their columns were taken up with nothing but lists of the dead. As if to match the war news, the weather turned dark and vicious, snow falling in Yalta for the first time anyone could recall. There were odd lights in the sky and the Tartar peasants told stories about seeing blood across the moon. Fuel was in short supply, then food, and long queues formed outside the bakers, but there was still no bread.

"And this in Yalta!" Maria Pavlovna said in amazement. "Imagine what it must be like in Moscow or Kiev."

Even before the Revolution, looters began appearing in Livadia on the outskirts of Yalta, and by September a dozen houses had been burned to the ground. At first, these bands were thought of as outlaws and shrugged off, but as the autumn wore on their ranks kept swelling, not only with deserters but with widows and children of men who had died. At the end of October, the shops along the promenade were broken into and sacked. In November, the villa next to them was stripped of everything and set ablaze. Maria Pavlovna appealed to Rashevitch for help, but by then he was fighting for his own skin and had no influence whatsoever.

One tear from Maria Pavlovna, one hint that her courage faltered, and Varka would have given way to panic herself, so terrified was she of the flames that at night formed a black-orange band around the streets of the New Town. Maria Pavlovna, though, did not lose her nerve. She took all her brother's notebooks and letters and deposited them in the vault of the English bank on Zagorodnaya Street. Paintings, portraits, and souvenirs went into the storeroom in the villa's cellar. Timbers were set ready to slam across the doors; the cistern was filled with water to use if sparks from the other fires spread that far. And when this had been done — when her brother's papers were safe and there was nothing left to defend except the house — she went to the village of Baukta and struck a deal with the smuggler Arseny to protect the villa with his gang.

This Arseny was a muscular, avaricious old Greek

who lived by a pirate's code. Maria Pavlovna had no scruples about playing the defenseless female before him, and this — combined with the money she offered — made Arseny agree to defend them. During the day, one of his Tartars would prowl the walkways; at night, Arseny himself would appear, settling himself in the garden on an old Ottoman carpet, a rusty shotgun with two huge barrels on one side, a bottle of *bouza* on the other.

At first, Arseny's protection worked, but then he began asking for more money. Again, Maria Pavlovna played the helpless female; again, Arseny was bribed into staying. But a few days later the same thing happened again, and this time Arseny threatened to lead the mob to the villa himself if he wasn't paid a hundred rubles at once.

He stood there in the kitchen when he said it, his scarred old body reeking of tobacco, his face cruel with self-satisfaction.

"My men are very restless, Missy. It is only with difficulty I restrain them. Times are changing for all in Yalta." He shrugged, playing the philosopher as he always did when at his most venal. "God is great, my friends. With his help you have nothing to fear."

Maria Pavlovna stood biting her lip. She was pale, but only with anger.

"You have friends among the mob, Arseny, this is true. I have friends among the court — yes, the court, in the Tsar's personal entourage — and they will see to it that you are crushed."

As smug as he was, Arseny hesitated. Events were happening too fast, the currents unleashed were too vague yet to say which party would be in power when things settled down.

"I will do what I can, Missy," he said. "My men claim there is gold in your villa. However —"

"Don't speak to me in lies, Arseny. I will pay you not a hundred rubles, but ten rubles. Here. For this, you will sell me your gun, and as for the rest, we do not need you any longer. We will defend the villa by ourselves."

Arseny twirled the ends of his mustache, obviously embarrassed to be spoken to in such a way by a woman. "You have the heart of a man," he said, with a mocking bow.

"No, Arseny. I do not have a man's heart. I have a bigger heart than that."

That night the mob came. Varka pleaded with Maria Pavlovna to keep the lights off, feeling the dark would somehow protect them, but she would have none of that and went from room to room lighting lamps in every window to defy them and show they weren't afraid. For the same reason, she took the gramophone and placed it near the window, playing her precious Chaliapin cylinders so that his voice boomed out like a cannon across the night. All the wine and spirits in the villa had already been destroyed; the two of them went around now barricading the weakest, most vulnerable doors.

At midnight, they heard a low rise and fall of sound that had no menace in it but the unstoppable monotony of surf. After that came a crackling, splintering sound as the looters, coming upon the fruit trees, ripped down their limbs. Varka crawled to the parlor window and peered out. There were figures swarming in the trees like apes, their coats hanging in patches that flapped back and forth as they climbed. They stuffed their mouths with fruit in their hunger; they hacked at the branches in hatred and rage.

"Varka! How many?" Maria Pavlovna called. She stood by the bookcase, Arseny's gun propped across a chair in front of her.

"It's all right, mistress. There are only ten, I think. They won't hurt us."

"Do they have torches? Do you see fire anywhere?"

"No torches," Varka lied.

She backed up slowly toward the middle of the room. The looters, sensing the house was undefended, moved in from the trees. They still didn't call out to each other, and the only sign of their presence was a rough tapping on the shutters as they circled the first floor probing for weaknesses. Maria Pavlovna ran frantically from shutter to shutter, as if to hurl her body against it the moment one should give way, but Varka remained crouched over in the center of the room. For all their danger, she felt a strange calm — a protective instinct that was so over-powering and certain it banished fear from her heart.

"Over here, mistress," she said softly, taking up the gun. "Here, come stand by me."

Maria Pavlovna was turning to say something when the door in front of her exploded in a cascade of splinters, knocking her back. An axe shot through the opening and chopped furiously up and down, narrowly missing her leg.

"Varka!" she screamed.

"Hurry!"

Maria Pavlovna turned so quickly she fell. Behind her, the axe ripped upward, creating an opening wide enough to admit a knee, then a shoulder, then a man's grasping hand. The black tip of a crowbar joined the axe and danced up and down beside it. Someone cursed, then a body threw itself against the door and the wood began splitting.

"Shoot!" Maria Pavlovna yelled.

Varka raised the gun to her shoulder but didn't fire. The door buckled inward, then flattened out. Buckled inward, then flattened out. Buckled inward . . .

"Varka!"

Her scream broke away in a crash as the window *behind* them shattered apart. Instantly, there was the overpowering stench of burning pitch. By the time Varka swung around, the looter was already through and scampering across the floor with his torch. He thrust it viciously at Maria Pavlovna's head, but she ducked away and his momentum carried him on toward Varka until the pitch seared her face. As fast as he rushed her, as blinding as the light was, her mind raced even faster, so that her finger tightened on the trigger and the gun exploded in her arms.

"Behind you!" Maria Pavlovna screamed.

Varka spun around to see the other, bigger man rushing at them through the door with an axe, and she fired again, the gun jumping against her cheek like a fist knocking her down, but not before the man threw his hands up to the black oozing mass where his eyes had been and screamed in horror and stumbled away.

"Varka!"

"They're gone, Maria Pavlovna!"

"Reload the gun! Reload it!"

"They won't come back."

"Varka! Are you all right? Oh, Varka! My precious precious Varka!"

"They're gone. See, there's his blood. The little one and the other both. They're gone. Shh now. It's all right, mistress. See, it's all right and Varka is with you and it's all right."

Trembling, neither daring to let the other go, they kept watch all night. At dawn, they bathed each other's face with water from the cistern, then — the gun reloaded now — went outside to await the sunrise beneath the black, twisted ruins of Anton Pavlovich's trees.

THE LOOTERS did not return. When it was obvious they were safe, at least for the present, Maria Pavlovna walked into town in order to send telegrams to Gorky and Bunin and other of her brother's friends — anyone who in the chaos of the times might cling to enough power to keep the villa from harm.

After she left, Varka began scrubbing the blood from the floor. She worked slowly and meticulously, not stopping until every trace was gone. There were two separate patterns, but they joined at the door and led out into the garden. One trail became thin and intermittent before it joined the road; the other grew thicker and richer looking, and it was this trail she followed. In the shelter of one of the unharmed almond trees she found the body of the boy she had killed.

He had leaned himself against the trunk to die; his arm was around the largest, mossiest root, as if he had hugged it in the final moments for warmth. Beneath his back, like Arseny's carpet, was a dark matted pool of blood.

The boy was thirteen at most, the age her own son would have been. The pellets had ripped through his throat, but above it his face was untouched. He wore a sleepy, contented expression that made her be very gentle with him. She dragged him to the edge of the garden where the sunflowers grew, and buried him there beneath the stalks, bending them crossways so there was no trace of any digging and Maria Pavlovna would never know.

That day, or maybe the next, the White Cavalry arrived, doing more damage with their horses in one hour than the looters had managed the entire night. At their rear rode Pavel Rashevitch, ridiculous in gold braid and a cone-shaped hat, but playing the hero nevertheless.

"My compliments to Madam Chekhova," he said, dismounting so clumsily his horse nearly staggered. "Tell her that a protective cordon has been established around the villa and the Bolshevik scum put to rout . . . And yes. That I'm hungry. Are there any *blinchiki?*"

For a time, under the Whites, things in Yalta returned to normal, or at least to the frantic, overheated frenzy that had passed for normalcy in the months before the war. The theatre started up again. The ferrys resumed service to Sevastopol and the shops were bright with necklaces and diamonds pawned by fleeing émigrés. Tempting as it must have been for her, Maria Pavlovna refused to believe in its permanence. Even during the depths of the Civil War, when entire regiments were switching allegiance daily, she never doubted which side would win, and talked quite openly about what she would do when the Bolsheviks took control.

"I have thought about it and thought some more, and it is only now that I realize what the people want is not the possessions here, not money or anything they can loot, but a share of the beauty. Do you understand this, Varka? They see my brother's villa shines with a certain radiance, and aren't sure why, and so it confuses them and makes them bitter and they attack like angry bees. It's the same with my brother's writing. It shines with a radiance in an age where everything must be dark in order to survive. In their hunger and fear they will want to destroy it, and it is up to me to show them this radiance isn't hostile, not against them, but theirs."

She was already talking about a museum, showing Varka the plans for it, explaining in great detail which of her brother's mementos would be displayed. Once the Bolsheviks were firmly in power, she began petitioning them for the permits necessary for the museum to open. Far from succeeding, these petitions only drew attention to what so far had been overlooked. Pavel Rashevitch, transformed by some miracle of survival from a proud White cavalryman on an undersized charger to a frightened Red functionary in gray canvas fatigues, came on Christmas Day to warn them the villa was about to be collectivized and the inhabitants turned out.

"I tried explaining about your brother," he said, smiling in a sheepish way that was particularly repellant. " 'Chekhov?' they said. 'The writer Chekhov? The name means nothing. The days of great houses are over with now. See that the villa is emptied at once.' "

By way of answering, Maria Pavlovna sent Rashevitch to town to buy two tickets to Moscow on the next available train.

"There's no hope of accomplishing anything here," she said, as Varka began to furiously pack. "Pavel Rashevitch will see to it the house is looked after for the time being. We can have Alexander Potapov to stay as well, poor man. I would go alone, but I'm too old for that now. I need you with me."

The next morning they began the long train ride north, crossing through the devastation left by the Civil War — the burned-out villages, the blackened farms, the skeletons of horses bleached the color of grain. In Moscow, they took a fetid room in an overcrowded hotel a block from the Kremlin. That same day Maria Pavlovna began the round of endless visits to endless ministries that were to occupy them not just for the next few days, not just for the next few weeks, but for the next eleven months.

It was the worst ordeal of their time together. Each afternoon Maria Pavlovna would come back to the room waving a slip of paper with a new name on it. This ministry might be useful in protecting Anton Pavlovich's papers — they must go there at once. As it turned out, this ministry wasn't the proper one at all; they must try this other ministry instead. No, she was mistaken there as well; there was a different ministry that handled the matter, only this ministry was no longer a ministry but a subministry and the officials there were helpless. And so on to another ministry where she was promised nothing definite. And so on to another ministry where she was advised to be patient. And thus with the ministry that might have protected the villa and thus with the ministry that was authorized to authorize museums and thus with the ministry that authorized authorizations and thus the sky got grayer and winter came and the treadmill spun faster but to no effect.

Varka never went in with her on these visits. She

could imagine the stuffy rooms in which Maria Pavlovna waited, the stale yellow light, the mealy faces of the men who told her no, and she preferred to take her drabness outside, where at least there was air. She stood on the street away from the traffic, peering through the snow toward the look-alike buildings, willing herself into something as impassive and unfeeling as their walls.

Long after dark, Maria Pavlovna would appear on the steps that led from the ministry's entrance, her shoulders slumped as they hadn't been even in the worst days of the war, her head bent in a peculiar way into her shoulder, as if she had just been whipped. She would stand there, the snow whitening her hat flake by flake until it quite covered it, and then — shaking it off like a young girl tossing back her hair — find somehow the strength to walk proudly down those marble steps, reducing the slumped-over miserable bureaucrats that climbed past her into the insignificance they deserved.

"I was mistaken, Varka," she said, with a smile at her own ignorance. "These were not the right people to ask for help. We will try somewhere else."

And hours later she emerged from the next ministry, the same ironic smile still in place, as if the expression were her own hardness, her own gray wall.

"Not here, Varka. Somewhere else."

Eleven months. Eleven months of noes and maybes and perhapses, and each time she swallowed it and pulled herself erect and came back to Varka with these same simple words.

"Not here, Varka. Somewhere else."

Only once did they take a holiday, this to visit Grachovka Street, where the Chekhov family had lived when they moved to Moscow from Taganrog in 1879. During the cab ride there, Maria Pavlovna sat on the edge of the seat, twisting her hands in excitement.

"It was a horrible old house. Horrible! Drafty and noisy and smelling of beets. But it had a yard and a trellis over which vines grew, and it was possible to lie there with your hands under your head and look up to where the sunlight came down through the leaves. I remember Antosha being furious with me because I treated the landlady with such respect. 'You're not a peasant anymore!' he would scream, literally scream it made him so furious to have us cringe . . . See? There's the river. We're almost there now . . . But Constantine Korovin used to come and draw sketches of us all, and Lika Mizinov, too, and we'd laugh at the slightest thing. Antosha brought his pens down to the yard and wrote his humorous sketches right there in front of us, and he would do perhaps three, then decide we still hadn't enough for supper, and so turn out three more. Michael ran them off to the printer and came back an hour later with enough rubles for a fete . . . Trubny Square. This was all brothels in the old days, and how those women frightened us with their frowns! Turn here, driver."

All during the ride Varka had watched Maria Pavlovna, taking delight in her delight, sharing the excitement in her eyes. Now these suddenly clouded and grew thin — the corners of her mouth trembled, then tightened into something hard. Varka turned to look out the window and saw . . . nothing. No houses, no shops, no sidewalks — nothing. There was a vacant lot the size of a square block and nothing on it except a scrub of old plaster and a haze of brick-colored dust.

"This isn't the right street, driver," Maria Pavlovna said. She said it slowly, like someone fighting to maintain control.

"Grachovka Street, ma'am. Or what's left of it. They're building workers' apartments."

"I said you're mistaken! Don't contradict me! Drive on, drive on!"

She fell back against the seat with her hand over her eyes, and it was a long time before she was able to say anything. "These Moscow drivers are notorious in their tricks," she said, forcing a smile. "Of course he took us to the wrong street to increase the fare. I would have him go back, but there's no time. We must get our rest for tomorrow. I feel certain we are on the right track at last."

A friend of Bunin's had recommended the Lenin Library as a possible source of protection, and it was here that Maria Pavlovna was concentrating all her efforts. It was hardly less labyrinthine than the ministries, but she was determined as ever and an answer was expected any moment. For her part, Varka had given up hope, and thought of nothing but the day-in, day-out necessities of caring for Maria Pavlovna and keeping up her strength.

"You are the foundation that supports me," Maria Pavlovna told her on a day when the news had been particularly bad. "Without you, I collapse."

Even the longest maze has its end. Eleven months to the day after they arrived in Moscow, the petition was granted — her brother's papers were to be established in a special archive within the library, while the villa was to become an official Soviet museum, with Maria Pavlovna herself as director. A fund was established to pay for repairs and upkeep; the day-to-day operating expenses were to come from selling admission tickets and commemorative editions of her brother's work.

On the day this was announced, they felt little joy but only the overwhelming desire to return to Yalta as quickly as possible, and they put off celebrating until they were actually on the train heading south. And even then it had been muted. They splurged on dinner in the dining car; for the first time in her life Varka tasted champagne. But the best part came after, when Maria Pavlovna fell asleep from exhaustion on the seat beside her. Varka covered her shoulders with a shawl so she wouldn't get cold. She folded her collar up around the bare spot on her neck, and then — feeling in her heart the delicious, intoxicating sense of safety that is indistinguishable from love — leaned across and kissed her sleeping mistress lightly on the cheek.

THE REST OF Varka's story doesn't take long to tell. Upon their return to Yalta, arrangements were made to turn the villa into the museum of which Maria Pavlovna had always dreamed. It had opened — the first visitors had come shyly in to stare in fascination at Anton Pavlovich's writing desk and books — when in the early dawn hours of May 11, 1927, after a night of strange tremblings, the Black Sea coast was struck by an earthquake that leveled half the house.

On that tragic morning when a full third of Yalta disappeared, the town's surviving telegraph office opened late. When it did, the first person standing in line was Varka, wrapped in the shawl that was the only personal possession she had saved, holding in her hand a message from Maria Pavlovna to the directors of the Lenin Library in Moscow.

VILLA DESTROYED, the message read. *CHAOS STOP. RUIN STOP. BUILDING AGAIN.*

PART TWO

ACT TWO

THE PARLOR of the Chekhov Museum, three days after the events of Act One. On the surface, all is unchanged, though the lighting is much brighter than before, focused in beams that illuminate the characters as they appear, then move restlessly on. In the background can be heard music — at first atonal and harsh, then vaguely melodic, with snippets from folk songs and dances. The music never decides what it wants to be, modern or old, loud or soft, but maintains throughout a mocking quality that seems the light's equivalent.

By the stairway, looking up it, stands Peter Sergeich Kunin, dressed in a shabby blue suit that suggests a military uniform. Impatient, he edges up to the first step, then the second, trying to understand the murmuring voices that come from above.

Tania Rashevitch, daughter of Pavel Rashevitch, enters left from the garden. She is nineteen, dresses in frocks like a small girl, wears glasses like an intellectual, yet has a woman's full body and walks with coy sensuality. Her hair is straw-colored; her face kittenish in the Slavic way. Not seeing Kunin, she makes right for the mirror hanging above the divan and stands there examining herself in obvious dissatisfaction. Turns sideways and raises arms like a ballerina doing a pirouette, goes up on tiptoes, then comes heavily down.

TANIA: *in a deep voice, imitating someone.* Tania, my little one. You will never fly.

Turns and catches sight of Kunin who is still staring intently up the stairs. Putting her hand over her mouth to stifle her giggles, she tiptoes up behind him and listens, too.

TANIA: What are they saying?

Kunin jumps. Turning, he takes her roughly by the arm and leads her away from the landing.

TANIA: Who's there? My father . . .

KUNIN: Maria Pavlovna and two Germans.

TANIA: *petulantly.* I hate my father.

KUNIN: What are you doing here? This isn't the time to pay calls.

TANIA: *mischievously.* Am I so unattractive to you then?

KUNIN: That's a line from a film. Why must you always pose so?

With that, Tania's playfulness disappears. Hugs herself and walks back to the stairs.

TANIA: My father, the saintly Madam Chekhova, and two fascists. Doing what? Parceling up the Chekhov empire? I don't envy those two. *Looks back at Kunin.* You've changed, you know. You don't laugh as much as before. You don't bubble over with ideas and extravagant imaginings. When I first met you I thought, Here is a writer. Here is a man who is in touch with the deep and true nature of things. You were my knight, my invincible defender. And now . . . You go sneaking around like a beaten dog, eavesdropping, saying disagreeable things. *Shakes head.* Never mind. We need friends in these times, not enemies. Have you been to town then?

KUNIN: No.

TANIA: Yalta has never been livelier. The cafes are crowded far into the night. The churches are open again, there are weddings and baptisms for the first time in twenty years. All my friends have taken jobs as translators and flirt with the officers over tea. The Germans are pigs, the Rumanians even worse, but when has Yalta been immune to pigs? There are stories though.

KUNIN: *quickly.* About what?

TANIA: No, I'm not going to tell you, Peter Sergeich. Your virgin ears are too pure. *Points.* What are they doing?

KUNIN: The Germans want the villa as barracks for their junior officers. Maria Pavlovna is objecting. Your father is playing go-between, trying to appease everyone and thereby save not only his skin but the modicum of honor he still retains.

TANIA: *whirling around.* She's just as bad you know. When it comes to appeasing morons, there's nothing my father can teach your patroness. Look around you. Look around you! All these absurd paintings. Goethe, Hauptmann. Why doesn't she just put a swastika on the wall and have done with it? She's spent the last twenty years sucking up to our glorious Soviet leaders and now that these leaders are to be German, she will suck up to them as well.

KUNIN: Her brother . . .

TANIA: Don't talk to me about her brother. This museum, this ridiculous glorification of a man who more than anything hated glorification . . . He would spit on it. He would spit on party hacks and party flunkies and all those moral idiots Maria Pavlovna finds so enchanting. His work is a direct contradiction of everything they stand for, and his sister far from honoring his memory is turning it into a mockery.

KUNIN: What would you have her do then?

TANIA: Learn from Tolstoy's daughter, Alexandra. Refuse to wear blinders. Speak out when writers are persecuted. Risk labor camp if that's what it takes. Risk exile.

KUNIN: Away from her brother's home?

TANIA: Do you know what she wants, Peter Sergeich? She wants his portrait hanging in the train stations in place of Gorky's. There is room for only one God in Soviet literature, and she wants Anton Pavlovich Chekhov to wear the blood-soaked crown.

She stares at him expecting an argument, but instead he walks over to the window and stares out toward the garden.

KUNIN: They'll hear us if you yell.

TANIA: I'm sorry, Peter. It's . . . I could tear out his heart. No, I could push it down his throat. Push it down to his chest, give him the manhood he never had. My father? How I hate the phrase!

Kunin remains by the window. His hand, rubbing the glass, becomes a fist that taps it and taps it again.

KUNIN: I can fire a gun. When we were boys in the Komsomol there was rifle practice every Sunday.

TANIA: Speak louder! *Leans over the railing to shout upstairs.* Defy them!

KUNIN: What I'm saying, Tania, is that despite everything I could be of use.

TANIA: The army? Don't be mad.

KUNIN: I've been thinking it over ever since the Germans arrived. A war is nothing more than the spirit of the times. A man is not immune to the spirit of the times. Therefore I feel deep within me — please don't laugh, Tania — deep within myself I feel the urgent need to kill.

TANIA: You have the wrong war, Peter. There are no syllogisms in this war.

KUNIN: I hate fascists.

TANIA: And our leaders are so much better?

KUNIN: You know I don't play that game.

TANIA: It's your clubfoot talking. A man wanting to prove his courage — it's the most common story in the world. Hitler wants to prove his courage. Stalin wants to prove his courage. Here the world is in flames and it's all because men want revenge for their infirmities.

KUNIN: Even so.

TANIA: *speaking slowly, with great precision.* We are living in an occupied city. We are living in an occupied city that acts like a liberated one. No one cares who the collaborators are and who are the patriots. Distinctions blur. We are prisoners in a backwater where nothing of significance will happen. And do you know why this is so? It's not because of tactics or geography, not at all. It's because when the war broke out Tania Rashevitch decided to play the dutiful daughter and return to Yalta from the conservatory, thereby insuring that a stupefying boredom would descend upon the city to the exclusion of all else.

KUNIN: *staring at her.* Come here.

Tania looks coyly over her shoulder toward the stairs, then starts toward him in obvious excitement. When she is halfway across the room, the door slams open from the kitchen and in walks the servant, Gerassim, carrying a vase of roses horizontally at his side. Tania stops and turns impatiently toward him.

TANIA: What is it?

GERASSIM: I have brought the flowers, Comrade Kunin. On the mistress's command, Comrade.

KUNIN: Don't use that word here.

GERASSIM: *without inflection.* I would like a word with you, Peter Sergeich.

KUNIN: About what? This is not the time for household matters.

Gerassim shrugs — from the waist to the shoulders, like a bear. Puts the vase down on the table with the proofs, then walks back toward the kitchen.

TANIA: Where did she ever find that one? He looks like . . . I don't know. An assassin. A white slaver. Someone dark and monstrous from a dream. Did you see the odd way he held those flowers? Like a ram.

KUNIN: He's an insolent . . . *Shakes head.* I don't like the man, but he does his work. The labor secretariat sent him last spring when Burkin joined the army. He comrades those Germans, they'll take him away.

Tania pulls a rose from the vase, presses it to her blouse, then takes a second and starts over to Kunin, holding it behind her back. She's almost there when voices are heard at the top of the stairs.

TANIA: Damn!

RASHEVITCH: Mind your heads now. We Russians are a much smaller race.

Pavel Rashevitch descends the stairs backwards followed by two German officers, then, after an interval, Maria Pavlovna. Tania and Kunin remain unnoticed in the shadows. The two Germans make a quick inspection of the stairwell. The taller conveys by his expression only boredom and apathy; the shorter, arrogance and disdain.

RASHEVITCH: You'll not find partisan scum beneath our stairwell, Herr Lieutenant. Maria Pavlovna will not allow it.

GERMAN OFFICER: *running his finger along the wall like a butler inspecting for dust.* How many in the house?

RASHEVITCH: Five, your honor. But once again, this villa is quite a landmark, mentioned in all the guidebooks. *Winks.* I hesitate to use the word in our impious atheistic state, but . . . Yes, a shrine, gentlemen. We in Yalta fully understand the necessity of procuring decent accommodations for your brave troops, who have liberated us from the Bolshevik jackals, and while personally it would give Madam Chekhova the greatest pleasure to have some intelligent conversation for a change rather than the didactic prattle of these Soviet butchers, there are certain considerations . . .

GERMAN OFFICER: There are no considerations. *Gesturing toward door.* Where does this lead?

MARIA: *with great dignity.* That is the door to my brother's study. I do not allow visitors in that room unless they have a special purpose. For instance, scholars.

GERMAN OFFICER: Then we will see it.

RASHEVITCH: Of course, Herr Lieutenant. Madam Chekhova will personally . . .

MARIA: The room is not open this morning. Next I will show you the kitchen and you will see for yourself how unsuitable it is for accommodating your brave men.

Rashevitch is horrified at her refusal — he all but covers his eyes — but the lieutenant contents himself with a scowl and follows Maria Pavlovna out to the kitchen. Rashevitch, with a bow, indicates the other officer should go first, and the two of them exit also.

Kunin stares in the direction they've disappeared.

KUNIN: Do you know "In the Ravine"?

TANIA: Of course.

KUNIN: It's the only story Chekhov ever wrote.

TANIA: *impatiently.* He wrote hundreds of stories.

KUNIN: Because there's that scene where Aksinia pours boiling water on Lipa's baby. I was thinking of that when I saw Maria Pavlovna just now. It's the most horrible thing in her brother's work, the culmination of all the misunderstandings, cross-purposes, and pain, and yet for us that scalding water is just the start.

TANIA: You talk in riddles. *Huskily.* Come here.

KUNIN: *to himself.* I received a medal for my marksmanship. I had the highest score among boys my age in Leningrad. I remember the sergeant who taught us saying "Ah, a pity you're not officer material, my boy!" He was an old man who had fought the Japanese in 1905. There was a bullet lodged in his neck, and he walked with his head tilted so. *Turns. . . .* Tania?

She is gone. He starts toward the opened garden door, then notices something on the floor. Bending down, he picks up the discarded roses.

POTAPOV: *offstage.* We'll ask you to kindly remain in single file as we continue on to our next room.

Enter Potapov from the right, followed at some distance by a small man with a military overcoat draped over his shoulder like a cape.

POTAPOV: *in a solemn voice.* We are now standing in the parlor of the late dramatist and storyteller Anton P. Chekhov. Of an evening he received his intimate guests here, often joining in their jokes and laughter before retiring. On the walls you will note portraits of many of his admirers, patrons, and friends. *Seeing Kunin.* Oh, hello Peter Sergeich. Just fancy, we have ourselves a visitor. Look. *Holds up a ruble. . . .* Moving on, we have on our right the bookcase of the late Anton P. Chekhov, containing many volumes personally inscribed by their authors in token of their great esteem.

The man in the military overcoat has been following Potapov with the same kind of solemn expression and at the same respectful pace. Now, though, he breaks away and moves as if magnetized to the table with the proofs. Stands there staring down at them in awe. Slowly, very slowly, reaches out a hand to touch the topmost page.

POTAPOV: You will notice the particularly fine morocco binding and . . . *Turning around; sternly.* Visitors will kindly keep with the guide at all times.

MAN: I'm terribly sorry.

Hurries over and stares bashfully at the books.

POTAPOV: It is not generally known, but Anton P. Chekhov had many interests besides literature and medicine. On the left, for example, you will take wry amusement in noticing his fishing pole, emblem of many happy hours spent on rivers and ponds.

MAN: *noticing Kunin.* I hope I'm not disturbing you. I wondered if the museum were open, the times being what they are, so I thought I'd come take a look. It's an honor. To be here at last is a . . . *Seeing the roses.* Well, I'm not disturbing you?

KUNIN: There's a regiment of Germans in the kitchen. One more won't hurt.

MAN: *with an apologetic smile.* My name is Rene Diskau.

He extends his hand, but Kunin doesn't take it. Diskau shows no offense — if anything, his smile becomes even friendlier — and he turns to examine one of the playbills mounted on the wall.

He's a man in his late twenties, short, with a dancer's precise body and the pale complexion of someone who acts. His head is surprisingly large, but so handsome and regular that the effect is of a fine china vase mounted atop a pedestal for admiration. His red hair lies in a dramatic sweep across his forehead; his eyelashes are curled and feminine over deeply set gray eyes. More than anything he resembles the famous Charlie Chaplin — not the Little Tramp of the films, but Chaplin without the mustache; the kind of man who dwells self-contained within his own radiance.

Removes his overcoat like a man who means to stay. Beneath it, he wears a double-breasted black suit, one arm of which hangs limp and empty by his side. Turns sideways, as if presenting the missing arm as evidence. His face, in the light, is not as flawless as it first appeared. There are stress marks on his forehead that wrinkle and curl independently of his expression. There's a throb visible beneath his left eye — a purplish vein lying close to the surface like a telltale heart. These things wind a tightness around his grace. As handsome and imposing as he is, there is something about him that stays clenched.

DISKAU: *reading the playbill in beautifully enunciated Russian.* On 31 January in this city will be given the premiere of *The Three Sisters,* a play by A. P. Chekhov.

Potapov, continuing with his spiel, moves from memento to memento without realizing Diskau is no longer following. Turning to illustrate a point, he sees Diskau across the room and hurries over, anxious not to be left out.

POTAPOV: I see you've met Peter Sergeich. Peter Sergeich is a young man of whom miraculous things are momentarily expected. He has been this way for quite some time now. *Laughs.* What you have there is the bill from the first Moscow performance. I myself well remember when Anton Pavlovich came to the Art Theatre to read his work. This would have been 1899. *Nods head up and down like a camel.* I was fortunate enough to have my stage directions from the master's own lips.

DISKAU: *mimicking perfectly not only Potapov's tone, but his self-important nod of the head.* Excuse me, and I myself was not alive at the time, but mustn't it have been 1900? Chekhov came and read the play to Stanislavsky's company in a hoarse voice that brought tears to the eyes of his listeners. I believe the exact date was November 23, 1900.

POTAPOV: That's as may be. Over here you'll notice a portrait of he who above all served as inspiration for the master's work. Yes, your compatriot, the great German dramatist Wolfgang von-something Goethe.

DISKAU: *with a wink toward Kunin.* Goethe? Horrible man. So artificial. I'm sure Chekhov would have despised him.

POTAPOV: And proceeding on with your tour, you will please note the expansive window overlooking the beloved garden planted and cared for by Anton P. Chekhov in those moments of respite from the all-consuming labors of the pen.

Diskau joins Potapov at the window. From the right enter the two German officers, followed by Maria Pavlovna, Rashevitch, and Varka. They come to a stop near the wood stove.

GERMAN OFFICER: *pulling a form from his portfolio.* The first detachment will take occupation of the villa tomorrow afternoon at fifteen hundred hours. The inhabitants will have twelve hours to pack their things. Is this clear?

RASHEVITCH: Very clear, Herr Lieutenant. *Turns toward Maria Pavlovna.* You have to understand these things from their perspective. These gentlemen work very hard. It's not easy finding billets, and what's more it will be officers who are living here, not enlisted garbage.

Maria Pavlovna's eyes close and tighten. She sways and motions Varka over for support.

MARIA: You'll excuse me, Lieutenant. An old woman with no one to rely on . . . My health . . . I feel I might

. . . *Then, realizing her helplessness is having no effect, straightens decisively and changes her tone.* We are not leaving my brother's house. The villa is a shrine, valued more in Germany than it is in Russia itself. Thousands of your countrymen consider my brother the leading writer of his day. Thousands more take a simple pleasure in reading his work. Go to the bookcase. Read for yourself the tributes written in his honor by German hands . . . To have our carpets torn apart by the boots of men who care nothing for literature, our furniture used as kindling . . . To have the villa become a target for bombs . . .

RASHEVITCH: *whispering viciously.* Eh, do you want to have us shot?

GERMAN OFFICER: *bored.* Very well. I extend the time to twenty-four hours. No more extensions will be made.

Makes a notation on the form, signs the bottom, then — keeping one copy — hands it to Maria Pavlovna. Her hands tremble as she takes it, and this time it's no act. Her entire body seems to wince.

DISKAU: *approaching from the window.* Excuse me?

Maria Pavlovna looks at him in astonishment.

DISKAU: May I just? There, thank you.

Takes the form gently from her hand, reads it, then rips it apart. Rashevitch, aghast, scrambles on his hands and knees to gather in the fragments — the effect is of a pudgy child scooping up snow.

DISKAU: *turning toward the German officers.* You are right about your extensions, Lieutenant. No more will be granted, since the villa is no longer being considered as a resort for your men. You have five minutes to vacate the premises.

GERMAN OFFICER: *with no letup in his boredom.* Very

pretty. Still, I may be excused if I question your authority.

DISKAU: *mimicking perfectly his tone and stance.* You are right to question my authority and I will see this comes to the notice of your superiors as a mitigating factor in the punishment you'll receive for your arrogance. You're not the only person in Yalta to carry papers. Here, read this and be quick.

Hands him his opened wallet. The officer takes a yellow form out, reads it, looks up at Diskau, then reads it again.

GERMAN OFFICER: You have impressive friends.

DISKAU: Friends who will gladly see to it that you are transferred to a post more hazardous than Yalta. A place where partisans are the enemy and not defenseless women. Would you enjoy that, Lieutenant? I know from experience that the partisans do lovely things to their prisoners . . . Four minutes.

GERMAN OFFICER: Still, it's a little vague about your rank.

DISKAU: It was Major until I was transferred. I'm afraid my ministry doesn't come under the jurisdiction of the Wehrmacht . . . Three minutes.

GERMAN OFFICER: Nor the Wehrmacht under . . . *Looks.* . . . The Ministry of Culture.

DISKAU: You have not read all the form.

GERMAN OFFICER: Correct me if I'm wrong, but wasn't it Dr. Goebbels himself who said "The minute I hear the word culture, I reach for my gun."

DISKAU: *smiling.* We who know the Doctor personally can indulge his exaggerations . . . Two minutes.

GERMAN OFFICER: *glancing at the form.* Still . . .

With this, Diskau's manner undergoes a complete transformation. No longer does he mimic the officer's cool tone and easy posture. His fist clenches, his eyes blink uncontrollably, and his skin flushes red. It's as if something comes over him that is molten, flowing from his legs up his torso toward his head so that each part of him in turn seems to stiffen and burn.

DISKAU: I'll show you not to bandy words with a Reich minister! I'll show you! You hear me, swine! You'll be shot, shot! . . . Pig! Moron!

Anger makes him incoherent. Advances upon the flustered lieutenant and screams unintelligible words at his face. The others look on in bewilderment; the lieutenant, unable to withstand such fury, backs away — slowly at first, then more rapidly, gesturing for the other officer to follow.

GERMAN OFFICER: *at the door.* A lunatic asylum. A perfect asylum!

Exits. Rashevitch, unable to decide who is in power, teeters with his arms outstretched like a rope in a tug of war, then follows the officers offstage.

POTAPOV: *yelling.* Mind the garden, gentlemen! Don't miss our mulberries! *Hurries after them.*

Diskau puts hand to forehead and spins around about to faint. Maria Pavlovna signals Kunin to bring over a chair into which Diskau immediately falls.

DISKAU: Thank you. My nerves . . . The swine! No, it's fine now. I'll soon be all right. To think we have such insensitive animals in the German army.

MARIA: Varka! Fetch some brandy for the Major. *Kneeling by his side, taking his hand.* You poor poor man.

He slowly revives. Wipes his forehead; plucks his clothes as if they are wet. At last manages a weak smile.

DISKAU: I take medications, and I'm afraid I've taken too much. *With a deep breath.* It's all very well to lose an arm, but it's a pity to lose your composure as well. *Pushing himself up.* Thank you again, madam. I believe I have the pleasure of addressing Maria Pavlovna Chekhova?

MARIA: *all but blushing.* But it is I who must thank you, Major . . .

DISKAU: *bowing, imitating her gentle manner and courtly tone.* Diskau. Rene Diskau.

MARIA: *softening her voice to match his.* You are quite our savior, Major Diskau. They would have taken our home, forced us to leave. My brother's clothes and belongings would have all been destroyed.

DISKAU: *whispering.* It's a dream for me being here. To think that in this very room the gentle Doctor Chekhov lived and wrote. And things are just as they were then, that's what is remarkable. I feel him. Yes, I can feel his presence. It's almost as if . . . *Spins quickly around.* There! No, but almost. Next time for certain.

MARIA: My brother had a particular fondness for the German dramatists. You see the evidence on the walls, but if anything his debt went even deeper. As you may know, it was to Germany that he made his last journey, feeling an overwhelming need to visit such happy and familiar scenes once again before he died.

DISKAU: *impatiently.* Yes, yes.

MARIA: You are a lover of his work?

DISKAU: From boyhood. *Walks over to the table.* Yes, it's just as I imagined. The proofs are back from the printers and sit waiting for the author to add those last refinements that will make the story come alive. Out in the garden, his beloved fruit trees wait for his gentle attention. Do you know, Madam Chekhova, I had the honor of translating your brother's early plays? They were little known in Germany, and while not the caliber of the later work, delightful romps that deserve to be performed more often. I had a theatre group in Dresden before the war, really nothing more than a cabaret, but we were honored to perform them to much success. Even Berlin noticed. I had it on good authority that Brecht himself was planning to attend before his . . . Before, that is. And then Reinhardt paid us the compliment of stealing one of our stagings.

MARIA: Diskau? Published in Dresden? The most delightful blue cover? You sent me a copy . . .

DISKAU: And you were so good as to write a note back.

MARIA: Rene Diskau! Varka, Peter Sergeich! Only fancy. Here we should be, at the darkest moment in the Chekhov Museum's history, at a time when all I've worked for was about to be destroyed, and who should appear but the German who above all believes in my brother's work. A fellow writer, a sensitive translator . . .

DISKAU: *nodding.* It's of the utmost importance to keep the museum in being. We in the Ministry of Culture have the opportunity to do great things in Yalta, despite the army's hostility. I, as minister, may be able to help in various ways. For instance, and excuse me for saying so, but I couldn't help noticing the paint on the way in was a bit shabby. We could see that repairs are made, things tidied up. We live in perilous times and much is uncertain, but there are . . . *Indicating Kunin and Varka.*

If we could only talk. *Shyly.* I haven't seen your brother's study.

VARKA: No one is allowed in the study.

MARIA: Yes, the study! Yes, we must talk. There is so much to go over, so little time. Here, follow me. *Over her shoulder.* No interruptions, Varka. Peter, you look foolish holding those roses, please find them a vase . . . You'll see for yourself, Major Diskau. Your translation sits on the bookcase within reaching distance of my brother's desk.

Maria Pavlovna holds her arm out and waits for Diskau to take it; together, they walk toward the study. The door closes behind them, taking with it a portion of the light. Varka and Kunin watch, amazed, as they leave; they stare toward the study door as if willing it into transparency. Neither realizes the other is there.

VARKA: She isn't well. Only this morning she took the last of the pills. She went dizzy when she stood up and would have fallen.

KUNIN: Minister of Culture! Leave it to the Germans to think that up . . . He seems made of rubber, Indian rubber. Something malleable and resilient. You yearn to squeeze him in your hand, then throw him down on the floor to watch him spring back.

VARKA: How they hum, it's just like bees. *Hugging herself.* Dark so early now. Why don't they paint the stars black and be done with it? Candles so dear . . .

KUNIN: I hate Tania when she's that way. There's a burr in her head and she shakes and shakes but it won't drop off. Still, Tania is right. Yes, there's the evidence right there. He's a fascist, the scum of the earth, and yet she takes him in the study and treats him like a king. You'd think it was a love duet they were singing.

VARKA: *bitterly*. She's always had a weakness for the pretty ones.

She exits down the tapering tunnel of the hall. In the parlor, the light quickly fades until the only illumination comes from the bluish radiance that frames the window. The darker it gets, the louder grow the voices in the study, though the words are still confused and indistinct. Someone laughs — it is high-pitched and feminine and impossible to assign. Kunin advances to the door, brings his hand up to knock, thinks better of it, and begins pacing restlessly across the room. The music, so low until now, swells to a noisy crescendo that matches the voices, then both abruptly stop.

For three full minutes not a sound is heard, giving the impression the act is over. Then, from the darkness near the proof table, a voice that seems twisted of thick black strands.

VOICE: In Kovrinka, they hanged all the women.

KUNIN: *startled*. What's that?

VOICE: They began with the men. They brought the children out to watch, and the children began giggling because they couldn't understand. It was like they watched a circus of dancing bears. To quiet their giggles, the Germans took their mothers and hanged them, too.

There's a scraping noise, then the quick flare of a match. In its reflection can be seen Gerassim, sitting slouched in the rocker by the proof table, his boots resting on its edge. Despite his words, his look is of total ease and contentment, more master than servant. Takes the match and holds it over the proofs as if about to light them, then with a soft, not unpleasant laugh, brings it instead to the Turkish cigarette that dangles from the corner of his mouth.

KUNIN: Fool! You'll burn them.

GERASSIM: In Borisovka . . .

KUNIN: Move your boots!

GERASSIM: They burned the churches. They filled them with women they had raped, then tossed in incendiary bombs. There were three thousand women taken from Kiev in the German advance, to be used in the soldiers' spare time. The pregnant ones were raped first. Many labors began early, and the babies were taken by the fascist medical officers and thrown against walls.

KUNIN: *advancing toward the glowing stub.* Those are lies. Propaganda. We've heard all that before.

GERASSIM: In Miestetchiki . . .

KUNIN: Lies! We've had twenty years of them now, and you expect me to believe . . .

GERASSIM: In Kerch . . .

KUNIN: *covering his ears.* Enough!

GERASSIM: In Kerch, they were set to shooting one another. Fathers their sons. They were forced to aim at their waists so the deaths would be slow. The women were ordered to dig the graves for their men. One of them escaped and reached our camp. She was a teacher of mathematics and used to counting. She counted six thousand bodies lying scattered across a football pitch. A German truck drove over them scattering lime.

KUNIN: *in a daze.* How do you know this? There's

been no news of any kind reaching Yalta. Only those . . .
Suddenly nodding. . . . So there are partisans even in Yalta.

Gerassim rocks back and forth. His face, always so
dark and passive, wears an expression of pleasure.

GERASSIM: There are patriotic Red detachments
everywhere, Comrade Peter. They are fighting the fascist
dogs in keeping with Comrade Stalin's personal directive
not to relinquish one inch.

KUNIN: I tried joining up. I took the train to Sevastopol, but they wouldn't take me. A leg and a half isn't
good enough, they said. We need whole men in the Red
Army, not men who are lame.

GERASSIM: For someone who is willing . . .

KUNIN: They wouldn't take me!

GERASSIM: Even here.

KUNIN: I begged and they wouldn't take me. *In a soft
and diffident voice.* How?

GERASSIM: *gesturing with his cigarette.* There are many
unlikely battlefields in war, Peter Sergeich. Many places
that will unexpectedly burn . . . For now? For now,
nothing. For now, the role of crippled noncombatant,
dabbler in the arts.

KUNIN: A spy, you mean. An informer.

GERASSIM: For now.

KUNIN: Where are the lines? Is Moscow taken? The
last we heard Leningrad was surrounded but still fighting. There is so little information. We could be on an
island towed out to sea.

GERASSIM: Do you doubt our final victory, Comrade
Peter? *Tilts head toward study.* Are you to be a collaborator
like our esteemed and venerable mistress?

KUNIN: *furiously, like a spoiled boy.* Out! Get out! You have your chores and see to them at once!

Gerassim continues to rock. Kunin stares toward him with his fists clenched, but is unable to meet his eyes.

KUNIN: What's that sound? Are they finished? *Looks behind him.* I have to see to something immediately . . . I have to . . . I have to clear the leaves from the gutters.

Exits left in confusion. Gerassim lifts his heels from the table with exaggerated slowness and brings them down to the floor. Stands, picks a piece of lint off his jacket as though it were a bug, then carefully dusts off his sleeve.

TANIA: *offstage.* Peter!

She enters breathlessly from the kitchen. At first, the darkness stops her like a wall — she looks around, doubting where she is — but then she continues on toward Gerassim.

TANIA: Where is Peter Sergeich? Varka told me he was here.

Gerassim looks down at her the way a hunter looks at a freshly killed rabbit. Laughs to himself.

TANIA: Well?

GERASSIM: Forgive me, Tania Rashevitch, but I would have thought you were the kind of woman who needed something other than a crippled boy.

Though Tania's face expresses outrage, her voice automatically becomes huskier, her gestures more flirting and coy.

TANIA: Don't you have work to do? I'll report you to Maria Pavlovna.

GERASSIM: I saw you watching me last week. When I stood beneath the pump washing.

TANIA: It's not safe to be alone with Tartar men.

The girls in school talk of nothing else. Animals. You should see the way they shiver when they say it.

GERASSIM: They are right to shiver. You are shivering yourself.

Tania starts to walk past him. As she does, he reaches out and grabs her roughly by the arm. She doesn't resist. He's about to kiss her — she has tilted back her head and closed her eyes — when he lets her go and laughs instead.

GERASSIM: A boy does not know the things a man knows, eh Tania Rashevitch?

Tania goes to slap him, but he catches her hand and presses it back into her shoulder.

GERASSIM: Tonight at nine. No one will notice us in the blackout. In honor of the occasion, I would like you to wear something white.

TANIA: Idiot!

GERASSIM: *with barely supressed anger.* Something white.

She pulls away from him and runs toward the garden door. She is about to rush out when she stops as if a noose has tightened around her waist. Turns slowly around. Stares at him with a resigned look that doesn't quite mask her mounting excitement.

TANIA: *helplessly.* Where?

Curtain.

KUNIN

ANY MEMORY that survives forty years is a work of
art. The same pain that made it so hard for Kunin to
remember would, by its price, revise those memories that
endured, pruning out the superfluous, eliminating the
trivial, moving around details until the dross of what really
happened became burnished into the gold of what really
was. So if old age had taken (taken hope, taken strength,
taken fear), it had also given back, narrowing his focus
until it became a sieve that trapped the impurities of the
past while allowing its general current to sweep through.

If anything, Kunin felt this effect too strongly. There were times when the synthesis of remembrance became too disciplined, too shaped, taking on a gravitational force that distorted every stray flash of memory that passed in its field. He would wake up in the morning beside the humming shortwave, his back sore from the armchair, his arms numb from stiffness, his eyes blinded by sunlight flooding in through the drapes. . . . He would wake in the morning longing for randomness the way other men long for coffee, an elixir unloosening the hardness of dreams.

But then mornings were always a bad time for him. After prying himself out of the chair — after a cautious knee bend or two — he fled his sister's cranky nagging to the refuge of the bathroom. The hot massage of the shower relaxed the tension in his remembering, set free expansiveness, so that the memories that had no place in the work he was building enjoyed their brief moment in the sun.

These morning memories were of two kinds. The first were completely frivolous, like bubbles, light and effervescent, so it wasn't so much their detail he was aware of as the constant imaginative popping as one succeeded the next. Maria Pavlovna spooning out her favorite English marmalade with the guilty, happy expression of a girl. Potapov playing patience; the way the cards seemed to startle him — how his mouth dropped open in astonishment as he picked up each one. The ivory coil Diskau wore on the small finger of his right hand, as if it were his knuckle made bare. These things were there, but of no significance, recalled only in passing, memory's froth.

The second kind — the kind he was apt to linger

over while shaving, his face puckered in the mirror's steam — were of undoubted significance, but only in isolation; true, but true in the wrong direction. And so while Maria Pavlovna's voice could most accurately be described as angelic, with a soft contralto register it was a pleasure to admit through one's ears, it was important not to remember it that way, since this made her seem too saint-like, tipped too far in one direction the generalized balance that makes up the truth. And her bad habits, too — her irritation, say, with all things mechanical; the furious, uncontrollable rages she went into if the telephone didn't work or the lights flickered off. To dwell on these was to tilt the scale too far the other way, paint her as shrewish, play up facts that lived alone and had never become enmeshed with any fate.

And likewise with Diskau's homosexuality. It had been there, it had undoubtedly been important, but not the kind of importance forty years takes notice of, so it was wrong to worry about it or waste any time trying to understand. Diskau loved men, but what of it? To remember him as a flamboyant queen would obscure the more salient, tragic aspects of his character. Kunin, if he thought about his sexuality at all, would remember him as perfectly average, the better to keep from following a wrong lead.

Facts always distort the truth. It was a fact that when Nina arrived and she and Kunin became lovers they had had five nights together, but to remember it as five would make their love sound almost permanent, while the only thing Kunin had been conscious of was how fleeting their time together was, not even a moment but an eternity removed from a moment, so that what he remembered was one night together and one night alone. So too Nina's death from tuberculosis complicated by typhus and influenza and a dozen other invasions in the early spring of 1942. He didn't remember the rapid wasting away, but only the very last moment itself, when the lines of her life and his life drew together into the same expiring point. And so too the face of the man he had been forced to shoot two months earlier. He didn't remember the contortions he went through as he fell, not the black jagged wetness across his chest, but only the relaxed softening of his mouth as he lay still.

In the shaping of his old age, Kunin remembered what he chose. Or at least sometimes. For once he let the genie out of the bottle, it was difficult to stuff him back in. Somewhere in the unfolding of things — somewhere between the time the Germans arrived and the time things started racing out of control — Tania had approached him in the garden and said roughly the following.

"I can see it when you're together. You and Diskau could be brothers. You're just alike."

It was a simple enough comment, said almost in passing, with no particular connection to what had happened just after or just before. And yet for forty years Kunin had wondered about those words, remembered them time and time again, and was no closer to understanding what had made her say it than he had been then. He was still a sensitive boy in that respect, tormenting himself over every analogy in which he figured, staring into the excruciating mirror people always hold up to the shy.

What made it worse was that Tania had said it. Tania of the voluptuous body that seemed to possess its own intelligence and curiosity, so that you didn't so much stare at and admire her breasts as have them stare at and admire you. Tania, who when all was said and done, had remarkable insight into a person's character, or at least its dark side. Tania who was in love with him and blunt.

"You and that Nazi could be brothers. Not only brothers, twins."

Because they were both crippled? Because Diskau's sleeve hung loose by his side and Kunin walked with a limp? But that wasn't a similarity at all, there being a world of difference between a sleeve that hangs proudly empty and a foot that merely drags. All the honor went to Diskau, for it was a brave thing to be armless in war — to display on your person the only evidence the century was interested in admitting, the evidence of what happens when metal intercepts flesh.

And so eliminating the obvious differences of manner, outlook, nationality, and allegiance, there was only one thing left to build an analogy on: their love of literature. But this was precisely the hardest similarity for Kunin to swallow. If Tania had based her comparison on their both being weaklings or moral nonentities, he would have found it much easier to accept. But to be told they both liked books? It was monstrous of her, totally mean-spirited, like being told he and Diskau were infatuated with the same woman.

This was the heart of the matter. As long as Kunin could remember, his love of reading — the places it could take him; the expansion it brought to his soul — was the deepest, most private thing about him, so that he found it impossible to believe anyone could share his love with the same passion. It was a boy's notion, all the more intense for that reason, and in school the teachers thought him stupid because even under the penalty of expulsion he never admitted to reading a book — this while he lay awake nights reading literally hundreds.

For the libraries were still open in those days. The authorities were going around making sure working writers were brought under control, but hadn't gotten around to the dead ones yet. At first, Kunin's favorites had been the adventure novels wrapped in faded yellow covers on the very bottom of the shelves. These were stories in the predictable style. Slavic heroes rescuing Slavic heroines from Tamerlane or Genghis Khan; sailors battling pirates in the Baltic; Cossacks chastising Turks. . . . Predictable, but to a boy in the frightened gray Leningrad of the Thirties, they were exactly like sparklers — wands burning just brightly enough to keep dreams alive.

In 1936, or thereabouts, an official was appointed to remove faded yellow books from lower library shelves. They were replaced with stories that were similar in tone, but done much less skillfully, as if the dissident poet or starving novelist who had been forced to write them had done it with a quarter of his heart. Young detachments of Red Guards, young detachments of Pioneer Women, young detachments of practically everyone, for the most part fighting counter-revolutionary saboteurs. It wasn't so much the plots that were bad, but the childish morals the authors were careful to include. The need to defecate regularly, the dangers of self-pollution, the importance of informing on parents and neighbors who in any way nonconformed. Kunin gave all this a good try, but his disgust soon forced him to look around for something better.

Then, too, that year saw the arrest of his father (or

his death, which in 1936 was much the same thing). A reclusive, studious man, he had specialized in astronomy in school and was put to work by the government renaming the constellations after revolutionary heroes. He did this successfully for a time, but then made the mistake of renaming Orion after Bukharin and was exiled to a remote village in the east. Kunin's mother, a translator of English, was arrested a month later, leaving the frightened fifteen-year-old to be watched over by his bachelor uncle.

Uncle Jacob was an engineer on a merchant steamer — a self-taught man of proud independence, away most of the time, hardly an influence. And yet he left behind something in his small flat that was: a fully stocked mahogany bookcase with the works of all the Russian masters. Kunin, from boyhood associating the best books with the lowest, pulled out a volume from the bottom shelf one day when a snowstorm off the Baltic had closed all the schools. It was in a dull-looking brown binding, but for lack of anything flashier he took it over to the egg-shaped stove that kept the flat warm and began reading a story called "The Overcoat" by someone named Nikolay Vasilyevich Gogol.

It was a story about an impoverished Petersburg clerk, who, having nothing in the world to draw comfort from except his overcoat, has it stolen from his shoulders one night as he walks home through a blizzard. As simple as the story was, it affected Kunin tremendously. His hands shook in horror the moment he realized what was going to happen; his soul wanted to leap out of itself to warn the poor man of what was in wait. When he finished, he was crying; he felt an unbearable pity that made him want to take all the poor lonely clerks of the world under his arm to warm them as if they were orphaned chicks. This was no adventure story to make him forget the dark smoky streets of his solitary wanderings. This was something that took those dark gray streets and made adventures of them.

The next story he read was in a different book by a different author. Fate working as it does, he was bound to discover it eventually; fate working as it does, he picked it up then because it was bound in the same American leather as the Gogol.

Third down in the table of contents was a story called "The Fish," and it was this he read first, one of his favorite pastimes being to drape himself over a bridge in the spring to watch the herring come swarming up the canals. It was a much different story than "The Overcoat," about peasants who have a huge pout trapped under some branches in a river and the commotion that ensues when they try to pull it out. But even though the story was funny, Kunin felt himself strangely moved — moved the way a boy can be on early mornings after a storm, when the washed air is so still and transparent that buildings, trees, and passersby stand out with a clarity that is breathtaking. Through this light he saw the greedy peasants and bumbling landowner; through this light he felt his hand grope beneath the branches for the pout's horny lip.

He turned back to the first page. The name on top was A. P. Chekhov. And just as there was a remarkable clarity to the story, there was a remarkable clarity to the name — a short jaunty bounce to it that sliced like a cleaver through all that was superfluous and old.

There were nine stories in the collection. Kunin was a fast reader, so he must have read all nine that very afternoon. But the odd thing was he didn't remember it that way. Since each story came to embody a different epoch in his life, his recollection spaced them out years apart; there may have been minutes between reading "The Fish" and "Ward Number Six," but his understanding needed a good four years to catch up, so it wasn't until he was a medical student that the last story made sense.

"The Kiss" came halfway in between. As with "The Fish," he was attracted by the title, not because he knew anything of kisses, but because he would have liked to learn. It was about a man who was just as lonely and timid as the hero in "The Overcoat," only this time he was an officer in a cavalry regiment on maneuvers. A landowner invites the officers to his home for a soiree; the hero, Staff Captain Riabovitch, feeling awkward and out of place there, wanders into a deserted, darkened room. He is just turning to go when a girl enters the room, embraces him by mistake, then vanishes in alarm, leaving Riabovitch haunted by the memory of her kiss and its "peppermint chill."

The fleeting sweetness of receiving that kiss followed by the eternal bitterness of its loss — this Kunin with his clubfoot and shyness knew all too well. Indeed, it seemed to sum up his predicament — to paint his future, and so in a complex way bring him comfort. He *was* Staff Captain Riabovitch. His cheeks always burned with peppermint chills from kisses never received from women who ignored him.

And then when he was eighteen and ready to take that first difficult step toward maturity — to think not of

himself all the time, but of ideas and methods and craft —
there was a story for that phase, too, a story called "Two
Beauties." In it, nothing happens. Or rather, things happen, but not in a plot, not in the way his earlier reading
had led him to expect. The narrator remembers as a boy
seeing a beautiful girl waiting on tables at a filthy inn on
the steppe, then remembers a later incident at a train
station when he glimpsed a beautiful girl on the platform
as his train pulled away. And that's all. Two beauties
seen in passing, and the rest is up to the reader's imagination.

It was here, in the contradiction between the preciseness with which the scene is painted and the vague-
ness of where it points, that the secret of Chekhov's art
seemed to lie. Here was a man who knew the meaning of
life was ungraspable, but that the grasping is part of it,
and so puts down both in every line, the yearning and the
defeat.

And not just in his fiction. After he had devoured
the stories, Kunin haunted the old bookstalls near the
Winter Palace until he found a cheaply bound edition of
the plays. The paper was so old it flaked apart on his
chest as he read, giving the effect of lives dribbling away,
and yet if anything Chekhov's message came through here
with even more force than in his prose — his insistence
that dreams are only dreams and never meant to come
true; that all love is unrequited and better off being so;
that art is our only glimpse of truth, though the people
who create it are as weak and foolish as the rest of us;
that despite all the bitterness, life must be plunged into
and embraced, the beauty and bitterness both.

"Chekhov?" his friends at the university would say

whenever he brought up the name. "A master, of course. Rather a miniaturist, though. Those sad little sketches." And then, remembering who might be listening: "And not much Socialistic fervor either."

Their reactions infuriated him. His friends, much as he treasured them, were too small themselves to see Chekhov's vastness. Taken all at once, read in huge doses, his work was epic, larger than anyone's. All those stories, all those farces and sketches and plays, each another small widening in an embrace intended to take in the world — to take in its pain and its beauty and extract from them the truth. In those first three stories and in all Chekhov wrote, Kunin saw the results of this transformation as clearly as if it were a machine marked *Life* on the first hopper and *Art* on the last. But stare as he might — read and analyze until the words turned into squiggles — he could never make out the gears and cogs hidden in between.

Faced with this mystery, Kunin had only one recourse: to make a pilgrimage and so approach it as closely as he dared. And since all the pilgrimages of youth are literal ones, he began by aping Chekhov in details of manner and dress, growing a beard, affecting a monocle, wearing a double-breasted overcoat with the collar turned up around his neck. This was the reason he had gone to medical college and not because of any aptitude; he was hopeless at memorization and the smell of formaldehyde made him retch. This was also the reason that given a summer's long vacation with nothing particular to do, he had made the journey south to Yalta, stopping to work when his money ran out, berry picking on the collectives, helping with the harvest, moving on when he had enough for train fare, begging rides on peasant carts, his skin getting tanner, his muscles gradually hardening, until he could swing a scythe all day without resting and his health had never been better.

By the time he reached Yalta it was already winter and his head was so full of the steppe and the stories he had seen there that all thoughts of a medical career were temporarily abandoned. When he approached the Chekhov villa that first evening, Maria Pavlovna had been standing outside beneath the orange trees to welcome him, though he had sent no message ahead and there was no way for her to know of his existence, let alone his arrival. She was waiting — she smiled her ironic smile and advanced toward him with her hand outstretched like a chatelaine whose skin and hair the sunset had turned golden. He remembered the warmth of her hand as it met his, the curiously masculine firmness with which it fastened, drawing him — by that contact, by that firmness she could only have learned from a brother — into the secret heart of something he had been seeking all along.

And this was what made it so hard for him to accept that anyone else could love literature precisely the way he did: that the pity and the compassion Chekhov's words evoked in him were caught up somehow in the skein of the massive egg-shaped stove in his Uncle Jacob's apartment, the dusty mahogany bookcase, the snow-covered Leningrad streets, the smell of wheat when it's freshly cut, the sight of the villa there in the darkness, caught so tightly there was no unraveling it, no comparison to be made between his love and an impostor like Diskau's.

Even if the tracks of their lives had converged there in Yalta, even if they happened to worship the same author, had pretensions toward art, there was still no reason for Tania to link them. For in that surface similarity lay hidden the essential differences Tania hadn't the insight to see. In the autumn of 1941, Kunin was still a young man who dreamed of emulation, while Diskau, having given up this ambition, had replaced it with something larger and more bizarre. Kunin was a dreamer in the conventional sense; Diskau a dreamer in the unconventional. Kunin was safe and harmless as only a would-be writer can be; Diskau as dangerous and unpredictable as a man who has failed.

For Diskau, on that November morning when Kunin was summoned by official courier to come at once to his office, had already crossed the point on which the Twentieth Century seemed to balance — the point where a man without talent, realizing he will never achieve knowledge, decides to achieve power in its stead.

THE GERMAN ministries were located in an old brick school building on the outskirts of town. Colder and gloomier than any prison, it seemed not merely to symbolize dullness but to actually exude it, so that the bricks were coated with a resinous gray. Vines climbed the walls but they were dead ones, suggesting bars. Out one window hung someone's underwear; beside it, mounted over an elaborate portal, perched a German eagle in bronze.

There were half-tracks and motorcycles parked in front, but Kunin walked past them into the entrance hall without seeing a single uniform. Instead, the place was swarming with German civilians, all of whom seemed cut from the same caricature, with oversized glasses and pasty white complexions, round shoulders and mean shrunken chests. Compared to the German officers who strutted along the promenade, they were miserable specimens at best, and yet here in the school they seemed to be in their glory and paraded up and down the stairway with briefcases under their arms as proudly as field marshals carrying batons.

God knows what they were there for. To feast off what was left, he supposed. There were elaborate placards over the old schoolrooms announcing the names of the various ministries. Ministry of Food, Ministry of Documentation, Ministry of Economic Re-allocation, Ministry of Administrative Services, Ministry of Cemeteries, Ministry of Race and Resettlement. Outside each one stood a line of people waiting patiently to be admitted.

Collaborators, he decided, with a shiver of disgust. But there was nothing to mark them as such; with their slumped, resigned postures they were quite normal looking, the kind who were used to waiting in line at Soviet ministries and obviously saw no difference between those lines and these. More sinister were the Tartar officials sauntering through the halls with their German counterparts. They were sleek looking and self-satisfied and the Germans held their elbows like pilot fish escorting sharks.

The Ministry of Culture was in the basement at the end of a dark hall. It seemed shabbier than the other offices, but was the only one with a placard printed in Russian as well as German. Inside was a room where students had once hung their coats; the hooks were low, not three feet off the floor, and there were bins around the perimeter for storing boots.

Into this cramped space two desks had been wedged. At the first, typing, was a young Russian girl. Seeing Kunin enter, she turned away ashamed. At the second, frowning at some files, was a man dressed in a sober-looking blue suit.

"Ah, there you are, Mr. Kunin," he said, pushing back his chair. "Thank you so much for coming. I'm Major Diskau's secretary, Hans Koenig."

The man stuck out his hand. He was a German about his own age, boyish looking and happily servile; his blond hair, combed straight over his forehead, gave him the appearance of a page.

"You may wait in the Major's inner office if you'd like. Will you be having tea?"

Kunin ignored him. The secretary smiled with that, as if willing to overlook his ill breeding. He opened a door in the wall that led to another room.

"He'll be with you shortly."

It was a conventional Russian classroom Kunin entered, with a large blackboard and high teacher's podium and glazed-over windows to keep daydreaming students from peeking out. In the center where the desks had been was a cherry-wood table, the delicate kind aristocratic women had once imported from France. On top were some papers and fountain pens; on the edge, a small oil portrait in an elaborate gold frame.

It was impossible not to feel fourteen there — feel that he had been kept after class and was now awaiting the teacher's mercy. To fight it off, Kunin picked up the portrait and went over to the window to study it in the light. It was of a young woman, pretty, almost Spanish in her darkness, but by the shape of her features — her thin neck and sensual face — unmistakably Slavic. Though the painting was of her head and shoulders alone, there was something else there in the background, a glimpse of an estate or manor house. Kunin was staring at it trying to make out the details when there came a soft, apologetic cough from the door.

"It's by a painter named Sobolev. Do you know his work? A perfect likeness, particularly the mouth."

Kunin looked up. There in the entrance stood Rene Diskau, his eyes blinking lazily like someone just woken from a nap. He was wearing the same black suit he had worn in the villa, but it seemed looser on him now, easier. His hair, rather than sweeping disordered over his forehead, was brushed into a part; his shoulders, rather than twitching, were steady, at ease. Even his empty sleeve seemed draped in a softer crease. It was as if an invisible fire had been melting him in the course of that week.

In the malleability of his features and tone there was no change at all. As before, he seemed to study Kunin's face with an eye toward choosing which role would be appropriate, finally deciding — seeing the hostility in his expression — to come across as manly and frank, with just a tinge of self-deprecation to make it go down.

"That was done when she was seventeen," he said, crossing to the window. "It was just after her first ball, so you can still see her excited flush." He glanced up at Kunin, smiling shyly. "My mother. Her family had an estate not far from here, near Sevastopol. Her grandfather was the General, Ivan Gavrilov. Before the Revolution came they were all smart enough to clear out."

He took the picture gently from Kunin's hand and stood there staring down at it in a pantomime of filial devotion.

"How she ended up marrying my father is a boring

story, so I'll spare you. But it was in Berlin before the last war. He was rich, of course. He was one of the few men in Germany who had the means to satisfy her tastes."

"Why was I called here?"

At first, it was as if Diskau hadn't heard him. He replaced the portrait on the table, then sat himself down in a chair on the far side. Lost in thought, his posture seemed to say. He leaned back and pointed in the vague direction of the window.

"You can imagine my feelings returning to her homeland. Here I was a lifelong student of Russia, a man who was raised bilingually, filled with stories of Romanov glory, and then to be suddenly set down in the landscape where it all happened . . . But please, have a seat. There, that's better . . . Well, you can imagine. I felt a great honor. To stand on the same soil as Lermontov and Pushkin. To see peasant villages come full-blown off the page, then to reach at last the Crimea . . . I was enthralled."

He laughed and shook his head. "As you see, I'm a sentimentalist. I've inherited that from her anyway, if not her beauty. All the Russian characteristics for that matter. Sentimentality, impetuosity, a taste for philosophizing, my love of literature —"

"Your courier said it was urgent."

"And so when I actually stepped foot in the villa of Anton Chekhov . . . When I saw at last the Yalta that figured so prominently in his work . . . 'The Lady with the Dog,' have you read it? It's one of my favorites . . . To do this was the culmination of all I had dreamed. No, more than this. Because to have the privilege of meeting his sister, to hear from her own lips stories about the master himself, this went beyond any dream."

Diskau was one of those rare Germans who decorated their talk with physical punctuation. At these last words, his fingers spread apart as if he were describing a fish.

"Madam Chekhova is a remarkable woman. I would use the word saint, but it hardly does her justice. For hours we talked, Peter. All afternoon there in his study. I wanted to take notes, but hardly dared for fear of losing a single word. The stories she tells of her brother, the memories . . . For instance, about his wife, Olga Knipper. We talked about her at great length. Apparently there was a time when Madam Chekhova was quite jealous of her. They had been friends before the marriage, and she felt her brother was being selfish in taking on such responsibility while ill. But after his death . . . Did you know he died in Germany? That he was particularly fond of German food? . . . After his death, they became friends again and were corresponding regularly until the war. And so she's lost track of her now, and fears for her safety. I've promised to do what I can to locate her. There are means, of course."

He wiggled his fingers toward the door like a magician — as if the current he needed was there for the summoning.

"But the truly exciting thing is that after all our talk, Madam Chekhova has graciously agreed to make me her brother's official biographer. Once all this . . . this resistance . . . ends."

He closed his fist. Kunin, who had felt like a timid

schoolboy until now, had become angrier and more jealous with each mention of Chekhov's name. This last piece of information, said so matter-of-factly, gave him the courage he hadn't found before.

"One of your soldiers almost shot me. For a joke, nothing more. There was a blankness in his face that was worse than any gun."

"I wonder. It's a small point perhaps, but had it ever occurred to you? I wonder how much she reads him. She's devoted to his work and has at her fingertips every edition ever printed. But does she read him? At night before retiring, does she open his books? You're her protégé, of course, and it occurred to me you might know."

"There are stories about massacres. Whole villages being burned. In Kovrinka, they hung all the women."

"Because she doesn't seem to understand her brother's art. I was speaking to her of the psychological undertones of 'Black Monk' and she looked at me quite blankly — I don't even think she remembered the plot. Because of this . . . If I'm speaking out of line, please be frank . . . But it seems to me, though I am struggling against the notion . . . Well, there you are. She's dedicated her life to preserving something she doesn't understand."

"And the Germans to destroying something they don't understand."

It wasn't a particularly killing line, but Kunin said it as if it were. Diskau, though, hardly noticed. His hand rolled idly back and forth over his papers; his head swayed sideways as if struggling against sleep. And yet when Kunin got up the nerve to meet his eyes, the effect was exactly the opposite. They danced back and forth with manic intensity, blinking furiously, refusing to focus. They reminded Kunin of a child's marbles suddenly scattered across the floor, and he had to restrain himself from reaching over to make them stop.

"There's another point," Diskau said softly. "No, not a point but a question. Has Madam Chekhova . . . She's never married, of course . . . But has she ever had a lover? Forgive me for asking, but I'm trying very hard to understand. To see such devotion in a sister is rare, and if I may be permitted to speculate about its origins . . . Do you see my drift? She must have been stunning as a girl. Of course, there's no question of anything unnatural, but sometimes even Platonic love can be carried to extremes."

With each word he spoke more slowly, like a top that's been winding down. And yet the spring in his eyes seemed wound even tighter, to the point where the contradiction became too much for him and with no explanation whatsoever he jumped up, grabbed his forehead, and stumbled awkwardly from the room.

Five minutes later he was back again, completely transformed. It wasn't just his eyes, which were steady now and focused. His whole face seemed to have changed — his complexion to have darkened; his throbbing vein to have disappeared. It was as if he had run outside to get a transfusion of fresh blood.

"Business," he mumbled. He opened a folder on the table, studied it, then looked back up with a serious and open expression that made Kunin feel he was seeing the real Diskau for the first time.

"I will admit mistakes have been made," he said quietly. "I will even say mistakes that go beyond the normal brutalities of war into a different category altogether. Your friends, whoever they are, are telling the truth. Though I don't know this Kovrinka, I have no doubt that the women were hung there, and at a hundred more Kovrinkas besides. What you have to consider is the military mind. They see an enemy and destroy it and the niceties be damned. That the land they are marching across has a culture — not only a culture, but a culture so glorious it's one of the justifications for mankind's existence — never occurs to them, and so they trample it like blindfolded elephants. If you only knew the opposition I've had to face in getting this ministry off the ground, the ridicule and contempt."

He paused, waiting for — what? Agreement? Sympathy? When Kunin didn't say anything, he got up and started pacing back and forth by the window.

"Our army is proceeding in a way guaranteed to make a conquered population rebel. Reprisals, the taking of hostages — it's barbaric, something straight from the Middle Ages. Whereas we in the administrative end of things . . . We who are getting the chance to prove our theories . . . We realize that the key to acceptance is exactly the opposite. We Germans must present ourselves to the Russian people not as conquerors, but as liberators."

"Butchers," Kunin mumbled, without heart.

"For now . . . yes. But this will change as conditions stabilize. As a point of fact, this has already changed, at least in Yalta. In Yalta, methods will be different. For one thing, there was little fighting here, so there isn't the sheer physical morass of it to untangle. No blood to scrub clean. Then, too, it's common knowledge that the Crimea has never been totally enamored of the Soviet regime. Nowhere were the White armies stronger, nowhere is Stalin hated as much as here. Between these factors we have ourselves a fertile ground for experimentation."

He came back to the table, his face shining like a boy's bursting with secrets.

"In Yalta, we will create a model for all the captured territories to emulate, not only in Russia but across the breadth of Europe as well. This will begin immediately. Correction — has begun. For we've started modest programs on every level. Language schools have been organized to fill the heavy need we have for translators. We've established an information office with Russian journalists, and our first newspaper should be out on the streets any day. There will be an art exhibit in the casino, paintings the Bolsheviks have suppressed. We're encouraging the Tartars to resume wearing their native dress — we're seeing to it that all the mosques are opened again. The churches too, for that matter. We're restoring to life all the cultural institutions Stalin has crushed.

"But these are small things," he said, with a dismissing shrug. "Beginning in December and continuing at two-month intervals throughout the year, the Ministry of Culture will be reopening the old Imperial Theatre and producing a complete cycle of Chekhov's plays. I've talked to Madam Chekhova about this, and she has not only given us permission but her blessing as well."

He glanced up to see Kunin's reaction. "*The Seagull* will be first," he added. "We start rehearsals on Friday afternoon with a reading of the complete play."

All through their conversation Kunin's reactions had

been lagging several seconds behind Diskau's words. Now each caught up with the other in a jolt hard enough to shake him.

"You're doing what?" he mumbled.

"We have his theatre. We have his sister. What more natural than to have his plays?"

"*The Seagull?*"

"Followed by *The Cherry Orchard, Uncle Vanya,* and *The Three Sisters.* We intend to give the one-act plays, too, but only as matinees."

Kunin felt like someone pushed off a cliff into clouds. Falling, he grabbed for the first thought that formed.

"You don't do plays in a war zone."

"On the contrary. There's a long tradition of Russians seeking out the theatre in perilous times. The first building restored after Napoleon burned Moscow was the opera house. During the October Revolution in Petersburg, Lermontov's *Masquerade* played to packed houses every night. Besides, think of occupied Paris. Never have there been so many plays mounted as this season. My friends write me that tickets are impossible to obtain."

"Comedies perhaps. Not Chekhov."

Diskau was ready for him. "Ah, but that's the very point! Because of war are we supposed to hide our best things underground like hordes of silver? Cherish our loves, but in secret? No, because they'll be burrowed out and destroyed like all the rest. Do you understand this, Peter? You can't hide your Chekhov until all this blows past, then have him rise again in the same untarnished splendor. Whatever isn't flaunted will disappear. And when I say disappear, I mean precisely that. Look at Germany.

Look at the books burned there already, and not just there but in Holland and Italy and France. Look at the Jew Mendelssohn. In Germany, no performances are allowed of his music, no mention of his name permitted. In a generation, Mendelssohn's art will have ceased to exist. And if the philistines can be so ruthless with a German, think how much more ruthless they will be with a Russian — a subhuman to their minds, a dirty piece of contemptible scum."

It was impossible to exaggerate the passion he put into these words. He bunched his shoulders together in excitement, leaned forward, and grabbed the edge of the table until his knuckles turned white.

"I can help save him, Peter. I can argue that his plays are useful for propaganda, and in that way save him. But I need help, and I need help from people who have faith."

When Diskau talked nonsense, Kunin found himself almost liking him — it was like watching the antics of a clown. But when he talked sincerely — when his ideas began making a bizarre kind of sense — he found himself hating him like he had never hated anyone before. His casual assumption that Chekhov was his now; the hint he was careful to give of the power backing him up; his shrugging, halfhearted dismissal of atrocity. Offered as the perversions of a sick mind they were one thing, but offered as salvations?

"You won't get anyone to come," Kunin said, his face turning red.

"Those who suffered under the Bolsheviks and are rejoicing in their liberation. Those German officers who are not SS brutes. Those lovers of drama who are tired of war. The curious longing for something to do . . . I expect a full house."

"The theatre is falling down. It's been vandalized out of recognition."

"Then we will fix it."

"There are no actors."

Diskau pursed his lips. His fingers, uncoiling from the table's edge, flitted back and forth like stamens.

"I'll admit this is a problem. A problem, but one we're well on our way to resolving. For instance, Olga Knipper. When we manage to locate her, she'll be brought here as Madam Arcadina, a role I understand to be among her finest. That corpulent fool who lives with you — Potapov? He's an actor and will be of use. My secretary, Koenig, has a theatrical background and will be taking a part. Even that girl Tania. Judging from her appearance she will make a fine Nina, and Madam Chekhova quite agrees. The other roles will be filled as we can. I myself will play Constantine Treplef."

He smiled — disarmingly. "It's a favorite characterization and something I've always longed to do. The young writer burning with ambition; the doomed, unrequited love. I find it very easy to identify with him . . . But here. I'm rushing now. I've been waiting all along for the obvious question."

"Which is?"

"Why are we doing *The Seagull* first."

Kunin sighed in what he hoped was an ironic manner. "Why are you doing *The Seagull* first?"

"It's odd that you asked that, Peter. I myself had planned on *The Cherry Orchard* first — starting at the very summit of his art. But Madam Chekhova insisted on *The Seagull,* and I've deferred to her wishes. To her, it's not about some wretched gull at all, but the phoenix. A disaster at its premiere, a triumph two years later — the effect on her was profound. We watch it and see a comedy about some literary types that veers brilliantly toward tragedy. She watches it and sees eternity — eternity and her brother's place in its midst."

Diskau shrugged. "Well, so be it. Eternity then — we have just the people to bring it off."

"Anyone who helps you will be a collaborator."

"A collaborator? . . . You know, Peter my friend, I've been watching you. Yes, throughout this entire conversation I've been studying you trying to understand your personality. And now I think I have it . . . The man who observes. The kindly, slightly cynical looker-on. Combine this with your medical background and I think you will be perfect in the role of Dr. Dorn."

Without waiting for his response, he stood up and gestured toward the door.

"I'm sorry you're not with us yet, Peter. But there are several considerations you should keep in mind as you debate your participation. The first is that there is a fine line between collaboration and cooperation. The war ends a certain way, collaborators are punished. The war ends another way, cooperators are rewarded. And there is no question that this war will end in the latter way. You are right to be skeptical of military communiqués, but in this case they happen to be accurate. Leningrad is cut off and starving, on the point of surrender. Moscow will be taken by Easter. The Crimea is conquered and the Caucasus will fall in the next offensive. Von Paulus is aiming for the Don, and all that will be left then is the mopping up."

This information was new to Kunin — he tried not to show its effect.

"Winter is coming," he said.

"Here in Yalta, a winter of plays. The war is over, Peter. The task for us now is to salvage what we can of Russian culture. I have a certain amount of power for good, and I intend to use it without scruple. My allies — and I count you among these — will find there is an important place for them in the new order."

"I'm not a collaborator."

"With Germany, no. With Chekhov . . . I think perhaps you are."

They were to the door now. Diskau held it open for him, but Kunin stayed put.

"Tell me one thing."

Diskau smiled. "Certainly."

"Why was I sent for? Why are you telling this to me?"

"Haven't you guessed?"

Kunin shook his head.

"Because I require your good opinion. . . . Thank you for coming, Peter. Mind your head now on that door."

ONE SISTER

ONCE UPON A TIME there lived a woman whose brother was the best man in the world. This first occurred to her at Easter when she was nine. She had rushed to her bed in tears from some forgotten humiliation in the series of humiliations that was her family's lot in those years, when even the purchase of a loaf of bread was something to be endlessly debated and there was never enough money for anything new. Living that close to the edge of things, it didn't take much to crush the spirit in a child's soul. A harsh word from their landlady (a pockmarked Little Russian who sipped vodka from teacups and mocked her to her face); a fresh example of her father's incompetence; a friend who suddenly turned on her and laughed at her ragged clothes. The exact cause was lost to her, but she remembered as if it were yesterday the desperation with which she threw her face against the rough fabric of her pillow, the way she hugged the mattress like a person suffering convulsions, how her breath ran away from her in a fury of anger, bitterness, and shame.

Through this and very gradually she became aware of a voice. It was her brother's — her brother who was sitting on the windowsill in his characteristic pose: legs hunched tight to his chest, arms clasped around knees, chin resting on the little bench thus created. Her tears came so fast she couldn't see him other than in outline, but she remembered his voice being pitched to the exact key of the sunlight — the gentle warmth of it, the way he spoke not of her humiliation but something apart from it, a funny incident he had seen that day, something perfectly trivial. The gentleness enveloped her sadness and lifted it bodily away so that within minutes she was laughing at his descriptions and quite unable to remember her agony's cause.

Always before she had taken this ability of his for granted. Antosha could trace little figures in the window frost and make her laugh; Antosha could demonstrate how to pinch candles back so their light would last longer; Antosha could show her not to be afraid. Antosha was the education their poverty denied her, and by this particular Easter her education had proceeded far enough to grasp the one important lesson she would have to learn on her own: that her brother Antosha was a truly exceptional being. The sun streamed in the window at his back, catching up his jacket in a soft fringe of yellow, blurring out his features until only this golden radiance remained, and she realized with a sudden intuitive knowing that she was finally seeing him as he really was — not the brother who always protected her, not the Antosha who refused to cringe, but something far beyond that: a boy who partook of sunlight, of glory, of an immaculate shining in.

So she wasn't surprised when later on, after they had moved to Moscow and things became both harder and better, he decided to study medicine. Even when he was a student, the people of Grachovka Street came to him with their illnesses, and he soon acquired a reputation far in excess of those corpulent, haughty doctors who treated only shopkeepers and whores. He was oddly gruff with his patients, would spend little time listening to their complaints, and yet he never refused them and his advice in almost all cases was direct and beneficial. It was as if he disdained his own healing capacity, thought it nothing special and was actually made angry by its expression. He was too conscious of the power of disease and fate to trust much in his own small power to alleviate them, and yet to Maria (who acted as his nurse in the worst cases, the ones where people were held) this power was immense and entirely mysterious, so that it only increased her awe and made her reverence him all the more.

It was largely the same with his writing. For him it was something he took for granted right from the start. From telling humorous stories to entertain the family he had taken to writing them down, selling them to popular newspapers for the miserably few kopecks they earned.

Again, Maria was in awe of this ability, but to him it was the merest commonplace and he became infuriated with anyone who treated him as superior. If anything, his modesty went too far, and he was slow in realizing how seriously knowledgeable people were taking his talent.

"See?" Maria would say, waving a review in his face to make him understand. "The *New Times* and a full column. They compare you to Turgenev, to Gogol himself. Here, look lower down. The reviewer speaks of you as the poet of wistful moods, a new voice in Russian literature demanding to be heard."

He laughed with that, quickly changed the topic to something else. But modest as he was, his power was steadily growing, until it encompassed not only the talent to make sad people laugh (a talent, after all, not much different from his talent in medicine), but the harder, more severe talent of making happy people cry.

"You must take off the blinders," he told her when she suffered some disappointment. "You must see things not as we wish them but as they are."

When his success lasted long enough that they began to fully believe in it, they bought a small dacha at Melikhovo, a short distance outside Moscow. This purchase, while establishing them in the country, complicated their life considerably. Now, not only were there parents to support, their feckless older brothers and Michael, who was just finding his way, but a whole army of uncles and aunts, nieces and nephews, friends, admirers, and hangers-on. In August there were so many guests the overflow slept in the corridors, and the only force standing between them and chaos was Maria's inflexible will.

For she was a tyrant when it came to her brother's

routine. Each guest upon arrival would be handed a sheet listing the rules and regulations governing the day. There was to be no noise of any kind in or around the south wing until eleven in the morning. There was to be no conversation about literature or politics for two hours after that. Antosha was not to be tempted with invitations to picnics or mushroom picking or fishing. Anyone who kept him up talking past midnight would be warned on the first occasion and on the second packed off to the station at Lopasnya in disgrace.

There were no exceptions. On the famous day when Tolstoy visited Melikhovo, it was Maria who arranged the fete in the garden, she herself who welcomed him to their home, not only with the peasants' traditional bread and salt, but with a freshly printed copy of the rules.

"Ah, and this is the famous Maria!" the great man said as he slid from his roan stallion and established his presence on the ground. "This is the warder of our Anton's brilliant cell."

She had blushed with that — blushed literally and with secret delight. She took great pride in her brother's fame and her own role in supporting it, became quite jealous of anyone who offered to help him in a similar capacity, and yet went out of her way to find allies among these people and thereby place his career on even firmer footing. It was she who read the proofs a final time for misspellings; it was she who handled all his correspondence regarding royalties and fees.

Of his writing itself she understood only parts. The feeling, the heart of it, she could grasp by instinct, but the subtlety, the stylistic touches that drove the critics to raptures, were totally lost on her. She accepted his talent as part of the mysterious radiance that had cloaked him in her eyes since childhood. In this radiance she placed all the faith of her religious instinct, all the certainty of a passionate soul. That his life was devoted to art was important, of course — it made her own task that much harder. But he could have devoted his life to selling vodka to the peasants and she would have worshiped him just as slavishly. He was a god to her first, a writer far second, and it was a long time before her priorities got re-arranged.

It was a day toward the end of summer when the burden of visitors, the constant financial juggling needed to keep things running, the demands of the peasants (who were refusing to use the school her brother had built them because a simpleton named Osip had seen there the evil eye) had all combined to overwhelm her and make her feel she couldn't go on. She was exhausted spiritually and her physical condition was poor — she was suffering one of the recurrent, unexplained headaches that settled in thorny bands across her eyes. She had tried at breakfast to go on as normal, but a harsh word from Antosha about the noise created by a threshing machine had sent her rushing across the veranda in tears. For the first time since moving to Melikhovo, she felt neglected — neglected and used.

There was a small copse of birch by the river where they would lie after bathing. Always before the peacefulness of the scene — the small oval leaves tossing against the sky, the rhythmic lap of the current as it swept past shore — had been enough to restore her and make her feel whole. This time, though, her agitation was too great, and immediately after sitting down she sprang back up again and marched across the lawn toward her brother's study with the intention of telling him exactly what was on her mind. It was time his precious solitude was shaken up a bit. It was time he recognized upon whose labor his writing was based.

His study was in the dacha's summer parlor — a small room facing the lawn with glass doors in the French manner. As furious as she was, she still found herself unable to march right in. For years she had insisted upon the sanctity of his mornings and it was hard to violate this rule herself. What was intended to be a loud, demanding rap on the glass door became, as it were, the tap of a beggar, and when minutes went by and he didn't respond, she tapped again even softer.

Still nothing. She bent sideways to peer in. There was his desk piled high with papers, but the wicker chair beside it was empty and pushed back. Gently, on tiptoe, she edged her way inside through the doors and pulled open the drapes.

The light, coming so suddenly, seemed to capture his shadow so that what she was first aware of was the trailing scent of his tobacco, the lingering sweetness of his cologne. His chair, set on casters, trembled slightly, as if he had just that moment gotten up. On his writing table between his pens and pince-nez was a large dollop of wet black ink. Papers — white papers, manila papers, yellow papers, papers with lines — lay in disorder everywhere, as if they had been tossed up in some whirlwind and left to fall where they might.

It was this blizzard of paper that affected her most of all. Those few times she had been allowed into his study she had been struck by how neat and orderly every-

thing was, as if no work had gone on there besides lei-
surely rumination. Because of this, because of the ease
with which so many things seemed to come to him, she
had assumed his talent was similar to his goodness, something he just had to let be for it to be. That it required
quiet she understood; that it required long hours alone in
his study she understood as well. But as to what went on
there, the turmoil and labor, she had always been blind.

Blind until now. For just as when she entered the
room and had the sensation of coming upon his shadow,
she had as she examined his writing table the further
sense that she was seeing beyond the shadow to his talent's inner source. For what was written on those confused, tangled pages was even more confused and tangled,
a maze of false starts and doubling backs and furious era-
sures. There wasn't a line that wasn't crossed out, not a
word that didn't have an alternate word scrawled in above
it, then a third wedged in above that. Whole paragraphs
were circled and recircled; whole passages were blotted
out and rearranged. Arrows swooped from the top of the
page to the bottom, words were forced in sideways, large
angry X's inked out pages on end. There were so many
lines and corrections that staring at them was like staring
at the sketchings of a lunatic painter, and even as evidence of sheer physical labor it was staggering, not to be
believed. On the dozen or so pages she could examine
without disturbance, there was only one word written
clearly enough to read, and it was written in capitals so
large and forceful it was as if she could hear him saying
it out loud and see the gesture that went with it, the
gesture a man uses who grapples with the essence of things,

the gesture of a hand slapped futilely against a forehead in an agony of impotence and rage.

DUNCE!

From this, she backed away. From this nakedness she backed away. She carefully placed the top page back where she had found it, took a last look around to make sure she'd left no trace of her intrusion, then went out the way she had come in, timing her footsteps to the noise of her brother's as he approached up the hall. The moment his hand turned the doorknob she stepped outside onto the lawn, taking the long way around to the kitchen where, such was her tension, she immediately screamed at Fekla, their serving girl, who was scrubbing out the pots.

"How long will it take you to learn! Silence! I ask of you nothing but silence until eleven!"

That moment in the study was a turning point for her. Having glimpsed the bitter physical and mental effort that went into her brother's talent, she was better able to accept those rebellious moments when her own lot seemed hard, better able to put up with the demands of running a school and nursing the peasants and the hundred and one other responsibilities she had gradually taken on. And to the admiration she felt for her brother was added a new emotion: pity. Not the pity that belittles, but the pity that elevates — pity that a solitary heart should have to grapple with the gods alone.

And so the Melikhovo years went on. They were happy ones for the most part, the long summer days being so precious that no one could bear to spoil them with arguments or gloom. In the afternoon there were expeditions in search of mushrooms, croquet games on the lawn, boat rides on the river, long conversations that were about everything and nothing at all. Her father kept a logbook, which every visitor was required to sign. Tchaikovsky, Svobodin, Gorky. . . . The list became more glorious with each summer, and her brother's reputation steadily grew.

Among these visitors was a friend of Michael's, Alexander Smagin by name. He was a minor official in the Moscow municipal administration — a stout, friendly man of forty, with commonplace features and no accomplishments worth mentioning. He was even a bit on the homely side, with ears that were floppy and sunburned and a chin that was far too broad. The only thing that saved him from complete nonentity was his affinity for children — the way his portly shape with its crisscrossed watch fobs, his open sparkling eyes, seemed to attract them like a magnet. Maria would come upon him in the garden struggling under a squirming heap of children of all ages, laughing uproariously as they tried to pin him down. And what was odd, this magnetism seemed to work on Maria the same way, so that when she watched him wrestle with the children — saw him with his shirt-sleeves rolled up, his wide shoulders glistening with sweat as he tumbled back and forth — she felt a vertigo not much different than the one she had experienced when she invaded her brother's study and stared down in confusion at the crossed-out lines.

Why this should be so bewildered her to no end. Smagin was a pleasant, approachable man, but when it came to ability, no match for her brother. The idea of him as a suitor was quite absurd, and yet it was in the role of a suitor that Smagin, after a quick trip to Moscow, now reappeared.

Strangely enough, it was her brother who commented on this first. Without provocation, without any discernible contact with the man, he began talking of Smagin in the most sarcastic and disapproving way. Smagin the boring bureaucrat; Smagin the well-meaning oaf. These remarks weren't addressed to Maria directly, but he always made sure she was close enough to overhear.

That her brother could even notice him — that of all the people to ever visit Melikhovo he alone was the one to provoke Antosha's jealousy — made her more curious herself, and she soon began noticing things about Alexander Smagin she had never noticed before. That he had a rich baritone voice that always made you think he was about to burst into song; that he knew interesting things about birds, and had the knack of picking them out from the foliage when no one else could spot them; that he could talk for hours about Russian icons and draw crude sketches to illustrate his points. She now went about finding ways to spend as much time in Smagin's company as she could, which wasn't difficult since Smagin was trying in his clumsy fashion to arrange the same thing.

And so they talked. Often, it was about quite trivial things. Smagin would see a cloud go by and call her over and carefully point it out.

"See, Maria Pavlovna? A stratocumulus, and you don't see many this time of year."

And she would look at the cloud and pretend to be interested and, when he turned to point at other clouds, stare at his broad honest face trying to decide why it brought her so much pleasure. Later, on their way down the hillside after berry picking, they lingered behind the others and walked side by side. The long afternoon shadows made Smagin talk about more serious things, but again in a simple, unexceptional way.

"There are those who claim the world is getting better and I count myself in their ranks. Why I can see it even in our municipal administration. Last year we were paid sixty rubles a month and this year we make sixty-one! Is that not progress?"

And he laughed at that and tossed back his head like he was gulping in sunshine, and again she was filled with happiness — happiness and wonder. Why she could find so much pleasure in Smagin's simple ways — she, a woman who had talked with Tolstoy as an equal — puzzled her and left her feeling girlish and unsure. She could listen to the loftiest talk imaginable and feel herself quite unmoved; Smagin talked of wood ducks and she felt open in herself a dizzying new world of possibilities.

One morning shortly before he was due to leave, Maria was in the parlor listening to a delegation from the village who were in hopes of honoring Anton Pavlovich on his name day the following month. As they were leaving, Smagin ducked his head in the door to ask if she had time for a walk.

"In a minute," she said curtly.

After the delegation there was a telegraph to dispatch to her brother's publisher, then letters to write, then a meeting with the headmaster from the Lopasnya school. By the time these chores were accomplished, it was noon. Maria, going upstairs to get some papers, was surprised to find Smagin still waiting in the hall, his broad planter's hat held bashfully in one hand.

"That walk, Maria Pavlovna?"

He said it so diffidently she laughed despite herself. Instantly, all the concerns that had seemed so urgent faded away into insignificance, and she rushed up to her bedroom for her shawl.

They walked together toward the river. It was a perfect September afternoon, the air balanced between the nostalgic warmth of summer and autumn's quickening coolness. It made Maria feel lighthearted and yet wistful; she remembered wishing the golden leaves, the fragrant breeze, the sparkling water would blend like that forever, wishing it so intensely it took her breath away.

Smagin was dressed rather formally, in a frock coat and vest. His manner seemed formal, too, as if he were nerving himself up to something. By the time they reached the riverbank and the bench propped there between two birch, he was perspiring freely and talking in riddles.

"You see, Maria Pavlovna. When certain . . . When affection . . . That is, in situations of mutual respect. The great esteem I feel for you . . . My own longing for children."

Poor man, she thought. But at the same time she felt sorry for him, she felt something else, something so new and delightful it made her want to stretch herself in pleasure.

Smagin was making her an offer. An offer. He was doing it as clumsily as one of the heroes in her brother's stories, stuttering and lisping, but there was no hiding the love that impelled the words, and his eyes met hers directly without shame.

"My prospects . . . The life we might lead together . . ."

I must say something back, she told herself. I must take his hand, smile, nod, show him that I love him, too. But despite her good intentions she remained where she was, standing next to him and not sitting, frowning and not smiling, doubt on her face and not love.

"Perhaps," she mumbled. "Perhaps, but —"

"I'm sorry?" Smagin said. "You whisper so."

Her voice seemed to jump out by itself. "It's impossible."

Desperation made Smagin eloquent. He took her hand and pulled her gently down beside him on the bench. "I understand, Maria Pavlovna. From seeing you together this summer, from hearing you talk, I know the great esteem in which you hold your brother Anton Pavlovich and the great responsibilities you have in assisting his career. I value his writing equally. There's that tale about the Moscow cab driver, the one where his son has died and no one will listen to his story of it and so he tells his horse. It's masterful — it made me weep . . . But our marriage will in no way change your relationship. Indeed, I ask for nothing more than that you continue to assist him as much as our new . . . uh . . . association permits. I would have spoken to him first, but Michael advised me to speak with you initially. Of course, we will do nothing without his permission."

"Of course," Maria mumbled. She felt quite dizzy and put her hand on Smagin's shoulder to steady herself.

"Yes?" Smagin said, squinting up toward her.

"Yes? Yes, of course. I'll talk to him at once."

"I'll come."

For the first time since reaching the river she was able to smile. "No, it's better this way. Wait for me here."

At that time of day it was her brother's habit to work in the garden behind the house. To get there, Maria had to cross an uncut meadow a hundred meters in breadth — time enough for her to frame all the arguments for and against marrying Smagin. Against were her own settled habits, her age, which made having children dangerous, her inexperience with men. Against was the fact she was indispensable to her brother's work, that his whole complicated tower of writing, friends, family, and home rested squarely on her shoulders, that her brother did not approve of Smagin. Against was every reason in the world, and yet *for* was the fact that she loved him, loved this unlikely man with a passion that scared her, and it was this that enabled her to wade on through the wildflowers though her every instinct was to turn back.

She came upon her brother's tools first, tilted sideways across a newly furrowed patch of brown-red earth. A little way beyond were his canvas gloves, palms facing downward, the fingers half-buried as if the gloves had been doing the digging by themselves. Other than this, there was no sign of him whatsoever.

Gone, she decided — for a moment, she felt a surge of relief — but then she noticed a path leading through the meadow grass where the blades had been freshly trampled. She started along it, then stopped and listened. There not ten meters ahead of her was the steady click of pruning shears interspersed with the harsher sound of her brother's cough.

She walked on more slowly. There were some apple trees planted there, little more than saplings, and the grass completely surrounded them like a woven Oriental screen. Toward the bottom of this screen and behind it was a convex bulge: the shape of her brother moving along on his hands and knees in time to the metallic clicking.

Weeding. For some reason this made her bolder — she quickly began rehearsing her words — but a second before breaking in on him, her shyness returned and she stopped. I can't go through with this, she decided. Then, knowing how anxiously Smagin must be waiting, she forced herself to begin. She was standing where the grass grew highest, as hidden and isolated as a penitent in confession. She couldn't see her brother from there; she only knew where he was because of the clicking sound and his hoarse raspy breaths.

"Alexander Fyodorovich has made me an offer," she said. "He's waiting by the river for my reply."

The clicking noise stopped. She waited for him to say something, then — when he said nothing — went on.

"He was very careful to assure me he knows how important I am here. We would naturally have come to you for your blessing earlier, but he's leaving and this was very sudden."

She paused again, but there was nothing. Above her, a bloated crow struggled up toward the sun.

"It's impossible, of course, and I told him so. The idea of someone my age being in love like a foolish girl. But still. Michael can help you with your appointments. We would be in Moscow during the winter, and I could oversee everything as before. Mother could come live with us, which would free you at least of that."

Nothing. No voice, no coughing.

"We could all spend the summers here at Melikhovo. Things will go on exactly as they do now, only I will have someone and not be left out."

Nothing.

"Your writing means everything to me. This will not change. My admiration for your work, my dedication to helping you . . . I've tried hard. If I have been at fault, for God's sake let me know."

She could feel tears welling up in her throat — she had to clench her fist to keep from crying out.

"I love him. You must know that. You above all. You create characters whose hearts are breaking from longing and now I am one of those and you must understand."

Nothing.

"I love him, Antosha. With your blessing, I will marry him when we return to Moscow."

Behind the grass, his figure moved.

"Say yes, Antosha. For the love you have for me, say yes!"

Very softly, with a slight hesitation as the two blades met, the shears resumed their clicking.

Maria spun around and ran back toward the garden. The grass, so pliant before, was now sharp enough to scratch her, and she beat it away from her face like a woman running from a mob. By the time she came to the meadow she had her tears under control, but her aching only went deeper, until she was all but doubled over from the pain. And what was odd, it didn't even seem her pain — seemed rather a pain born of sympathy for the man she had just left and the man she was running toward, so that what she felt wasn't unrequited love or outraged justice, but a mother's helpless pity for the follies of her sons.

Smagin was standing by the river exactly where she had left him, though his pacing had churned the bank to mud. His face brightened in expectation when she approached; he hurried toward her, then suddenly stopped.

"Have you spoken to Anton Pavlovich then?" he said.

She nodded, though it was agony to move her head.

Smagin sensed her hesitation and gestured toward the river to make it easier. "I saw a merganser while you were gone. He flew along the surface like he wanted a cooling sip."

He said this in a peculiarly high-pitched voice, running his finger along his neck and a raised greenish welt she had never noticed before.

"Then you have spoken to Anton Pavlovich?"

She wanted to explain, but her throat was too dry for words, her tongue too swollen, and she only stared at him in confusion.

Smagin forced a smile. "Please share with me his comments."

Nothing.

"Did he grant us his approval?"

Nothing.

"For pity's sake, tell me!" Smagin cried, his voice breaking like glass. "Don't torture me like this! What did he say?"

But she couldn't get the words to form, didn't have words for it, was struck dumb by her aching and couldn't even find enough strength to shrug. Help me, she said with her eyes. Hold me, feel for yourself what is going on in my heart. But she was too inexperienced to convey this by a look, and Smagin was too bashful to seize it by himself and so the two of them stood there with their eyes dumbly on the ground and not each other.

"It was a reddish merganser," Smagin said at last. "It flew by me here and then over the bathing shed, poor thing."

He left the following morning without saying good-bye. Before Maria could come to grips with what had happened, she was caught up in the kind of domestic and artistic crises she alone could untangle. Fekla announced she was pregnant and wouldn't name the father. The village elders decided for a third time they were closing down the school. The Art Theatre cabled from Moscow that the printed text for her brother's new play differed from the manuscript in several important respects. By the time she had set these things to right, the scene on the riverbank already seemed a distant memory, something from another life.

And yet its effects lingered on. In taking up again the burden of domestic detail, in setting her brother's affairs back on track, she felt the same wave of self-pity that had made her storm his study on that August morning years before. At first, she assumed it was only temporary, something that would pass, but as the months wore on and the family returned to Moscow, the feeling only intensified, until there wasn't a moment of the day or night when she wasn't consciously fighting it off.

What this "it" was, she couldn't quite say. A feeling of being cheated; the conviction she had lost her chance — a combination of negative emotions too black and tangled to fully understand. Its chief manifestation was a deep, inescapable bitterness that came over her like a temptation. She would be sitting at her desk correcting proofs from the latest story when Smagin's face would appear on the page before her and she would have to force herself not to tear the proofs apart from anger at the memory of her brother's silence. Other times the temptation was more general, so that her pleasure in attending the plays was spoiled by her jealousy, and she found herself picturing revengeful scenes where she stormed out of the theatre during the applause.

As hard as was the sheer physical labor involved with her responsibilities, as complicated the skein of family, teaching, and art, this was much harder, far and away the most difficult thing life had brought her. Antosha had betrayed her; Antosha had kept her from the happiness that was her right, but far worse than these things, he had placed this bitterness between himself and the one who loved him most, and so raised higher the wall over which she must climb in order to help him.

His illness was worse now, his lungs torn by hemorrhages at the first touch of cold, but he still saw truth too clearly not to be aware of this himself. In his way, he tried to make it up to her, was explicit now in singing her praises and even went so far as to make some halfhearted attempts to introduce her to eligible men. She was cold to this — there was no escaping the fact their relationship was much more formal than before. If anything, their estrangement forced her to turn more and more to his writing for solace, and she began rereading the early stories for the first time in years. It was as if the whole episode was meant to prepare her for the time when her brother would be gone and all that would be left to love was his essence: the simple radiance of his words.

There were relapses, as it were. In moving the

household from Melikhovo to the warmer Yalta, she felt a wrench of separation that made her moody for months. Even worse was the moment when Antosha telegrammed from Moscow to say he had married — this without warning or preparation of any kind. That he should be so greedy for personal happiness brought back all her old resentment, and it was weeks before she could bring herself to cable back congratulations, months before she could force herself to greet the bride.

But even this resentment didn't last long. It was obvious now that her brother was dying, and she spent as much time with him as possible those last months, sitting there on the bed beside his ghostlike transparency, hearing in the choked whisper that escaped the blankets what exactly his intentions were in regard to his work. Burn this, he said, crossing out a title with his weak, trembling finger. Save this. On the day of his funeral, with half Moscow in attendance, she stood alone in front of the other mourners in the place of honor. Though tears filled her eyes, she forced them back and held her head up higher, conscious that her appointed task in life was only now just beginning, and that whatever was left of personal longing must be ruthlessly throttled before it interfered.

She remembered Smagin only occasionally. A certain tinge to the light in early fall; the sight of two lovers walking shyly hand in hand. For a time these were enough to bring the pain back, but soft and distant enough that it took on a bittersweet quality that was not totally unpleasant. After the proposal, Smagin had broken off all contact with the family, so they heard little about him.

When she tried to picture what he must be like now, it was as a happy, rolling hill of a man upon whose fleshy slopes sons and daughters scampered in delight.

With time, she realized her brother's opposition to the match had been completely justified. The joys she found in hard mental labor; the unique satisfaction of sharing a great artist's dedication and being his support; her pride in carrying on. Compared to these, the satisfactions of a traditional marriage would have seemed banal and stale. She knew this intellectually as it were — cold-bloodedly and not in the heart.

As it turned out, she did see Smagin one last time. It was five years after her brother's death. She had gone to Moscow to arrange for the first complete printing of his work since the 1899 edition — a project to which she had devoted every ounce of her energy for the last three years. The publisher's was in one of those narrow side streets that crowd against each other in the Kremlin's shadow, where the sunlight only touches for an hour each day and the people turn moldy in the perpetual gloom.

She had finished her errand and was waiting on the street for a cab when a man brushed past her with his head bent into his scarf. Smagin, she thought. She turned and watched as he continued up the walk. She was wondering why her imagination should picture him so vividly just then when he turned and came back to her. It *was* Smagin, though so thin and emaciated-looking that at first she didn't believe her eyes.

"Yes, it's me, Maria Pavlovna," he said, smiling bashfully. Then, seeing her glance run up and down his coat: "I've not been well. But never mind that. Look at you! Here it's been at least ten years and you seem younger than you did then."

At first, their conversation ran along the usual lines. Smagin had heard of her role as her brother's literary executor, and asked intelligent questions about the new edition. For her part, she had trouble thinking what to say. She knew that rather than stand there in the cold street where pedestrians brushed rudely past them they should find a tea shop where they could talk, but she was too shy to suggest it. In this respect, it was as if no time had elapsed since that moment on the riverbank when they had been unable to find the courage to break through each other's unease.

"No, I've never married," Smagin said, with a little laugh. "So no children for me then, though I have my niece, Natalia, who's twelve and already being spoken of as a great beauty. But tell me this, Maria Pavlovna. Do the mergansers still fly along the river at Melikhovo?"

When she told him she had never gone back, his expression, so bright and rigid, relaxed into something sadder. "No, I'm a bachelor," he said, as if for emphasis. "I have status, a position as director of the municipal administration, more money than I can easily spend and yet . . . Well, you see me, Maria Pavlovna. I have success of a worldly kind and yet I feel empty and for me nothing counts."

With that, her old pity came back in redoubled force — she began to reach her hand across to take his arm — but then she saw with alarm that he was losing control of himself, beginning quite openly to weep.

"I am alone in the world, Maria Pavlovna, as you

yourself are alone. And yet you are not yet forty and there is still time. You are still a young woman, Maria. We made our mistake, but there is still time to correct it."

He was sobbing so much his face became splotchy, then distorted and grotesque. She turned away from it in horror and began walking slowly up the street.

"There is still time, Maria Pavlovna!"

It was as if all her bitterness were rising up to mock her, springing back after she had throttled it for so long, and she covered her ears and kept on, longing for him to follow and stop her and yet walking even faster for that reason.

"Maria Pavlovna, there is still time!"

And then she was crying, too, but there was no going back as much as she longed for it, nothing to do but continue walking toward the murky gaslight at the street's far end, her head held high with the pride of a Chekhov. Smagin's voice was still clearly distinct, as if it came through a wire that connected them, but she swung her arms to break it and walked even faster, onto a new street, faster and faster. She tried summoning up her brother's face to gain courage, but the image wouldn't come and instead she saw the faces of all his characters, the poor, the saddened, the solitary, and then she realized she wasn't imagining them at all but making right toward them there in the middle of the pavement, the dense throng of the heartbroken, their collars turned up against the cold, and just when she decided she must swerve to get around them, Smagin's voice faded away into silence, the crowd parted, and she was accepted into the space Antosha had left for her there all along.

PART THREE

ACT THREE

THE GARDEN of the Chekhov villa on the afternoon of the reading. Wicker lawn chairs arranged in a semicircle beneath lime trees. In the opening that remains, an overturned fruit box suggests a conductor's podium or miniature stage. Neatly arranged on each chair, a thin sheaf of papers. In the background, neglected garden tools, old croquet mallets, a trellis thick with vines. Beyond these, a faint white shining suggests the stuccoed roofs of the distant town.

From the chairs, the lawn falls away into a lower terrace fringed with ornamental shrubs. This creates a two-tiered effect — the lime trees and chairs as upper stage, the smaller square of grass as lower stage.

Despite the fruit trees, it's clear the weather has turned sharply colder. Shadows cover the ground in a sawtooth pattern; the light that remains is the thin color-less veil of late autumn. Fallen leaves scratch across the lawn singly and in pairs. The wind rustles the papers on the chairs, and here and there the topmost ones blow away, joining the leaves.

Enter Tania right, totally absorbed in reading from a script. She's wearing a white summer frock that, jux-taposed against the grayness, gives the effect of a wistful, impotent rebellion. Stops near the overturned box, frowns, then with a sudden defiant motion whirls around to face the empty semicircle of chairs.

TANIA: *reading from the script.* Men and lions, eagles and partridges, antlered deer, geese, spiders, the silent fishes dwelling in the water, starfish and tiny creatures invisible to the eye. These and every form of life, yes, every form of life, have ended their melancholy round and become extinct . . . *Pauses, shakes head in dissatisfaction, then continues with a different emphasis and much faster.* Men and lions, eagles and partridges, antlered deer, geese, spi-ders, the silent fishes dwelling in the water . . . *Impa-tiently turns page.* Thousands of centuries have passed since this earth bore any living being on its bosom. All in vain does yon pale moon light her lamp . . . *Hesitates, raises hand to point, then quickly lets it drop again.* All is cold, cold, cold. Empty, empty, empty. Terrible, terrible, ter-rible.

While she is reading, Maria Pavlovna enters through a gate on the lower lawn. Her complexion takes on the quality of whatever light she is under; in the autumnal shadows, her skin appears flushed and dark.

MARIA: Men *and* lions, eagles *and* partridges, antlered deer, geese . . .

MARIA: Again.

TANIA: *turning suddenly.* Who's that?

MARIA: *closing her eyes.* Again!

Tania takes a few steps toward her in confusion. At the moment she seems about to burst into tears, her expression hardens into something mean. Though she reads again, the words come out sounding cynical and old.

TANIA: Men and lions, eagles and partridges, antlered deer, geese, spiders . . . It's so absurd.

Maria Pavlovna walks toward the upper stage so quickly and forcefully it suggests she wants to shake her. With a great effort at self-control, stops herself and takes Tania gently by the hand, sitting her down in a chair beside her.

MARIA: You're making fun of the words.

TANIA: But it is! Empty, empty, empty. Cold, cold, cold. Absurd, absurd, absurd! This war is absurd and Peter is absurd and that German major is worst of all.

MARIA: *patiently.* What is Nina feeling here?

TANIA: It's impossible to know!

MARIA: You are Nina. You are the central character around whom everything in *The Seagull* revolves. Here in the first act that means being the naive and innocent heroine of Constantine Treplef's play. You're in love with the young writer, in awe of the stage, a girl who dreams of being a great actress, full of excitement and wonder.

The play Constantine mounts for you in the garden may be overwritten and ridiculous, but to Nina it is the most important thing in the world. You must read it that way, with rapture.

TANIA: *softly, looking back toward the villa.* They're hoping I fail, goddamn them.

MARIA: Once the reading begins I must leave to get things organized in the theatre. Posters to be made, tickets printed . . . Something as simple as props, they're not to be obtained, not even on the black market. And to find a stuffed seagull! . . . But never mind. There's miraculous news. I've found the last three stagehands left in Yalta — three ancients from my brother's day; I'm really in awe of them — and we'll begin cleaning things out of the greenroom later this afternoon . . . Now please. Read it to me once more. Include all the passion of a young girl's dream.

TANIA: They think it's beyond me, make jokes and ridicule me at every chance. But finally here is my chance to laugh at them . . . *Reads.* I am alone. Once in a hundred years I open my lips to speak, and my voice echoes sadly in this emptiness and no one hears.

Stops as voices are heard approaching from the left. A moment later, the participants of the reading begin to enter in twos and threes. There's great variety in their manner, from Potapov, who smiles brightly and slaps everyone on the back, to Kunin, who hangs back from the others and sulks. Bringing up the rear are two German soldiers toting a newsreel camera; Diskau waves them off to the side where they are less noticeable, then stands talking animatedly with Rashevitch and Koenig.

As they sort themselves out around the lawn chairs,

the conversation is general and indistinct, though from time to time snatches of conversation become audible through the hum.

POTAPOV: Once more into the breech, Varka my girl! The first reading of the play has long been one of my favorite moments in the dramatic arts. I well remember . . .

VARKA: *sternly, all but trembling.* What is expected of me? What am I meant to do?

POTAPOV: Sit near me, my pet, and I will coach you when it comes your turn. Ah, there's Tania! Our Nina, and how fine she looks in her frock. *In a whisper to Varka.* She's somewhat, uh, voluptuous. But never mind. Fashions in Ninas do change. *Louder.* Tania! Let me congratulate you and kiss your hand!

KUNIN: *stopping Gerassim.* I must talk to you immediately.

GERASSIM: *whispering.* Not now, you ass! Later.

RASHEVITCH: This farsighted policy of conciliation is winning the populace to your side, Major Diskau. Yalta has never been livelier and everyone speaks of the German troops with the highest praise. Those Bolshevik bastards must be shitting in their pants from envy.

DISKAU: *ignoring him, turning to Koenig.* See that those cameramen mind their manners. And see to it that Madam Chekhova is taken care of, understand? I don't want the old bitch left alone.

POTAPOV: The buzz of anticipation, the scripts lying in wait there on the chairs . . .

VARKA: *staring at Maria Pavlovna.* It's good for her. To have her mind on something keeps her young and so it's good.

TANIA: You've come, Peter Sergeich. You've deigned to grace us with your presence.

KUNIN: Hello, Tania. You're looking well.

TANIA: Don't patronize me.

GERASSIM: *with exaggerated servility.* Is everything arranged to your satisfaction, ma'am?

MARIA: Very good, Gerassim. And I'm pleased that you're taking a part. True, Yakof never says much, but he does have some lines.

GERASSIM: I am too ignorant to be in a play.

MARIA: And here is the man whose inspiration this was!

DISKAU: Shall we begin, Madam Chekhova? I believe everyone is here now. If you will permit me, I'll take your arm.

Leads her over to the assembled chairs.

MARIA: Please be seated everyone. First, I want to thank you all for joining us in our effort to put *The Seagull* back into the theatre where it belongs. When I think of the effort still ahead of us, the difficulties yet to overcome, the dark times we live under, I become quite faint. When I look at your faces, when I see the enthusiasm there and remember what it is that unites us, I feel confident and able to go on. With your help, my brother's work will shine again.

POTAPOV: *clapping.* Brava, Chekhova!

The others clap uncertainly. Maria Pavlovna holds her hand up for silence.

MARIA: I've set a busy schedule for myself today. The carpenters Major Diskau promised us are due to begin their repairs to the theatre and I must be there to superintend them. I have a meeting with our costumer, then after that I must meet with the translators in order that our programs shall be bilingual. But I wish you every success, I congratulate you on your dedication, and I leave you in Rene's good hands. Thank you all. From the bottom of my heart, thank you all.

DISKAU: *loudly*. Thank *you*, Madam Chekhova!

There is perfunctory applause. Maria Pavlovna says something to Diskau, then starts toward the gate on the lower stage. Before she can open it, Kunin steps out and confronts her.

KUNIN: I've been trying all week to speak to you alone. They stand guard over you like a prisoner. You're in great danger, Maria Pavlovna. You are in danger of being taken for a collaborator with the Germans, and furthermore . . .

MARIA: *turning on him in fury*. Don't speak to me in that tone, Peter Sergeich! It is I who am outraged. I hear nothing but bad things about you, and it wounds me to the heart. You above all. I took you into the villa as if you were my son. I trusted you as the custodian of all my brother stood for. And how is it you repay me? By refusing to take a role in his play.

Kunin steps back, shaken by her vehemence.

KUNIN: I . . .

MARIA: You are a traitor to art, and I can say it no plainer.

KUNIN: *forcing himself to remain calm*. You are mistaken, Maria Pavlovna. It is I who mean you well. *Waves hand*. The Germans are your enemies.

MARIA: Because they intend to perform my brother's play?

KUNIN: Look up there at their cameras. They film every detail for domestic consumption. The atrocities, the massacres — the cameras record them all. And now it's this play. Diskau is using the Chekhov name strictly for propaganda.

MARIA: I will speak to him. The cameras will be removed.

KUNIN: It's not enough.

MARIA: How dare you! How dare you! I am the caretaker of my brother's work and it's up to me to decide what is proper for his memory and what isn't. Are we to hide his work in a closet until the world recovers its senses? Are we to be cowards and not fight for his sake? Unless my brother lives through the worst of times, he will disappear. Whatever is not flaunted is destroyed.

KUNIN: *grabbing his head in a pantomime of agony.* His words. His very words!

Paces back and forth across the grass trying to regain control of himself.

KUNIN: I don't doubt your good intentions, Maria Pavlovna. There's no question of your dedication. But don't you see? Anything connected to the Nazis will be tarnished, and not just temporarily but forever. You can't use evil. Evil uses you.

MARIA: *staring toward the lime trees, not hearing.* I tried calling off *The Seagull* once before, did you know that? It was in 1898 when the Art Theatre did a revival after no one had dared a performance since the Petersburg fiasco two years before. I went to Stanislavsky and begged him to find an excuse to cancel it. I was so afraid another failure would kill Antosha that I literally went down on my knees and begged him to call it off . . . But it went on despite me and it was Antosha's greatest triumph and

I have never stopped hating myself for my weakness and lack of faith.

KUNIN: Everything was different in your brother's day. There was no Stalin, no Hitler. There is a war now and . . .

MARIA: There is no war.

KUNIN: *startled.* What?

MARIA: You mentioned war. There is no war. There is only this. *Points to the circle of chairs.*

KUNIN: *shaking his head as if to clear it.* You have to explain your theories, Maria Pavlovna.

MARIA: Only this exists. This play, putting it on despite the difficulties. In forty years what will this war be? A line in a textbook, nothing more. And yet what Antosha wrote will still move people and make them feel for hundreds of years . . . You talked about evil. I'm not afraid of it. The light in my brother's work is stronger than any darkness evil can bring.

KUNIN: It's not as simple as that.

MARIA: *holding up her hand.* You disappoint me, Peter Sergeich. I will not forgive you until you agree to take a part.

Kunin is trying to summon up the strength to argue with her again when Koenig approaches from the upper stage.

KOENIG: *smoothly.* We have a car waiting to drive you to the theatre, Madam Chekhova. If you will permit me.

MARIA: *as she follows him through the gate.* Remember what I said, Peter. I have the right to test the loyalty of my friends.

Exits. Kunin stands alone, his arms heavy and useless by his side. Slowly, grudgingly, his attention is captured by what's happening on the upper stage. A light rain is falling now — the participants in the reading are turning up their collars, using the scripts to cover their heads. Diskau alone ignores it. He paces back and forth in the opening between chairs, talking simply but with great sincerity and force. He's dressed in a khaki fatigue shirt with wide flannel trousers; his red hair is heavily pomaded and brushed straight back. His features glow with such vivacity he could almost be pregnant; there is that kind of robust good health about him, as if everything in his life has been swelling to this point.

DISKAU: Shall we get down to work, my friends? I'll be as brief as possible in my remarks. This small group represents the essential nucleus of our company, though we'll have some additions before the staged rehearsals get under way. As you know, I've instituted measures to locate Olga Knipper, and we expect her to take on the vital role of Arcadina. We'll also recruit some local actors for the smaller roles as need dictates. We enjoyed a similar mix of professionals and amateurs in Dresden and so I'm expecting great things . . . As you know, the performance is scheduled for New Year's Eve, giving us little over a month to get ready. But not to worry. By then we will be so polished that Chekhov's lines will come to us more easily than our own thoughts . . . Are there any questions so far? No? Well, I can think of one. Why exactly are we here? What is this mysterious reading all about and why doesn't this foolish fellow shut up so we can start? All perfectly natural questions, and all simply answered. To get the feel of it. To get our feet wet. Chekhov is always deceiving us with his simplicity, but this afternoon we will go along with his deception and keep things straightforward and plain.

Reaches down to take a script off a chair. Rather than open it, rolls it into a baton, which he uses to emphasize his points.

DISKAU: Shall we all turn to Act One? Again, the plot is simplicity itself. We start by a lake on the estate of a wealthy landowner named Sorin. Sorin, to put it bluntly, is a nonentity and well aware of the fact. He will be played with gripping authenticity by our good friend Pavel Rashevitch. *Rashevitch pops up from his chair oblivious to the irony.* Thank you, Pavel Rashevitch. Now much more important is Sorin's sister, Madam Arcadina. She's a famous actress, no longer young and bitterly aware of the fact. In the absence of Madam Knipper, I will take the liberty of reading her lines myself to move things along. With her in constant attendance is her lover, a famous writer named Trigorin. He's an intelligent man, inclined a bit to melancholy and totally selfish. We are honored to have a veteran of the Moscow Art Theatre taking the role, Alexander Potapov. *Potapov, wearing glasses, rises to his feet and bows gracefully.* The other main characters are Madam Arcadina's son, Constantine Treplef, an aspiring young writer played by myself, and the girl with whom he is desperately in love, the immortal Nina. *Tania stands up without taking her eyes off the script; smooths down her dress with a gesture more vulgar than coquettish.* Thank you, Tania my dear. In the first act all these characters gather around a makeshift stage to witness the performance of a play Constantine has written for Nina. Right from the start we have the tension between comedy and tragedy, love and unrequited love, to say nothing of . . . Yes, Alexander Potapov?

Potapov tilts his head to one side.

DISKAU: Of course. A thousand pardons. In the smaller roles helping us out we have Varka as the maid . . . *Varka, prodded by Potapov, stands up and blushes furiously.* And in the role of the servant Yakof, the servant Gerassim. *Gerassim hangs his head in a convincing pantomime of groveling respect.* There is also the important Dr. Dorn, the world-weary cynic who alone has faith in Constantine's talent, and we are hoping to have a peculiarly fitting actor for this role very soon . . . Any last comments before we begin?

Rashevitch clears his throat, is about to say something, then thinks better of it and merely coughs.

DISKAU: Speaking for myself as director, I'm looking forward to taking a totally fresh look at the play. Chekhov's style — it's the quality that attracts me most. What we must keep in mind is that *The Seagull* was revolutionary for its time, a deliberate experiment in dramatic technique. The slightest of plots, no crises worth mentioning, characters who talk past each other, spill out their souls in passionate monologues, then sputter off into trivialities . . . These are all Chekhov's inventions. The person watching Chekhov can't grasp too hard, but must let it be — let *life* be, and sit there watching with a mixture of passivity and wonder. It's up to the actor to convert the audience to this mood . . . And in this connection. There's a certain dated mustiness to his work that needs updating in order to make it more relevant — a certain fin de siècle kind of slackness. But I'm getting ahead of myself now. Let's read through the first act and perhaps I may be permitted a few suggestions here and there regarding tone.

A gust of wind sweeps across the chairs, blowing away the scripts. Confusion — frantic grabs, curses, general milling about. Several minutes go by before everyone is seated and the reading begins. The rain has let up, but the sky is darker than before and the characters, hunched over their scripts, are silhouetted and momentarily frozen in black, as if partaking of the cloud's substance. The one column of light that remains slants down to where Kunin paces back and forth across the lawn.

Enter Koenig through the gate. Looks toward the chairs, then shakes his head with a wry smile.

KOENIG: He's forgotten me again.

KUNIN: I always thought Germans were famous for their directness. *Sighs.* Who's forgotten you and why?

KOENIG: I've been given a part. Medvedenko, a humble schoolmaster who is in love with this Masha woman. Rene says I'm to play him with latent bitterness, like a young Stalin. Do you think that's right? Here, listen . . . I love you. I cannot sit at home for longing for you. Every day I come four miles on foot and four miles back again and meet only with an "I can't" on your part. Naturally, I have no means. Why should anyone want to marry a man who cannot even feed himself?

KUNIN: He's no Stalin.

KOENIG: But Rene says so. Rene has great insight into these matters. He's a theatrical genius, don't you think?

Koenig says everything with an upward tremble of his lip, a cross between a sneer and a sob. His face is handsome in the conventional Nordic way, but pasty, with skin that seems rolled out from beneath a pin. He wears a short mustache in imitation of Hitler, but much lighter, almost fuzz, and it gives him a look of evil boyishness.

KOENIG: He was quite active in the theatre before the war. He attended the Sorbonne for a winter, but he was too original and spirited for them and so they kicked him out. He spent a year on Capri writing a novel, but it was too futuristic to get published — I've read it in manuscript and it's breathtakingly conceived. But after that was a year in Munich as manager of one of his father's factories — it was a farce, an utter farce — and so he helped himself to some of papa's money and founded his own little theatre with a distinctly left-wing bent . . . Of course, there was art in his blood all along. Do you know the story of his mother? She was a Russian and a beauty, though a notorious whore. Rumor has it she screwed everyone in Berlin above the age of sixteen before syphilis finished her career. Rene was devoted to her. I forget her rank, but it was at least countess. She left the Crimea well before the Revolution.

KUNIN: And now her son has come back.

KOENIG: Not directly. He was stationed first in a little village called Zhukovo. A wretched hole on the edge of the world. On the edge, so you had to be careful at night not to walk into the void from sheer madness at the fleas and the stench. It was bad — a very bad time for him. The army in its infinite wisdom chose him to head an anti-partisan unit. It was his fluency in Russian, of course; they thought he would be good at interrogation. But between you and me, it was a fiasco right from the start. Rene was far too gentle for the job. He actually released some of the partisans his men had captured. They were boys, beautiful boys, and he couldn't bring himself to have them killed. *Frowns.* It was very bad for him after that. A *close* thing. There were enemies who had it out for him anyway because of his . . . sensitivity . . . and so it was a wonder he wasn't shot. Men are shot for less, you know.

Wipes the end of his mustache off with a satin handkerchief, studies it, then folds it back up in his pocket.

KOENIG: You can hardly blame him for what happened. In his charge was a band of partisans that had just been captured. I say partisans, but they were more like gypsies. Refugees. A traveling circus of some kind — a few clowns and a woman who had stumbled into one of our tank columns. I think Rene actually liked them, and had the clowns show him their tricks. It was only his anger at being called too lenient that made him do it.

KUNIN: Go on.

KOENIG: He killed them. The men anyway. He had the clowns dress themselves in their costumes, then shot each one in the stomach. No, right above their stomachs . . . Right *there.* He did this himself, though he could have easily arranged a firing squad. But the worst part was what he did afterward. Before their bodies had even stopped twitching, he took his revolver and shot himself in the shoulder . . . Right *here.* It happened so quickly it was impossible to say whether it was an accident or whether it was deliberate. And if it was deliberate, was it from guilt or was it because he realized killing partisans wasn't enough to prove his courage and he needed a sterner test? It's a great mystery to me still. But there was blood all over the ground and Rene stood there serenely bleeding and then my head swam and it all became one.

KUNIN: And the woman?

KOENIG: *puzzled*. The woman?

KUNIN: Did he shoot her, too?

KOENIG: *offended*. Of course not. The woman was quite stunning. He had her sent to an SS brothel outside Kiev. A *puffhaus* they call it — the SS are so quaint. But it was a terrible misfortune for him. Terrible. It was after this episode that he began using drugs.

Glances over to catch Kunin's reaction.

KOENIG: And everyone speaks of you as so observant! But of course he does. Morphine, and in increasingly larger doses. The doctors started him on it, and since then he's developed a taste for the other kinds as well. It helps him forget and does no harm. But that was the reason for his discharge, not the shooting. He was ordered back to Germany in disgrace. Anyone else would have gone, too. His father had enough well-placed friends that a safe appointment in a Berlin ministry could have easily been obtained. But such is Rene's love . . . No, such is his passion for the Russian land that he used this same influence to get his appointment to Yalta.

Beneath the trees, the light becomes brighter and indistinct snatches of the reading can now be heard. Diskau walks around the ring as each new character speaks, and stands beside whoever is reciting with his shoulders bunched together in intense expectation.

KOENIG: After his success here, he will move on to Moscow and take charge of everything related to culture. He will use his power to make Russian art, music, and literature shine as they haven't since the Tsars. He has all the details written down in three thick notebooks there in his office. There will be a new Bolshoi, a new Hermitage, uncensored editions of all the great plays the Communists have banned. And though he will do this in the end, the timing is quite tricky. A lot depends on how well this *Seagull* comes off. The propaganda people — Goebbels himself — will be watching the experiment with the greatest interest. If the play is a success, if it convinces the intelligentsia of our good intentions, Rene's conciliatory policy may soon be adopted on a far greater scale than Yalta alone . . . And Rene will not fail to make this a success. His dream shines too fiercely to be quenched.

Stares up toward Diskau, and while there is no mistaking the awe in his tone, there is a nervous edge to it as well.

KOENIG: I hope he remembers to take me to Moscow with him when he goes. *His voice lining out into a whine.* Ah, Masha, if only someone would write a play and put it on the stage showing the life we schoolmasters lead! It's a hard, hard life!

Walks to the upper stage and slumps down in an empty chair without being noticed. Everyone watches Diskau, who paces with great energy, now reading from his script, now reciting lines from memory, emphasizing each phrase with a different gesture: a slight questioning shrug; an impatient wave of the hand; a nervous tilting forward on the balls of his feet.

DISKAU: *reading Constantine's lines.* I regard the stage today as mere routine and prejudice. We must have new forms. That's what we want. And if there *are* none, then it's better to have nothing at all . . . I am sorry I have a famous actress for a mother, and I feel that if she had been an ordinary woman I should have been happier. Her drawing room filled with nothing but celebrities, actors, and writers, and among them the only nobody is myself, tolerated because I am her son. Who am I? What am I? I am twenty-five years old and a perpetual reminder to her that she is no longer young.

RASHEVITCH/SORIN: *squinting, running his finger along the lines as he reads.* What kind of man is this Trigorin? I can't make him out. He never talks.

DISKAU/CONSTANTINE: Famous already before he's forty and sated with everything. As for his writings . . . What shall I say? Charming, talented . . . but . . . You wouldn't want to read Trigorin after Tolstoy or Zola.

RASHEVITCH/SORIN: I love literary people, my boy. There was a time when I passionately desired two things: I wanted to be married and I wanted to be a literary man . . . May I read that again, Major? My throat. This fucking weather . . . I wanted to be a . . . *And* I wanted to be a literary man, but neither came my way. Ah! How pleasant to be even an unknown writer, confound it all.

DISKAU/CONSTANTINE: I hear someone calling . . . I cannot live without Nina. Even the sound of her footsteps is charming . . . I am insanely happy!

As the reading continues, Potapov slips quietly away for a cigarette, cradling his stomach in his hands as if to keep it from betraying him. When he joins Kunin on the lawn, he sighs with relief.

POTAPOV: Say what you will, Peter, acting is labor — coal mining, something stooped. *Lets his stomach drop, then dusts it off.* I noticed you talking with that sly

Koenig man. Have you ever seen a weasel with its leg caught in a trap? You don't know whether to pity it and let it loose or bash its head in with a hammer. My inclination with Koenig is for the hammer.

KUNIN: How long is this going to continue? There's someone I must speak with.

POTAPOV: But still it's good to be back. I feel juices flowing in me that have been frozen far too long. And of course Trigorin is a classic role. The secret is to stare above everyone's head and always let the others act to him.

KUNIN: You were best.

POTAPOV: *beaming.* I was, wasn't I? And it's not a contemptible company, either. I've acted in many far worse professional assemblages. If it's true that Knipper is coming, we shall be first-rate. I for one am terribly impressed with our German friend over there. I was prepared to be dubious, but I can now announce I am totally won over. The man is an actor; I can give him no higher praise.

KUNIN: He's a fascist.

POTAPOV: He *is* Constantine. He is that nervous bundle of ambition and doubt. He is totally in love with Nina — you can see it in the way he positively blushes when she's there. When he recites his lines he forgets Diskau and becomes enmeshed in the role, with just the right shadings. Listen now, here's what I mean.

DISKAU/CONSTANTINE: My love, my dream.

TANIA/NINA: *agitated.* I'm not late . . . surely, I'm not late.

DISKAU/CONSTANTINE: You've been crying.

TANIA/NINA: It's quite true. My father and his wife

won't let me come. They say you are all Bohemians . . .
They are afraid of my becoming an actress. But I am
drawn toward the lake like a seagull. My heart is full
of you.

POTAPOV: *whispering.* See what I mean about his conviction? But why does Tania shake her hips like that? She
plays the ingenue, not a striptease artist.

TANIA/NINA: Trigorin will be here. I am afraid of
acting before him. What wonderful stories he writes!

POTAPOV: *still whispering, but with more urgency.* Don't
bark the words, Tania! Caress them. Caress them, my
girl!

DISKAU/CONSTANTINE: *coldly.* Does he? I haven't read
them.

TANIA/NINA: Your play is very hard to act. There are
no live people in it. And I think a play ought always to
have a love interest.

There's a pause. Diskau goes over to Tania, puts
his arm around her shoulder, then leads her off to one
side.

POTAPOV: He's telling her to relax. She's much too
nervous. But still, her approach is all wrong and she's
like a bird who wants to be in the air but doesn't know
how to get there. But she has the play scene. If she pulls
it off . . .

KUNIN: You're not staying?

POTAPOV: The famous Trigorin is in need of refresh-
ment. But he will return. *Looks toward the chairs.* Poor
girl. I do hope she finds a way.

Exits through gate. Kunin starts to follow, then remains. Diskau leads Tania back into the opening between

chairs and helps her mount the overturned fruit box. She rubs her hand nervously around her opposite wrist; she tosses back her hair and takes a deep breath of air, as if she is about to dive off a cliff.

DISKAU: *softly.* Are you ready then, Tania?

Tania nods — hesitantly, then with sudden determination.

DISKAU/CONSTANTINE: Harken ye venerable shades that hover in the nighttime over this lake; send sleep upon us and let us dream of what will be in two hundred thousand years.

TANIA/NINA: *turning to face the trees.* Men and lions, eagles and partridges, antlered deer, geese, spiders, the silent fishes dwelling in the water, starfish and tiny creatures invisible to the eye. These and every form of life, yes, every form of life, have ended their melancholy round and become extinct . . . Thousands of centuries . . .

DISKAU: *tapping his script against his leg.* I'm sorry, Tania. That's very good, but a shade too forceful. Remember, you are acting a girl who is acting. Say it more preciously. Again, please.

TANIA/NINA: Men and lions, eagles and partridges, antlered deer, geese . . .

DISKAU: Soften your consonants.

TANIA/NINA: Spiders, the silent fishes dwelling in the water, starfish . . .

DISKAU: *closing his eyes.* Again, please.

TANIA/NINA: Men and lions, eagles and partridges . . . I'm trying, aren't I trying? . . . Antlered deer . . . These and every form of life . . .

DISKAU: Don't skip. *Turning to the others.* We've been

working hard and I think everyone deserves an intermission before we start Act Two. Tania? If you will remain, please.

The others get up in obvious relief. They wander off through the garden, all except Koenig, who remains slumped in his chair, peering out between his interlaced fingers. Last to leave is Gerassim, who stops before the overturned box to stare at Tania with mocking respect, then continues down to the lawn of the lower stage.

GERASSIM: Pretty words. Do you like pretty words, Comrade Kunin? Pretty words are to me like stool that drips forever before coming out. Words should be like hammers, short and abrupt.

KUNIN: You took on a role readily enough.

GERASSIM: I was ordered to by our mistress — and for now it suits me to obey. *Shrugs.* Besides, it's the perfect cover. People will look at me on stage and see only scenery.

KUNIN: I've been waiting to talk to you.

GERASSIM: And yet all the time I was sitting there I had the urge to vomit. Actors are like people going around holding their bowels in their hands, wanting us to admire the stench.

KUNIN: I want to . . . What's the phrase? Join. Help you. Enlist. I want to join the partisans.

GERASSIM: And what makes you think I know anything of partisans?

KUNIN: Don't take me for a fool.

GERASSIM: We are in need of men, Comrade. Half-men, no.

KUNIN: If you mean my foot . . .

GERASSIM: I mean your mewing, stinking mind with all its bourgeois sentimentality. It's not a weapon we need.

KUNIN: I can fire a rifle.

GERASSIM: As can a thousand million other fools . . . Do you know anything of knives? Anything of explosives? What's needed nowadays are men with talent for assassination or mass liquidation, nothing in between. Understand? A single death may be of value to us and so too the death of several thousand, but killing hundreds is for mediocrities.

KUNIN: Pretty words.

GERASSIM: Pretty deaths.

KUNIN: I'm tired of riddles. I want to fight.

GERASSIM: The partisans do not exist solely to prove your manhood. That's what the Tanias of this world are for. Or perhaps you couldn't find your manhood there, Peter Sergeich?

KUNIN: You're a filthy bastard.

GERASSIM: *laughs.* You're too hostile. It makes you conspicuous. You're like a hedgehog, whereas what we require in Yalta are rabbits — rabbits who follow orders. Do you have too much pride to follow orders? You follow Maria Pavlovna's — follow them too well. We don't want men whose loyalties are divided.

KUNIN: We've had an argument. She's . . .

GERASSIM: Say it.

KUNIN: Stubborn, naive. She loves the Germans and I hate them. *Shrugs.* And now they've offered me a part in the play.

GERASSIM: *his expression immediately serious.* Who offered you?

KUNIN: Diskau. The part of Dorn.

GERASSIM: When?

KUNIN: Earlier this week.

GERASSIM: *after a pause.* Take it. Hide your hostility, make things up with Maria Pavlovna, go along with this farce, and then . . . There may come a time when it will be useful having you in the center of things here. In the meantime, you take orders from me alone.

KUNIN: I understand.

GERASSIM: I understand, Comrade.

KUNIN: I understand, Comrade.

GERASSIM: I understand, Comrade Gerassim.

KUNIN: I understand, Comrade Gerassim.

GERASSIM: *smiling.* The first lesson. There will be many more. Follow me.

The two of them exit through the gate. In the resulting silence — in the twilight of the late afternoon — Tania's voice becomes distinct. She is alone on the box, Diskau and Koenig standing to the side in her shadow. Her body slumps from exhaustion; her blouse is transparent with perspiration, revealing the jut and separation of her breasts.

TANIA/NINA: Like a captive flung into an empty well, I know not where I am nor what awaits me. One thing only is revealed to me, that in the cruel and stubborn struggle with the Devil, the principle of material forces, it is fated that I shall be victorious. Till then, there shall be horror and desolation. Behold, my mighty antagonist the Devil approaches. I see his awful, blood red . . .

DISKAU: You mumbled it. Please don't mumble.

KOENIG: *giggling.* You can see her nipples. *Holds his*

hands up and twists them around. They're like pinkies, like thick ugly pinkies.

DISKAU: *with a tone of utmost weariness.* Once more please.

TANIA/NINA: Till then, there shall be horror and desolation. Behold, my mighty . . .

DISKAU: *abruptly.* Thank you. That's all we require.

TANIA: *in confusion.* Do you mean I'm done? There's more. There's the scene where I come out and flirt with Trigorin.

DISKAU: Yes, thank you very much, my dear. That won't be necessary. *Drawing Koenig aside.* She's hopeless. We'll have to find someone else.

KOENIG: Who? Actresses in wartime don't exactly grow on trees.

DISKAU: I have an idea. Wait a moment and let me think.

Paces behind the chairs, rearranging them absentmindedly. Tania looks from him to Koenig, not sure whether to remain on the box or step down. The wind springs back again and she shivers.

DISKAU: Do you remember that girl? The one we captured in Zhukovo with the circus?

KOENIG: The willowy blond? Of course. Those SS stallions will have screwed her into sawdust by now.

DISKAU: *thoughtful.* Perhaps. Perhaps not. I want you to go to Kiev and fetch her for me. Leave this afternoon and take a medical orderly along. I'll write out the necessary orders.

KOENIG: I've forgotten her name.

DISKAU: I remember seeing it in her during my interrogation. Something inside that the dirt and filth couldn't hide. Defiance, passion. She was an actress, or so she said. I should have been more careful with her. But perhaps it's not too late.

KOENIG: The SS won't be pleased to lose their plaything.

DISKAU: I'm not afraid of the SS.

KOENIG: I'll fetch her. If she's alive.

While they talk, Tania continues hugging herself, as if to hide her nakedness. She brings her hands up to her eyes, then slowly lets them fall.

TANIA: I'm not to do Nina, then? I knew it. I thought I would at least try. Are there any other roles? I don't want a major role, but something . . . I would do anything. You see, they laugh at me, and so there must be something to throw in their eyes, and I'd even . . .

KOENIG: *in a high mincing tone.* She's propositioning you, Rene. Be careful now.

DISKAU: *scowling.* Leave, goddamn you.

Koenig clicks his heels and raises his arm in a Nazi salute. Exits, leaving Tania and Diskau alone. Diskau leans over a script and begins marking it with a pencil.

TANIA: Anything . . .

DISKAU: *writing.* We need new forms in politics, too. An end to this liberal . . . sentimentality. *As if only now remembering her presence.* What's that? Oh, of course. Of course you may have a part. We need someone yet for Masha, do you know her? The girl who is helplessly in love with Constantine, yet who settles for Medvedenko — the one who wears black and takes snuff. Here, it's a very important part. We'll just have you read the first line by way of audition.

TANIA: *taking the script from him in gratitude.* Here?

DISKAU: Go ahead then.

TANIA: *reads.* I am in mourning for my life.

DISKAU: Coarser.

TANIA: I am in mourning for my life.

DISKAU: *smiling, bringing finger to his lip.* Perfect. Perfect, my dear. Masha to the flesh.

Curtain.

KUNIN

HE KNEW he should get out more. The doctor had told him so during his last exam — the one deduction her slow, suspiciously gentle stethoscope had made. She had written a prescription for an hour's walk per day regardless of the weather, then, as if to get him started, walked with him down the clinic's hall, sending him out the door with a push that was as firm and encouraging as a mother's.

She was right, of course. Despite his retirement, he maintained a large correspondence with Chekhov scholars throughout the world, and he could easily spend the day over letters. Added to these were his household chores. On alternate weeks he took complete responsibility for the cleaning while his sister worked on her own correspondence at the district library.

But even alone the flat did funny things to him. There were times after lunch when the walls, rather than closing in on him as walls are supposed to, seemed to do just the opposite — seemed to expand and then soften, taking on fleshy qualities of sensitivity and touch, until he felt he was dwelling within a larger skin. A spot of grease on the plaster tickled him exactly like a spot of grease on his nose, and he couldn't relax until it was wiped off. A hesitant throb to the heater worried him just as much as a hesitant throb to his heart, and he would pause in his typing waiting for its normal rhythm to resume. He had spent sixty-some years learning to be the custodian of a crippled body, and now here he was faced with a new body, a clumsy overheated boxed-in one, and to keep it functioning he had to be carpenter and electrician and plumber rolled into one.

It was this he fled from every afternoon around three, umbrella in hand. He felt some relief the moment he stepped into the hall, still more when he descended the stairway and walked outside. But even there the sense of confinement still affected him. The sky with its pestilential grayness; the look-alike architecture that was turning Moscow into a monstrosity; the television tower with its phallic posturing; the impassable moats formed by the new loop roads. The flat was a box, the building a bigger box, Moscow a bigger box yet, until the world seemed a series of nesting boxes, large on top of small, the kind a child might stack together on an otherwise dull day.

Was Russia worse in this respect? He supposed so, but he wasn't sure. He had traveled to Western Europe frequently in the Sixties, in attendance at one scholarly conference or another, and it seemed to him there were just as many boxes there as in his own country. The architecture was just as square; the temptation to pigeon-hole your thoughts just as compelling; the air just as noxious and thick. In Russia, the boxes were hard and impermeable; in the West, gooey and soft, capable of stretching. But in the end, goo was just as inescapable as iron, and though several of his colleagues had defected at these conferences, he himself had never been tempted.

Or tempted just once. There had been a symposium on pre-revolutionary Russian literature at Edinburgh in 1969, chaired by himself. He had spent most of the time gaveling to order a floor torn between the noisy fulminations of a French Marxist and the crackpot theorizing of an American professor in beads. To flee such nonsense, he had prevailed upon his host to take him on a weekend drive to the northwestern coast.

They had parked on a hillside covered with heather and yellow broom. It was a beautiful spot, with a view toward the Hebrides, and they were there in time to watch the sun go down over the sea loch at the hill's base. The sky turned crimson, then a softer red, then crimson again, all within the space of a few minutes. A moment before the red became so dark it was indistinguishable from black, a last solitary ray of sunlight shot across the ocean between islands, coloring each one as it passed in a soft wave of molded purple that blended them into a continuous expanse, until the seascape resembled the outline of an enchanted, unreachable land. Watching it was like peeking out from beneath the boxes to a world of horizontal planes, and this moment, simple and brief as it was, opened something in him that neither the flat with its stuffiness nor Moscow with its grayness had ever managed to fully shut.

This was what he sought in his afternoon walks — not expanse, but glimpses that reminded him expanse was still possible. A few blocks from his flat the narrow streets opened into Trubnaya Square with its flower market, and a few blocks past that, opened further into a park, and there in the center of this park was a small rise on top of which was a bench commanding a view of the few hundred square meters of green that seemed half the world. Down below in the sailing pool, geese splashed furiously and noisily honked. There to the left, young boys circled under soccer balls and called out one another's name. Behind him, young mothers pushed their carriages where the walk slanted downhill, skipping a little to keep up, so that babies, carriages, and mothers seemed driven by a fresh and exhilarating wind.

To the park! Box with the most holes in it, outpost of nature, the pensioner's friend!

He spent an hour there on afternoons when he still felt the old tug of schedules, three hours on those rarer afternoons when he remembered that rushing was no longer for him. By five, the mothers had left for their husbands, the soccer players gone home to their books, and the park would be given over to strolling young couples waiting patiently for dark. They were little more than children most of them — teenagers, with the pudginess of babies and the same unsure movements, so that they kept their arms around each other not out of love, but merely to keep from falling down.

But he thought of them with irony, not malice, and even his irony couldn't last long against their innocence. When they passed the bench they always made faces, irritated that an old man should take up such a fine spot, but they quickly got over it and moved on toward the trees with soft, throaty giggles that were indistinguishable from coos. What they actually did there in the dark he couldn't imagine. Fornicate? Not likely. Cuddle? Help each other learn to talk?

The teenagers were as much a part of the park as the squirrels, and he welcomed them. It was different with the slightly older couples, those acned men in uniform who led their women — their purple–eye-shadowed women — stiff-armed across the grass like prisoners. He didn't think much of soldiers and romance, not the contemporary version anyway. It was a conscript army without a cause, and their love seemed the same way, forced and pointless. Most of them seemed filled with an aggressive kind of self-pity, mad that they should be forced to have haircuts and wear such stiff, ridiculous clothes. They swaggered a lot. Most of them, the women more than the men, seemed drunk on insignificance.

It would take a war to change that. A war would make them tragic enough, those it didn't kill in the first five minutes. He himself was an expert in wartime love, that peculiar sub-category in the larger subject of love in general. He knew nothing of marriage or affairs or juvenile romance, but had specialized strictly in the wartime version, three months of it anyway. Three months, or —

in a rough calculation he was constantly updating — one three-hundredth of his life.

Not much of a figure, even compared to a teenager's, but when he thought back on it, it seemed a miracle that he had ever loved at all — loved with that kind of intensity. For loving in wartime had been the most courageous thing he had ever done; far more courageous, for instance, than killing someone. Loving in war had made a man out of him. Loving in war had been his education in humanity, the grounding in heartbreak anyone needs before being free to understand.

One three-hundredth of his life to be thought of in the remaining fractions, obsessively at times, randomly at others, but always futilely, to the point where he felt like a myopic scientist examining a specimen of pure spirit through a microscope that was cracked. At times, he let his irony carry the analogy even further and pictured his thoughts being printed as a thesis, to be distributed to the military at large. *Wartime Love, Generalities and Conclusions, by P. S. Kunin, Socialist Hero of Wartime Love First Class.*

It wouldn't be hard to make a list. He could start off with the way wartime love magnified even the smallest gesture into something symbolic and universal, so that holding hands became the very epitome of union and you couldn't do it without a certain defiant set to your expression.

How the most common subject of conversation in wartime love was the future — future plans, future dreams, future meetings, even though the chances of there being a future together were laughably slim. "When this is over," lovers said, though there was nothing sadder, since what they were longing for was a time when their love wouldn't be so desperate and intense.

How in traditional war, the danger only reinforced the usual order of things between men and women, the man going off to battle, the woman staying home. How in the Twentieth Century this had all been reversed, since neither lover at parting knew which was most at risk. In this sense, wartime love was a love between equals — equals in the dangers they faced and the courage needed to survive them.

How wartime love was the widest, least selfish love, taking in not only the other, but every victim in the war's path, it being impossible to stand before a firing squad and not feel empathy for those against the same wall.

How in wartime love sex wasn't the easy thing popular literature painted it as, but something much more difficult — something that had to be struggled for, all but reinvented. In traditional war, men and women might copulate with the lust of dying salmon, but in Twentieth-Century war, in total war, it was just the opposite, and the proper analogy was to those lonely species facing extinction that lose the breeding instinct and so acquiesce in their destruction. To copulate in some circumstances is to say no to life, and at other times to say yes, and it was this constant tension between the two that made sex in wartime an indescribable brutality or an exquisite tenderness and nothing in between.

How stupid it was for an impotent old man to generalize about sex.

How they had once lain beneath a flowering almond in the villa's orchard — how the petals blew down and buried him, making her laugh, until suddenly she became frightened and pawed desperately at the flowers to clear him off.

How much he still longed for a child to remember her by.

How when he had held Nina, when she tilted her head against his shoulder and closed her eyes, he had been holding the pain of the world. How he had shuddered at this, but never — not then, not in the forty years since — let go.

THE REHEARSALS were held in the greenroom while repairs were made to the stage. Despite Diskau's promises, the Germans had done nothing to rehabilitate the theatre, and it was only through Maria Pavlovna's own efforts that any work was being done. By beggary, by threats and outright bribes, she had managed to assemble what few carpenters Yalta could still produce, and while the youngest of these was past seventy, the theatre was being roughed somehow into shape. The footlights had been rewired and tested; the mildewed boards in the stage replaced; the lobby swept clean and fumigated; the windows forced open to admit air.

Save for the play's actual direction, Maria Pavlovna was taking care of all the details, even the food. Since rehearsals lasted from morning to midnight, it was necessary to serve lunch in the greenroom to save time. A board was laid across some trestles and plates arranged. Varka, frowning severely, served out the bread and cheese. At first, there was fresh fruit as well, but at the third rehearsal there were only figs — small figs, as hard and flinty as clams.

There was grumbling at this. Kunin had enough irony

to find it amusing, but the pleasure he took in watching Alexander Potapov scratch his stomach like a forlorn orphan was soon transformed into something very different, this by the simple opening and closing of a door in the dusty, prop-crowded corner to his left.

At first, glancing up, he saw nothing. That a new person had come into the room was apparent only by the reactions of the ones who stood closest to the door — Rashevitch and Tania. On their faces came expressions so mutual it was as if their muscles had synchronized, startled eyebrow for startled eyebrow, dropping chin for dropping chin.

For a ghost had entered the greenroom, the ghost of a woman. She wore a skirt of soft material that drooped from her waist like a shroud over a skeleton, with no fullness in it, no movement or life. Her thin gray sweater was the same way, lifeless and still. The only motion apparent at all was the trembling of her shoulders and the slight tilting of her head to offset it; it was this gesture, simple as it was, that first convinced them she was actually alive.

Everyone stared. The woman took a step further into the room, staggered, then suddenly straightened, the way a sapling snaps to attention after a wind. Drunk, Kunin decided — the certainty of that first impression shamed him for the next forty years. With a drunk's difficult dignity, she shook herself closer to the vertical and advanced deeper into the room.

If it was hard to make sense of her, it must have been all that much harder for her to make sense out of them. In circling the room — in staring at the opened scripts, the cane-backed chairs, the impromptu stage with its overstuffed sofa — her eyes met the table with the platters of bread and cheese; met the table and on it became fixed. Her first step in that direction was quick and automatic, as if she had been yanked, but her next steps were slower and more controlled, so that she approached the table with the fastidious reluctance of a debutante at a ball.

There was more light in that part of the room. Beneath it, the woman's features became more distinct. She had straw-colored hair that stopped over her shoulders in a jagged edge. Her eyes, the little Kunin could see of them, were oval and dark, suggesting a gypsy's. Her cheekbones were strong and prominent in the same manner, Asiatic in their sharpness, but there was a softness about her mouth and chin that suggested great vulnerability, setting up by this contrast the puzzle that was beauty's start.

And yet she wasn't beautiful, not anymore. Kunin judged her to be in her late twenties at most, but atop her beauty was a layer of suffering as thick and pasty as makeup. Her cheeks were puffy, bruised an ugly blue. Her lips trembled involuntarily, sending up answering twitches by her eyes. Her forehead was red and angry-looking, the hair above it parted to expose the roots, giving the effect of an invisible hand yanking her scalp forcibly back. Her body was emaciated, devoid of air. Above her shoulders, like a necklace, was a livid white scar.

Like a whore rouged with suffering, Kunin thought. The first strong emotion he felt toward her was the urge to reach over and scrub all the suffering away.

And since there is a current in first moments, the woman must have in some way accepted his thoughts, so that her next gesture was to bring one hand up and gently touch her face, as if to make that first tentative cleansing by herself. Her other hand, with the same difficult self-control, reached down for the uncut loaf of bread. She touched it — she patted it the way a blind man pats a wall — then with a clumsy twisting broke off a small piece of crust.

She brought it back up to her mouth — the slowness was terrible. At the touch of it against her tongue, she closed her eyes. Satisfaction, relief — they were both evident on her face. But something deeper and more subtle as well, not merely the satisfaction of hunger, but the satisfaction that comes when a person regains touch with the person they once were.

The bread was dry, difficult to swallow, yet the moment she finished she reached down for more, this time with the shameless grab of starvation. She ripped off chunks with both hands, stuffing them in her mouth so fast that pieces fell out and she choked. Beside the bread was a platter of cold potatoes, and she reached down and grabbed these, too, just as greedily. In between swallows she must have realized she should be using a fork, but when she reached for one it dropped out of her fingers and fell with an exaggerated clatter against the floor.

The others watched her eat with expressions that ranged from Potapov's obvious pity to Tania's obvious disgust. The only surprising reaction was Maria Pavlovna's. On her face was a look Kunin could only describe as recognition — not the recognition that comes upon seeing a person again, but the recognition that comes upon seeing a person for the first time. The woman was *known* to

Maria Pavlovna already, at least in outline — there was no mistaking her amazed little nod.

And so she went up to her. She spoke very quietly so the others couldn't hear, but it was obvious she was introducing herself, saying something gentle to put her at ease. The woman gave her a grateful smile, but there was no letup in her eating — she brought the bread up to her breasts as if to hoard it beneath her blouse. Maria Pavlovna, to share her embarrassment, began eating some herself, making the tearing off of huge pieces seem perfectly normal. Because of this, because of the vivid darkness in their eyes, Kunin was reminded of mother and daughter — a mother and daughter sharing a secret and not bread.

They were eating, surrounded by everyone's stares, when Diskau plunged into the room, his rolled script tucked beneath his belt like a gun. That he had used the lunch break to take drugs was obvious, at least to Kunin. His body pulsed with energy and he literally skipped across the room, all but flapping his arm from sheer vitality.

"I want to introduce someone," he said, raising his voice to the level he saved for acting. "May I have everyone's attention, please?"

He was over to the woman now. She cringed when he took the bread from her, but he was too close to notice. Like a fussy hairdresser, he brushed the crumbs from her mouth, tapped his wrist under her chin to make her stand straighter, then stroked the red spot where her hair had been yanked back.

"This is our Nina," he said, beaming like a sculptor unveiling his latest work. "Nina has come to Yalta to help us with our play."

Nina — it was as though he had christened her, and despite all that happened after, they never found another name for her and Nina she remained. Partly this could be explained by the mystery of her origin, her own reticence in talking about it, so that she came to them unencumbered with anything so ordinary as a name. But at a deeper level there was a quality about her that suggested the Nina of the play — a girlish defiance visible beneath the makeup of bruises; a naive ambition that was smothered but not yet extinct.

That she was an actress was obvious right from the start. Diskau, to his credit, started rehearsing with Act Two, where her role was shortest. He stood next to her to help coax her through her lines, but she shook off all his promptings and recited the part by herself. That the lines thus recited were mumbled and indistinct — that they came in a hoarse whisper suggesting a scar in her throat beneath the scar on her neck — didn't matter. In her simple, girlish inflection, in the way she shut out everything but the words and the role so that nothing existed in the room besides the imagined life she was making real, her theatrical background shone through.

Or tried to shine through. For along with her weakness was a distracting roughness that made her gestures seem stiff and overdone, her acting too brittle and forced. At times she would stop altogether and let her shoulders go limp, closing her eyes as if to recall something essential about herself the way she had when she was eating. Toward the act's end, when she talked of enduring the hatred of her nearest and dearest in order to be an actress, suffering poverty and disillusionment if only to demand glory in return, a semblance of volume and strength crept into her tone. Listening, Kunin found it easy to imagine someone throwing a dead seagull at her feet in despair at not having her love.

It was just a flash; a moment later she was stuttering again and coughing uncontrollably. Diskau wanted to go back to the middle of the act and start over, but Maria Pavlovna wouldn't let him.

"That's enough for today," she said, climbing up onto the stage. She had a shawl with her and draped it over Nina's shoulders. "We're going home for a proper rest."

Diskau flushed with that; he didn't like to be crossed, even in small things.

"She can't go yet." He brought his arm up and appealed to the ceiling. "I cannot endure this continual *meddling*."

Maria Pavlovna, who was already helping the woman down, stopped and faced Diskau with an expression that was part anger, part surprise. Her next words were spoken very slowly and distinctly.

"I am taking this poor girl home."

Diskau smiled and made a slight bowing motion; it was a tribute to his acting that it came off as sincere. "Why of course, Madam Chekhova. That was exactly what I was about to suggest." He snapped his fingers. "Koenig? See these ladies are escorted back to the villa at once. Drive them yourself if you must. Our next rehearsal will be at seven tomorrow morning."

With her arm around her waist, Maria Pavlovna guided Nina toward the door. Diskau applauded as they went past him; Nina flinched from it as from a slap. So unmistakable was the hatred in her eyes that Kunin could feel its intensity all the way across the room.

Diskau would have had to have been blind not to see it himself. During the break, when he joined Kunin by the samovar, he was shaking his head in what was obviously meant to be admiration.

"A veritable wildcat, eh, Peter my friend? Such passion in one so weak. But she's rather fine, don't you think?"

He didn't wait for an answer, but gestured toward the stage. "I'm dissatisfied with Trigorin. Oh, not Potapov — he acts well enough. But the whole conception. Your Chekhov is regrettably lax on symbols. The seagull for instance. More could be made of that. It's all a question of capturing the decadence at the Nineteenth Century's core. But why is your Chekhov so timid in saying so? Why didn't he give us more lines? He's badly in need of updating. The musicality of his lines is astonishing, but he's so maddeningly vague . . ."

He talked nonstop for the next forty minutes, alternating sharp insights into the play with complete nonsense in a dizzying whirl. Kunin had only to nod now and then to keep him going. As before, he had the sense that the longer you let Diskau talk, the closer he would come to spilling out something real.

"I feel frustrated that I can't get everyone to go along. They go along — it's not that. But they don't *see* the work as I do, and we're talking from separate visions. It's times like these when I wish I had remained a writer. The solitary life of unending toil — it's the German in me, I'm afraid. The Russian half craves action and applause. How to unite them? How? It's one of my obsessions. Once the fighting ends we'll set up an exchange of Russian and German youth, with special hostels where the talented may intermingle and so combine the intuition and passion of the Russian soul with the intelligence and order of the German. I have the details written out in my notebook already . . .

"The final act — of course it all comes down to that. Constantine's empty success as a writer, Nina's reappearance after two years away on the stage, their confrontation, the heartbreak . . . Has anyone ever captured the bittersweet quality of love any better? Sometimes I feel the first three acts are only a kind of comic stretching exercise for this one final leap into tragedy. Everything points toward Act Four — that's the secret of directing *The Seagull* . . .

"And while I think of it, Peter. I must compliment you on your Dr. Dorn. Just the right touch of understated irony. I'm so pleased you're with us now. I understand your hesitation, the way loyalties are jumbled, but we're pragmatists, you and I . . . Now it will only take Olga Knipper to make our company complete. I'm very close to her, Peter. I have information that she was living in Moscow as recently as October. When the city is taken we'll find her and bring her here at once . . .

"Can't you see her acting with our Nina? Her voice is weak, of course, and she will insist on rolling her shoulders in that abominable Stanislavsky style, but we'll soon cleanse her of that . . . I found her myself you know. She was near starvation and quite sick . . . In a brothel, actually. An SS brothel up near Kiev. They don't keep their women long, I'm afraid. They toss them out like so much waste. She would have starved but for me. A third-rate actress judging by the companies she performed in before the war. All this dreary social realism. She played factory girls for months on end."

He glanced up at Kunin to see the effect all this was having, then frowned and hurried on.

"I foresee great things for the girl. I want you to help her in any way you can. Should I say it out loud? . . . Well, I won't. But I watched your eyes when she crossed the stage. Like magnets. And she's not diseased, by the way — the SS are quite careful about that . . . But no matchmaking for me. I've a meeting this evening with the propaganda people about a possible broadcast. I believe things are coming together splendidly, don't you?"

It wasn't until six that Diskau dismissed them. By the time Kunin walked the cliff road back up to the villa, it was already dark and Nina was ensconced in the small guest bedroom overlooking the sea.

"She's weak," Maria Pavlovna said, when he asked about seeing her. "I don't want her disturbed until her strength comes back."

She assigned Varka as nurse. At breakfast she could be seen carrying a tray up to Nina's room, her back bent into the slant it had become now, her head lowered to match it, her eyes gauging the effort between steps. Afternoons she took Nina walking in the overgrown part of the garden where the earthquake had spared the old walls, letting Nina lean on her, all but serving as her crutch. There were early buds on the apple trees, and Varka led her from one to the next, as if by doing so she could inhale their fragrance and by some miraculous emulation blossom herself.

A week went by before Nina began taking these walks alone. Varka helped her to the gate, then with the look of an anxious mother not at all sure her child can walk, let her proceed by herself toward the first bench.

Kunin was in the habit of spending part of the afternoon there himself, so it was inevitable they would meet. At first, he made no effort to speak with her; she would walk past the tree against which he sat reading and for all the attention she paid him he could have been bark. Dressed in a simple white shift, her shoulders covered by one of Maria Pavlovna's shawls, she still retained that wraith-like air of her first appearance, and it was only her sudden, shattering coughs that made her human. At their sharpest she would double over, surrendering completely to the pain that wracked her, not straightening again until minutes after the last spasm when she would uncoil herself and slowly shiver, like a rabbit emerging from the safety of its den.

At these times she wore the solitude of the very ill, and he knew it was useless trying to break through. Even later, when her strength increased and the color returned to her complexion, she still seemed contained within an impermeable glass ball, and his shy attempts to speak with her were met with uncomprehending silences and abrupt retreats.

That he longed to speak with her went without saying. The contradiction between the beauty of her features and the pain that masked it, her soft voice, which seemed scarred, her oddly contemptuous manner of staring, the way she had suddenly appeared from the battle zone like war's emissary — these put him through an agony of confused emotions, ranging from pity on one hand to desire on the other and touching every shading in between.

Half in love with her, frightened, he took what he could from the distance. Besides the walks in the garden, the only time Nina left her room was for rehearsals. These had been increased to two a day as the date for the performance grew near. Everyone showed the strain of this — arguments became frequent — but Nina most of all. Physically, she continued as before, no better, no worse, but her acting showed definite signs of deterioration. She gestured too stiffly, with too much exaggeration, suggesting not Chekhov, but murals and posters and revolutionary art. She mumbled too much, swallowed a third of her lines. She portrayed youth not as someone who was living it, but as someone who was afraid of losing it, and this brought a hysterical quality to her characterization that made everything seem forced. Time and again she stopped in the middle of her lines to stare down at the stage with her peculiarly inward look, as if trying to remember something about herself she had long since forgotten.

"I'm sorry, it's been so long," she mumbled whenever Diskau corrected her. These occasions were frequent. Nina was marching where she should glide — Diskau must correct her. Nina was flirting with her body and not her eyes — Diskau couldn't have that. Nina was too harsh when she kissed Potapov and must be gentle — hadn't Diskau shown her twenty times? Diskau never raised his voice when he said these things, was in fact quite patient, but there was an edge in his manner that suggested a lion tamer needing only to show a glimpse of the whip to command obedience. Nina cringed every time he came near.

A week before the dress rehearsal, after a particularly long and grueling day, Kunin was in his bedroom writing in his journal when there was a loud knock on the door behind him. It was Varka, wrapped in a robe that gave her the thick, solemn appearance of a monk.

"The mistress would like to speak with you," she said.

"Now? It's after midnight . . . In the parlor?"

"In his study."

Had it been God's study, she couldn't have said it with more reverence. Kunin put his shirt on and followed her down the stairs. Varka tapped twice on the study door, opened it, then pushed him firmly in.

It was darker in the room, the only light coming from a candle on the desk, and it was a few moments before Kunin's eyes grew accustomed to the dimness. Maria Pavlovna stood by her brother's bookcase looking down at two volumes that lay open beside each other with their edges touching. Her hair, always so tightly arranged, hung down to her shoulders; the candlelight turned the auburn a garish red, so that the effect was of gray hair rinsed with dye. She seemed stooped over compared to her usual posture — buckled. Rather than the neat, old-fashioned skirt and blouse she usually wore, she had on a loose peasant robe that made it seem the proud discipline in her had been snipped.

"It's not the same," she said quietly, talking more to the books than to him. "In Antosha's version, the peasant girl twirls through the wheat like a ballerina. In Diskau's version, the peasant girl swaggers through the wheat like a gypsy whore."

She shook her head. "I've been comparing translations. Rene's are good, but he changes things. Not often, but now and then. A word, a phrase — a piece of description. My German isn't very good and I realize the difficulties. But tell me this, Peter. Why would anyone want to change my brother's words?"

"Vanity. Power. He's a complicated man."

Maria Pavlovna gave no indication she had heard him. She crossed over to the picture of her brother's patron, the editor Suvorin, and stood looking up at it as toward an icon.

"I've just left Nina's room. We were talking, but now she's asleep. I stayed for a few minutes watching her. I thought it so odd."

Kunin knew what was expected of him. "Odd in what way, Maria Pavlovna?"

"That eyes like hers could ever close."

So quiet was the room that Maria Pavlovna's whisper made the candle flicker. She tilted her body until she sheltered it and the flame straightened.

"She's a fine actress despite everything. The conviction she puts into her words, the way her expression wraps itself around every syllable. All our other actresses have been spoiled by this Gorky monstrousness, quite ruined. They've been fed realism like so many cows, and they've lost all sense of naïveté. There hasn't been a Nina in Russia in thirty years. . . . Oh, I know what you're going to say. I anticipate you, Peter Sergeich. She's awkward with her hands, too stiff and formal. But our Nina is there beneath that, I sense it. People always stiffen under pain and talk formally. It's up to you and I to free that Nina and let her flourish."

Kunin waited for her to explain just exactly how they would do this, but she abruptly changed tacks and glanced up at him with a lighthearted smile that had too many lines in it to be genuine.

"I've been meaning to thank you, Peter. I feel so much better having you in the play. Our argument was

such a burden. And your Dorn is excellent, quite professional. I draw strength from your presence. Like a birch
that puts on young leaves. No, that's not very good. My
brother would smile. But you catch my intention. I'm tot-
tering now and I need your support."

Help, support, assistance — Maria Pavlovna was always asking for one of the three. But there was something new in the way she said it, a tremble in her voice
that was so naked it embarrassed Kunin and he rushed
into the silence with the first words that came into his
head.

"It's an interesting role. I enjoy it in a way. Everyone claims your brother split his personality between Trigorin and Constantine, but I feel much closer to him as
Dorn. Acting an older man forces me to drown something
childish in myself, something I'm finished with. . . . I
especially enjoy the part where I tell Constantine how
much his play moved me. And then it's nice being someone who's survived so many affairs."

Maria Pavlovna smiled. "I was always a bit in love
with Dr. Dorn. Maxim Fedorovitch played him in the
first performance. Have you seen his picture? After the
play ended, half the women in Moscow would be waiting
outside the theatre hoping to speak with him. And this a
man of sixty."

"But still, it's a difficult thing. It's hard for me to
say the lines."

"Of course it's hard."

Kunin took a deep breath. "With the war, it's hard
to think about plays."

Maria Pavlovna glanced over at him, then crossed to
her brother's leather divan and sat heavily down. Kunin

expected a strong reaction from her — he all but braced himself against the bookcase to wait it out — but her voice, when she spoke, was quiet and oddly resigned.

"Everyone is putting difficulties in my way. Everyone, even my friends. They warn me to be cautious, advise me the play would be better off not performed. At best they consider me the tool of the German major. At worst, a deliberate traitor. But whom do they think my allegiance is to? And when it comes to that, we Russians ourselves are the worst offenders. Here in Yalta there is a municipal administration so-called. This municipal administration so-called has now taken it into their heads to forbid the play. Forbid it and do you know on what grounds? Do you know on what grounds, Peter Sergeich?"

Kunin shook his head.

"The plague. Typhus and influenza. They've made their appearance in Yalta, a few cases on the outskirts, and because of this the cowards want to forbid all assemblies, which is fine with their masters because they want to forbid the same thing."

"The Germans? The performance was their idea."

Maria Pavlovna made an impatient gesture with her hand. "No, not Rene. The others — the ones in the military. There's a decree being posted tomorrow forbidding gatherings of more than two without a special permit. They're scared — I could see it in their eyes when I went to apply for one. They have the look men have just before they cut and run."

This was new information to Kunin. He was still trying to decipher its significance when Maria Pavlovna reached into the pocket of her robe and took out a piece of paper.

"And now this."

She threw it down on her brother's desk. It was soft and dirty, the wrapping from Turkish cigarettes. Across the side, in pencil, were scribbled two lines: *We know how to shear fascist sheep.*

Kunin looked up. "Where did this come from?"

"It was left pinned to my coat at the theatre."

"It's a joke."

Maria Pavlovna shook her head. "Partisans," she said. She spit the word out like a gypsy.

It seemed strange hearing her say it; a moment before, Kunin would have guessed she didn't know what the word meant.

"The closer we come to putting the play on, the more our enemies will try to stop us. I've explained all this to Rene, but he doesn't listen. He refuses to understand. A word from him and all these regulations and permits could be done away with at once. I've appealed to him a dozen times, and yet all he cares about is the acting and leaves everything else to me."

"He's the Minister of Culture. Not just in Yalta, but the entire Crimea. I assume that carries a certain power."

"All he talks about is power! It's in his power. Thanks to his power. By using his power — it's like a holy man bragging of God. Let's see your power then, I told him. Bring Olga Knipper here so we can have our Arcadina rather than endlessly promising us her. Tell the military that no permits are necessary to perform Anton Chekhov. Throw a cordon of guards around the theatre so no partisans sneak through. If everyone is determined to stop our play, then we will force it into existence despite them, but I can't do it alone. . . . I need him, Peter. Why doesn't he move to put things right?"

Beside the desk was one of those oddities of which her brother had been fond: a stuffed mongoose he had brought back from Ceylon. She went over to it, brushed the dust from its shiny, intelligent snout, then turned and faced him, her hands pressed to her waist as if steeling herself for a great effort.

"It's late and I'm sorry to keep you. The fact is I need your opinion as a doctor."

"I'm not a doctor."

"But the closest I have. Is Nina physically capable of acting her part or isn't she?"

"It depends on what you mean by capable."

"I see the strain on her. I've seen the way she collapses after rehearsal. Even when she acts — that terrible tightness. It's as though she's bursting with her own story and needs to tell it before she can play my brother's. But why doesn't she confide in me? Why the deliberate mystery? At times she trusts me like a daughter, and then not a second later she treats me like her worst enemy. We've talked, and yet I know hardly the slightest thing about her. Hardly the slightest thing."

"She needs time."

"She coughs blood, did you know that? She begged me not to tell anyone. My brother begged me, too. It was at Melikhovo the first time, when we were alone together in the kitchen. In his entire life it was the only thing that made him ashamed."

Kunin knew Maria Pavlovna wouldn't let him go

without an answer. He thought for a few moments, then spoke very carefully.

"She has tuberculosis, of course. Probably long-standing, though it would take a chest specialist to confirm that. It's been aggravated by malnutrition. I would say she's susceptible to a host of things right now. Typhus would be a possibility. It's good that Varka's nursing her."

"But good enough? Answer my question. Am I putting her life in danger by letting her act?"

"If it were only a matter of three acts there would be no problem. She could husband her strength, pace herself. But in the final act? She's on stage longer, there's so much emotion . . ."

Maria Pavlovna closed her eyes. "Tell me!"

"Yes, Maria Pavlovna. You are putting her in danger."

She nodded — whether to confirm she had heard him or confirm his opinion, Kunin couldn't tell. She turned around, walked over to the study's fan-shaped window, and stood there staring into the curtain as if into stars.

Kunin knew what she was going to say. She was going to argue with him, dispute his conclusions. She was going to beg him to obtain stimulants and drugs to keep Nina going until the performance was over. She was going to sacrifice Nina to *The Seagull* because in the end her brother's work was so important it demanded human sacrifice. She was going to prove her saintliness by giving up the woman closest to her heart, and he shuddered for them both.

Maria Pavlovna turned around and faced him.

"There will be no play."

Her words, said so softly, jolted him like a fist below

the heart. Not a fist — a kick. The kind of kick that propels a person toward maturity whether he wants to get there or not.

"That might be too drastic," he mumbled, taken aback. "I suppose she could go on. If she were cared for properly. There's the morale factor. Tuberculosis is as much psychological as physical at her stage. Perhaps we should leave it up to her."

And though he realized it only when it was too late, this hedging was precisely the cruelest thing he could have done to Maria Pavlovna, holding out hope to her just when she had rejected it. Seen in this light, what happened next was entirely his fault.

Maria Pavlovna began to cry.

He had seen her cry before, of course, but always because she wanted to — because tears were weapons in getting her way. These tears were different. They weren't wrung from her and splotchy, but the waxy beads of an old woman that seem part sweat, so they emerge from a body that's learned sadness and not just the eyes.

"I'm sorry, Maria Pavlovna?" he said, unable to make out her words.

She struggled to shape them, the tears down to her lips now, becoming perversely dewlike just when they were at their most bitter. He crossed over and took her firmly by the shoulders. It steadied her, but then he felt a shudder go through her body, then another one, then a third. Between each spasm her back noticeably stiffened, as if she were willing iron into her flesh, but the metal never quite succeeded in catching and the throbs kept flooding back. If I let go she'll fall, Kunin decided, but the moment the thought came to him she broke away with a violent gesture and stood by herself near the desk.

"Take her away!" she said, her voice shrill and desperate. "Escape with her — leave at once! I will arrange things myself. There are smugglers who trust me. You can be taken to Turkey. The two of you must leave immediately!"

It came in a spasm and Kunin waited until it passed. "We can't leave, Maria Pavlovna," he said quietly. "It's too late for that. . . . Are you feeling stronger now? Shall I call Varka?"

But she was beyond his solicitude. Again, as calmly as ever, she stroked back her hair, the strands yellow in the declining candlelight. When she spoke next, it was more to the desk than to him and there was nothing tremulous in her tone, nothing except the bitter irony from her eyes.

"Yalta," she said. "How he *hated* it."

She was still standing there when Kunin let himself out into the hall. He closed the door carefully, then started across the parlor. It was two by the clock. To soften his footsteps, he took the pantry staircase up to his room. It had three turns in it, three separate landings. At the highest was a window the size of a porthole and enough moonlight to illumine something that he thought at first was a sack. When he stepped to get around it, he nearly tripped from astonishment. A hand touched his ankle and the sack moved.

"Shh," someone whispered.

It was Nina — she was huddled against the topmost step like someone taking shelter by a cliff. Before he could make sense of her appearance, she tugged him down beside her and whispered again.

"Hear? She paces like that all night in the hall."

Kunin tilted his head the direction she pointed. A few feet beyond them the floorboards creaked with a splintering noise, relaxed with a softer one, then creaked again. The pattern of sound was so intermittent and yet so purposeful it was easy to picture Varka's labored steps.

"She lost a child when she was young, did you know that? I kept waking the moonlight was so bright. They always take children away. In Riga where we did *Dead Souls* there was a landlady who paced that way. Katerina — such a happy name, though she was wretched enough. She's searching for her baby."

The words came in a strange order, disjointed, and he had to pay close attention to keep up. His emotions were still colored by his conversation with Maria Pavlovna, so it was hard to detach his listening from the turbulence he had just been through.

"I couldn't sleep," she said again. "In Riga, I could never sleep it was so oppressive. Do you think Varka was once pretty?"

Leaning against the step, pressed against each other, they listened to her footsteps. When the sound reached the far end of the hall, Kunin twisted slightly so that his shoulder no longer interrupted the moonlight and it continued on toward Nina's face.

That close the mask of pain over her features seemed partially askew, so that the cheek facing him was soft and unblemished, vibrant with life. A curl of hair hung down over the edge of it like an earring that was magnetic — he felt an irresistible impulse to touch a finger to its yel-

low. Below it, closer, her neck was exposed by the loose-
ness of her robe. There was the thinnest line of powder
between her scar and her shoulder — the smell was lilac
and comforting.

Comforting, at least until she turned and faced him.
There was no mistaking the pain then. Meeting the hollow of her eyes, he felt the shamed impotence a man feels
when he watches a woman giving birth. But no — that
was wrong, too. She looked like a woman who had just
had an abortion, not given birth. A woman who had not
been delivered of anything but a woman from whom
something had been stripped away.

"Where are you from?" he whispered, groping for a
place to start.

"In Minsk —"

"You were born in Minsk?"

She smiled. "In Minsk, there was a boy like you. He
acted with us, then left — I'm not sure why. The good
ones always disappeared. You're the writer everyone speaks
of. I've seen you reading in the garden."

There was a patient firmness in the way she said
this — it was as though she had removed his hand from
her breast. By it, he understood she didn't want him
probing too hard, and it was up to him to explain first.

And so — stumbling at first, shy — he explained. He
told her about growing up in Leningrad and all the books
he had read there. He told her about his uncle and his
father, who named constellations. He told her about his
pilgrimage across Russia to Yalta in the last summer of
peace when the black earth of the steppe had been his
bed at night and tall fields of wheat had sheltered him
from the sun. He told her of his plan to go back to med-

ical college once the war ended and the books he would begin writing once he had time.

But what was strange, the more he explained, the more certain he became that none of what he was saying would come true — that he would never go back to school again; that he would never get around to writing his stories down; that the war itself would never end. What he was telling her was reverie, the idle dreams of a boy, though he had gone beyond boyhood now and entered a realistic world in a brutal century where dreams came true only seldom. He would never be a doctor, let alone a writer. Never. But since maturity gives as well as takes, there was comfort to go along with the disappointment — he felt the exhilaration a man feels in braving a naked fact alone — and so there was no regret in the way he talked, no apology. He knew it was important for her to see the dream he had emerged from before seeing anything else.

She listened to him carefully, alternating her eyes between the moonlight and his face. When he finished, she stretched herself the way a girl will at the end of a story and glanced expectantly up at him, as if prompting him to recite the last line.

"And so now you live in Chekhov's house," she said.

"And so now I live in Chekhov's house."

"We did *Cherry Orchard* in school. That was years ago, before truth became unfashionable. There, you hear? She's outside my door wondering if I'm asleep. A seagull — I am a seagull. I should be rehearsing even now. I wonder what kind of man he was."

"Chekhov? It's strange, but I was just thinking about

that. This was his favorite staircase, I'm told. When Olga Knipper . . . Do you know who she is?"

Nina's eyes widened. "To act with Olga Knipper is the dream of my life."

"When she visited before they were married, he would sneak up these stairs so they could spend the night together. Maria Pavlovna was living here then and they wanted to spare her feelings." He smiled and patted the step below them. "Dusty pantry stairs. Up you crept the famous Anton Chekhov, lustful as a cat."

She laughed and immediately covered her mouth — not to keep Varka from hearing, but at the surprise taste of the sound. "But what kind of man?" she insisted.

Kunin thought for a moment. "Serious. Detached. More pragmatic than his stories, not as vague. A man who deliberately kept himself immune from his era. A shy lover. It's hard to say, really. He had no vanities."

"I love his plays best. He's the only Russian to understand a woman's heart. To the others, she's either a virgin or a whore. In the provinces the directors put you in something white and lacy or red and torn, and pat themselves on the back at their brilliant costuming. We did *Three Sisters* in Kazan once. I played Irina and felt somehow she was me. But it was poorly received. Did they actually forbid Chekhov once or was he just frowned on? I can't remember. Do you know Anya in *Cherry Orchard*? It's Irina again, only not as intellectual."

For a moment, she talked easily without constraint. The roles she had played, the roles she wanted to play, the roles that might someday be hers. She sounded like a girl whose head was filled with nothing but flighty ambition, and it made Kunin remember Diskau's dismissal of her as a third-rate actress. But it was just this contrast between the endurance of her hopes and the evidence of what she had been through that made him listen so intently. In talking to her his dream had evaporated, but here hers was in full flower despite everything, and there was something magic in their crossing that equalized the difference in their ages and brought them together.

"And now Nina," she said, finishing. "Nina is the greatest role. To play Nina successfully — no, brilliantly. To play Nina brilliantly is every actress's dream. There, do you hear? Nothing. Varka has gone to bed. Once again she's realized she will not find her missing child by pacing, and so she must go to sleep and get her rest." She brought her hand up and touched him lightly on the arm. "We must get our rest, too."

She started to get up.

"There's one thing," Kunin said.

"Yes?"

He shook his head. "Nothing."

There was no canceling the play for her. Even to mention the possibility would make her hate him. Instead, he held his hand out — she was so light it needed only the slightest tightening to help her up.

"Tiptoe," she whispered. "Like Chekhov going to Olga."

They said good night in the hall. Kunin didn't want to leave — he could think of a hundred questions he wanted to ask — but after a few commonplace remarks about the next day's rehearsal he started back toward his room.

Her cough made him turn around. She was standing

outside her door, her hand on the knob, her face turned as if she were trying to make something out there on the floor. My clubfoot, he decided — she's staring at my foot. In the dimness it was hard to be sure, but her expression seemed to convey both surprise and great gentleness, as if despite all the times she had seen him only now was she really seeing him. And the odd thing was he wasn't ashamed of this, even though he felt naked. There was pity in the way she stared — not pity that was cheap and condescending, but the pity that widens into compassion and sees in one man's pain the pain of the world.

Dignified by her eyes, strengthened, he walked to his room.

HE WOKE late the next morning. The others had already left for the theatre and so he was forced to walk there through a black squall blowing in from the sea.

The rehearsal was on its way to falling apart by the time he arrived. The heat in the theatre had failed and everyone was shivering. The German engineers were building anti-tank barricades out on the promenade and the pounding of the jackhammers forced everyone to shout. There were rumors of a great battle to the east — in the wings, Rashevitch and Potapov whispered of nothing else. To top it off, the lights started blinking, blinding them one moment, blacking out the next. Diskau, ignoring the distractions, fastened his attention on Nina and refused to let go.

"You're too naive. She's ambitious. Her naïveté is a pose, a relic of Nineteenth-Century Romanticism. She knows what she wants by now and she'll do anything to get it."

He kept hammering away at her, insisting she say the lines with the inflections he gave her. This was at the beginning of Act Three, where Nina debates whether or not to leave home to become an actress — where she hands Trigorin the locket with the name of his novel on it and the reference to the lines "If you ever need my life, come and take it."

It was an important scene, but not one that called for any special histrionics. Nina, though, acted it badly, with too much emotion. Diskau kept circling her all the while, whispering the lines a syllable ahead of her, shouting "No!" at every third one, making her repeat them again and again. It was obvious to everyone that her fear of him only made her act worse. Kunin, watching from stage left, stood it for as long as he could.

"That's enough, Diskau," he said. He walked rapidly across the stage and stood between them. "Let the woman act."

Everyone froze. The lights, so wobbly until then, stopped so the three of them were in its circle. Kunin's back was to Nina so he didn't see her reaction. At first, Diskau seemed too stunned to react at all, but then with a slight feline smile he bowed and took an exaggerated step backwards out of the light.

"I appreciate your help, Peter," he said loudly. "Thank you. Shall we continue?"

And that was the end of it. The rehearsal went on in its stumbly fashion, Diskau turned his attention to the others and nothing more about the incident was said. Its real significance only Kunin understood. In the moment he had faced Diskau down, beneath the irony of his smile, beneath the mocking salute, there had been something else, something Kunin had been too dense to notice before.

Fear. Fear not of him, but of Nina. He was afraid of Nina. Challenged the slightest bit, he had shied away from her like a hangman whose victim springs back to life.

Had she sensed this herself? Her acting showed signs of improvement during the afternoon — she spoke with more confidence, and didn't press quite so much. She even allowed herself a tantrum — this directed toward Varka of all people, who crossed in front of her before the right cue.

That evening, after they had returned to the villa and were walking through the rain-soaked garden, Nina took Kunin's hand and held him back so the others went in ahead.

"Thank you," she whispered.

Embarrassed, Kunin shrugged. "I was worried for you."

But she wouldn't let him be embarrassed. She rose up on tiptoe and kissed him lightly on the cheek. Her face came away for a moment, then she leaned back and kissed him even more lightly on the lips.

"Thank you," she said. She hurried toward the house.

All through their meager dinner Kunin kept staring toward her, willing her eyes to meet his, but she kept them fixed on her plate and seemed half-asleep. That night Kunin paced his room in a fever of impatience, unwilling to let sleep rob the moment in the garden of any of its luster. When the morning came he went right to her room intending to speak with her, but Varka — who was immune to tantrums — was there ahead of him; she already had Nina wrapped in Maria Pavlovna's sable coat and was now making last-minute adjustments to her hair.

At the rehearsals, Nina hardly looked at him. That night she walked quickly into the villa and didn't catch his hint to hold back. She didn't talk to him at dinner and she didn't talk to him again the next day, and not for three days after that, until his agony at her silence became unendurable and all he could think about was why she had become so cold.

On the fifth night, as he tried to focus his exhaustion into sleep, there was a scuffing noise outside in the hall. Varka, he decided — he rolled over and shut his eyes. But a moment later there was another sound, this one on the door — it was as if someone were stroking it with their hand. He had just sat up and thrown back the sheet when the latch clicked, the door opened, and into the room stepped Nina.

She wore a white slip that stopped just over her knees. In the dark, her face was vague and he couldn't see her expression. There was motion, then a silken sound — he realized she had pulled the slip up over her head. There wasn't much difference between the white of her slip and the white of her skin; her nakedness came to him instead as a sudden lightening in his soul, so that he felt himself nearly choked by a rush of joy.

Exhilarated, afraid, he got up from his bed very slowly. She waited by the door for him. He touched her first on the cheek. When he tried to turn her face toward the light coming in through the window, she took his hand and moved it down to her neck and its scar.

"I tried to stay away," she whispered. "I tried so hard."

He let his hand stroke the line above her shoulders, afraid more than he had ever been afraid of anything that he would somehow hurt her. When he leaned to kiss her neck she took his hand and brought it to her forehead and the red mark where her hair had been tortured and pulled back. It was as if she were guiding him to what was most secret in her, the places he had to know first before he could understand.

"Not inside me," she said softly. "I've been hurt and we can't."

He nodded, though he was too inexperienced to understand. He slid his hands down her shoulders to her breasts, then to her waist, then knelt in front of her and pressed his head against her thighs to stop his trembling. He felt her hands in his hair — felt them slide around so she was pressing his face into her, and then she came to her knees, too, and they knelt by each other trying by soft touchings to find a way to obliterate their separation. He could sense her fighting toward him from the depths of something — when he kissed her breasts he felt the shudders rise up her chest.

When she shuddered, he held her tighter — it was the one thing he understood he must do. She leaned back and pulled him down with her, but still it wasn't close enough and she had to whisper again to hold him back.

"I'm torn."

There was a moment when he didn't hear her, then a moment past this when the only thing he wanted was to hurt her hurt, feel it and so absorb half its pain. He stroked his hand between her legs and she shuddered and bit her lip to keep from crying out. He stroked her again, but there was hurt everywhere he touched and no entry past it, no way around. They could fight together toward climax but never reach it, for there could be no release in love for them, no ending, and all they could do for each other was to cling like this in the cold darkness and whisper to each other and strain together toward the same distant thing.

THE STEPPE

I ACTED BADLY in Kiev. My lines were lies so I
mumbled them. Children of the heroic motherland. Let
none yield without taking a fascist with them heroes of
socialist labor. This while I waved a red banner from my
gun. And what was odd, the people still came and still
applauded so you'd think we were putting on Ibsen. There
were queues out in front even though the first Stukas
were coming in and there was talk of evacuation. They
were starved for theatre and pretended what we were giving them was bread. I acted badly so as not to embarrass

them. By the second act most left. A few pretended to the end.

How can you pretend in an age when all is pretense?

Fewer came every night. There was a war; no one told us where. When you play factory girls all you think about is vodka. When Semechny didn't come and Kovrin took his part I knew the Germans were closer. There were five in the audience that night. We were in Kiev to stiffen morale.

Kovrin called me into his dressing room. "You are mocking us again," he said. "I see in you the spirit of defeat."

This for form's sake.

"You're pretty in that tunic. I wager you're even prettier with it off."

A face the color of a cheap canvas briefcase. Our director, Kovrin. A politically reliable man.

"And don't stare at me so. I'm lonely, is that a crime? Besides, you're too talented to remain in this dump. I'm going to Moscow, did I mention that? A special plane to fly me out. My own theatre, too. The classics, not this crap. I'll need someone with your spirit."

I didn't sleep that night. The rooming house where they kept us was near the railroad yards. There was a rumbling noise that peaked and grew fainter. Men swore and it didn't come in a buzz like when they were drinking but singly and distinct. Toward dawn there were children singing marching songs. I could picture them holding hands and slept to it. When I woke up it was sunny and quiet. I went immediately to Kovrin's room.

When I first became an actress I fell in love with anyone who was famous just because I was so certain

they had an insight into truth. Not for advantage. I scorned
their offers of help and took small roles in the provinces
so they wouldn't think me a whore. None of them had
truth, of course. I became pregnant by one but the child
was taken away from me before I could hold it. Is that
truth? A baby boy, a baby girl? I don't know which it was
so where do I begin in telling you?

An airplane to Moscow — that was truth. So I went
to Kovrin's room. Maybe he was going to be given his own
theatre. Maybe he was going to do the classics. Maybe he
was in need of an actress with range. At least the Kovrins
don't insult you with flowers and talk of love. I walked
up the stairs toward his room and all the doors were open
in the hall and sheets were lying disordered on the floor
and no one was about.

Yes, I went to him — you should know that about
me. What's that line in the fourth act? Early tomorrow
morning I must travel to Yeletz third-class with peasants
and at Yeletz I shall have to put up with the attentions
of the educated shopkeepers.

What sweet bliss that would be! The educated shopkeepers I learned to handle before I was twenty and young
commissars with their zeal and factory chairmen with their
bellies. I learned to put them off with coy smiles and
acquiescent nods, learned their cynicism and put it to
good use. I have a performance tonight. Perhaps tomorrow? Do leave me your card. But after that there were
always the Kovrins with a new role to offer, the Kovrins
with their magic carpets that would whisk me away. I
walked up the stairs to him wetting my lips to make them
more alluring, unbuttoning my blouse so there would be
no question of any illusions.

The attentions of lecherous directors! How sordid! And yet compared to the rest that was paradise, too, and just when I thought I had reached the end and touched bottom the bottom fell away so I dropped spinning through blackness where there was no question of giving yourself to someone but where everything was taken. Taken, that is, with a knife pressed to your throat so you wouldn't struggle. And even here, at the bottommost rung, there were gradations to be observed, so that the worst ones weren't the ones who came and took you quickly in rough uniforms, not the brutal ones who put their hands in you and tore, not the ones who took turns and swarmed over you like swollen ants. The worst were the ones without expression, the pasty ones, the ones who entered you like they were dead.

Here, feel my throat — feel it there. The young ones mostly. Because terror was the only thing that reminded them they were human. With wire, sometimes cord. The gentle ones used cord. They came when you screamed so you learned to scream quickly. Because they had lost their fear of death and needed it from a woman more than warmth.

There was no plane ride to Moscow. Kovrin's room was empty. He had left his briefcase on the bureau and the bed was soiled with the reek of his pomade. Like a rat from a sinking ship — it's strange how comforting such expressions are. I went through the briefcase looking for money. Kovrin was a great one at flashing papers at you to prove his importance. They were gibberish and in a fury I ripped them apart.

By the time I finished I felt tired. The sun was high now and hot enough to make plaster sweat. Where the rumbling of the trains had been came the peeping of birds. I walked down the stairs on tiptoe. There was no one about. In the silence, in the emptiness, it was as if everyone had caught a line pulling them to safety and I alone had let go.

Alone and then not alone. Besides actors, the boarding house took in circus performers, ballerinas, mimes — anyone who could content themselves with its filth. Crouched beneath the bottom landing were three members of the Stepanoff Circus. Stepanoff's wife was closest — a fleshy woman with steel-rimmed spectacles, famous for her tyrannies. Behind her, cowering in the shade of her ample rump, were Misha and Emil, the circus's two clowns. They played Siamese twins in their act and would try to get on a bicycle together or eat the same chicken with one fork. Even away from the circus they were constantly in each other's company and there was a synchronization to their movements that made the bond seem real. They had come to our performance every night. Each tried to outdo the other in the ferocity of their applause.

The Stepanoff Circus. Like us, sent to Kiev to stiffen morale.

Stepanoff's wife, seeing me, put her fingers to her heart and made them flutter. "We thought you were Germans," she said.

"Germans," Misha said, trembling.

"Germans," Emil said, the tremble exaggerated.

They looked to me for help. Not because I was stronger, but because I was the one to come down those stairs first. Understand? They had spent the morning waiting for German jackboots and my sandals had appeared in their place. In gratitude, they would have given their allegiance to a cat.

"There's not much time," I told them. "Go to your rooms and take only what you need. We must leave at once."

I was playing a role — I admit that now. To the barricades, comrades! Heroic Russian womanhood to the fore! And yet how else was I to get them moving? In a few minutes they were back down with their belongings. Misha and Emil brought their clown suits and wore them wrapped around their necks like silk bedrolls. Stepanoff's wife lugged a cardboard suitcase tied with belts. There may have been food left in the pantry but none of us remembered until later.

I had them to the door when Stepanoff's wife threw her suitcase over and sat on it with her arms crossed like a spoiled child.

"I'm not leaving," she said. "Modestus promised to come back for me. He said he was only going to check the tiger."

Luckily for her I was still in my role. "Very well. We'll leave you here. Besides. They say the Germans only rape the pretty ones."

She was up in a flash. The three of them followed me out to the street.

It was much harder outside. In a house you have a proscenium, a platform, even lights. Outside there's none of that and it's harder to frame your thoughts. I remember how hot it was. The heat shimmered above the railroad tracks and bent them. The yard was deserted. Back toward town we could hear windows being shattered by looters. Higher, in the distance, rose a pillar of iodine-colored smoke.

"Stukas," Emil said. "They won't be long."

We started east, spacing out steps to match the ties. There's that line of Gorky's about how difficult it is to walk on tracks without looking backwards expecting to be smashed. It's true. You look back often and it makes you trip.

There was no sign of life until the edge of the city, where the shacks began. Sparks from passing locomotives had scorched the shrubbery and the embankment was blistered with roots. At the bottom sitting on cartons were peasants waiting for what would happen to happen. The older ones seemed amused by us and pointed, but the young ones — the women in kerchiefs — scowled and searched the ground for something to throw. Emil turned somersaults on the cinders for them, but even then they didn't laugh. They peered toward the smoky line of the city and cursed us for bringing this upon them and wiped their foreheads in the heat.

Past the shacks the countryside began. The first stragglers were here pushing their carts. They didn't look up at us. They were townspeople, pale and unsure. Most of them were loaded down with too many possessions and barely able to move. Children rode the bundles like they were camel humps. The sight made Stepanoff's wife begin to wail.

"There's a child involved," Emil explained. "She is missing him with her husband."

"No time for that," Misha said bitterly. "There; he's fed him to the tiger. Hear that bitch? Keep on! Keep on!"

We had to use the embankment to get past the carts. They were more numerous farther out of town. Old men, exhausted from pushing, collapsed in the sun. Unwilling to leave the tracks, people defecated where they were and the stench was overpowering. A plane slanted down and took pictures out its window and everyone turned their faces away in shame. Where the grade dropped we could see over the carts to a line of people extending in a column halfway to the horizon so that it seemed the whole of Russia was fleeing east. After finishing with us, the plane flew straight along the column at a height of a dozen meters, roaring its engine to scare everyone and cause panic. Beneath it, like wheat parting in the wind, the bodies went prostrate and lay still.

Prostrate and still. I've made it seem lyrical. But then the air stank of shit.

The closer we came to the head of the column the more aggressive and frightened everyone became until it took shoving and shouts to keep our place. At the same time there seemed to be more uncertainty regarding direction. The stream that had come out of Kiev so solidly was now breaking up into smaller rivulets. A family would start out at a right angle to the tracks, then another family would take a chance and follow, and then a third, so that smaller columns were constantly forming and it was hard to know which lead toward safety and which toward German tanks.

It was Misha, the ruthless one, who made us stop.

"We'll never make headway against this mob," he said. "The Panzers will come and roll us up like this." He tightened his fist until the blood was squeezed out and spat on it for good measure.

But still, he looked to me for a decision. I shaded my eyes and turned around in a circle searching for something that offered promise. In the distance, so vague and hazy it seemed a mirage, was an apple tree. It was probably the only apple tree for a hundred versts but compared to the cindered wasteland by the tracks it was an orchard.

"There won't be food staying here. It's like following locusts. We'll head south and see what happens."

Those first few steps. Does a minnow know such torture in leaving the school? Our foolishness was so evident no one else broke off to follow us. After a few meters the railroad was out of sight and the only thing left of the moving column was the dull plodding rustle of the shoes.

It didn't take long to reach the apple tree. Emil ran ahead but was standing motionless when we got there. There were no apples, of course. The limbs were shredded and pointy, as if someone had sucked them in an attempt to find nourishment.

"Ah well then," Emil said. He dug down into his pocket. "I've been saving this for such an occasion."

It was a plum cake, the small kind they sold at the theatre. He divided it into thirds, refusing to take any himself. "Too fat," he said, patting his stomach. "Here, miss. You take some. It will do you wonders."

We walked south through sunburnt farmland without trees. There were no cows, no grass. Misha scratched the soil with his finger but no grain had been sown. Stepanoff's wife whined about her feet hurting but we didn't talk.

Toward dusk it became cooler. Behind us the sun

flattened out into a sunset so beautiful it made me ache. Just before the light disappeared there was a terrible sound in the distance. Roars, pounding — it came to us in a vibration through the ground up our feet. "Don't look!" Emil yelled, but I did. There was a column of smoke toward the railroad tracks — one column, two columns, then a solid towering curtain. The sunset, catching it, turned it red so it seemed like blood pouring up into sky. We turned our backs on it and walked on.

Walked on to a place out of history. Is that what we were seeking all along? There in a grove of parched willow, an old manor house that collectivization had missed so that it stood proudly shuttered to the century, beams nailed in X's across the doors. We tried breaking in to escape the cold, but the beams were too thick. It seemed haunted besides — not by anything evil, but a spirit so pure we didn't want to infect it. In the mud where the garden had been were some broken corncobs. The rooks had picked the kernels off the tops. The ones on the bottom may have been edible, but we weren't hungry enough to turn them over.

Misha made a barricade of timbers from an old fence and we slept in its shelter. "To protect us from lions!" Emil laughed, but it seemed cozier there. We made mattresses of wild hemp and lay back facing the stars.

We told stories. Emil and Misha had led adventurous lives and had appeared in circuses not only across Russia but in Austria and Poland as well. Emil would start the stories off, turn to Misha for their middles, then take the endings upon himself. The two of them fussed over each other the way old bachelors will and went to great pains to make sure the other was comfortably settled. Misha talked in a bitter way, but he was the softer of the two and was dependent on Emil's common sense.

It was warm listening to them — the cold didn't bother me. When they finished they insisted I tell them stories in turn. "About the theatre," Emil said. "You actresses. Always a new part to take. I wonder what it must be like."

So I told them stories, some funny, some sad. They fell asleep to the last one. I covered them up with their silk costumes so they wouldn't get chilled. When I stepped back from them I was reminded of a photograph I had seen in a paper not long before, a photograph of German parachutists lying dead in a field. The fabric of their chutes had settled across their bodies in billowy folds. It made me shiver seeing that. I wanted to reach out and touch them back to life.

I may have slept a little. When I woke up the stars were so thick it was impossible to find black in between. There were stars like that over the lake where we lived when I was young. Wildflower stars, my father called them. Our dacha had a lawn without trees so nothing hid them. I was a seagull then — there's that line from the play. But Nina came to me and I was gladdened by it the way you feel gladdened by a shooting star. I felt closer to her dream than ever before. To be a great actress! How vain it was in the midst of war. And yet I felt a great responsibility, as if I were the only actress left in the world, the only one left who understood what it was to transform yourself into another person and so escape. I felt awed by this and my head spun with an exhilaration I had never known on the stage. To act beneath stars! To be illuminated by that light! I felt what I feel now when you hold me. Anything is worth this certainty. Hunger. Fear. Anything!

If only it would last! Before dawn the stars widened and disappeared. Misha was grumbling in his sleep. Emil got up and pulled apart the barricade so there would be no trace of us. Stepanoff's wife stood by the manor house beating two sunflowers together in a futile attempt to find seeds.

That morning was the first time we missed food. Not nourishment, but the ceremony of eating. It was cruel to start walking without that solace — cruel not to be able to divide a piece of bread and make fun of its meagerness. The hunger itself was still manageable, at least for a while. Walking, I was vaguely aware that something wasn't right, something more basic than disorientation or fatigue or the threat of Germans. The longer we walked, the more definite the feeling became, until it was localized in the small of my stomach. I'd always thought of hunger as something distant like Jupiter or Mars and now here it was and I was walking through it trying to understand how it could be located inside me now and not somewhere impossibly remote.

It was a brutally hot day — the sedge grass curled into itself in withered clumps. Stepanoff's wife insisted we were heading the wrong direction. Emil tried to reason with her, but I could tell he had doubts of his own. Misha kept urging us to walk faster and yet kept falling behind so that after every hundred meters we would have to stop and wait. He was limping and embarrassed. He walked with his hands in front of his groin like a naked man.

"Ah well," Emil said when we stopped next. "He doesn't like to mention it, you know."

"Mention what?" I said.

"His piles. They're bleeding, you see. It's agony for him to walk."

We were all blistered by then. We tried walking barefoot but the stubble of the dead corn ripped our feet apart like spikes. We walked toward the sun and when it got behind us walked in our shadows. When we came to a birch copse, Emil would shimmy up the highest to look around. We were afraid not only of Germans but partisans. There were stories about what they did to stragglers caught in their territory.

I don't know how far we managed that second day. Not far. We stopped after dark in a forest of spruce. There were corncobs on the edges where the rooks had dropped them and this time we weren't too proud to turn them over. The pellets were so hard and brittle they turned to dust on our tongues.

There were no stories that night. I slept fitfully to a rumble in the distance like the trains leaving Kiev. The others were slow in waking. I went to the edge of the forest and found a spring where I could wash. As the water streamed down my face — as I shuddered in its coolness — I opened my eyes and saw something that made my heart stop. There falling away from the forest to the east, a plain so wide it exploded my notions of vastness in a glance. I rubbed my eyes the way a child will, not believing them, but when I looked again I recognized it the same instinctive way I had recognized hunger. Coarse grass, black earth, purple sky. The steppe — and on it nothing except the shadows of clouds.

There were no crops growing there, not the wheat or rye you might expect. The morning wind was at my back but when it fell down to the plain it rustled nothing and passed over the blistered land without a trace. The emptiness terrified me more than the vastness. There was no feature on which my eyes could rest — no focus but the negation of all focus. Nothing but the lilac-colored horizon that seemed too distant to be real.

I had just decided to go and wake the others when there was the crackling of branches and a hand against my arm.

"That was very close," Emil said quietly. "Very close. It's a wonder they didn't turn into the woods."

He pointed to the left. There where the grass bent back were two parallel lines of choppy black dirt.

"German tank," he said. He went over and touched the tracks with one finger like someone testing an animal's spoor. "Ahead of us somewhere. When the sun gets higher we'll see his dust."

After skirting the forest the lines dropped straight to the plain. There was something terrible in their straightness. Anything human would have faltered at that vastness, swerved back and forth in hesitation. But not these lines. They were out to humiliate space.

That's what was so frightening. As fast as we had walked the war had gotten ahead of us. A plane passing anywhere across the sky would spot us instantly. But where else could we go? The steppe lay between us and safety and had to be crossed. Not saying anything, tucking the last of the corncobs beneath our belts, we helped each other down the bank and started at a clumsy trot toward the sun.

At first the earth was cool and playfully yielding, but then it grew deeper and for each new step we had to grab our knees and yank our feet back to the surface. After an hour of this our legs ached unbearably. The last of the corn was soon gone. We turned through bird droppings looking for bits of grain. About noon the land ahead of us cracked apart and we came to the lip of a deep gully. At the bottom, like a miracle, flowed a river.

It was a muddy river, little wider than a Moscow street, but with enough current in the middle for a small band of rapids. The sides were slower and darker looking, overhung with willow. The secret way it cut through the steppe attracted me and made me feel lighter. The others, seeing the rushes along the edges, thought immediately of food.

"There'll be frogs there," Misha said. "Crayfish if we're lucky. All kinds of fish. I suppose it's fit to drink besides."

We would have gone down to it instantly but for one problem. The river flowed south a short distance, then — from what we could see of it — looped in a bend toward the west.

We took a vote. Misha was for following it. Stepanoff's wife cried and wouldn't vote. Emil hesitated, looking to me. I felt if I could touch the water I would know.

I spoke very carefully.

"Judging by what we can sense the war is moving east. Our soldiers are there somewhere but we don't know how far. The chances are good we'll stumble into a battle trying for them. If we move west there's a possibility we can slip under the war and emerge on the other side. I know that sounds muddled, but it's the best I can do.

Our only chance is to put our backs to the war and keep moving."

While I talked, Emil stared toward the river.

"The Black Sea," he said at last. "It goes there. I can smell the salt."

And though we were hundreds of kilometers from any sea, it did seem that way — seemed like we could smell salt flats and iodine, hear the crash of surf where the river emptied into a gulf. It decided us in the end. We needed to align ourselves with a hope and a direction and in that featureless plain the river was the only thing possessing either.

We raced one another down the bank. There were berries growing at the water's edge and we threw ourselves at them until our mouths were purple and we laughed from sheer joy. We ate a bushel each, but it still wasn't enough and we combed the shoreline for more. Out in the middle of the river a fish jumped. When the outermost ring of its splashing touched shore I wanted to grab it and tug him somehow in.

We spent the night where a trickle of water entered the main river. The moon was bright enough that I could see my face when I washed. Like the berries it made me laugh. Was this the beauty that had driven the educated shopkeepers of Yeletz mad? It was the face of a woman who played the matronly parts — the flint-faced mean ones who are always being rude to the servants in the first act.

And do you know a secret? The worst part of suffering comes not during its middle but when it slackens. That night lying alone away from the others I gave myself over to despair. The food, the comfort of having those riverbanks towering above us like castle walls, the soft

lap of water past my head. The contrast with the war
was too great. I thought of my child, my unknown child.
I tried to picture its place in the chaos and by concentrating transfer all my courage to its heart. Do you understand how a woman can feel that? You do because I
sense you're doing the same with me now so that I feel
stronger every minute we talk. But it was impossible for
me then. I couldn't picture it because I didn't know if I
should picture a boy or a girl and so all my pity was wasted.
Having no child to feel sorry for I felt sorry for myself
and cried that night like I had never cried before, until
finally it was all wrung from me and I lay still.

Across the brook, Emil whispered toward Misha's dark
shape.

"And then once we cross the sea we'll come to Turkey. Harems, my boy. All the good tobacco you want,
none of this cheap Russian cabbage. It will be paradise
for us then, Mish my lad. Turkish women are four feet
high."

A nightingale started up back in the berries. On the
water something coughed like a gull.

We followed the river for eight and a half days. The
berries gave out after the second. We combed the weeds
looking for freshwater clams but there weren't any. There
were mushrooms but they made us sick. Without line we
couldn't catch fish, though we threw stones in the river
and tried grabbing them with our hands. On the third
day the water took on a silvery color with pinkish streaks.
Misha balanced his way out on a log and dipped his finger
in to taste it.

"Oil," he said, puckering his mouth.

"Are you sure?" Emil called.

He tasted it again, then held up his thumb so we could see the stickiness.

"There's been a battle," Emil said. "Upstream somewhere. We'll probably see bodies floating down before long."

There were no bodies, not then. Instead came that endless flow of spent oil. We couldn't drink from the river anymore. To go with our hunger we had thirst.

"You've led us here deliberately!" Stepanoff's wife screamed at me. "You're jealous because you can't have Modestus and so you've led us here to die!"

She had abandoned her suitcase now. Her favorite dress she wore tied around her middle like a truss. When she called for her child I could sympathize with her but she had stopped calling for him now and talked only of her own suffering. She ate dirt from her fingers. Emil said it was turning her insane.

That evening there was a thunderstorm without rain. Long after the lightning disappeared the rumble remained until at last we understood it was tanks. "They'll not come down here," Emil said, but we decided to keep moving during the night and slip past them.

We waded through the shallows so as not to leave tracks. When the moon was straight overhead we stopped for a rest. There beyond the bank the sky was yellow. A village probably. The yellow was welcoming and soft. I left the others beneath some willows that extended out over the water, then climbed up the bank toward the steppe to have a look.

There was a village there — a cluster of shacks around a church and a mill. It was set at least a kilometer from the river but so flat was the land leading up to it I could see it perfectly. The empty grain ricks, the wash set out on poles to dry. Everything seemed quiet there and normal. I could even smell mutton being fried. The moonlight slanted down off the church dome to coat the streets a bluish silver.

I was torn between wanting to get closer and wanting to go back for the others. I decided to wait in the grass. Later — it must have been minutes — I heard a tinny sound that had a curious lilt.

Music.

Martial music, the happy kind I had heard that night in Kiev when the children were evacuated. I raised myself on my elbows for a better look. Down the main street proceeding at a snail's pace was a large truck with something mounted on the back that looked like a basket.

"The war is over!" a voice announced. It was metallic and scratchy and the Russian was terrible. "All civilians are to remain inside and await further instructions."

The voice repeated this over and over, only pausing so the music could have its chance. When the truck reached the end of the village it continued out across the steppe, its headlights bouncing up with each rut.

"The war is over!" the voice cried. The lights blended into the stars and disappeared.

I slid back down the bank. The others weren't in the willows where I had left them. I was about to whisper their names when I saw Misha further along on a small sandbar. He seemed to be wrestling with something but at first I couldn't understand what.

"Over here!" Emil hissed. "It's Stepanoff's wife. She heard the radio."

Misha tried to hold her but she was beating at his

face with her hands, writhing in desperation. "Don't you hear? The war is over!" she shouted, breaking away from him. "There's no excuse for us now. I'm going up there and talk with them. I'm going to tell them how you kidnapped me. I'm going to tell them where you are!"

Misha made another grab for her but she spun away into the water. "Jew!" she screamed. She put her arms over her head like a ballerina and began wading sideways through the current toward the far bank.

The water was too deep for Misha and Emil. Without thinking I rushed in after her. She was already over to the shallows, where her steps became quicker. I had to lunge across the mud. She was halfway up the bank but I grabbed her ankles and we slid down again into the river. Immediately, I felt her nails on my face. She kicked toward my groin the way she must have kicked toward Stepanoff's when he was drunk. I pulled her closer — her spectacles made a gouge down my forehead to my cheek. She pressed her hand on my head to force me under and my lungs filled with water and I closed my eyes and let the current tumble me downstream. When I fought my way back to the surface she was nowhere to be seen. I searched the bank on that side while Emil and Misha searched the opposite one. In the middle of the current streaming like weeds from a rock were the shredded remnants of her dress.

"Drowned," Misha said when I joined them. He spat on his hands. "Good riddance."

I didn't say what I was thinking: that she may have made it up the bank to the German truck. It was better to think her drowned. Better to choke off her memory the way she had tried choking me. Exhausted, numb, we spent that night and the following day hiding in a cave where the sand had given way. The river was wider here, more exposed. It was safer to move after dark.

We made better time without Stepanoff's wife. There was no whining, no melodramatic scenes. On the best nights we seemed to blend ourselves with the river until the current was established in our hearts. On other nights we had to tear our way through dams formed by drifting branches, make constant detours, cross and recross the river for the gain of hardly anything. The branches had a way of tugging you back just when you thought you were free of them. Tugging you back and forcing you under so that it was like running a gauntlet of a thousand rough hands.

Days were best. We would find a place where the reeds grew thickest along shore. Emil and Misha would lie together near the bank and I would find a spot closer to the water so I could hear it when I slept. The reeds were a golden color, starchy and warm. When you lay on them you could feel their spring. I liked that. I liked the rectangle of sky the reeds admitted. Across it flew countless birds. Geese, plover, lapwing, snipe. No matter when I opened my eyes they were there slanting across the blue as they followed the river — birds and butterflies and blowing leaves, until it seemed all nature had aligned itself with that flow. At dawn and at dusk the cries of geese were so loud we had to cover our ears — our bodies trembled at the thrill of it and the force. Why were there so many there? The war, Emil explained. They were fleeing it the same way we were.

"Beautiful creatures," he said. He took his cap off and bowed as they settled. "But you know, miss. I think what geese like best is mud. Lots of warm mud. I wonder now . . ."

Lying there, possessor of a small corner of sky, sheltered by those reeds, I had the illusion of escape. To dwell there forever was my dream. I indulged it each day and at night it maintained me and at dawn I embraced it again.

But there was no question of staying. The oil had caught up with us again so that the river was shiny and unfit to drink. There was a fungus growing on the dead trees but we were afraid eating it would make us sick. We tried eating weeds but it only gave us enough strength to want more. Even the geese tormented us now. We made clumsy attempts to snare them, but they always flew away at the last moment and our hunger made them seem even more beautiful and noble than before.

No water, no food. And Emil was right about the mud. On the fourth night after Stepanoff's wife drowned the riverbank abruptly flattened and we entered the domain of an immense marsh. There was mud everywhere, deep as our waists. We detoured to the left to try and find solid footing, got lost on an island, nearly drowned in some quicksand, had our eyes blinded by midges, then — with all the detours and doubling backs — lost the sense of where the channel was. We groped our way on for hours but the mud only grew thicker, the vegetation more impenetrable and dense. At each step we let up bubbles of marsh gas. The smell was smothering and bad.

"The river's gone," Misha said bitterly. "There's nothing for it but the steppe."

Emil held our waists to steady us. "Misha's right. The river is gone here. But rivers come back."

We looked at him carefully.

"It's just this," he explained. "This marsh doesn't go on forever. The river is bending here, making an oxbow. If we can cut across the steppe to where the bend uncoils we'll be on the river again further downstream where the going is better. I'm not sure how far we've come now. But if we move a little each night eventually we must come to the sea. It stands to reason. We can hide in the dunes there. We can live on shellfish. We can wait the war out in the sand . . . If there are no Germans on the steppe."

He said this very softly. His next words were softer yet.

"Or we can try the marsh."

They looked to me for a decision. Off to our right I could see the terraced leveling where the steppe began. I remembered the truck I had seen last time. I remembered the lilac-colored plain past the forest and how it had terrified me. How it terrified me and how if you flinch before terror you are lost.

"The steppe," I whispered.

We started at once. As low as the bank was there, the sides were formed of clay that kept slipping away in our hands. Misha burrowed his head into it and grabbed onto some roots. We used his shoulder as a step and pulled him up in turn. At the top all was still. We waited to make sure no one was about, then started running. The soil was soft and yielding — a promenade compared to the mud. We made good time. It was frightening not to have the willows to shelter us, but we took some comfort from the darkness of the night. The moon was too weak to do anything but marble the blackness with thin white veins.

So closely had we become tied to the river that we

could sense where it lay and make for it instinctively like cattle. It was a kilometer ahead of us — a flesh-colored phosphorescence that rolled toward us like a cloud. I was in the rear following the others when Misha made a little coughing noise and abruptly stopped, his hands continuing forward and windmilling like someone on the edge of a cliff. Emil ran into him and went through the same gestures, making it seem as if they had chosen that ludicrous moment to resume their act. But when I joined them they weren't smiling. They were pointing at something long and sullen in the dirt.

It was a body — a man's body. It nestled in its own impression the way the corncobs had nestled in theirs. "Don't look," Emil said, but it was too late. The body was naked and swollen, the flesh peeled from the sun. Insects formed an X across a dark puckered indentation in the chest.

"Civilian," Emil said. "Shot in the heart, poor bastard." He bowed toward him the way he had bowed toward the geese.

We stepped around him and kept walking. Ten paces beyond was another body, this one with its hands lashed together. We stood staring down at it for the same minute of horrified sympathy, then stepped around it and kept walking. To its left was another body, this one with a burlap bag tied around its head, and we stepped around it more quickly. We stepped around a woman's body, then a child's body, then a man and another woman, until to avoid them we lost the thrust of our direction and became disoriented. "This way," Misha said, but when we followed him we came to the place where the bodies were piled thickest. We realized now that there weren't a scattered handful but hundreds — that the steppe resembled a graveyard that had been overturned by a giant spade. Each body shaped its own ridge of pinkish moonlight, some gentle and tapering, others bunched and abrupt. In between each body was a litter of shell casings. Shells, bodies, shells — then just bodies alone.

There was no telling how long they had lain there. There was no smell of decomposition, no sign of struggle. Each one was terrible to look at but after a while we stopped looking and became blind to them and only felt infuriated they should block our way. Misha tripped over a body and swore at it — Emil did the same. We saw now that they lay in concentric rings, the men on the outside, the women further in, the children toward the center, so that the mounds became smaller the further we went on. I was mad at them for blocking us from the river, still madder at their supine posture and ridiculous submission. On your feet! I wanted to scream. Show your courage! March! Maybe I did scream in the end, I don't remember. I didn't cry. We walked and there was no end to them so at last it didn't seem as if we were walking through space at all but through time — that these infinite moundlike things were the hollow digits of time's end.

"Can't go on," Misha grunted. "Can't go on. Can't go on." He said the words over and over, stepping across the bodies to their rhythm. "We'll turn," Emil said. We started retracing our way back through the women. We knew it was away from the river but we couldn't face the bodies anymore, not just the horror of them but the sheer physical ordeal of climbing across their flesh. Just as the horror had become wound so tight it had disappeared, it now unraveled again so that we had to back through all the jarring gradations that separate indifference from fear. When we came to the outermost body on the outermost ring dawn was starting to break in the east so that the last mound was gentler looking and more distinct. It was a man's body, face down so we could see the burnished creases on his neck, his light boyish hair, the rough homespun fabric of his vest. He lay alone with his hand stretched east as if he had grabbed for the sunrise in his death agony. The hand was splayed, tipped with dirt. I cried seeing his hand. Emil and Misha. We all cried. Our journey across the bodies had been to that.

The sun came against our faces like a hand turning them aside. To our left was the marsh with its mud. To our right were the bodies. We walked straight ahead toward the east because there was no other choice. There was no shade on the steppe, no trees, no shelter of any kind. Our only hope was to move quickly. Our only hope. I remember Misha used that phrase and we all nodded, though hope was already gone.

I suppose we walked an hour in all. It was hot and there was a purring sound off to our right. I was ahead of the others. The glare blinded me and at first I saw nothing.

"Ah well," Emil sighed.

I turned around. He was squatting down on his haunches the way a peasant squats. He smiled at me in resignation and lifted his arms. I couldn't understand that smile. I couldn't understand when I looked and saw Misha running in a circle there over the dirt — running furiously, his shirt flopping open, his small arms pumping up and down. Around and around he ran, churning up a cloud of dust that followed him like a yellow cyclone. And then I realized the dust wasn't from his running but from a motorcycle racing around him in circles, making him run for the sport of it . . . and that waiting patiently beyond in the trampled steppe grass, its turret swiveling the way a child's head swivels at the circus, was the square brown shape of a tank.

When Misha fell the swiveling stopped. Like we were children, the Germans came and took our hands.

But that's not the end. Where they took us, what happened then. It doesn't matter. The end is this, what I'm telling you now. Misha, Emil, and I. We were right to follow the river. We were right to leave it and then seek it again. We were right to speak of hope at the very moment it was gone — right to run across the steppe toward the illusion of safety. And beyond these things is something more, something I only discovered here in your arms sheltering me the way those reeds did so that I am safe. My life had been a journey long before I set out from Kiev and all along waiting there were those bodies stretched across time so there was no way around.

No way around. But this is where we were wrong. For the bodies do end. I know that now. Survival is a height and love is a higher one and from them I can see every dead soldier, every dead child, every dead Pole and Russian and Jew, every last pathetic victim of our century's puckered kiss, and as far as they extend it's not in endless circles but finite rings. They end and if we had found more courage within ourselves we could have gone through them and so gained the river once again. Somewhere in our tragic time the bodies end and we have to keep walking until they are past.

The bodies end.

Hold me.

PART FOUR

ACT FOUR

BACKSTAGE AT the Imperial Theatre the night of the dress rehearsal. A narrow metal cage with pulleys and levers. Above it, bunched velvet folds of the curtain. Copper wires strung up in haphazard fashion. Scenery flats tilted against a wheelbarrow. A small mahogany table with decanters of mineral water. A garden bench upside down. Everything is swollen by the darkness and distorted; the effect is of awkward cubes, crooked cylinders, misaligned planes.

To the left past the curtain a small portion of stage

is visible: boards polished blond by time; a cracked green
footlight. Occasionally the actors' legs come into view,
but this is all. Their feet make a tapping sound as they
move, and like all sounds from the stage, it comes magnified by its own echo.

By the cage paces Gerassim smoking the black stub
of a cigarette. He is dressed in costume — a simple blue
jersey not much different form the clothes he normally
wears. It's too small for him and he pulls constantly at
the sleeves.

When the cigarette is finished he tosses it aside
and stands listening to the voices on the stage. One is
Diskau's in his role of Constantine. The other, reciting
Madam Arcadina's lines, is mannered and unpleasantly
shrill.

DISKAU/CONSTANTINE: Please change my bandages,
Mother. You do it so well.

ARCADINA: It's almost healed up. There's hardly anything left there. Do you promise not to play at suicide
again while I'm away?

DISKAU/CONSTANTINE: I promise, Mother. That was
in a moment of despair when I had lost all self-control.
It won't happen again . . . These last few days I have
loved you just as tenderly and trustfully as when I was a
child. I have nobody left now but you. But why in God's
name do you submit to Trigorin's influence?

ARCADINA: You don't understand him, Constantine.
He has the noblest nature in the world.

DISKAU/CONSTANTINE: The noblest nature in the
world! Here you and I are almost quarreling about him
and where is he? In the garden laughing at us, improving
Nina's mind and trying to persuade her he's a genius.

ARCADINA: This is mere envy. Conceited people with no talent have no resource but to jeer at really talented people. It relieves their feelings no doubt.

DISKAU/CONSTANTINE: Really talented people! I am more talented than all of you put together if it comes to that. Here, I tear off these bandages! You apostles of the commonplace have taken the front seat in all the arts for yourselves and call nothing but what you do yourself legitimate and real; you persecute and stifle all the rest . . . The day of reckoning is coming. There will be chaos and blood, a great purging conflict from which art can be saved only by those who are persecuted and looked down upon now . . . I don't believe in any of you. I don't believe in you and I don't believe in him . . . If only you knew! I have lost everything. Nina doesn't love me and I cannot write anymore. All my hopes are lost.

During this, Kunin enters the backstage area from the right. Hesitates when he sees Gerassim, then continues on more slowly, making no effort to hide his frown. His face has been made up to look older for the role of Dr. Dorn; his hair is powdered gray and he wears a double-breasted suit of heavy serge. Stops near the cage and stands listening to the voices with Gerassim.

KUNIN: So he's found his Arcadina.

GERASSIM: Anna Repin. I knew her quite well . . . Once upon a time.

KUNIN: A whore off the street. And we were promised Chekhov's wife.

GERASSIM: If the fascists took Moscow.

KUNIN: Has Maria Pavlovna been here?

GERASSIM: Our mistress? *Laughs ironically.* I haven't had the privilege of serving her today.

KUNIN: I don't envy Diskau when she finds out. A whore for Arcadina and wholesale changes in her brother's lines.

GERASSIM: *stroking his leg.* Anna's a talented woman. In her own sphere.

Laughs again, then pulls over a stool and sits down. His self-assurance, his irony and lazy contempt — all these are evident in the way he slumps. Kunin moves the curtain aside to peek at the stage, then pulls it abruptly back again, muffling the voices.

GERASSIM: Ah, his sensibilities are outraged. His beloved theatre defiled by a woman of the town. But Anna's not that bad. A bit scratchy is all. I think it adds a badly needed touch of realism. All actresses are whores.

KUNIN: *sourly.* So you've become a critic then.

GERASSIM: I've been thinking, yes. About these characters in the play. It's interesting to speculate about what became of them afterward.

KUNIN: Afterward?

GERASSIM: In the Revolution. What's the landowner's name, the one Rashevitch plays? Sorin? Well, we know what happened to landowner scum. The schoolmaster Medvedenko, too. A bourgeois sentimentalist of the worst kind. It's only a question of whether they survived the first round of liquidations or lasted to the second . . . His wife, Masha, would have joined us; I admire her realism . . . Madama Arcadina? Here I admit there are possibilities. She was flexible and there was need for flexible people in those days. The ones who liked to dramatize themselves found the Revolution very tempting. I see her taking the lead in a patriotic film by Comrade Eisenstein and ratting on the younger actresses to keep her place . . . But I'm guessing here. With the writers I'm much more certain.

KUNIN: *in an attempt to sound bored.* Tell me then.

GERASSIM: Trigorin, the older one, would have written flattering odes to save his skin. A Trotskyite probably — we knew what to do with his kind of decadence. A bullet to the forehead like we settled Mandelshtam and the Jew liar Babel . . . Constantine would have survived much longer. That burning self-righteousness; with the right amount of pressure, it could have been turned to something useful. A man like that, all you do is wave the scent of interrogation before their nose . . . whisper the name Lubyanka softly in one ear . . . and they soil themselves in an effort to please. The intellectual ones always break first. They talk of art and poetry and things that make a decent man want to puke, then rat on each other worse than thieves . . . Constantine. I'll tell you about your Constantine. He ratted on Trigorin so he could have Nina and then he ratted on Nina and had her put away as well. He's hiding in a safe zone right now, the bastard. Some writers-union dacha with women and plenty to eat. He's there writing poems about spilled Russian blood, and when we finish with the fascists we'll finish with him.

KUNIN: It's easy to be contemptuous.

GERASSIM: And harder to act. *Stretches.* Well, we act, too. It's time you knew when.

KUNIN: We'll talk here?

GERASSIM: Why not? It suits me. *Cocks his head to the side.* To balance their prattle, our deeds. Or is it that you're having second thoughts about joining us?

KUNIN: *flustered.* No, of course not. I've been waiting for you to be more definite.

GERASSIM: You sound like Constantine.

KUNIN: I wouldn't rat on anyone . . . To use your phrase.

GERASSIM: *with an appraising frown.* No, I don't think you would . . . Do you know how to handle a pistol?

KUNIN: A rifle. I told you that.

GERASSIM: But a pistol. Be specific in your responses.

KUNIN: I can learn.

GERASSIM: It will have to be a pistol. Do you know that stretch of beach east of Yalta? We'll meet there Tuesday morning before dawn. I'll show you. All that's required is to hit a target three meters away.

KUNIN: I'm listening.

GERASSIM: I have hopes for you, Comrade Kunin. And to spare your indecision I'll put it as plainly as I can. A series of counterattacks are planned for this winter all along the front, from Moscow to the Don. We've managed to check the fascist invader, now it's time we threw him back. To coincide with the offensive, it's been decided to strike a blow in drowsy Yalta to show the fascist dogs that even here they are doomed. A series of assassinations will begin New Year's Eve. Our first will be so spectacular that all Yalta will be forced to notice.

KUNIN: *doubtfully.* The night of the performance?

GERASSIM: New Year's Eve — like I said.

KUNIN: The symbolism.

GERASSIM: You're learning.

KUNIN: Who?

GERASSIM: It's been decided that the first target should not be military. They protect their own. If we shoot a general, there would be reprisals and this is not something we desire at this time. No, our first target will come from the ranks of the fascist officials. *Smiles and points briefly toward the stage.* We shall begin with the elimination of our beloved Minister of Culture.

KUNIN: Diskau?

GERASSIM: To kill Rene Diskau will be to explode this farce of German sympathy once and for all.

Kunin stares at him in disbelief, then turns abruptly around.

KUNIN: It won't be easy.

GERASSIM: Are you backing out?

KUNIN: *angrily.* I only said it won't be easy. He's never alone.

GERASSIM: I'll take care of his lover. A bullet in the stomach so he remains alive to tell the others how horrible it was. You'll finish Diskau yourself in the head.

KUNIN: Assassination?

GERASSIM: Elimination. Elimination of him, elimination of his brotherly sham.

Kunin, in a daze, starts for the stage, then stops and turns around. Walks over until he stands only a few inches from Gerassim's face. Meets his stare without flinching. Speaks very slowly and distinctly, emphasizing each word.

KUNIN: I don't want it here in the theatre, understand?

GERASSIM: The setup is perfect. All these shadows.

KUNIN: Not here. The Germans will take out their vengeance on Maria Pavlovna. They'll burn down the theatre at the very least.

GERASSIM: *shrugging.* Very well . . . At his flat after the performance is over. He always returns through the Zarechye the same way. We'll be waiting for him the moment he walks in. No one will connect it to your beloved mistress. We'll arrange to have a boat left on the beach so they think we slipped into town from the sea . . . My men have their plans all made. They'll hide us afterward in the mountains, then smuggle us out to Turkey once the search is called off. And they won't search long — the Germans themselves hate his guts. In their eyes, he's a rich pansy with crazy ambitions. No, Comrade Kunin. There will be no reprisals for the death of Rene Diskau.

POTAPOV/TRIGORIN: *from the stage.* I have no will of my own. I never had will of my own. Weak-kneed, flabby and submissive; everything that women hate. Take me, carry me away, but never let me stir an inch from your side.

GERASSIM: *viciously.* Putrid shit.

KUNIN: I hear the others coming.

GERASSIM: They think it's something important and real and yet all you have to do is puff on it and it comes tumbling down.

Reaches into his pocket and takes out something metallic and stubby. Holding it to the light, he flicks it open — a knife.

GERASSIM: These wires control the lights. Here. *Throws knife to Kunin.* Cut that wire.

KUNIN: *bewildered.* For what purpose?

GERASSIM: Cut it!

Kunin hesitates, then shrugs. Reaches up for the closest wire, tugs it down, cuts it in half. Immediately, the light on the stage darkens.

POTAPOV: *from the stage.* Damn!

DISKAU: *further away.* It's a footlight. Someone fix it at once.

GERASSIM: *smiling*. Very good, Comrade Kunin. I had my doubts — until now. I think when Wednesday night comes you'll pull the trigger after all . . . and that will be the signal all Yalta awaits.

A confusion of voices is heard from the left. The first one to enter the backstage area is Tania in a shapeless black dress that blends into the curtain. Stands staring at the two men from the distance.

GERASSIM: *nodding toward her*. We'll have to compare notes sometime, Comrade. Tania's really quite good, almost Anna's equal . . . She goes about with the fascist officers, did she tell you that? To the cafes with them, then back to their quarters. It's astonishing the secrets they tell her. Germans instinctively trust her kind of cynicism . . . and her kind of tits.

Gets up from his stool, stretches lazily, then walks past Tania into the dark portion of the wings. A moment later Nina appears in a costume — a white dress with a girlish collar and puffed, lacy sleeves. Tania stares at her with an oddly frightened look, starts to say something, then turns and strides quickly off toward the stage.

KUNIN: You're here.

NINA: *spinning around like a ballerina*. You see? They've been fixing my costume. Now I am nineteen again thanks to Varka's skill.

Kunin walks over to her and takes her face tenderly in his hands.

KUNIN: You're so pale.

NINA: It's nothing. My nerves.

KUNIN: You've been pushing yourself too hard.

NINA: Varka's been nursing me. Have you seen her? She rehearses her two lines constantly. She couldn't bear the thought of my being on the stage without her being able to come out and help me . . . Is it time to start yet? I worried I might miss my cue.

KUNIN: Sit here on this stool. Let me feel your forehead.

NINA: *turning her head away.* It's fine. Listen . . . I've made up my mind beyond recall; the die is cast. I am going on the stage. Tomorrow I shall be gone from here; I am giving up everything and beginning a new life. I am going to where you are going . . . to Moscow. We shall meet there.

Kunin applauds, but it irritates her. Frowning, she gets off the stool and paces nervously back and forth.

NINA: I've acted wretchedly so far. I could see poor Potapov twisting this way and that trying to pry the words out of me. When they did come out they sounded wooden and false.

KUNIN: You're exaggerating. I was enthralled.

NINA: It's just so infuriating! I feel the role as I've never felt a role before and yet I still can't fit my body to it. My muscles seem detached from my brain and my nerves are scattered. I tell my eyes to close and it takes thirty seconds for the message to get there. They open and close of their own volition, like shutters flapping in the wind.

KUNIN: It's your weakness. Malnutrition slows the reflexes. It will pass when you gain back your strength.

NINA: Only four more nights before the performance . . . Tomorrow I shall be gone from here. I have made up my mind beyond recall . . . Is that better? I must get it right this time.

She says this looking past the curtain toward the stage. Crosses herself for luck in the old Russian fashion. When

Kunin comes up to her, she turns and embraces him desperately.

NINA: I'm frightened!

KUNIN: I'll be with you.

NINA: That's all I want. Just say that again and again and again.

KUNIN: I'll never leave you.

They hold each other with a tightness that cannot last. Nina puts her head on his shoulder and closes her eyes. From the stage comes Diskau's voice.

DISKAU: Louder, don't mumble! You're doing it deliberately to spite me and it won't be tolerated!

A shudder runs through Nina's body and she lets go. Kunin looks at her anxiously.

KUNIN: His voice alone terrifies you.

Nina shakes her head.

KUNIN: I need to know. It's painful and it's terrible of me to ask, but . . .

NINA: *biting her lip.* No.

KUNIN: But I need to, don't you see? I must know everything about him in order to understand.

Nina looks at him carefully, then finally nods.

NINA: He's the one who interrogated us. Misha first, then Emil, then me. He was very polite. Charming even. You know how he can be when he wants to. He didn't believe for a second we were partisans. He explained he had a certain quota to fill and was putting us down in that category just to be tidy . . . I only saw him twice after that. On the day he shot them he had one of his fits. It was before he shot them. He was furious — he screamed in German so I didn't understand. He was composed when he actually pulled the trigger. He had them put on their clown suits and I remember Misha's excitement because he thought they were being asked to do their act . . . Diskau sized them up to see which would suffer more from watching. He offered them a cigarette and saw which one let the other take it. He shot Misha, then he made Emil kneel down over his body . . . He put gloves on to shoot them. I remember the leather was the color of cream. When he finished, the muscles on his face began twitching and then on his neck and then the revolver went off again and he was standing there holding his arm.

She says this hoarsely, in little more than a whisper, but there is no emotion in her tone. Finishing, she looks at Kunin as if to ask if that were enough.

NINA: I know what you're thinking. How can I act with him after that. How can I be so inhuman.

KUNIN: Don't . . .

NINA: *whispering now.* He saved me from the SS after all.

KUNIN: And gave you to them in the first place.

NINA: *passionately.* But it's because I *am* inhuman, don't you see that? All my career I've acted badly because I've never been able to forget my hates and loves and my own personality. I was never ruthless enough before. I never had the key. Now I throttle myself and it's only Nina that survives and nothing else matters. Diskau approaches me at lunch and I have to restrain myself from plunging the bread knife in his chest, but step onstage and I see in him only a boy named Constantine who is in love with me and half out of his mind from jealousy . . . Everything in my life before this . . . all the humiliations and defeats and mind-numbing mediocrity . . . all the horror . . . all these were only a preparation for Wednesday night. I can feel it — can feel my life drawing to a point. Nothing Diskau's done can rob me of my triumph. I'd act with the devil if that's what it takes.

Doubles over and coughs — uncontrollably, her whole body bent in spasms. Kunin stands by watching helplessly. He reaches to take her arm but she breaks away.

NINA: Don't tell Maria Pavlovna. I beg you!

KUNIN: You're ill. You can't act in that state.

NINA: It's nothing. Here. You see? I'm standing straight as a guardsman . . . There's my cue. Come with me and be my strength.

KUNIN: *softly*. He won't hurt you again, I'll see to that. You can forgive, but not . . .

NINA: *not hearing*. Come.

Takes his hand and leads him toward the stage. As they disappear past the curtain they pass Potapov, Tania, and Rashevitch, who file offstage wearily, in single file.

POTAPOV: We're going on a break then. We won't be long.

The three of them stop near the table with the mineral water. Potapov is dressed in pin-striped trousers and a corduroy vest; his hair is dyed brown to make him look younger. He pours some water, but none of them drink. At first, they hardly seem aware of each other's presence.

POTAPOV: It's abnormal. To change lines like that without the author's approval. Unprecedented! . . . Rotten liberalism . . . Bourgeois falsifications . . . The bankruptcy of freedom . . . See how heavily they come off the tongue? Trigorin wouldn't say any of this and yet Diskau insists. He's added them in pencil to the script.

TANIA: She looks pretty in that dress. I want to hate her, yet I can't.

POTAPOV: Still, what if I refuse to say them? What good will that do anyone? Diskau will send me away somewhere cold and what good will that do anyone? You can't deny it, Tania. Men have been sent away for less.

TANIA: What difference does it make? He's changed my lines, too.

POTAPOV: And if Maria Pavlovna finds out? She's off trying to convince people to come Wednesday night, literally stopping them on the streets and begging, but when she finds out?

RASHEVITCH: There's something different in Yalta. I can't put my finger on it yet, but things have changed.

TANIA: Peter's found his love and flaunts her to make me suffer. He's blind to her faults. Her vanity and ambition would be monstrous except for weakness, which makes her quaint.

POTAPOV: If it bothers you so much, quit.

TANIA: *hugging herself.* If it were only that simple! Masha *is* me — Diskau was right about that. Spiteful, jealous, condemned to love someone who hardly notices my existence. Even my lines are perfect . . . I have a feeling as if I had been born ages and ages ago . . . I drag my life after me like the train of an endless dress . . . Masha, twenty-two years old, of no occupation, born into this world for no apparent purpose.

POTAPOV: *yawning.* Most convincing.

TANIA: Of course. It's me, as I told you. The night of the performance will be my wedding night, and when I recite Masha's lines I will become her . . . *Making her voice much lower; with an odd determination. . . .* and thus escape my fate, purge it, shed it off from me like a snake its hated skin.

POTAPOV: All this philosophizing.

TANIA: I'm Masha then, and yet with this absurd schoolgirlish crush on the Nina I ought to hate. It's not even her I admire — it's the shadow of what she's been through. *To Potapov, suddenly.* You're a pathetic man.

RASHEVITCH: For the longest time I thought the Germans were the real ones at last. The masters, the incarnation of power. And now . . . I wonder. Guards on all the avenues. Trucks leaving through the night. The casino empty of officers. Soldiers who are sullen and withdrawn. They're nervous, not like conquerers at all, but men who are trapped . . . What can it mean?

POTAPOV: Diskau's improving Chekhov? Forgive me, but Chekhov cannot be improved . . . This coming sanguinary chaos. I can't say it! . . . I suppose I could . . . This coming sanguinary chaos. This coming *sanguinary* chaos.

He's repeating the phrase to himself when Diskau strides backstage followed closely by Koenig. The latter is dressed in sloppy tweeds as the schoolmaster Medvedenko; the former is dressed as Constantine — very simply, in a white linen suit. His face is red with excitement; his body pulses with shocks of uncontrolled energy.

RASHEVITCH: *with a touch of surliness.* Good afternoon, Major.

Diskau ignores him. Goes over to the table, pours himself a glass of mineral water, then spits it out in disgust.

POTAPOV: I congratulate you on your new Madam Arcadina. She has tremendous, ah, potential. Tremendous potential.

DISKAU: Thank you. *Pauses.* Do you mean that ironically?

POTAPOV: I feel there are rough edges, but nothing I can't help her with in the three days we have left.

DISKAU: The roughness is part of my overall conception. We need her vigor, her fresh . . . *Sees his words are having no effect; furiously.* You will not meddle with her, understand? She's a better actress than any of you and I won't have her slandered!

POTAPOV: *confused.* I just . . .

DISKAU: *beside himself.* I won't take any more of your criticism! You've been sniping at me ever since rehearsals began. Making fun of me when my back was turned, trying to upstage me, ignoring my suggestions. I'll fire the lot of you and start over again with real actors. Real actors, do you hear me! . . . Back to your places! Back at once!

So abrupt is this outburst the others don't know how to react. They look at him with fear, but with a curious sympathy, too, and it's only when Koenig motions with his hand that they exit toward the stage. Koenig remains behind with Diskau, who slumps on the stool, his head in his hands.

KOENIG: They're Philistines. Don't let them annoy you.

DISKAU: My pills? Do you have them?

KOENIG: *mischievously.* Your candy? No, it's all back at the flat. Now is not the time for sweets.

DISKAU: I need them.

KOENIG: It's as I explained. The situation has changed. It's time we changed with it.

DISKAU: *in a voice little more than a whisper.* Nothing's changed.

KOENIG: The offensive is stalled outside Moscow. Leningrad is surrounded but shows no sign of giving in. This week along the front the cold reached a temperature of thirty-five degrees below zero . . . The Russians don't retreat anymore, but keep probing our lines in ever stronger patrols . . . There is already talk of evacuating the Crimea. We must adapt ourselves to the new situation before it's too late.

DISKAU: Meaning?

KOENIG: The Russian can't be won over by sympathy, only by the lash. This is obvious to everyone now. The plan of offering ourselves as liberators is no longer applicable.

DISKAU: *as if he hasn't heard.* Anna is not that bad an actress. She will stumble and act confused but no one will notice. Arcadina is supposed to overact. Besides, our audience will know nothing of drama. Brilliance would be lost on them.

KOENIG: The strategy of reconciliation has to be repudiated or we can expect to suffer the consequences. The Wehrmacht won't look with pleasure on anyone claiming to be the Russian's friend . . . My plan is this. Go to the SS. Tell them a plot has been uncovered — you don't have to say about what. Name everyone here. Potapov, Kunin, Chekhov's sister. Have them arrested. It's the only way to salvage any credit.

DISKAU: Don't talk nonsense.

KOENIG: I have the papers all drawn up. All that's required is your signature and the arrests can begin.

Diskau gets up from the stool. For a moment, he seems his old self. His gestures are broad and theatrical; his movements graceful, those of a dancer, so that he prances upon each word.

DISKAU: Wednesday night they will all be there. They will all be there, Hans. Field Marshal Manstein with his ribbons there in front. His staff on the side smiling when he does, frowning when he does, farting when he does — can't you see them? Behind him on the aisle, General Von Kloster with his ridiculous stomach. Dietrich Englehart from the Foreign Ministry. Dorborg with his mistress. Behrens and Tienappel sitting slumped in the back. The lights will shine off their medals and blind our eyes. They won't understand a word of Russian, yet they will smile and applaud just the same. And do you know why, Hans? It's because what they fear most, the chaos of words, will be ordered and tamed. They will see what we've created here. They will see what can be accomplished by a man who understands the Russian heart. They will remember the name Rene Diskau when victory is complete.

KOENIG: *his voice rising to falsetto.* Arrest them. Sign the papers. I will fetch your candy for being such a good boy. All this will seem like a dream . . . Yes, I see them, too. Von Kloster with his ridiculous stomach. Dorborg with his mistress . . . Shh. Close your eyes.

Diskau closes his eyes. Koenig stands behind him and gently strokes his forehead.

KOENIG: I can feel you softening. There, let me smooth this one line.

DISKAU: *plaintively*. Why would you have me arrest them? They're innocent. I've grown fond of them.

KOENIG: For the two of us. For our future. I tell you times have changed.

Continues stroking him, then suddenly brings his hands away as if burned. Diskau's eyes remain closed.

DISKAU: Don't stop.

KOENIG: *stepping back; in a loud, formal voice*. Good evening, Madam Chekhova . . . *To Diskau, in a whisper.* The dried-up bitch. Arrest her! Arrest them all, do you hear!

Maria Pavlovna steps out from the corner where the curtain is tightly bunched. She's dressed in a heavy sable coat that makes her look tinier and frailer than usual; the fur's rich darkness brings out the intensity in her eyes. She crosses directly to the cage and pushes up the largest of the two levers. Immediately, the backstage area is flooded in blinding white light.

MARIA: Tell him to leave.

DISKAU: Leave.

KOENIG: I hardly think . . .

DISKAU: Leave.

Koenig smiles. Makes a mocking bow in Maria Pavlovna's direction, then exits in a mincing strut that flaunts his effeminacy.

DISKAU: It's good to see you, Madam Chekhova. You're looking radiant.

MARIA: Spare me your flattery.

DISKAU: We were concerned about you. No one could say where you had gone off to. We were counting on your presence at the dress rehearsal.

MARIA: There are no posters up in town. Tickets

have not been distributed. You intend to perform my brother's play in secret like something shameful.

DISKAU: Posters were prepared as you know. I myself supervised their design. But certain unforeseen contingencies have made it necessary to postpone their placement and . . .

MARIA: I am an old woman, Major Diskau. I have no time for prevarication.

DISKAU: . . . and modify our plans. It has been decided that in light of the number of German officers to be in attendance the local population will not be admitted to this first performance. There are security concerns, naturally. Later, if conditions permit, we may reconsider this and have further performances for the Russian inhabitants alone.

MARIA: So we're to be performing animals.

DISKAU: Hardly performing animals.

MARIA: I have saved some of the posters. Varka and I have spent the afternoon placing them in prominent positions throughout Yalta.

DISKAU: *smiling.* If you permit me. With the military situation as it is, it will take a brave person to risk being seen reading them.

MARIA: Then only brave people will come.

She takes a step toward the stage and listens.

DISKAU: It's our new Arcadina.

MARIA: What you don't know, Major, is that I made it to the dress rehearsal after all. I was sitting in the stalls where I missed nothing.

DISKAU: *nervously.* And?

Maria Pavlovna doesn't answer, but turns and stares

at him in contempt. Diskau acts oddly relieved at this; his body, so rigid before, relaxes into a slump.

DISKAU: You're right, of course. Anna's no actress, poor thing. I held out the prospect of a bright new dress and introductions to staff officers and she couldn't refuse . . . I really did think we could bring Olga Knipper here. We almost had her. One more push and Moscow would have fallen and I would have gone there in person and persuaded her to come.

MARIA: And so you bring a whore in her place.

DISKAU: *taking a deep breath.* Because of this, because of other considerations I can't go into, I feel it would be best if *The Seagull* were temporarily postponed.

MARIA: Postponed?

DISKAU: Until the military situation is clarified.

Maria Pavlovna brings her hands to her head, then her heart, then swings them frantically back and forth; it's as if she doesn't know where to put them and is furious at this and not Diskau's words.

MARIA: I will not let you fail.

DISKAU: Pardon?

MARIA: *shouting.* How dare you! How dare you talk of postponement! I will not hear of it. I have put up with German flattery and German lies and German contempt for all my brother stood for, but I will not put up with that. The play goes on as scheduled New Year's Eve.

Diskau starts to say something, but she continues shouting.

MARIA: I refuse to accept your failure! Here, look. You are one of my fingers and I won't let you fail. Do you understand that? From this moment on, you have no significance whatsoever except as a tool. I have not worked as hard as I have in order for a coward to run in terror at the last moment. The performance goes on.

DISKAU: *with the hint of a sneer.* But you told me to get rid of Anna. Without an Arcadina, there can be no play.

MARIA: Then I will take the role myself.

DISKAU: *incredulous.* You?

MARIA: *in a sugary voice.* I would like you to write my brother's biography, Major Diskau. You are the only one who understands the deep recesses of his soul . . . There on the wall is Goethe, my brother's inspiration, he loved Germany so . . . I can't act then? I can't play a role? I will play all the roles if that's what it takes. *The Seagull* will be performed Wednesday night on schedule and nothing you can do will change that fact.

DISKAU: Ah, the final consummation. The sister becomes her brother's character before an audience of true believers. The prospect must be very gratifying. However, to those of us with official responsibilities . . .

MARIA: *ignoring him.* You will have no contact with any member of the cast until the night of the performance. You will say my brother's lines exactly as they are written. You will not disturb those posters that are in place. You will allow civilians to come. On Wednesday night you will arrive here two hours before the performance begins and then come directly to me for your instructions.

DISKAU: I am not a child.

MARIA: You are not a child, Major Diskau. For the next three days you are the thumb of my right hand. After that . . . *Snaps her fingers* . . . You are nothing.

Diskau straightens to attention with an exaggerated click of the heels. Salutes.

MARIA: *disgusted.* Away from me.

DISKAU: What I have refrained from mentioning is this. Rumors have reached me of a plot involving members of this cast. I cannot say more at this time, but there are reasons for postponement far more serious than any I have mentioned.

MARIA: Nothing.

· Exits slowly right. Diskau hesitates, then hurries after her.

DISKAU: I'm trying, can't you see that? Do you know how impossible it's been?

After they leave there are several minutes of silence. Then, from the stage and very faint, the actors' voices.

NINA: I am going to where you are going . . . to Moscow. We shall meet there.

POTAPOV/TRIGORIN: How beautiful you are! I shall see these lovely eyes once more, this expression of angelic purity . . . My darling!

Curtain.

KUNIN

A WOMAN NAMED Clavdia came in the evening to prepare their dinner. She was a Georgian, stout and crafty, but with enough beauty left between the creases to show how she had managed to attract three husbands in her prime. Her life now was mainly vicarious; she was the authority on all the scandals in the building and would unpack them, as it were, with the groceries, so that the latest doings of so-and-so on floor such-and-such would come with the sound of cans being slapped down on the counter as punctuation. This was bad enough with the adulteries and petty thieveries, but certain stories made her so furious that the cans, held sideways, would all be smashed.

"Can you imagine the disrespect? Young Dymov, the oaf. He pushed his way to the head of the queue as if he were Comrade Brezhnev himself. And this while there were heroes of the Patriotic War waiting patiently for bread. Their ignorance! They think the world was created the day they were hatched. It makes your blood shrivel!"

And she shuddered at this, as if her blood had indeed shriveled at the thought her generation's dead were being so quickly forgotten.

Once dinner was over and she had left, there was an hour, perhaps two, until his sister went to bed and he could have the radio to himself. He used this time to read — mainly history books now, and not just Soviet ones but editions his friends would send him from abroad. It was illegal, but the censors were too lazy to open them. Even if they had, the books were all about the war. The censors, young men in their twenties, wouldn't have found anything subversive in events so remote.

When he first retired, his ambition had been to read every word ever written on the years 1941–45, as if by doing so he could find a clue toward solving the puzzle in his heart. He had started with the official Soviet histories. Massive, exhaustively detailed, they were scrupulous in explaining what, but useless in explaining why. The American versions were rather better on why, but much weaker on what; they came from a culture whose face hadn't been wiped in blood. Both versions made the mistake of confusing effect, which is obvious, with cause, which is obscure. The disintegration of Capitalism; the legacy of Versailles; appeasement at Munich. All sounded very plausible, but not by the only measure that counted for him now: they had nothing to do with what he had seen.

If he still read them, still begged his friends in Britain to send him the latest volumes as they came out, it was only because he needed periodic strengthening of his conviction that the historical approach was all wrong — that history had lost itself in the brutal maze of the century. As learned and sincere as historians were, too many looked for truth where it couldn't be found: in great events; in the lies and falsehoods of great men. To make truth from this kind of raw material was clearly impossible. At best, all it could hope for was the truth of the daily newspaper on a larger scale; the truth, that is, that combines trivial facts with inflated language to form a malleable nothing that could mean anything anyone wanted it to mean. And so too with television and films. They couldn't add verisimilitude to the historical record — far from it. If it was easy to lie in print, it was even easier to lie with film, where the falsehoods were injected directly into the recipient and not filtered out by a screen of thought.

The historians were wrong on another level, too. They assumed the war was over — that certain years could be sealed off and packaged and stored away up on the shelves. But the war wasn't over. The rot had settled too deep. In France was a school of historians who claimed the extermination camps were a myth. In Cambodia, extermination camps had been reinvented. In Germany, an American president placed a wreath on SS graves. In Poland, survivors of Auschwitz were spat at in the streets.

In Africa, a leader modeled himself on Hitler and employed former Nazis as advisers to his troops. In Argentina, police torturers wore swastikas on their uniforms and mocked their victims with stiff-armed salutes. In Israel, weapons were made for the fascists in Johannesburg. In Japan, scholars rewrote textbooks to show the war was only an aberration and no one was to blame.

The butcher's bill was too high and mankind hadn't finished paying. Only the power of words could settle the evil dust raised by those years, but here as the Twentieth Century came to an end, words themselves were under assault, from a dozen different directions, so that it wouldn't take a Homer or Thucydides to pronounce the war's epitaph, but someone whose imagination was a thousand times braver — some great heart who found the courage to wrench back the language from the politicians and the dictators and the propagandists and so find the balm to assuage all the pain.

The beauty that comes between hearts. The bravery that sees truth square without taking comfort in lies. The perpetual endurance of the solitary and poor. History knew everything, but it didn't know these. It had taken him ten years of hard reading to reach a conclusion he had known all along: that truth lay in the individual and not en masse; that every word of every formal history ever written was at some fundamental level false.

"There is no war," Maria Pavlovna would say. "There is only art."

He had smiled at the time, more at the obvious satisfaction she took in making such sweeping assertions than at anything else. But now that he was nearing seventy himself, he realized that a weakness for sweeping assertions was one of the chief characteristics of old age. The points you cared to make became fewer the older you grew, but they were held with more intensity, so that you were constantly faced with the temptation to deepen your voice and make everything a pronouncement.

"Stalin?" Maria Pavlovna said whenever the name was mentioned. "To me it sounds like a railroad station where the flies cover the buffet. To talk of Stalins is to give up on life."

He had smiled at her for that, too, but he realized now he himself had been the naive one. For since that time he had witnessed history in person, or at least a corner of it — history complete with its great men. Three of them to be exact: Churchill, Roosevelt, and Stalin as they posed for photographs outside the Livadia Palace of the Tsars at the conclusion of their meeting in the liberated Yalta of 1945. There were five lines of troops stationed around the square to protect them, another line of mounted police around that, but thanks to an official he knew, he had found a spot close to the front where he could peek through the forest of helmets and see.

He hadn't seen much. A glimpse of Churchill's pink skin. Roosevelt palsied and frail, his pant legs stretched tight by invisible steel. Stalin's white uniform, with a dab of grease below the collar the shape of a mushroom. (In later years the three images would combine until he pictured everything in the history books against a hallucinatory backdrop of pink greasy steel.) As hard as he stared at them, as hard as he tried to understand, it was impossible to find any link between their appearance and the suffering the world had just been through.

At first this angered him; he wanted to shout "Old

287

men!" at the top of his lungs. But gradually, as they arranged their flabby faces into the wary smiles history would
record, he began to feel only pity — pity that such harm-
less-looking gentlemen should be made to stand outside
on a day without shade.

Mummies — it was the best description he could find.
Perhaps like Napoleon and Alexander I, they would come
to life someday in the work of a Tolstoy or Stendhal, but
judging by the type of men who trailed after them, there
were no Lev Nikolayevichs present in that square. Courtiers, flunkies, they had the bland expressionless faces of
the men whose turn was now coming: the think-alikes,
the interchangeables, the men without allegiance, thought,
or spirit. Yes-men, bureaucrats, timeservers — a vile
enough term had not been invented.

"Our Joseph dwarfs them all, eh Comrade Kunin?"

The official who had gotten him his privileged spot
poked him in the ribs. This was none other than Pavel
Rashevitch himself. His star was in the ascendant again.
While the secret police were busily executing all the officials who had been involved in the German occupation,
Rashevitch had saved himself by a self-abnegation so ab-
ject that it made his previous self-abnegation seem like
bombast in comparison. Having confessed to being a Brit-
ish spy, confessed to entering a correspondence with
General Montgomery, confessed to writing messages in
chalk on top of the Yaila cliffs, he was now busy drawing
up detailed lists of his confederates. As a reward, there
was a place waiting for him in KGB counterespionage —
or at least so he claimed. He spent an hour in the morning over his shaving now, trying to make his face as smooth
and lifeless as the courtiers he envied.

"Look, here he comes!" he whispered, tugging Kunin's arm. He was beside himself with awe, and wiggled back and forth as though clearing the space necessary to prostrate himself in worship.

Stalin, in crossing to a black limousine, passed within fifty meters of where they stood. Kunin couldn't help thinking how easy it would be to shoot him if he'd had a gun. His neck above the mushroom would have been the spot to aim for; if nerves made the bullet go high, there would still be the head to interrupt it.

The thought of this caused Kunin to laugh out loud, so that Rashevitch looked up at him in alarm.

"What is it, Comrade? Please lower your voice!"

He hadn't bothered trying to explain, though the joke was funny enough. All the events of the war, everything that had happened, the virtual destruction of Yalta by the fleeing Germans, the intensity with which he had lived the last four years, the love he had buried, and its end result was this: to make him an assassin who thought strictly in terms of trajectory and range.

He wasn't proud to remember this. But then, that was his sweeping conclusion, the one he was fond of making whenever his sister stirred from her own reading to ask if he were enjoying his book.

"History," he said, slamming it down on the end table like Clavdia her cans, "is nothing else than the worst examples."

THE TUESDAY morning Kunin learned to fire a pistol was one of those winter days by which Yalta's reputation had been made. What clouds there were seemed mild and inoffensive — little white puffs that drifted in from the ocean to look things over, then blew like petals away. The southerly breeze was scarcely noticeable, and it came warmed by the fragrance of almond and lemon. It was a heavy, lazy smell in summer, but now, in the sparkling December sunlight, it seemed more diffuse, more invigorating. Kunin, hurrying past it, felt like someone going to a picnic.

He kept to the grassy terrace that paralleled the road east from town, detouring inland to get around the one bored guard the Germans had bothered posting, then swinging back toward shore when the terrace became limestone and broke apart into cliffs. Where the coastline began curving toward the south was a small cove. Cypress grew in a fringe around the top; at the bottom was a narrow, self-contained crescent of white sand. To someone who didn't know the way, the cliff was jumbled and featureless, but just below the lip was a rough smuggler's path that switchbacked its way to the beach.

Kunin let himself down as carefully as he could, but his foot gave him trouble and he frequently stumbled. The ocean looked calm from above, deceivingly so. The swells rushed into the cove with tremendous force, gathering themselves into a huge paw as the cliff walls narrowed, rising up for momentum, then — after the briefest of hesitations — pouncing gleefully on the sand in a heavy thud.

When he reached the beach he called Gerassim's name, but there was no answer. The sand on that side of the cove was littered with fishing floats the current had carried in from Turkey — the yellow glass was dimpled and rough. He was bending down to examine one more closely when there was a clicking noise and the press of something cold at the base of his neck.

"One step forward and slowly turn around."

When Kunin turned it was to see Gerassim pointing a pistol at arm's length toward his face. Only gradually did he bring it down. His expression was as blank and cold as the gun.

"Not a sound," he whispered.

He stepped past Kunin and squinted up toward the cliff.

"Did anyone follow you?"

"No."

"The facist sentry?"

"Sleeping."

Gerassim put his hand on Kunin's chest and shoved him back toward the rocks where they were out of sight. They waited there for what seemed a long time — long enough for the tide to come in and wash away their footprints. When no one else appeared down the path, Gerassim finally began to relax.

"You're late," he said. "We were to meet at dawn."

"I had to be careful. Varka is up before that. She would have thought it suspicious."

Gerassim nodded. He seemed smaller than he did indoors, but quicker, so that his movements were ferret-like and swift. He was dressed in black canvas trousers and a tattered sweater that reeked of olives. His eyes, usually so heavy, darted about like Diskau's when he was drugged.

He leaned forward and stuck his hand between the rocks. It closed around something, came back out, and uncoiled with the twisting flourish a magician gives in finishing his act.

In his hand was a pistol, small and blue — the twin to the one he had pointed at Kunin's face. He blew on it to get the sand off, held it up so the sun caught the metal and brightened it, then fit the grip carefully to Kunin's hand.

"Italian-made," he said. "There aren't four in the entire country. The fascist doctors will scratch their heads when they dig the bullet out."

He pushed himself to his feet, then held his hand out to boost Kunin up. Past the rocks was a small dune where the sand had been dampened tight by spray. Gerassim squatted down and shaped something in its middle like a boy making castles.

"There," he said, patting it.

It was a sculpture — a sculpted man's head. He gouged his fingers into the middle for eyes, poked out a mouth, then stepped back to admire his handiwork.

"Not a bad likeness, eh Comrade? Notice the slope of the forehead. I've always noticed that in our friend Diskau. His brow offers itself to the world like a target . . . Here, like this."

He loaded Kunin's pistol, then took the bullets out and made Kunin do it himself. When the time came to shoot, Kunin started walking toward the rocks to get some distance, but Gerassim ordered him back.

"It's vanity to go farther. You'll either kill him close or you won't kill him. And don't think about aiming. You intellectuals think too much as it is. Hate your target, then point your hand toward your hate. The pistol knows what to do."

Kunin fired off five rounds. The first three went high, but the next two struck home, scattering apart the sand in matching whirlwinds.

"Good!" Gerassim shouted. "Again!"

At each shot, Kunin braced himself for the sound, half-expecting it would bring a squad of Germans racing to the cliff. But there was no sound — nothing except the vague tingling jar of the recoil up his arm. The rock and sand absorbed the report like layers of felt.

After each series Gerassim reshaped the head, then had Kunin fire from closer range; by the third, he was pressing the gun barrel directly against the sand. He tried to imagine Diskau's face as he squeezed the trigger, but it was impossible. It was as if he had moved so close his features had blurred into a generalized grainy evil it was his duty to blast apart.

"Good! Again!"

He fired twenty times in all. Each new shot released a small amount of his adrenaline, yet the overall amount kept building until he felt a giddy bursting sensation that left him dizzy.

"That's enough for now," Gerassim said, kicking the sand. "You're a marksman — I'm very impressed. Our poor friend Diskau is turned into gruel."

He led the way to a small indentation in the cliff where he had stored some bread and a flask of wine. Kunin thought again of a picnic, but by now the sun had gotten caught up in the clouds and it was colder. While they ate, Gerassim busied himself cleaning his pistol. He talked about the advantages and disadvantages of aiming for the neck, but said nothing of the logistics of the assassination or the timing. When Kunin brought the subject up, he only shrugged.

"Scared for your skin, are you? Our comrades will get us off. By this time Thursday you'll be puking your guts out in the bottom of a boat bound for Turkey."

Finishing his gun, he took Kunin's and quickly had it apart. He wiped each piece with an oiled cloth he took from his rucksack, then held it up to the light to make sure he hadn't missed any spots. It was impossible to exaggerate the pains he took over this. For the first time since Kunin had known him, he actually looked like a servant — a servant devotedly polishing the family silver.

It was this hint of softness beneath the cynicism — if only a softness for automatic weapons — that made Kunin say what he said next.

"You knew there would be no echo when we fired the gun. You knew about this cave. You knew the tide would be out so we would have the beach."

He didn't seem to hear.

"Do you come from around here?" Kunin asked.

Gerassim fit the trigger guard back into the grip, snapped it to make sure it was the proper tension, and only then looked up.

"Tell me, this, Comrade Kunin. Your crippled leg. Does it hamper you in fucking?"

Kunin felt the muscles tighten in his face, but he kept his temper. Gerassim coughed up spite the way sick people coughed up phlegm, and there was no getting to the inner man until a certain quantity was passed.

"Even so," Kunin said quietly. "I wondered."

Gerassim looked at him, then shrugged. "There to

the right of the cliff. Walk inland a hundred meters, you come to a grove of cypress bent like witches. In the middle is a pile of boards. Those on top are black and slick from sheep dung. The middle ones have spiders. The bottom ones, the ones the rains haven't rotted, still have traces of paint."

It was the start of a story, but he didn't finish it, not immediately. Instead, he leaned slightly to one side and spread his arms apart with a curious yearning gesture, as if to embrace the bright crescent of beach on which they sat.

"I'd come here alone just to get away. The birds kept me company. I learned to shoot with a rusty muzzle-loader I stole from my uncle. I shot the birds in the end. I'd yell to warn them first, then pick them off as they circled back . . . I went there before meeting you. There are rusted cans scattered about, pieces of glass. My father thought it would be romantic to have a house overlooking the ocean."

"You lived up there?"

"He was a schoolteacher. He wanted to initiate the peasants into the joys of self-sufficiency. A generation removed from serfdom himself and already he could sentimentalize them and call them his flock . . . And do you know what else my honorable father did for his romantic amusement? He wrote poems. Wretched poems. He thought of himself as a poet. The sole support of a wife and four sons, and he wrote poems and made them live in a shack with no heat and never managed to understand why the peasants detested him."

He nodded to himself and glanced down at his hands. "My honorable father," he mumbled. "They couldn't protect his family. His wretched poems couldn't bring them bread or warmth or medicine. When the counter-revolutionists came, my mother died and then my brothers. Disease, starvation — call it what you like . . . His friends were painters and composers. Yalta nonentities who thought themselves the equal of Tolstoy and Tchaikovsky and wondered why no one agreed. They couldn't protect us either when I went to beg. When drink finished him off, none of them bothered attending his funeral. I buried him in the cypress and when I finished I pissed on his grave to oil his way straight to hell."

He spat toward the sand, then tilted his head toward Kunin's with a sly expression. "Am I boring you, Comrade Peter?"

"No."

"Because there's more. For the longest time I thought an unsuccessful poet was the most contemptible thing in the world, but then I discovered that far more contemptible and wretched was a successful poet, someone who actually had managed to get his drivel published. They were there in Moscow when I moved there to study engineering. Artists who flirted with revolution and inspired us with patriotic odes while they sat in the cafes swilling vodka with their whores. They were more sensitive as to rank and reputation than the worst Romanov scum, and if you were a Tartar or even a Georgian they'd look down their noses at you and sneer in disgust."

While he was talking a gull wheeled in from the ocean, then a second, then an entire flock, so that his last words were formed of the same tight shrillness as the birds' call. He looked up at them angrily — he raised his pistol as if to fire, then thought better of it and smiled.

"Looking for corpses. I admire gulls. They learn fast in war."

He pushed himself to his feet, brushed the sand off his trousers, then took a step toward the inrushing tide.

"Once the fascists are defeated the poets will be of use . . . for an interim period. They will bury the dead beneath pompous odes and so help us forget all the more quickly and get on to rebuilding the state. My honorable father starved because no one would publish his poems, but we will publish everyone's poems. They'll be given jobs teaching harmless things in university, but in return they will work for us just as surely as an ironworker or a tractor driver . . . Not right away. Perhaps not for fifty years or a century, but someday not far off we'll start phasing them out. There will be no further need for their ornamentation. We will make them geldings first, then eliminate them entirely. They'll go without a fight, too. They'll summon up the energy to mewk out some self-pity toward the end, but by then no one will be listening. In the meantime, we won't let them write lies about us or hinder us. We won't permit the untalented ones the comfort of illusions. We will make them admit their impotence and dig their own graves and when they've done all that they'll be gone. In a hundred years, maybe sooner, they'll all be gone.

"Taste the air?" he said, sniffing. "That metallic sweetness? It's building on now to storm."

He took the pistol from the oiled cloth and rammed home a fresh clip. As before, he squatted down to fashion something in the sand. It wasn't a head this time, but something rectangular and large.

"A mural!" he shouted. "A mural painted by one of our illustrious heroes of art!"

He spun and fired from the hip. A spurt of sand fell out from the corner. He fired again and the whole edge jumped away. He fired three times with his own pistol, his hand burping spasmodically, then fired off a clip from Kunin's until the rectangle was trimmed into a square half its original size.

"A painting now!" he yelled.

He fired again and again until the sand exploded so fast there was a cloud streaming back from it and it seemed liquid. "A book now!" he yelled, and then when that was blasted away and there was nothing left but the merest bubble, he took careful aim, the pistol held in both hands, and shouted again.

"A poem!"

And with that the bubble fell away, just disappeared, with no report, no muzzle flash, no echo, making it seem as if all Gerassim had to do to erase it was will the energy from his hands. He nodded to himself in satisfaction, then stooped down to collect the spent bullet casings that lay like cigarette butts around his feet.

"Wait ten minutes before you leave!" he shouted. "Tomorrow night at the theatre. You'll receive your instructions then."

He walked across the sand toward the cliff. Halfway there, he stopped and looked back.

"It's a steep climb. You'll need some help. Here, come with me — I'll give you a hand up."

"I can manage."

Too late, he realized how much it had cost Gerassim

to make the offer. He scowled at him in unmistakable hatred, turned, and continued on toward the path. In five minutes, maybe less, he was lost in the mica flash toward the top.

Kunin counted off the time before he could leave. When ten minutes were up, he remained where he was — his hands under his head, his legs stretched flat across the sand. The amphitheatre's air was so self-contained the strengthening breeze couldn't dent it, and the temperature was still relatively balmy — balmy enough that he soon fell asleep.

When he woke it was to the tide playing with the laces of his boots. It was coming in slowly, probing its way up the shingle, and it seemed like hours between the first gentle tugging sensation and the impact of wetness against his skin. For a time he was able to remain there with his eyes closed, imagining Nina was lying there next to him. So real was this dream — so intensely did he wish it — that it seemed when he opened his eyes that the damp sand had molded itself to the contours of her body and taken on the soft fragrance of her hair.

She wasn't there. He sat up quickly, with a sudden burst of bitterness that came against his stomach like a fist. He pushed himself to his feet, started toward the path, then changed his mind and came back again. Before leaving, it was important to try to understand — to arm himself not only with a pistol but with something approximating the truth. He limped along the highest ripple of sand, detouring to his right when the tide surged in, dropping back again toward the ocean when it ebbed back out. He had the feeling the truth was right there above his head somewhere, but maddeningly vague, and he kept swinging his arms out and clapping his hands together as if to trap it like an irritating fly.

Some things were obvious at least. All along he had thought that by letting himself get caught up in Nina's fate he would be swept along with her until all his doubts and hesitations vanished. She was like a meteor he was clinging to as it shot across the sky. For a while he had been able to go with her — holding her, he felt borne away toward a new universe of splendor — but the speed was becoming too much for him, the ride too dizzying, and the emotion he felt now was the bitterness antecedent to letting go.

His fate — his gravity — was stronger than hers and couldn't be escaped. He saw that fate just as clearly as if it were a huge tranquil planet that had risen there above the sea, consisting not only of his ordinariness, but the ordinariness of millions like him, so that he was pinned in solidarity to the mass of it while Nina circled in brilliance high above. He couldn't devote himself to one intense thing and burn with it like she could. He couldn't forgive his hurt and build from it — could neither forget nor forgive his way toward freedom. He was the kind of man who would lead a productive but solitary life, respected by many, loved by few. He was the kind of man whose advice and sympathy would help others to their martyrdom without partaking of any of its glories himself. He was the kind of man who would study life with an artist's distance and perspective without being an artist. He was the kind of man who would write epitaphs in his head without being able to deliver them — the kind of man, that is, who would spend an entire lifetime mourning the love of a few seconds.

He had once loved a Nina. It was the only obituary he would ever need.

But as bitter as this understanding was, it was matched by an odd sense of release that made him walk faster the further along the beach he went. His fate was there waiting for him, but not until after Wednesday night. In the thirty-some hours in between anything might happen. Anything might happen yet! In the foreshortening of war, thirty hours was enough for an entire life. It was as if his youth had been compressed into a layer of incredible density and richness by the weight of time, and from the core of it he felt a surge of energy and passion little different from the one he had experienced when he first took Nina in his arms. Anything might happen. For the next thirty hours he was the freest of men.

And what was odd, besides all these other emotions his heart still had room for one more, one that contrasted so ludicrously with his sadness it was all he could do not to laugh out loud. The way his head spun when he tried to remember Dr. Dorn's lines, the butterflies in his stomach when he thought of acting before an audience, the dramatic challenge of the final act. To go with his real fear, he had a bad case of stage fright, as if everything in his life had come down to the difficulty of posing, posing correctly and with grace.

His pacing had carried him to a jetty formed by boulders fallen from the cliff. The western curve of the crescent, it separated the amphitheatre from the unbroken wall of rock leading back toward Yalta. The incoming tide had most of it awash — there was a rattling, hissing noise as the foam gathered and tossed the smaller pebbles like so many dice. He stood there at the edge of it, his back pressed tight against the cliff, watching with curious indifference as the tide rushed in and cut him off from the beach.

It didn't take long. With each new surge the water rose higher, until the tide had thickened into heavy green waves. By wading, by forcing his way, he might have managed to retreat the way he had come, but he had no wish to. The desperate something in him — that last rebellion of youth — turned him instinctively toward danger the way a moth turns toward flame. To his left was the beach and the path up the cliff, cut off by six feet of water; to his right, ten kilometers of abrupt limestone cliff where the surf lay waiting to crush anything interposing itself between its sweep and the rock's base.

Trapped then. He looked both ways and took a grim satisfaction in the fact.

There was a third way — at least possibly. He turned and craned back his head so he could study the cliff that rose directly behind him. It was high, but the fallen boulders had created a staircase he could follow to the spot where the cliff swelled out into a mossy buttress. Past this he couldn't see — that would be the risky part. If the top half of the cliff were steep and smooth he would be stranded there with no way down.

He looked out to sea where the storm waves were building, looked up again toward the bulge, then with an ironic, why-not kind of smile, started scrambling his way up the rocks.

At first it wasn't bad. The rock had a gritty quality that made even his clubfoot adhere, and in the space of a few minutes he was up the first shelf. Climbing, he remembered the morning he had scrambled across another cliff — the infinitely remote morning when he had gone to fetch the portrait of Goethe for Maria Pavlovna. He had felt caught up in a larger inertia then, as if the force propelling him down the cliff were the suction of the approaching war. He had let himself drop down to it; now, with difficulty, he was climbing back out.

The grade steepened beneath the buttress, and he could feel his heart pump faster as a result. He could see now that the cliff was split in the widest part the way fresh-baked bread is split, so that there were grooves of light-colored rock where he might find a route. It gave him impetus up the next stretch. With each new step he led off with his crippled foot, even if to stride with the other were more natural. On the easy stretches, anyway, he wanted to let his weakness lead the way.

He was sweating profusely by the time he made it to the grooves — his shirt was as cold and heavy as chain mail. There was a ledge there wide enough to sit down, and even though it was greasy from spray he was grateful for the chance to rest. Thirty meters below was the ocean — the overhang cut off the rest of the cliff so he was looking straight down into its depths. It was surprisingly transparent from that height. He could see the current waving the seaweed back and forth in a way that was oddly beckoning, as if the greenness were calling him down. There were turquoise rocks, silver flashes his imagination shaped into fish. He stared for a long time. It gave him a sleepy sensation — a drowsiness that made him want to close his eyes and go limp.

He had to force himself to start up again. He traversed to his left to get around a bad stretch, only to come

onto rock that was slipperier than before and steeper —
steep enough that he had to use his hands for balance.
They were soon numb from the blood rushing back down
his wrists; at every third step he brought them down again
and shook them as hard as he could to restore circulation.
Even worse, as each new wave hit the cliff a tremor raced
through the rock and vibrated his legs, giving the effect
of a giant hand trying to shake him off. He had to flatten
himself to the rock in order to resist it; his mouth came
against the dirt and the acid, scaly taste made him gag.

He still had his perspective — at least a shred of it.
He remembered the time the German soldiers had aimed
their rifles at him, tried to compare the terror he felt then
with the fear he was experiencing now. In the first, man's
indifference to his life had humiliated him, cheapened
him, tore something essential from his center. Now here
it was nature's turn to threaten him and yet he didn't
feel humiliated at all — quite the opposite. The waves
pounding upward toward his feet, the rock breaking away
beneath his hands, the tug of gravity. It was nature's indifference at its most palpable, and yet by defying it, by
continuing on, he felt uplifted and dignified and made
whole.

He knew one thing: if he fell, it would be in strain-
ing to go higher, not collapsing from exhaustion where he
was. He groped with his hands until he found a knob of
rock that seemed solid, then, by jamming his good leg into
a crevice, managed to boost himself up onto the highest,
deepest of the grooves. Once there he was able to bring
his head back far enough to see past the buttress to what
was left of the cliff. To his relief it wasn't sheer, but

relatively broken — it sloped back from the overhang at an angle below vertical and there were roots and hummocks to use as holds.

It had started to rain now — cold hard drops that stung like hail. The easy grade to the right was shaped like a fan and gathered in every drop of water that hit the cliff, making it far too slippery to climb. To the left was an alternate way that would have been a boulevard for anyone with normal legs, but for him it meant leading off with his clubfoot — and not by choice this time either.

"Carefully, Peter," he said. "One . . . two . . ."

He reached as far as he could, spread out his fingers, then swung his foot across the cliff as his hands tightened on rock. He brought his right leg over, balanced for a moment, then repeated the maneuver, this time stretching even further. Each time he did this his hands managed to find an adequate hold, but his foot bounced off like a mallet, refusing to adhere, and there would be a moment of slipping before his right leg came over and took up the weight.

Later he would wonder how long it took him to reach the top. Minutes? Hours? He remembered Nina telling him how when she had walked across the dead bodies on the steppe it had been like crossing the boundaries of time. He could understand that now. It seemed he had always been groping this way, hands trembling from effort, skin scratched and bleeding, rain pouring down his eyes — seemed he always had been and always would be, so there was no end. The crack he balanced across gave way to another crack, then a small ledge, and with each new step he had to concentrate his energy on the lump in him that was weakest. He almost fell once, twice — almost fell a dozen times. His lungs burned so much that falling would have been a relief, and the higher he climbed the more he longed for the rush of wind that would soar through his throat as he plummeted down. It was the temptation of vertigo that threatened him most. It was the irresistible urge to let himself go.

At the top was a Y-shaped rock barring exit from the cliff. Its right side was split by a wide and easy crack, but he saw it was a trap leading to a vertical drop, and so instead he led off with his left foot and went up the hard way, kicking wildly, groping, until finally he managed to get his elbows higher than his shoulders and with a last convulsive pushing heave himself up and over the top.

There was grass there, wild grass soaked with rain. Meeting it, he collapsed in exhaustion and rolled inland from the cliff's edge, giving in to gravity at last. When he stopped there was the burning taste of vomit at the back of his throat and he was staring faceup into the gray sky. It was opaque and streaked with oily clouds and yet it was so beautiful he yelled from sheer joy — yelled and yelled again until the seabirds, huddled there out of the storm, rose and flapped away in dignified protest.

It was sleeting now, sleeting buckets. He blew on his bleeding hands to warm them, pressed them deep within his jacket, then turned and hurried through the darkness toward home.

ON THE EVE

IT WAS A TOY of infinite capacity, the box of childhood Diskau's mother had given him for being a good boy
and not telling — small, secret, and wooden, with royal
ladies stroking the heads of ivory unicorns and knights
dueling dragons with sapphire eyes and a lid that fit snugly
with a smooth silver hinge. Into it had gone everything
that had tormented him for the last fifteen years, reduced
into little square packets that nested one inside the other
until all that remained was one neat comprehensible decorated treasure with the ladies who stroked unicorns and

the knights that killed dragons and the lid that was easily closed.

Space was inside and infinity and emptiness, one inside the other like clever nesting boxes, and the only thing left to fit in was the harmless little doll, the man-doll in costume his mother had given him for being a good boy and not telling. He took it by the middle and stuck it in sideways, but the lid wouldn't close over its funny round belly. He took it by the legs and wormed it back and forth like a wire, but the lid wouldn't close over its funny round head. He crumpled its stuffing into a ball, cracked the legs toward the neck, stamped the other boxes to make room, stove it down with his fist. He had almost succeeded — the lid was a centimeter from shutting — when the stuffing sprang back again, the doll's legs flew akimbo, and out of the box in a whirlwind rushed the space and infinity and emptiness he had tried so hard to squeeze in.

And what was so hard was that his emotions flew out with them, uncoiling from the neat and malleable to the huge and out of control in a spiral of petulance into anger into desperation into fear. He was left breathless by the rush of it, felt his insides scoured by a metallic bore. He groped wildly for some water, knocking over the carafe Koenig had left on the table beside the pills. He watched it leak onto the miserable shred of olive carpet, counting the drops as they fell. One, two, three. He reached his hand out and stroked with his fingers trying to urge them back into the fallen carafe. Two, three, four. Drops the color of wine. Four, five, six. Drops the color of burgundy. Five, six, seven. Drops the color of blood. He pushed them sideways but they flattened and turned sticky, and gentle as he was with them they wouldn't slide back over the carafe's rim.

There was a storm outside. He could feel the throb move through the window up the floorboard through the table to his arm. He turned his head — heavily, like someone opening a spigot. Snow crept beneath the door, an oozing mercury iridescence. In its light he could see simple things. The wobbly oak table on which his arm rested near the pills. The porcelain washbasin with its pendulous lip. A bookcase with his revolver. An icon in ghastly colors, gut-tinted and pale. Koenig asleep in bed, covers down from his naked shoulders, the small of his back pinching and relaxing with each breath. All these things he had managed to press in the box first, and so they were the last to fly out again, damp from the darkness, crenellated with thought. He waited, measuring them. Only when they were back in place there in the present, only when they were inflated and hard, could he begin the delicate job of restuffing.

He reached across the table for the pills. They were round-backed and brittle, the same pale color as the flesh in the icons. He shook them loose of the bottle, spread them apart like marbles, then started counting the total, moving them as he did so from left to right beneath his inspection.

Nine. Cut in half that gave eighteen. Eighteen divided in half gave thirty-six quarters, but quarters weren't enough anymore — quarters left him with a centimeter of lid he couldn't quite shut. Halves this time. Halves, and if that didn't shut it, three quarters.

He slid his hand across the felt matting until it found the razor blade, then brought it back again and began cutting. He did this slowly and carefully, squinting like a jeweler, his tongue flicking across the chemical aftertaste on his lips. His hand always trembled in excitement, but by concentrating his focus and slowing down his breaths he was able to fit the razor's edge in the exact center, then — with a slight tapping pressure — cut the tablet in half. Pressing the sides back together, he repeated the same action on a perpendicular axis until he had four pie-shaped wedges arranged in the chalky dust of the cut.

He separated two of these wedges, hesitated, then separated out a third. Using his thumb and the tip of his pinky, he placed the wedges in the acid spot beneath the back of his tongue. They only took a few seconds to melt. He closed his eyes in happiness as the familiar bitterness shuddered its way down his throat.

It took effect slowly, more slowly than it used to. When the doctors first gave it to him back in Zhukovo the bitter taste would be followed by a jolt of brightness so sudden and dazzling it was as if a window had been thrown open in his soul. Air streamed in and light and color, washing out his center, blending him into whatever world he focused on so there was no division between what he desired and what he possessed. Bitterness first, then the jolt of a cell miraculously thrown open, allowing his mind to escape the heavy, immalleable bars of his flesh and exist instead in shining particles.

In the Zhukovo days. Now it took effect more slowly, the bitterness coming down in clotted dabs that brushed his heart without exploding. Or rather they did explode, but in slow motion, the particles dividing themselves so slowly he could never pinpoint the exact line between his heavy sensation and the euphoria. It was merely a question of waiting though. Merely a question of focusing on something simple so the particles would have a center to spread from as they drifted apart.

Koenig's head — he would focus on that. It lay on the pillow like a spot left by a messy pen — black and featureless and irritating, so that he felt the urge to rub his wrist over it and smudge it out. It was a ludicrously small head, offensively small. It was small because Koenig's thoughts were small; it didn't take a massive cavity to contain slyness and cynicism and servility. A head that size could only be aware of smallness, so there was never any conflict in him, never any compulsion to fit things in. Only the talented were tormented by the hugeness of things. Only the talented would lie awake through a blizzard seeking the magic secret of reduction. Small minds went into boxes and large minds were the boxes themselves — the toy box, the box of childhood his mother had given him for being a good boy and not telling.

He pointed his fingers and snapped them and Koenig's head dropped into the box with a little skittering noise like a dried pea. The bed went in after, then the chairs, then the bookcase and revolver with an insucking whoosh, then the room itself compressed into a tiny cube hardly taking any space at all, merely a fraction of the box's one corner, so there was room for all the rest.

He wanted to pause here, hold the box up to the light to admire its uncluttered squareness, but there was a distracting noise behind him as the wind shot through the vacuum where the walls had dissolved. The wind tried to encircle him, reduce him in its chill the way he had reduced the room, but he was vaster than the wind and it was no trick at all to open his arms to it and hug it and roll it up into a smooth cylinder that stacked neatly on the cube.

This was instantaneous, with no effort, so that he was hardly aware of the compressing factor at work at all but only a gradual and exhilarating widening of his focus — a widening and hardening both, so that his thoughts were like a giant pincers slowly opening. The farther apart the jaws spread the more that came within their scope, until not only Koenig and the room and the wind were enveloped, but Yalta itself out there in the darkness, the evil-smelling city with its aristocratic pretensions, the provincial second-rate Yalta that had dared ignore him — Yalta with its Turkish indolence and nauseating palms, Yalta the sprawling lump of insignificant nothing his pincers encircled and pressed into dots.

Pincers in the first stage, but pincers were for those content with mediocrity, and if he waited long enough — if he didn't force the euphoria but merely rode it — they changed into something vaster and more circular: a thick tubular ring that pressed not by snapping but by a slow irresistible constriction. He closed his eyes and inhaled the damp blackness until all the torments of his life rushed in close to his center, where their mass widened the ring even more. When it was at its widest — when it was so large and enveloping there was nothing left outside — he slowly let his breath out and began squeezing the ring shut.

Yalta was in there, and not just Yalta but the entire Crimea, and not just the Crimea but the Ukraine and the Urals and the great Russian cities, and not just spread out on a map but particular and detailed and sharp. The rusty columns of dust that slanted across the sunset after a month with no rain; the sky with its clouds that were vaster than some countries, so that to walk below them crushed you between infinities and made you feel flat; the way the horizon never came closer but always seemed to recede; the feeling the steppe gave you that mud was the basic element of the world and not just any mud but a viscous cream-colored mud — that man was made of mud and condemned to mud and mud in his very essence; the stinking hovels of the peasants, where copulating pigs squealed beside nursing babies; the beggars who were so desperate they threw themselves on top of tanks screaming for alms; the scabby trees with their tangled shafts; the way the beggars and the mud and the trees never ended but kept on unrolling forever until they formed an immense ring whose circumference was only slightly smaller than the circumference of his imagination. Russia was the vastest thing there was, the inescapable great fact, Easternness and Anarchy and Chaos, and yet he managed to shrink it anyway, its beauty as well as its horror, slowly and patiently the way a boa constrictor crushes its prey, until finally it was box-sized and manageable and easily stored.

Into the box beside the cylinder of wind and the cube of furniture — Russia, the whole of it, a puce-colored shell.

He was usually able to rest at this stage, hold the circle back, catch his breath. But the triumph of fitting the first things in so easily sent a surge of adrenaline through his veins that it would have been suicide to resist. It was as if he had taken a separate pill and the two powders were racing each other down his chest — insight for insight, exhilaration for exhilaration — until the ring of his imagination clenched down the way the heart muscle clenches, enveloping his tormentors and squeezing them into shape.

The great Russian writers, Dostoyevsky and Tolstoy, Chekhov and Turgenev, Gogol and the others. Their faces merged into a grinning mask little smaller than the mass of clouds he had already circled, a composite monstrosity tormenting him not only by the glory of their beards and the power of their foreheads and the sensuality of their lips, but in the mildness of their expressions and the beauty in their eyes, so that they were handsomer than any film star, more virile than any soldier, the very incarnation of all that he longed for, grace and beauty and power and strength. They were bigger than he was and knew more secrets, but he reduced them and put them into the box, and not only writers but the remoras who fed off them, the Berlin directors who had rejected his plays, the Jew academics who sneered at his stories, and not only their corpulent faces but the faces of the officers who had mocked him for his softness and called him faggot, Doerr and Ulbricht and Schrier — a whole line of pasty-faced nonentities stretching back to his masters in school who took delight in caning him for a lying braggart, caned him until the blood stained his trousers just because they didn't recognize he spoke to them from his dreams.

Into the box beside the shell of Russia and the cylinder of wind and the cube of furniture — tormentors, the lot of them, a flat doughy cake with a raisin for each head.

They went in so fast it created a blur and a rushing sensation so that he imagined he was running across the sand-colored boards of a stage. He felt excited at this —

felt lifted out of himself the way he did whenever he took on a new role — but a moment later the excitement gave way to uncertainty as he realized the stage boards were moving beneath his feet. At first he had trouble accepting this — he hopped sideways to get off a faulty plank — but the stage moved on that side, too, forcing him to spread apart his arms to keep from falling headfirst toward the footlights. "Cross to stage right," a reedy voice kept saying — "Cross to stage right!" But he couldn't cross to stage right, couldn't even stand where he was, because beneath his feet the stage kept rolling, faster and faster, making him run as furiously as he could just to stay in place. He couldn't afford to take his eyes off his feet and look up, but when he did he could see the stage didn't come to an end at the proscenium but extended through the theatre walls, spreading out in a varnished platform that was just as flat and bare as the steppe. He was startled by this, shaken, but not so much that he couldn't surround it in his circle, turn the expanding edge back around into itself and narrow it down.

Into the box with the cake of tormentors and the shell of Russia and the cylinder of wind and the cube of furniture — the stage in its infinity, a splinter of wood.

And if he could put nightmares there he could put anything in, even though he felt himself swaying now, felt his head become a crazy bucket of color, all browns and yellows and rusts. As they blended they took on odd shapes and surprising consistencies so that he saw the girl Nina staring upward from a pool of brownish red, her face confronting him as if it were his own reflection, feminine and mild, only she was spitting at him — spitting a

thick black substance that burned his eyes. With his thumb
he erased her face into the brown pool, but in the brown
pool was Chekhov's sister with the maddening certainty
of her smile, only she wasn't paint now but a lump of
marble he didn't have time to crush. He scooped the paint
between his hands and poured it into the box, then lifted
the marble and dumped it in after, and big as it was there
was still room left for all the toys of his childhood as well.
The metal rocking horse his mother had given him for
being a good boy and not telling. The wooden train his
mother had given him for being a good boy and not telling. The floppy giraffes and sickly-looking rhinos and er-
mine muffs and everything else she had given him for not
going to his father and telling — into the box, into the
box with the royal ladies stroking the heads of ivory unicorns and the knights dueling dragons with sapphire eyes,
until it was bursting with toys and there was hardly room
for the most important things, the hardest sharpest most
unboxable things, the long carpet of the hall up which he
tiptoed at night when his father was away and the darkness scared him, the strange overcoat hanging not on the
hatstand but disordered on the floor, the vest beyond that,
the shirt beyond that, the trousers and stockings beyond
that, the heavy oak door at the clothing's end, the door to
his mother's bedroom that slowly pried open, the candles
by the bedside with their tulip flickers of light, his mother's creamy shape against the red silk of the bed, the
creaminess enveloped by a coarser male thrusting, the way
her boobies spasmed, the way her hips heaved and tightened, heaved and tightened, the groans that couldn't come
out of her at all but must be torn from some spirit there

in the darkness, a passionate spirit that murmured and screamed in a language he was even then old enough to recognize as Russian.

Into the box with the passion, the guttural syllables, the wet matted hair, the twisting and the groans — his mother and her nakedness, and not just his mother but the doll she had given him for being a good boy and not telling, the man-doll in clown costume, all red and polka dots and satin. There was a space left below the rim where he could press it, but the clown was a stubborn clown, a bad stubborn selfish clown, and refused to fit in — sideways or endways or upside down it wouldn't fit in, until he sobbed from frustration and tore its head off in fury and with an ecstatic savage motion rammed its carcass into the toy box and slammed the lid shut.

THE SEAGULL

THE SEAGULL

THE IMPERIAL THEATRE in Yalta, New Year's Eve
1941.
　　At first all is darkness. There's the plaintive music
of a far-off cello finishing a chord on its deepest note.
From this sound others arise, pitched at the same low
key: a distant air-raid siren, a distant foghorn, the faint
sorrowful wail of a mother calling for her child. These
blend into a note far lonelier than the cello's, swelling to
a pitch that is unbearably poignant, then stopping all at
once, as if a string has been severed. In its place come

homelier sounds from the theatre's interior: the squeak of seats; a raspy cough; the vague unintelligible murmur of voices left and center. These will sharpen as the light very gradually brightens, establishing a correspondence that lasts throughout the act — the brighter the light, the cleaner the sound.

The stage is divided into thirds. The left is the actual theatre stage, set with furniture and props, among which the silhouettes of the actors are frozen in tableau: one pours tea; another readies a coat; the third points a cane.

To the right of this traditional stage, connected to it by a narrow band of blackness, are the wings as they were in the previous act, with the cage and the samovar table and the thick gathered folds of the opened curtain. They frame another, larger grouping of silhouettes who stand closer together than those on the left and tilt their heads in that direction as if listening.

To the right of the wings is a second band of blackness, then the hazy outline of a small dressing room set somewhat higher than the wings. A chest of drawers sits in one corner. Above it, an unlit light bulb dangles from a cord. Toward the back, a dressing table over which someone slumps, head on arm. While the other silhouettes suggest by their rigidness great anticipation and excitement, this one suggests the exact opposite: exhaustion and lifelessness and despair.

The voices on the far left become more distinct. Simultaneously, the light widens on that side from the bottom of the stage toward the top, revealing first a crease of brightness, then a horizontal band, then the entire left bathed in footlights. The play is in progress and the effect is dazzling. The vibrant motion, the colorful costumes, the yellow light. Coming so hard upon the darkness, the effect is like a heart-quickening rush of cool air.

The setting is for the final moments of *The Seagull*'s third act: the dining room of Sorin's house. Doors right and left. Sideboard. Cupboards with medicine bottles. Table. Trunks and hatboxes; preparations for departure. Rashevitch as Sorin is hugging Maria Pavlovna as Arcadina with one arm and struggling to put his coat on with the other. As the theatre is transformed by the costumes and lighting, so too are the actors; they seem magnified in this scene, vitalized, their every gesture partaking of splendor.

RASHEVITCH/SORIN: Time to be off, Irene. You musn't be late, confound it all. I'm going to get in the cart.

MARIA/ARCADINA: Good-bye everyone. If we're alive and well we shall meet again in the summer. *Varka, as the maid, kisses her hand.* Don't forget me. *Gives Varka a ruble.*

VARKA/MAID: Our humblest thanks, lady. A good journey to you.

MARIA/ARCADINA: Where's Constantine? Tell him that I'm off. We must say good-bye. *To Varka.* Think no evil of us.

Exit all right. Stage empty. Noise of farewells and departures behind the scene. Varka comes back for a basket of plums and exits with it.

POTAPOV/TRIGORIN: *coming back.* I've left my stick behind. I think it's out there on the veranda. *Goes left and meets Nina entering.* Ah, it's you. We're off.

Nina's face flushes with the excitement of a young girl; her tone is a perfect mix of love, vulnerability, and defiance.

NINA: I felt we should meet again . . . Boris Alexeyevitch, I have made up my mind beyond recall. The die is cast; I am going on the stage. Tomorrow I shall be gone from here. I am leaving my father; I am giving up everything and beginning a new life. I am going to where you are going . . . to Moscow. We shall meet there.

POTAPOV/TRIGORIN: *looking around.* Stay at the Slavyansky Bazaar. Let me know at once. Molchanovka, Grokholsky's house . . . I'm in a hurry.

NINA: *pleading.* One minute more.

POTAPOV/TRIGORIN: *murmuring.* How beautiful you are! What joy to think that we shall meet again so soon. *She lays her head tenderly on his chest.* I shall see these lovely eyes once more, this inexpressibly tender charming smile, this sweet face, this expression of angelic purity . . . My darling!

A long kiss.

The curtain falls in a horizontal band of blackness across the left. In reflex, the light brightens on the center as the actors come off into the wings — Potapov in great excitement, flourishing his fist; Nina slower and more reluctantly, her head bent down into her shoulder, her lips moving slightly as if she's already rehearsing her next lines. Waiting there to meet them are Maria Pavlovna, Kunin, and Varka, who applaud in delight. Rashevitch and Tania stand aside with shy, embarrassed expressions like spectators at a wedding. Koenig, slouched on a stool, takes swigs from a metal flask and arranges his mouth into drunken sneers. Behind him, Gerassim stares intently toward the black band on the far right and nervously rubs his wrist.

POTAPOV: *throwing his arms around Nina in an exuberant bear hug.* A triumph! A performance that will live forever!

Nina smiles, struggles halfheartedly to remove his arms, then surrenders and with a little sob of happiness hugs him back. Potapov kisses her on both cheeks, then turns to face the others.

POTAPOV: I tell you this in all sincerity and from fifty years' experience on the Russian stage. Never have I seen acting so real and convincing and heartfelt. Never have I been so moved. When she handed me that locket as a token of her love, I felt tears rushing to my eyes, actual tears. *Leans toward Nina and hugs her again; softly, in a whisper to her alone.* Brava, my girl. Brava!

MARIA: One act left to go. Are the props in place? The writing table's not where it should be, further to the left.

POTAPOV: And you, too, Maria Pavlovna. It is impossible to act badly with you on the stage. I see in your conception traces of every great Arcadina from the last five decades. A woman fighting desperately for her youth — a living woman, a woman who laughs and cries and feels . . . Peter. An excellent job. Dorn to the flesh. Worldly and wise, though if you don't mind my saying so, a little less of that cane twirling in the final act.

Maria Pavlovna goes over and takes Nina's hand. Holds it for a moment, then presses it to her cheek and kisses it softly.

MARIA: Alexander is right. You are my brother's creation come to life. *In a whisper like Potapov's.* You're almost there now. Almost there. Courage!

KUNIN: *puzzled.* There wasn't any applause.

POTAPOV: Yes. Well . . . They were too moved for applause. Yes, that's it. Too moved.

VARKA: I counted ten in the audience. I could see them through the footlights.

KUNIN: I counted twelve. I was looking when I first came out. None of them look German.

POTAPOV: The acoustics are different in an empty theatre, and yet there was a vibrant something sitting there watching us — I could sense it . . . Ten brave hearts. Here, we'll send out Tania. Tania, my pet. Peek out from the curtain and count how many heroes have defied these Nazi bastards in order to come and witness history.

KUNIN: *to Nina.* Are you all right? No more of that dizziness? *Pulls chair over.* Here, sit and rest while I take your pulse.

POTAPOV: *pacing up and down in a frenzy; to himself, to everyone.* And he dared tinker with the master's lines! He dared for one moment think he could actually improve them! Here, I've written down his changes on my wrist in case I forgot. I'll rub them out just like . . . this! *Crosses himself.* My apologies, Anton Pavlovich. I will apologize on bended knees in heaven. *Shakes head.* Our Major mumbles his lines and gropes through his part and then retreats to his dressing room like a coward. *Advances to the right and spits.* There, Minister of Culture! This is what I think of you and your glorious German race!

RASHEVITCH: *nervously.* He might hear you.

POTAPOV: I will yell louder to make sure! Death to all fascists! Let them eat grass!

Tania hurries in from the left. She is breathless and her face shines with excitement.

TANIA: There are twelve. They are sitting scattered about in the darkness and I could only see their silhouettes. Three in the orchestra. A few in the parterre. Four or five in the balcony. I couldn't make out their faces very well.

KUNIN: Any German officers?

TANIA: All civilians, I think. No Germans.

VARKA: Standing and stretching are they?

TANIA: Leaning forward mostly. Sitting, their arms on the seats in front of them. They stare toward the stage and look nowhere else.

MARIA: *shaking her head.* There are hundreds.

TANIA: Twelve, Maria Pavlovna. I counted them twice.

MARIA: The theatre is full. And not with hundreds either, but with thousands. Thousands, a hundred thousand. The ones you see are merely their representatives. Everything will be crushed in the world but this will not be crushed.

POTAPOV: Thousands! I can hear the applause.

MARIA: If only one came we would still have gone on. In my nightmares, no one came.

POTAPOV: In mine, too.

KUNIN: They're the brave ones — like you said.

MARIA: And now everyone must rest. There are still ten minutes until the final act. Nina, I insist you go to your dressing room and lie down.

TANIA: *timidly.* I'll take her, Maria Pavlovna.

Maria Pavlovna hesitates and starts to say something, but Tania hurries on.

TANIA: None of you trust me, I can see it in your eyes. You're afraid I'll contaminate her with my sadness. *Goes over to Nina.* May I help you? Here, please take my arm.

Leads her toward the darkness with a combination of tenderness and great respect. Nina leans on her gratefully; despite her assurances, it's obvious she's exhausted and badly in need of rest.

MARIA: *watching them exit.* What do you think, Peter?

KUNIN: *shrugging.* Her pulse is racing. I don't like the color of her cheeks — it's as if she's burning.

MARIA: And her biggest scene left to go . . . *Taking Peter's arm.* We have business to take care of. *To the others.* Please ready yourselves. Varka will help you with your costumes.

The two of them disappear into the black band on the right. Footsteps are heard ascending an iron stairway; a few moments later the dressing-room door creaks open. Maria Pavlovna pauses to catch her breath, then enters, followed closely by Kunin. He gropes to find the light bulb, then pulls the cord.

The light is weak, but enough to illuminate the room in more detail. A battered horsehair chaise in one corner, the springs showing through. Old photos on the wall. Discarded costumes scattered about in dusty mounds. A stack of tattered, dog-eared scripts. A window the size and shape of a porthole.

At the dressing table, Diskau leans forward with his head resting on his arm, immobile. Before him a cracked mirror captures a corner of his face; his skin is doughy and thick-looking, with a brown crust visible across his upper lip. Before him is a semicircle of medicine bottles mixed in with cans of greasepaint and powder. His hand, blindly groping, knocks one of these over, then goes limp.

Maria Pavlovna takes all this in, then walks over to the dressing table and touches his shoulder with a gesture that is surprisingly tender. She strokes the back of his head the way a mother would her son.

MARIA: We need you.

DISKAU: *groaning.* No.

Stirs himself; brings his head up with a tremendous effort.

DISKAU: The gracious victors. Here to gloat, are you? Charming. *Tries unsuccessfully to stand.* I know what you're going to say.

MARIA: The last act is about to begin. Here, I'll help you get ready.

DISKAU: *viciously.* Stand back!

MARIA: *calmly.* We need your help or the play can't be finished. Constantine's scene is next.

DISKAU: I know I've acted badly. My wooden interpretation isn't deliberate wood — far from it. Neither is my . . . How shall I put it? Vacant stare. All natural and unaffected . . . Well, what of it? There's no one here to see my disgrace. It's hard to be inspired by empty seats.

MARIA: Tania counted twelve.

DISKAU: Twelve!

He laughs — laughs uncontrollably, rocking forward on his seat, tears coming to his eyes, his fists beating against the table in delight.

DISKAU: Twelve in a theatre built for a thousand! That's delicious! That really is delicious.

MARIA: *to Kunin.* How much time?

KUNIN: Five minutes now.

MARIA: *turning back.* We'll have to start again with your makeup. Here, look in the mirror. It's smudged.

DISKAU: I'm finished.

MARIA: Don't talk nonsense.

DISKAU: *stubbornly, his face set like a boy's.* I'm finished, I tell you. We're all finished. All of us stuck in this wounded aberration of a century . . . Not a day's journey from here boys are dying in agony because their anuses are freezing shut, do you know that? They're freezing to death while a few meters across from them other boys are ripping apart horses and crawling into their flesh to stay warm. That's nothing to the real horror, either. And what's really ironic is that we think we can escape in the end, one horrible war and it's past us, but we'll all end up paying, you wait and see. Mankind's going to have to bleed forever for the sins of this year.

KUNIN: The Germans . . .

DISKAU: Oh yes, we Germans — we're to blame . . . You Russians fight in the depths of winter when anyone with decency would fight only the cold. Crushed beyond all hope, you spring back up again and go for our throats . . . Koenig is right. You should all be exterminated. You talk of culture and art and pride yourselves on your Tolstoys and beneath it all you're nothing but barbarians.

Turns and mumbles something toward the mirror.

MARIA: Speak clearer.

DISKAU: *shouting.* Ovens!

While he is talking, footsteps are heard on the iron

stairs leading up to the dressing room. The door opens —
Gerassim silently enters. Kunin sees him, but the other
two don't. He puts his finger to his lips and backs up into
the shadows.

MARIA: *to Kunin.* Time?

KUNIN: Three minutes now.

MARIA: *desperately.* What will it take?

Leans over the dressing table and speaks to Diskau
in a low, urgent whisper.

MARIA: They're laughing at you. Rashevitch and the
others. They're taking bets you'll quit like a coward and
refuse to go on.

DISKAU: *groggily.* They win.

MARIA: They're making fun of your missing arm. They
call you cripple. They say you were never meant to act.

Diskau reaches for one of the bottles, unscrews the
cap with fussy preciseness, then takes out a pill. Holds it
up to the light and squints at it in satisfaction.

DISKAU: Your friends should bet on pills, not people.
This one, as you'll notice, is green. It's green and round
and when I swallow it there's not an actor in Europe who
can touch me. *Unscrews another bottle.* This pill, as you'll
see, is white. You will notice it's cut in quarters. With
this pill I am no longer Europe's greatest actor, but it
hardly matters.

KUNIN: *quietly.* Listen.

From far to the left can be heard the first lines of
the final act; the distance gives them the same wistful
effect of the cello note.

TANIA/MASHA: Constantine Gavrilovitch! Constantine Gavrilovitch! . . . There's no one here. How dark it
is out in the garden. They ought to have that stage pulled

down. It stands bare and ugly like a skeleton, and the curtain flaps in the wind. As I came by here yesterday evening I thought I heard someone crying there.

MARIA: *to Diskau*. Potapov will give you your cue soon. You have to go on.

DISKAU: They all despise me. The Germans despise me because I'm too lenient, the Russians because I'm too harsh . . . And do you know what else, Madam Chekhova? I have the distinct impression your brother would have despised me, too. *Holds hand up as if to block any disagreement*. Yes, despised me. Despicably despised. But that is satisfactory to me. To be despicably despised by a Chekhov is something of which to be proud. To come within a great man's notice even as a worm.

Holds the pills up, shrugs, then swallows the green one.

DISKAU: *matter-of-factly*. They never take long.

MARIA: My brother put himself into Constantine. Constantine was Antosha in his worst moments, all he feared to become. Empty and silent and without direction.

DISKAU: Exactly.

Turns and faces the mirror. Slowly, yet with expert and experienced motions, begins applying makeup to his face.

DISKAU: I've seen pictures of your brother toward the end. A sickly man, for all his youth. Here, I'll make my forehead ashen and gray. A pince-nez, of course. Here, how's that? A pallor on the forehead and a pince-nez for his nearsightedness and I'll walk bent over and frequently cough . . . Just a little more shadow beneath my eyes. The bruises attendant upon seeing into man's soul . . .

I will complete my role, Maria Pavlovna. I will act as I have never acted before out of my respect for your devotion. For the next thirty minutes my soul will be Constantine's, my fate his . . . There. A little more paleness in the cheek. And there. I will be authentic down to the last detail and when people look at me they will see death's shadow.

MARIA: *going over to him.* Take my arm.

DISKAU: Gratefully. *Struggles to his feet, then leans on her. In a firm voice.* Rene Diskau. Man of a thousand talents but no accomplishments. What he might have done with the help of a sister like you.

Maria Pavlovna staggers under his weight. Kunin goes over to assist, but she waves him back. With Diskau on her arm, she walks slowly toward the door. The moment they exit, Gerassim steps out from behind the chaise.

GERASSIM: *in a hoarse whisper.* After him, fool! Don't let him out of your sight.

Shoves Kunin toward the iron stairway; the two of them hurry down the bare X of it toward the wings. Maria Pavlovna, at the bottom, has let go Diskau's arm. His ironic smile has given way to a set look of purpose. He forces himself to stand straighter; he brushes off his collar, then his sleeve, then his cuff. The fussiness seems to tranquilize him; by the time he walks past the curtain toward the stage he appears dignified and composed.

MARIA: *turning, looking wildly about.* Nina? Is that you? Come here quickly and hold my hand.

Nina, who has been standing with Tania and Potapov, goes over and stands beside Maria Pavlovna near the gathered curtain; she is trembling and has a shawl draped over her shoulders. Maria Pavlovna takes her hand.

MARIA: There, he's beginning now. It won't be long before your cue . . . Peter? Darken the light so we can see.

The contrast in the lighting brings the left stage into focus. It is set for the final act — the drawing room of Sorin's house, now converted into a study. A glass door in the back leads to the veranda. Besides the usual drawing-room furniture, a writing table stands to the right; a bookcase, books on windowsills and chairs. It is evening. Twilight. One lamp is lit, with shade. The wind howls in the trees and chimneys.

Diskau stands at the writing table staring down at the papers scattered across the top. Picks one up, studies it, then lets it fall. Suddenly looks up and stares toward the audience with a puzzled blankness, as if he's forgotten what he's there for. Walks slowly toward the glass door, his eyes fixed on the stage as if measuring it — as if re-familiarizing himself with every feature. Teeters. Comes back finally to the table. Shrugs.

DISKAU/CONSTANTINE: *in a faint, indistinct voice.* I have talked so much about new forms, and now I feel that I'm slipping back little by little into the old clichés. *Reading.* "The placard on the hoarding informed the public . . . Her pale face framed in masses of dark hair . . ." Informed the public; framed in masses . . . How cheap! *Scratching it out; his voice starting to strengthen.* I'll begin with the hero being woken by the sound of rain, and throw the rest overboard. The description of the moonlit night is tedious and artificial. Trigorin has worked himself out a method; it's easy for him. The neck of a broken bottle glimmering on the mill dam and the black shadow of the waterwheel, and there's your moonlit night complete; but here I am with my tremulous rays and the twinkling stars and the distant sound of a piano fainting on the perfumed air . . . It's frightful! *Excited now, his voice filling the theatre.* Yes, I'm coming more and more to the conclusion that it doesn't matter whether the forms are new or old; a man's got to write without thinking of form at all, just because it flows naturally out of his soul. *Someone knocks at the window by the table.* Who's that? I don't see anything. *Opens the glass door and looks into the garden.* Someone ran down the steps. Who's there? *Goes out; walks quickly along the veranda outside and returns a moment later with Nina.* Nina! Nina! *Nina lays her head on his chest and sobs unrestrainedly.* Nina! Nina! Is it you? I had a sort of presentiment; all day my heart has been in anguish. *Takes off her hat and cloak.* Oh, my dearest, my loveliest! She has come at last! We mustn't cry; we mustn't cry!

NINA: Is there anyone here?

DISKAU/CONSTANTINE: No one.

NINA: Lock the door; they may come in.

DISKAU/CONSTANTINE: Don't be afraid. No one will come.

NINA: *looking him hard in the face.* Let me look at you. *Looking around the room.* How warm and cozy . . . This used to be the drawing room. Am I much changed?

DISKAU/CONSTANTINE: Yes, you're thinner and your eyes are bigger. Nina, how strange it is to see you at last! Why would you not let me in when I visited you? Why have you not come before? I know you have been here nearly a week. I've been to the inn several times every day and stood under your window like a beggar.

NINA: I was afraid you must hate me. I dream every night that you look at me and do not recognize me. If only you knew! Every day since I came I've been walking up here by the lake. I've been so often near the house but did not dare to come in. Let's sit down. Let's sit here and talk and talk. How pleasant it is here, how warm and comfortable . . . Do you hear the wind? There's a passage in Turgenev: Blessed is he who sits beneath a roof on such a night, in his own comfortable room . . . I am a seagull. No, that's wrong. *Rubs her forehead.* What was I saying? Yes . . . Turgenev . . . And the Lord help all homeless wanderers . . . I'm all right. *Sobbing.*

DISKAU/CONSTANTINE: Nina! You're crying again . . . Nina!

NINA: I'm all right. I feel the better for it . . . I haven't cried for two years. Yesterday evening I came into the garden to see if our stage was still standing. It's still there. I cried for the first time in two years, and felt relieved and easier in my mind. See, I'm not crying anymore. *Taking his hand.* So you've become a writer. You're a writer and I'm an actress. We're both caught up in the vortex. Once I lived so happily, with a child's happiness; I would wake of a morning and sing with glee; I loved you and dreamed of fame. And now? Early tomorrow morning I must travel to Yeletz, third-class, with peasants, and at Yeletz I shall have to put up with the attentions of the educated shopkeepers . . . How brutal life is!

DISKAU/CONSTANTINE: Why Yeletz?

NINA: I've accepted an engagement there for the whole winter. I must start tomorrow.

DISKAU/CONSTANTINE: Nina, I cursed you and hated you at first; I tore up your letters and your photographs but all the time I knew that my heart was bound to you forever. Try as I may, I cannot cease loving you, Nina. Ever since I lost you and began to get my stories printed, my life has been intolerable. How I have suffered! . . . My youth was snatched from me, as it were, and I feel as if I had lived for ninety years. I call to you; I kiss the ground where you have passed; wherever I look I see your face with that caressing smile which shone upon me in the best years of my life . . .

NINA: *wildly.* Why does he say that? Why does he say that?

DISKAU/CONSTANTINE: I am alone in the world, unwarmed by any affection; it chills me like a dungeon and whatever I write is hollow, dull, and gloomy. Stay here, Nina, I beseech you, or let me come away with you! *Nina puts on her hat and coat.* Nina, why are you doing that? For God's sake, Nina . . . *He watches her putting on her things.*

NINA: My trap is at the garden gate. Don't come and see me out. I'll manage all right. *Crying.* Give me some water.

DISKAU/CONSTANTINE: *giving her water.* Where are you going to?

NINA: Back to town. Is your mother here?

DISKAU/CONSTANTINE: Yes . . . Uncle was taken ill on Thursday; we wired for her to come.

NINA: Why do you say you kissed the ground where I walked? You ought to kill me. *Leaning against the table.* Oh, I am so tired! If I could only rest . . . if I could only rest. *Raising her head.* I am a seagull . . . no, that's wrong. I am an actress. Yes, yes. *Hearing laughter, she listens, then runs and looks.* So Trigorin's here, too . . . *Coming back to center stage, the spotlight narrowing on her alone.*

Yes, yes . . . I'm all right . . . He didn't believe in the
stage; he always laughed at my ambitions; little by little I
came not to believe in it either; I lost heart . . . And on
top of that the anxieties of love, jealousy, perpetual fear
for the child . . . I became trivial and commonplace; I
acted without meaning . . . I did not know what to do
with my hands or how to stand on the stage. I had no
control over my voice. You can't imagine how you feel
when you know that you are acting atrociously. I am a
seagull. No, that's wrong . . . Do you remember, you
shot a seagull? A man comes along by chance and sees
her and just to amuse himself, ruins her . . . A subject
for a short story . . . No, that's not it. *Rubbing her forehead*. What was I talking about? . . . Ah, about acting.
I'm not like that now . . . I'm a real actress now. When
I act I rejoice, I delight in it; I am intoxicated and feel
that I am splendid. Since I got here I have been walking
all the time and thinking, thinking and feeling how my
inner strength grows day by day . . . and now I see at
last, Constantine, that in our sort of work, whether we
are actors or writers, the chief thing is not fame or glory,
not what I dreamed of, but learning to endure. One must
bear one's cross and have faith. My faith makes me suffer
less, and when I think of my vocation I am no longer
afraid of life.

DISKAU/CONSTANTINE: *sadly*. You have found your
road, you know where you are going, but I am still adrift
in a welter of images and dreams, and cannot tell what
use it all is to anyone. I have no faith and I do not know
what my vocation is.

NINA: *listening*. Shh . . . I'm going. Good-bye. When
I am a great actress, come and see me act. You promise?

And now . . . *Shaking his hand.* It's late. I can hardly
stand up. I'm so tired and hungry.

DISKAU/CONSTANTINE: Stay here. I'll get you some
supper.

NINA: No, no. Don't see me out; I can find my way.
The trap is quite near . . . So she brought him here with
her? Well, it's all one. When you see Trigorin, don't tell
him I've been . . . I love him; yes, I love him more than
ever . . . A subject for a short story . . . I love him,
love him passionately, desperately. How pleasant it was
in the old days, Constantine! You remember? How clear
and warm, how joyful and how pure our life was! And
our feelings — they were like the sweetest, daintiest
flowers . . . You remember? *Reciting.* "Men and lions,
eagles and partridges, antlered deer, geese, spiders, the
silent fishes dwelling in the water, starfish and tiny creatures invisible to the eye — these and every form of life,
yes, every form of life, have ended their melancholy round
and become extinct. Thousands of centuries have passed
since this earth bore any living being on its bosom. All in
vain does yon pale moon light her lamp. No longer do the
cranes wake and cry in the meadow; the hum of the
mockingbirds is silent in the linden grove . . ." *She embraces Diskau impulsively and runs out by the glass door.*

DISKAU/CONSTANTINE: *after a pause.* I hope nobody
will meet her in the garden and tell Mother. Mother might
be annoyed.

For two minutes, using one hand and the weight of
a book, he silently tears up all the manuscripts on the
writing table as the stage directions require, but there are
another two minutes after that during which he tears the
already shredded pages into even smaller pieces, throwing

hind him. He waits a second, then kicks out the legs of the chair so that Diskau goes sprawling across the floor.

Diskau lies there laughing and babbling like a baby. Gerassim kicks him in the side — kicks him dispassionately and mechanically, the way he once hacked apart the portrait of Tolstoy. Diskau curls himself up into a ball for protection and tries to roll away.

GERASSIM: *standing over him.* Behold the Minister of Culture. *Kicks him in the groin, again and again.*

KUNIN: Don't.

GERASSIM: Shoot him.

KUNIN: What?

GERASSIM: Shoot him!

KUNIN: *backing up.* You said later. In his flat with no one around.

GERASSIM: The plan's been changed.

KUNIN: *facing him, the pistol at his side.* You intended it this way all along, didn't you? You said it would be later on in his flat so the Germans wouldn't connect it with Maria Pavlovna and so arrest her. But it's her you've been after all along, isn't it? *Waves his arm around.* It's this you hate; all this. You want the Germans to destroy this for you.

GERASSIM: Shoot him!

When Kunin still hesitates, Gerassim snaps back the slide on his own pistol, places his boot on Diskau's neck, and aims toward the base of his skull. Kunin swings his arm toward Gerassim as if pointing. His pistol goes off with a thin, toylike crack. Gerassim collapses immediately, shot in the chest. He falls dead onto Diskau's legs. Diskau — delirious now, feeling the pressure — embraces him and rolls with him and laughs manically.

Kunin drops the pistol. For a full minute stands there looking down at the two of them. As Diskau's laugh becomes softer his legs separate and Gerassim's body rolls off him onto the floor. Kunin reaches down and picks up his pistol, reaches over for Gerassim's, then goes to the window and throws both pistols outside.

Voices can be heard from the distant stage. Kunin shakes his head as if slapped. Turns and hurries over to the door, kicks away the chair, then comes back again and stands for a final moment over Diskau, who lies tightly curled in a ball — rocking, sobbing, chewing for comfort on his fist.

Kunin pulls the cord on the light bulb and exits in darkness. His steps are heard on the iron stairway as he races toward the wings. Pauses there, smooths down his clothes, and stands squinting toward the bright white light from the stage. Rubs his hand compulsively on his suit coat, as if trying to polish it clean. Taking a deep breath — forcing his expression to lighten — he walks out onto the stage in the tall, dignified posture of Dr. Dorn.

Varka as the maid stands by the writing table holding out a tray to Maria Pavlovna as Arcadina and Potapov as Trigorin. As Kunin approaches, she hands a drink to him and curtsies. They all raise their glasses in a toast. Tania as Masha comes in holding a stuffed seagull and hands it to Potapov.

TANIA/MASHA: Here's the thing you were talking of, Boris Alexeyevitch. You asked to have it done.

POTAPOV/TRIGORIN: *looking at the seagull.* I don't remember. No, I don't remember.

MARIA/ARCADINA: Put the claret here on the table.

We'll drink while we play patience. Now come along and sit down, all of you.

A muffled popping sound behind the scenes left. Everyone starts.

KUNIN/DORN: *rubbing his hand on his coat, faster and faster.* It's all right. I expect something's broken in my medicine chest. Don't be alarmed. *Exits and returns a moment later.* As I expected. My ether bottle's burst.

MARIA/ARCADINA: *sitting at the table.* Good heavens. I was quite frightened. It reminded me of that time when Constantine tried to . . . *Covering her face with her hands.* I feel quite faint.

KUNIN/DORN: *taking up a magazine and turning the pages; to Potapov.* There was an article in the paper about a month or two ago . . . a letter from America, and I wanted to ask you, among other things . . . *Puts his arm around Potapov's shoulder and brings him to the footlights . . .* I'm very much interested in the question . . . *In a lower tone.* Get Arcadina away from here at once. The fact is, Constantine has shot himself.

Curtain.

As it descends, none of them move. The light brightens evenly until the stage and wings are bathed in the same luminescence, but no one moves — not Kunin there by the footlights, not Potapov standing next to him, not Maria Pavlovna frozen over the writing table with the cards.

Motion resumes. Maria Pavlovna breaks away and runs toward the right, where Nina stands waiting wrapped in her shawl. The two women embrace as if they are the only two persons left in the world — desperately, passionately, tears streaming down their faces. Kunin starts toward them, then stops and with a little nod forces himself to step back to the side where he's not in the way.

POTAPOV: Still no applause. The ovation should be deafening.

VARKA: *peeking through the curtain.* They are applauding. Listen.

TANIA: *joining Varka.* I can see them distinctly now. There's a fat one sitting in the orchestra with a serious expression. There's a woman with her child up in the balcony — she looks to be twenty.

VARKA: An old man and a woman holding hands . . .

TANIA: A young girl with opera glasses. A man in formal dress!

MARIA: A meek little stooped man? I stopped him on the promenade. He was so frightened of the Germans he literally shook with terror, and yet he took my hand and kissed it and promised me he would come.

VARKA: They are applauding! They're getting to their feet and applauding.

POTAPOV: Two dozen of them at least! More coming in all the time. Hear it? Feel the way it catches at your throat? That's applause for you. They want us out. Curtain calls everyone!

There's great excitement. Nina breaks away from Maria Pavlovna and goes about taking everyone's hand, trying to pull them toward the curtain, but they stand back and smile at her and indicate by their gestures that she is to go out alone.

The lights flash off, then on again, narrowing into a single focused beam. The curtain parts. Nina steps to the front of the stage and stands there with her head down, as if she can't stand the pain of being recalled back to herself. The illusion of youth has vanished from her face; she appears before them as she really is — a person worn by life, an ill woman nearing thirty, the scars and bruises visible for all to see.

The applause mounts until it echoes in the deserted theatre like the applause of a million hands. When it reaches its peak, she raises her head and proudly nods.

From out of the darkness someone throws a rose and it lands in tribute at her feet. She picks it up and holds it in front of her with both hands. She holds it in front of her with both hands and kisses it as if it were a chalice and brings it high over her head until the light surrounding her fades and all that is left is the heart-shaped rose there in the darkness, the one shining unquenchable thing, and when it is established there long enough for its memory to become eternal, the curtain falls again and the play ends.